Fergus McNeill is a Scottish author and award-winning interactive entertainment developer. As well as writing crime novels, he has been creating computer games since the early 1980s, writing his first interactive fiction titles while still at school. Over the years he has designed, directed and illustrated games for all sorts of systems, including the BBC Micro, the Apple iPad, and almost everything in between. Now running an app development studio, Fergus lives in Hampshire with his wife and teenage son.

You can read his blog at
fergusmcneill.blogspot.co.uk

Facebook
www.facebook.com/fergusmcneillauthor

Twitter@fergusmcneill

CUT OUT

Nigel never meant for it to happen. At first, he just wanted to be Matt's friend. But quickly his fascination with his new neighbour drifts into obsession: rearranging his furniture to recreate the layout of the rooms downstairs . . . buying the same clothes . . . going through Matt's post; his things . . . becoming Matt, without him ever knowing. And it would have been all right — no harm done — if Matt hadn't brought the girl home. When things spiral out of control and the young woman goes missing, Detective Inspector Harland has to unravel the disturbing truth. But there's far more to the case than meets the eye . . .

Books by Fergus McNeill
Published by Ulverscroft:

EYE CONTACT

FERGUS McNEILL

CUT OUT

Complete and Unabridged

CHARNWOOD
Leicester

First published in Great Britain in 2014 by
Hodder & Stoughton
London

First Charnwood Edition
published 2017
by arrangement with
Hodder & Stoughton
An Hachette UK company
London

A catalogue record for this book is available from the British Library.

ISBN 978–1–4448–3357–7

Published by
F. A. Thorpe (Publishing)
Anstey, Leicestershire

Set by Words & Graphics Ltd.
Anstey, Leicestershire
Printed and bound in Great Britain by
T. J. International Ltd., Padstow, Cornwall

This book is printed on acid-free paper

For Eve & Francesca
Without whom . . .

Yesterday, upon the stair,
I met a man who wasn't there
He wasn't there again today
I wish, I wish he'd go away . . .

from 'Antigonish' by Hughes Mearns

1

Detective Inspector Graham Harland nosed the car into a cobbled alleyway and bumped the passenger-side wheels up over the kerb. Switching off the engine, he leaned forward, gazing up through the windscreen at the old, industrial building — three storeys of sturdy Victorian brickwork, illuminated against the darkness by the steady flash of blue lights. The arched windows were bricked up and sealed beneath decades of masonry paint, while spiked iron railings and aluminium-cased security cameras crowned the upper floors. But it was the murals that held his attention.

Burning bright against the grime-blackened walls, a host of nightmarish images reared up — sinister, subjective, suggestive. Stencilled creatures stood ten feet tall above the cracked pavement, wreathed in slogans, while aerosol figures twisted themselves around the architecture of the upper storeys, leering down out of the gloom — different styles and colours, yet somehow the characters danced together to form an unbroken skin, stretched out across the nightclub's walls.

Ahead of him, Harland could see a small crowd of ghouls — shuffling silhouettes pressed up against the gently twisting police tape, all eagerly staring towards the lights of the ambulance and the patrol cars.

Waiting for the body to be brought out to them.

He sighed and sank back into the seat, his watchful gaze flickering up to the reflection in the rear-view mirror. He looked tired. The strobing blue lights glinted cold in his eyes, casting shadows beneath the high cheekbones, picking out flecks of silver grey in his short, dark hair and in the stubble on his angular jaw.

'Shall we?'

Beside him, Detective Sergeant Russell Pope stared at him with small, expectant eyes, one pudgy hand on the door handle, inquisitive and eager to poke around the scene.

Just like the bloody ghouls.

'Might as well,' Harland said. It was a narrow alley, and he watched Pope struggle to clamber out without banging the passenger door on the adjacent brick wall, then turned away and got out himself. Standing up and stretching his tall, lean frame, he briefly thought of lighting a cigarette, but the chill touch of a breeze that blew across the cobbles dissuaded him. Not now. He'd have one later. Afterwards, when he'd really need it.

Pope was staring up at the building, head back, his lips slightly parted as they always seemed to be when he was thinking.

'Know anything about this place?' Harland asked, slamming his door and walking over to his colleague. He'd heard of the Jahanna club but had never been in.

'Not much,' Pope said with a shrug, turning back towards him. 'A few drugs busts, the odd fight. Nothing out of the ordinary. Locals and students, I suppose.'

Harland glanced up at the mural, noting the eerie, psychedelic nature of the figures. Above him, a painted octopus held two giant pills marked *Truth* and *Freedom*.

'Not my sort of place,' he mused.

They made their way along the alley, pushing between the milling onlookers, and the snatches of murmured speculation. A tall, uniformed officer stepped forward briskly to intercept them as Pope went to duck under the blue and white cordon tape, but relaxed as the shorter man flourished his warrant card.

'DS Pope and DI Harland, CID.' A little pompous, but Harland was too weary to make anything of it tonight.

'Evening, sir.' The officer nodded, lifting the tape for them.

'All right, Johnson.' Harland nodded as he stooped beneath it, then walked a few paces away from the ghouls. 'How's it going?'

'Fine, thanks.' Johnson had been welcome back-up during a difficult arrest on the Lawrence Weston estate last year. In the confines of the alleyway he seemed an imposing figure, with broad shoulders and a square jaw. 'They got you working for Central now?'

'That's right.' Harland maintained his dead-pan expression. 'We solved all the crime in Portishead so I've come to help you sort Bristol out.'

As they talked, he let his gaze sweep the crowd of onlookers, noting the average age, the way people were dressed, looking for anything out of the ordinary . . . but it seemed to be just the usual bunch of misfits — faces painted pale, and eyes sunk in shadow from the street lamps. The only one who caught his attention was a wasted-looking man in his thirties who appeared to be blatantly skinning-up a joint, despite all the blue flashing lights.

He sighed and turned back to Johnson.

'Everyone inside?'

'I think so, yes. DS Linwood was talking with the ambulance crew . . . ' Johnson turned and pointed towards the club's main entrance — a vaulted archway lined with stencilled yellow teeth, and double doors painted like a lolling tongue. 'Just through there.'

'Thanks.' Harland glanced over at Pope, then gestured towards the building. 'Lead on.'

* * *

The double doors opened on to a small foyer, wallpapered with posters. One showed a girl with a rapturous expression on her upturned face, and blood running out of her ears, except the blood was blue. Harland paused to look at the image.

Not a quiet place, then.

Ahead of them, a long black-walled corridor led into the club, with recessed spots in the low ceiling casting pools of illumination onto the chequered lino floor. At the far end of it, a knot of people stood in the light, talking quietly. One of them looked round, excused himself from the group, and hurried over to meet them. He was a wiry man, with short brown hair and a suit that looked as though he slept in it.

'Evening sir, evening Russell.' He smiled — a bundle of nervous energy and quick movements.

'Evening,' Harland acknowledged him. He'd got to know DS Jack Linwood quite well in the first few weeks following his transfer to Bristol CID and, while he'd found his new colleague's relentless enthusiasm a little wearing, it was infinitely preferable to being teamed up with Pope. 'Who was first in on this one?'

'Ambulance crew beat us to it.' Linwood jerked his head towards the green-and-yellow-clad paramedics he'd been talking to. 'They were here a few minutes before PC Hopkins and Reed in the area car. Do you know them?'

Pope shrugged and shook his head.

'Not yet,' Harland replied, 'but I suppose we will before the night's out.'

Linwood smiled.

'Well,' he said, beckoning them to follow him, 'I reckon everyone will want a look at this one.'

'What are you on about?' Harland frowned.

'You don't know?'

'I know you're starting to annoy me.'

'All right, all right.' Linwood held his hands up. 'Just making conversation. Come on, you're going to like this.'

He led them down a wide set of steps that opened out on to the main dance-floor area — empty now, but still heavy with the smoky reek of dry ice and the sharp tang of sweat. Huge colourful shapes were suspended from the high ceiling, giant paper butterflies and vast canvas flowers twisting slowly in the gloom above. A brightly illuminated bar area ran along one wall, and several police officers were standing there, along with a couple of vacant-looking kids who, judging by the logos on their T-shirts, were members of staff.

Linwood led them across to the far side of the room, where another officer was pulling off a set of blue paper overalls beside a scuffed metal door marked *Men Only*.

'Suit up,' he said brightly. 'It's in there.'

* * *

The toilets smelled of bleach and liquid soap. A battered vending machine hung from the wall by the door, supplying the late night combo of breath mints and condoms, and glassy puddles meandered out across the tiled floor from beneath the urinals. A photographer, wearing white overalls, was crouched on one of several steel stepping-stone plates, training his lens into the farthest of the three graffiti-covered stalls. There was a soft click, and a glaring flash lit the walls.

Harland blinked and lowered his eyes, his own overalls rustling as he stepped carefully from one steel platform to the next. His shoes were wrapped in protective plastic coverings, but in here he was glad of any excuse to keep his feet from touching the floor.

The photographer studied the screen on the back of his camera, then glanced up.

'Want me to . . . ?' He gestured towards the door.

'No, it's fine.' Harland shook his head. 'You carry on.'

He took another step towards the photographer, and another, then paused as the scene inside the toilet cubicle came into view.

It was the body of a man, slumped down in the corner at the side of the porcelain bowl, like a puppet with its strings cut — legs splayed wide, bald head slumped forward. The arms were stretched out horizontally — one along the back wall, one along the inside of the stall — palms outward as though in surrender.

Another click and the camera flash glared back from an ugly wet stain on the crotch of the dead man's jeans. His skin looked sallow, but he didn't appear to be that old. Brilliant white trainers, a slim red zipper top — expensive clothes that passed for stylish among the younger generation — and the dark shadow on his scalp suggested he was bald by choice rather than age.

Harland crouched down, wanting to see the victim's face, frowning as he leaned forward to —

Flash.

'Shit!' He stumbled back, putting a hand on the floor to steady himself, as he glared up at the photographer. '*Just* . . . just give me a second, OK?'

Wiping his fingers on the leg of the overalls, he realised that his pulse was racing.

Breathe.

Turning back, he leaned in closer, trying to

discern something in the alien expression on the dead man's face. It looked almost foetal — eyes squeezed shut, lips pressed together . . .

'Superglue.' Linwood's voice came from behind him. 'Or some other sort of fast-bonding stuff. Someone sealed his eyes, nose and mouth. Even his ears.'

Harland recoiled slightly, as the awful expression before him suddenly made sense. Slowly, he turned to look at the man's outstretched arms.

'And glued his hands to the walls,' he murmured. 'Like posing the corpse for us.'

He started to get to his feet, glancing down to make sure he didn't misjudge his position on the stepping stones.

'Was this done to him post-mortem?' He hoped it had been, tried to stop his imagination careering into the claustrophobic horror of what it might have felt like to be conscious, aware.

'No,' Linwood said quietly. 'He was alive.'

And now, Harland noticed the small peels of bloody skin, an angry blemish on the tiled white wall behind the body.

'For fuck's sake.' He averted his eyes, staring up towards the merciless glare of the ceiling lights — anything to burn the image out of his mind — forcing himself to breathe steadily.

Breathe.

This poor bastard had been so desperate to breathe that he'd torn the skin off the back of his head, trying to thrash himself free himself before he suffocated.

'Sir?'

Get a grip. Don't try and empathise with the victim.

Turning away from the body, he waved for the photographer to continue, then picked his way stiffly back towards the door, where Linwood was watching him.

'Told you,' the younger man said.

Harland shook his head, composing himself. He couldn't let the Bristol team think he was squeamish.

'Do we know who he is?'

'That's the good news,' Linwood said. 'One of the bar staff knew him. Ever heard of the French Connection?'

'The film?' Harland asked, puzzled.

'No, a nasty piece of work called Arnaud Durand.' Linwood nodded towards the toilet cubicle. 'He's better known to his friends as the French Connection.'

'Let me guess . . . because he's French?'

'I suppose there's that too,' Linwood conceded, 'but mostly because he's your friendly local dealer.'

Harland pictured the miserable toilet cubicles, their doors covered in scrawled obscenities, imagining dull-eyed junkies slipping inside to score.

'Makes sense,' he said. 'What about the paramedics? Did they disturb anything?'

'I've spoken to both of them,' Linwood replied. 'He'd already been dead for some time when they got here — they went to check his airways, saw what had been done to him, and stepped back. They know the drill.'

Another flash lit the room. Harland turned to look back at the row of stalls. From here, the body was hidden, but he could still see the man's face in his mind, yearning for air.

Breathe.

'Must have been subdued,' he scowled. 'You don't *let* that sort of thing happen to you.'

Linwood tapped his chin thoughtfully.

'The paramedics said there's a lot of trauma to the back of the skull, not just around where the glue was.' He gazed across the room towards the cubicles. 'I don't know . . . maybe somebody bashed his head in, knocked him out first. Then they'd be able to stick him to the wall, and finish off doing his eyes, nose, mouth.'

Harland looked at him and nodded slowly.

'And then the poor bastard woke up.' He shuddered. 'Come on, let's get out of here. I need some air.'

2

The headquarters of Bristol CID were in a boxy grey building — three storeys of concrete and glass that loomed over the surrounding sea of anonymous industrial units and warehouses. From the small square windows, Harland could gaze out across the car park to the unceasing flow of traffic on the Causeway flyover, and the trains crawling in and out of Temple Meads station. But not from his desk.

Since he'd transferred here, his new desk was one in a cluster of four, tucked away into a corner of the largely open-plan offices. His neighbours were Linwood, who he generally found useful to talk with, and Pope, who he did not. The fourth spot had remained vacant since his arrival.

There were no photographs or other decorations cluttering his workspace — just a series of yellow Post-it notes along the bottom edge of his computer screen, a stack of folders beside the phone, and a jotter with curled pages that served as both notepad and mouse mat. The only personal item was a coffee mug that he'd brought with him from Portishead.

For now, he was sitting on the edge of Pope's desk, which always seemed tidy enough to have lots of clear surface area, and afforded a better view of the whiteboards. There were two of these, arranged side by side on one of the thin partition walls. At the top of one, the name *Arnaud Durand* was written in blue capital letters, but you could still see where Linwood had written *Le French Connection* then rubbed it out.

Pope had wheeled his chair back a little, and was hunched over cleaning his glasses. Linwood, sitting at his own desk, looked expectantly at Harland.

'What does it say?' he asked.

'So far it's pretty much what we expected,' Harland murmured, leafing back to the first of the printed pages he'd been studying. 'Preliminary medical report confirms several blows to the back of the head. Not enough to fracture the skull, but probably enough to leave the victim unconscious. No indication of anything sharp being used, and no sign of any weapon at the scene, so it could suggest he had his head banged repeatedly against the wall. SOCOs will let us know for sure, but it fits with your idea, Jack.'

'That he was knocked out first, then glued into place,' Linwood explained to Pope.

'Or posed,' Harland added.

'Why seal the nose and mouth if you've already tried to kill him by smacking his head against the wall?' Pope asked him. 'Why not just whack him a few more times and finish the job?'

It was a fair point. There were simpler, quicker ways to kill someone.

'I don't know,' he replied. 'Perhaps it's a kind of message, or a warning. Perhaps it symbolises something.'

'Or maybe Durand's killer was just making sure that he was dead,' Linwood mused. 'You wouldn't want your victim waking up again.'

'Except he did wake up,' Pope observed.

'Yeah.' Harland bowed his head and rubbed a weary hand over the short hair at the back of his neck, trying to release some of the tension in his shoulders. He'd come across his share of bodies in the past, but the thought of being sealed inside your own skin . . .

'Well, I don't suppose he could have struggled for long,' Linwood was saying.

'Long enough.' Harland turned to shoot a bleak look at him. 'He'd almost ripped enough of the skin to free one of his hands.'

Linwood shifted uncomfortably in his seat.

'And nobody heard anything.' Pope shook his head. 'Still, I suppose his mouth was sealed . . . '

Harland thought back to the poster in the club foyer — the girl with the bleeding ears. A noisy environment would hide all sorts of sounds.

'Anyway,' he said, leaning forward and getting to his feet, 'cause of death was suffocation.' He held up the report for a moment, then threw it across to land on his own desk. 'You can read the gory details later if you really want to.'

It would be easy enough to get distracted by the gruesome manner of Durand's death, but there were other facts to consider, and he didn't want the team to overlook anything. Shaking his shoulders to loosen them, he walked over to the whiteboard and picked up a marker.

'The body was discovered by a bartender . . . ' He spoke slowly, uncapping the pen and noting the solvent smell of the ink. 'Who were the last people to see him alive?'

Pope leaned forward, his elbows on his knees. 'We interviewed all the staff,' he replied. 'Nobody remembers serving him, but one of the bouncers saw him coming in around ten.'

'Bouncer's name?'

'Something Davison . . . ' Pope frowned for a moment. 'Gary, I think.'

'OK.' Harland nodded to himself, the pen squeaking across the board. 'Jack, how are we doing with the CCTV footage?'

'Well, we've lifted everything we can from the club and the surrounding streets,' Linwood replied. 'I took a quick look through the interior stuff, and it just shows Durand going from the door, straight down to his little office in the Gents. There's a couple of nods and greetings on the way, but he doesn't stop for a proper chat with anyone.'

'OK. Let's prioritise getting an ID for everyone he said *bonjour* to.'

'Already on it.'

'No cameras in the Gents, are there?' Pope asked.

'Nah.' Linwood leaned back in his chair. 'And the one that's nearest the toilet door isn't well placed for a good view of people's faces. We're having to cross-reference with the one upstairs by the main entrance, so we can figure out who's who.'

'Let's get a couple more people on it,' Harland told him. 'We need to get a line on everyone who went in or out of there. What time was he found again?'

Linwood consulted his notes.

'Half eleven, maybe a little after?' He shrugged. 'Emergency call was logged at eleven forty.'

'All right, so we work backwards from eleven forty. Hopefully we'll get lucky and find someone who comes out of that door and leaves in a hurry.'

'Smart people don't hang around after wasting someone,' Linwood agreed.

'Smart people don't kill their local drug dealer with superglue,' Harland sighed, leaning back against the whiteboard. 'What are you frowning at, Russell?'

'I was just wondering,' Pope said slowly. 'If Durand's a dealer . . . then where was his protection?'

Harland stared for a second, then waved the pen at him.

'Good question. A drug dealer, on his own in the stalls with a load of gear . . . ' He wrote *Protection?* on the board and underlined it. 'Did he have somebody watching his back? Did he know all his customers?'

'I'm guessing he knew his killer at least.' Linwood looked at them both. 'I mean, there's faster ways of doing someone in, right? What happened to Durand was . . . well . . . *personal*, you know?'

'Most likely,' Harland agreed. He added *Personal? Knew his killer?* to the board. 'Could have been one of his customers . . . '

' . . . or a robbery?' Pope suggested.

Linwood shook his head.

'Durand had . . . ' He flipped forward through the pages of his notebook. ' . . . here we are, he had over a hundred quid in his wallet and another three hundred in his socks, plus about two hundred quid's worth of gear in his pockets.'

'Then it's a hit by a rival dealer?' Pope asked.

'That makes more sense.' Harland nodded, staring at the board. He turned to Pope. 'Who's your friend in the drug squad? The one with the accent?'

'Barclay?'

'Yeah. Speak to him, see if Durand was the subject of a hostile takeover. Even if there's nothing definite, do some digging, see if he might have been treading on any toes.' He scrawled *Rival dealer hit?* in the middle of the whiteboard, hesitated, then circled it. 'Jack, you carry on working up a list of names from the club.'

He replaced the marker pen on the shelf at the bottom of the board, then turned to face them. Some victims attracted less sympathy than others, and he could read in their eyes how they felt about Durand.

'I *know* we're talking about the murder of a drug dealer . . . ' he began.

'Yeah, I suppose it was almost a public service,' Linwood grinned at Pope.

'Hey!' Harland snapped. 'I don't care who he was. Understand?'

The others fell silent, Linwood's face reddening slightly as he nodded in contrition.

Harland shook his head and turned back to the board, staring through the scrawl of words to that struggling figure in the cubicle . . . the awful, voiceless panic.

'There are simpler ways to kill someone,' he said. '*This* . . . this one bothers me.'

* * *

It was a cool May evening and the sun was low in the sky, throwing long shadows across the narrow incline of Stackpool Road, with its tightly huddled houses. Harland managed to squeeze the car into a cramped space, and got out balancing the pizza box carefully, enjoying the warmth of the cardboard against his palm. He tried not to resort to takeaway food too often — cooking helped pass the time in the evenings — but tonight he couldn't be bothered with the thought of preparing a meal.

Walking back down the hill, his gaze flickered from one window to another, affording him glimpses of the stories that played out in his neighbours' front rooms. A new drum kit for the Christian couple who lived three doors up from him — they seemed nice enough people, and the music was never loud enough to bother him. Next door to them, he could see the hunched form of Mrs Denby, bathed in the blue glow of the TV screen as she ate from a tray table propped up in front of the sofa. Another day spent in her dressing gown, not leaving the house — he wondered whether she was ill or whether she'd lost her job? Then the watchful face of the Wentworths' large tabby cat, its unblinking stare following him as he passed — it always sat there when they were out.

And then he was at his own house — a tidy two-bedroom semi, with a square of gravel where the front garden used to be. Unlocking the door, he stepped into the gloom of the hallway, scuffing a couple of pieces of junk mail aside with his foot, the sound uncomfortably loud against the heavy silence.

He stood for a moment, listening. The place seemed to have grown steadily quieter in the months since Kim had moved out — that same awful stillness that had smothered the house after Alice's death, rolling back in like fog on the evening tide.

He pushed the door closed with some reluctance, sealing himself in with the memories once more, and trudged through to the kitchen. Placing the pizza box on the table, he grabbed the pepper mill from the counter and a beer from the fridge. Then, pulling up a chair at the table, he opened the box and leaned forward to inhale the aroma — ham and pineapple. He *was* extremely hungry. Perhaps the evening wouldn't be so bad, and at least there would be no washing up.

Later, when he was full and beginning to feel tired, he pushed his chair back and got to his feet, closing the lid on the last slices of pizza and putting the box in the fridge for breakfast. Then, glancing at the clock, he washed his hands at the sink, and went to the back door. The bolt was stiff, but he drew it across and stepped outside into the back garden — a narrow strip of city sky, sandwiched between the neighbours' high brick walls. Lighting a cigarette, he leaned against the door frame and looked out over the tangle of bushes and unchecked weeds, then lifted his eyes to the shadowy clouds of evening.

He wondered where Kim was now. Back in Taunton at her sister's place, maybe? Or had she moved on, found somewhere new, somewhere without memories? He hoped so.

It would never have worked out for them — not with the way they'd been thrown together. She'd been the first woman since Alice, and everything had happened in the wrong order — a relationship in reverse.

He took a final drag on the cigarette and stubbed it out against the brick wall, grinding the glowing ember until the last sparks were extinguished.

It was only after she'd gone that he realised they'd never had a proper first date, never just sat there enjoying a drink and a laugh, getting to know each other . . .

But he still missed her, especially late at night, when the house was at its emptiest. Sighing, he turned around, stepped back inside and pulled the door quietly closed behind him.

3

This part of the CID building always seemed to have a quiet calm about it. The AV suite was at the far end of a long first-floor corridor, away from the bustle of the operations area. Slatted blue blinds kept the daylight out, while a bank of monitor screens lit the rooms with a cool, electric glow. Harland stared at the different images — frozen moments captured on the nightclub's CCTV — then leaned forward in his chair and lifted his mug from the long, curved desktop.

'So you've been through all of this?' he asked.

Linwood nodded quickly.

'All the interior stuff anyway,' he said. 'I've got some officers who normally work Central or Stokes Croft putting names to faces.'

Harland sipped his coffee.

'And there's nobody here with form?'

'Nothing significant so far.' Linwood shrugged. 'A couple with possession charges but no real villains.'

Harland put the mug down, then slumped irritably into his chair. He'd been sure they'd turn up *someone* in the place with a record of violence — the sort of character you'd want to keep close if you were carrying gear or cash.

'It doesn't stack up,' he muttered. 'I can't help thinking Pope was right about Durand having someone to watch his back.' He frowned then shot his colleague a meaningful look. 'And you *know* how much it pains me to say that.'

Linwood's face split into a broad grin. 'I know.'

Harland shook his head and sighed.

'He must have had *someone* keeping an eye on him.'

They sat in uneasy silence for a moment.

'Did you want to take another look?' Linwood asked, reaching across and pulling the keyboard towards him. 'These are the different camera views.'

'This is all of them?'

'All the interior ones from the lower level, yes.'

'Go on, then.'

Linwood hit the Play button and the images on the monitors suddenly jerked into life — blurred monochrome figures weaving between one another as they drifted silently through the frame, clusters of people moving together, dancing to an absent beat.

Harland leaned forward, elbows on the desktop, watching the muted action unfold. He'd been sure that a dealer — even a small-time dealer like Durand — would have some back-up to make sure he wasn't robbed. On the screen in front of him, he watched people going in and out of the Gents, but nothing caught his eye.

'How long do you think it took?' he mused. 'To subdue Durand, do all that to him, and stay with him till he stopped struggling?'

'How do we know our man didn't just glue him up and leave him?' Linwood asked, then shook his head as realisation dawned. 'Ah yes, of course — cause of death was suffocation, so the gluing, struggling and death must have happened in the space of a few moments. Still, I reckon the killer could have been in and out of the Gents in . . . what, five minutes?'

'That's what I was thinking,' Harland said, then straightened, frowning as he glanced between the images before him. Something wasn't right. 'Jack?'

'What?'

'These are *all* the camera views from the downstairs area of the club?'

'Yeah. Why?'

Harland leaned over the desktop, pointing an accusing finger at the upper corner of the screen, indicating a grainy shape in the gloom above the dance floor.

'So where's the footage from *this* camera, then?'

Just a few grey pixels, but there could be no doubt about what it was. And none of the views on the other screens came from that angle.

'Sir?' Linwood was suddenly at a loss. Blinking at the image on the screen, he shook his head, then looked round. 'I'm sorry, I didn't . . . '

Harland held his gaze, letting him suffer for a moment.

'You're sure they didn't give it to us?'

'They said that this was everything they had and I didn't . . . shit, sorry sir.'

Harland sighed. It was an easy mistake to make. On another occasion it might have warranted a rebuke but, to his credit, Linwood looked suitably mortified by his oversight. There was nothing to be gained by punishing him further.

'You're very *trusting*,' he observed, pausing until Linwood lowered his gaze, then quietly adding, 'That's not a good quality for people like us.'

'No, sir.'

Harland turned back to the screens, peering at the missing camera for a moment, then pushed his chair back from the desk. It wasn't much, but it was somewhere to start.

'Come on,' he said. 'We're going to take another look at that club.'

⋆ ⋆ ⋆

The place looked different in daylight. Beneath the grey of the overcast sky, the old warehouse seemed smaller, and the writhing mural creatures were now only paint. There was no muffled music, no clamour of voices in the street, just the dull rumble of traffic from the nearby main road.

Parking opposite the front of the building, they walked across the smooth cobbles and stepped in under the awning. Harland pushed the intercom button beside the closed doors and turned to Linwood.

'What did you say the manager's name was?'

'Jones.'

'OK.'

They stood in silence for a moment. Harland turned back to scowl at the intercom, then jabbed the button again. Eventually, it crackled into life and a voice said, 'Yeah?'

'Detective Inspector Harland and Detective

Sergeant Linwood, Avon and Somerset police.'

A pause, then, 'Yeah?'

Harland bent closer to the intercom, annoyed.

'So are you going to let us in or what?'

'Sorry, yeah.'

There was a metallic click and a buzzer rattled noisily. Linwood grabbed the handle and pulled one side of the double doors open, then followed Harland inside.

* * *

The man who met them in the entrance foyer had a vacant expression and a mouth that seemed to hang open. He was young — early twenties probably — but darkness around the eyes and several days' stubble made him appear older. His faded T-shirt might never have been ironed and there was paint on his jeans and trainers.

'All right,' he said. 'You here about that dead guy in the toilet, are you?'

His mouth seemed barely to move, as though he only had the energy to speak with his tongue.

'You must be the brains of the operation,' Harland told him, keeping a straight face.

'Dunno about that.' Seemingly unaware of any sarcasm, the man pushed a hand through his hair, which looked as though he'd just got out of bed. 'I only do maintenance an' stuff.'

'Well, we're here to see Jones.'

'Manager's not here, not till tonight. Just me at the moment.'

'No matter,' Harland said. 'What's your name?'

'Kevin.'

'Well, Kevin, maybe you can help us.'

* * *

They walked downstairs into the main room of the club. The long bar was in darkness but a series of naked bulbs hung from the high ceiling, casting a dim, even light across the whole space. Harland walked out onto the middle of the empty dance floor, turning slowly round to look up at the different cameras on the walls.

'Kevin?'

'Yeah?'

'You said you do the maintenance, right?'

'That's right.'

'These cameras work, do they?'

'Yeah.'

Harland nodded to himself, glancing round casually, then pointed at the wall near the Gents toilets.

'What about that one?' he asked.

'They *all* work.'

'Where's the recording set-up?'

'Office,' Kevin replied, with a sullen upward glance. Harland wasn't sure whether he was expressing exasperation or indicating the floor above.

'Can you show us?'

'Suppose so.' An indifferent shrug. 'This way.'

* * *

The upper floors of the building, where the club's clientele didn't go, looked as though they'd been preserved from the time of Brunel, but not preserved well. Perhaps *untouched* since the time of Brunel, Harland thought as he gazed up at the crumbling brickwork of the stairwell, the air stagnant with the smell of damp.

At the top, the ringing echo of his shoes on the rusty iron steps was replaced by the gritty crunch of masonry dust underfoot. Linwood placed one hand on the metal rail that ran along the wall, then quickly brushed his hand off on his trousers.

'Watch yourself there.' Kevin glanced down at the fragments of glass on the floor, below an old window. One of the panes had been patched with cardboard and black electrical tape. 'Mr Jones' office is down this way.'

He led them along a short, vaulted corridor. At the end, beside the propped-up wreckage of a giant paper butterfly with torn wings, was a featureless door, painted in grey wood primer. Harland noted that the locks were new.

'In here, is it?' he asked, not waiting for an answer before moving forward and trying the handle.

The door opened on to a large, shadowy office. Colourful, tie-dyed sheets had been nailed across the pair of tall windows in the far wall, casting a dim hue over the room. A high-backed leather chair sat behind an impressive, glass-topped desk — someone might have had aspirations, or delusions of grandeur when they first set up here, but as Harland glanced around the room, he saw that the reality wasn't quite as glamorous. The pale leather sofa was stained and scored. The glass coffee table was weighed down by a collection of empty bottles and overflowing ashtrays, while the floor was home to old pizza boxes and spilled bundles of promotional flyers. A shrivelled condom was draped over the lip of a large plastic bin.

Living the dream.

Surveying the office, Harland knew exactly what sort of person Jones would turn out to be.

Opposite the sofa, on a small table flanked by ugly steel shelving units, two monitor screens glowed in the gloom, each one divided into four, with a different security camera view in each quarter.

Harland walked farther into the room, pausing by the screens, noting the old PC tucked away under the table.

'It's all recorded here?' he asked, turning back to Kevin, who was leaning up against the door frame. 'On the computer?'

'That's right.'

'Can you show my sergeant how to view the old footage?'

Kevin regarded him doubtfully.

'It'd be a big help,' Harland continued, doing his best to sound friendly. 'Save us coming back?'

'I suppose.'

'Really appreciate this,' Linwood said, smiling, as they all gathered round the computer. He sounded genuinely enthusiastic, but those sorts of emotions came more easily to people like him. 'If you just get me started, I can take a look through and you can get on with whatever it was you were doing.'

Kevin gave a non-committal shrug. If the state

of the upper floors was anything to go by, he hadn't been getting on with much.

* * *

It quickly became clear that the missing camera footage wasn't going to be as useful as they'd hoped. Kevin had lost interest and gone downstairs, leaving them to stare at the screen where events from the evening of the murder were unfolding at fast-forward speed.

'I thought we'd have a better view of the door to the Gents,' Linwood sighed. 'But this is hopeless.'

Harland nodded. The wings of the lower-hanging paper butterflies all but obscured the door, and the only new thing they could see was the adjacent wall where one of the club's bouncers stood with his arms folded — a single stationary figure watching the milling crowd.

'Maybe it was a genuine mistake,' Linwood continued. 'Maybe they just forgot about that one camera.'

Harland glanced across at the list of folders on the second screen, arranged one above the other.

'I don't think so,' he frowned. 'It would have been simpler to dump *all* the footage, but someone took the trouble to give you everything *except* this view.'

Linwood shrugged, then turned his attention back to the screens.

'Well, there doesn't seem to be anything interesting,' he muttered. 'And that bouncer would have jumped in if there was any trouble.'

Harland leaned forward.

'Do we know him?' he asked. 'The bouncer, I mean?'

Linwood reached into his pocket and drew out a notebook.

'Jason Kerr,' he said after a moment. 'Don't worry, we checked all the staff. None of them have any previous.'

Harland continued to stare at the screen.

'Was he in the Gents at all?' he asked.

'Just once, I think . . . earlier in the evening,' Linwood said. 'Didn't see much of him on the other camera footage.'

Harland nodded to himself.

'You wouldn't have, not if he was parked in that corner all night.'

An idea was beginning to form.

'Come on,' he said, standing up. 'Let's get out of here.'

⋆ ⋆ ⋆

Kevin was at the foot of the stairwell as they came down the last flight of steps.

'You off, then?' he asked. There was nothing in his expression to indicate whether he was pleased to see them go or not.

'Yeah, we've got to get back to the station,' Linwood told him. 'Thanks for your help.'

Kevin gave him a blank look, then walked through to the entrance foyer with them.

'The manager will be sorry he missed you,' he said as he opened the door, then stood and watched them leave.

'Yes,' Harland murmured to Linwood. 'I think he might be.'

* * *

A fine drizzle touched their faces as they stepped out under the grey skies and walked back to where they'd parked.

'So what do you want to do?' Linwood asked as he settled into his seat. 'Come back later and speak to Jones?'

Harland allowed himself a thin smile.

'Sometimes you get more from the monkey than you do from the organ grinder,' he mused.

'Sir?' Linwood frowned.

The patter of rain filled the silence, and Harland peered out through the droplets on the window to consider the old brick building.

'You said there were a few people done for possession there, right?'

'Yes . . . '

'Make a list, and maybe check for anyone else who's been busted in there recently. I want to know who they were buying their gear *from*. Keep it nice and low-key for the moment, but we need to establish if there were any other dealers operating in there.'

Linwood stared at him blankly, then nodded.

'So you're thinking it was a hit by a rival dealer?' he asked.

Harland glanced at him.

'What? Oh, I suppose it might be . . . '

Linwood looked at him, puzzled. 'But?'

Harland started the car, then left it to idle for

a moment as he stared out at the murals.

'Pope asked about who was watching his back, right?' he said.

'Yeah.'

'OK, so what if we do some digging and we *can't* find any other dealers working here? What if Durand had an exclusive?'

'Sorry sir, I don't follow . . . '

Harland leaned back into his seat, ordering his thoughts.

'It's a popular club, right?' he explained. 'Plenty of room for more than one dealer. So if he *did* have the place to himself, who do you think he was paying off? Who was making it happen?'

'You think he paid that bouncer to keep an eye on him?'

'Perhaps. But it wasn't the bouncer who conveniently forgot to give us the footage from that camera. Who backed up the data for you?'

Linwood looked at him. 'It was the manager. Jones.'

'There you are.' Harland nodded. 'He was involved, or he was turning a blind eye. Either way, I'm sure Jones can shed some light on who might want Durand out of the way.' He put the car in gear. 'Find him for me.'

4

The rain clouds had passed and it was a bright, warm evening as Harland dashed between the tables lining the pavement outside the steak-house. Ducking in under the shadow of the broad canopy, he could see Mendel through the window — his former sergeant would have arrived on time, of course, solid and dependable as ever.

Once inside, he slowed his pace, getting his breath back as he walked across to where his old friend was sitting, and patting him on the back.

'Sorry I'm late,' he apologised, sliding into his seat.

Even hunched over the table, Mendel was a big man, with broad shoulders and tidy black hair. He sat back in his chair and made some show of consulting his watch, pointedly raising an eyebrow before his serious face split into a broad smile.

'Evening, Graham,' he said.

'There was a broken-down lorry at the roundabout,' Harland explained. 'Traffic was backed up, right along Feeder Road.'

'Yeah, yeah, *course* it was,' Mendel grinned. ''Cos you're normally so punctual.'

Harland chuckled to himself, glancing round the room, his eye lingering on an attractive brunette near the doorway. This place had become a regular haunt since he'd transferred out of Portishead and it had a quirky, down-to-earth atmosphere that he found pleasing. A huge porcelain bull's head gazed out from above the service counter, and the wallpaper was a subtle pattern of butcher's cow diagrams, endlessly repeating around the walls . . .

. . . but the sizzle and smell from the kitchen were making him hungry. He reached for the familiar menu, then glanced up at the Specials board and quickly down at his watch.

'Damn!' It was later than he'd thought. The place did an excellent steak meal deal for fifteen pounds if you ordered before seven, but it was already ten minutes past.

'What's the matter?' Mendel looked at him.

'It's after seven,' Harland scowled. 'I missed the early dinner special.'

The big man shook his head.

'No you didn't,' he rumbled. 'I already ordered it for you.'

'Thanks.' Harland put the menu down and sat back in his chair, relieved. 'But how did you know what I was going to have?'

Mendel raised an eyebrow again.

'Because you always do the same thing when we come here,' he sighed. 'You look at the menu, then order the special.'

Harland glanced at him, slightly aggrieved.

'I'm not *that* predictable, am I?'

Mendel stared at his beer glass, his brow furrowed in thought.

'Yes, you are,' he said, nodding. 'But it's my turn to pay this week, so it's kind of a win-win situation.'

Harland tried to find fault with this.

'I could have been late,' he pointed out.

'You were.'

'All right, *later*. Or I might have had to cancel altogether . . . '

'Then I'd have had *two* steaks.' Mendel shrugged. 'Again, win-win.'

Harland gave in and laughed.

'Fair enough,' he conceded. 'I notice you didn't order me a beer, though.'

Mendel raised his own glass.

'You CID boys don't miss a thing, do you?' he grinned.

* * *

The beer was ice cold when it arrived, and Harland savoured his first sip as he gazed out of the window at a group of office workers arranging themselves round one of the pavement tables. The brunette was among them, but she was smiling and chatting with a man in a suit.

He put his glass down and looked up to find Mendel watching him.

'So what is it?'

'What do you mean?'

'I know that look,' the big man said. 'Something's bothering you . . . something you're working on?'

Harland lowered his eyes. He knew better than to try to bluff his old partner.

'There was a murder in Stokes Croft,' he said slowly. 'It was . . . well, it wasn't pretty.'

'It never is,' Mendel observed. 'But you knew

there'd be more of that when you transferred to Bristol.'

'Yeah.' Harland frowned as he stared at his beer glass. He'd dealt with murders before, seen death up close. Why should this one feel any different? 'It's just . . . there was something really *awful* about this one.'

Mendel gazed at him.

'Stokes Croft,' he mused, then nodded in recognition. 'The drug dealer they found in that nightclub?'

'Yeah.'

'What about it?'

Harland glanced up at his friend, then stared down at the table, picturing the unnatural expression on Durand's face — mouth sealed, nostrils squeezed together, eyelashes crusted with a sheen of solvent tears. It wasn't so much the murder that bothered him. It was the thought that someone could do that to another human being — do it, and pose them, and then watch them struggle.

'You heard about how he was killed?' he asked.

'Ah, yes.' Mendel gave him a grim nod. 'I know the one you mean now.'

Harland felt a twinge in his shoulder and raised a hand to rub some of the stiffness away.

'While I was taking a look at the body . . . ' He broke off, shaking his head.

Can't see, can't hear, can't breathe . . . tearing your own skin trying to get free . . .

Mendel sat quietly, giving him time.

'I just . . . *hate* the thought of it,' Harland continued. 'What kind of sick mind does something like that?'

'I don't know,' the big man replied. 'But you'll stop him.'

Harland looked at him and gave a non-committal shrug.

'I suppose.' He turned to gaze out of the window again, staring up at the sunlight on the windows of the big hotel across the road. 'Seeing someone killed like that . . . it really got to me, know what I mean?'

'Of course I do,' Mendel said. 'But dwelling on it won't help. Just catch the bastard — that's the only thing that'll make you feel better.'

He raised his glass in grim salute.

'Amen to that,' Harland agreed, lifting his own glass. 'Anyway, it's not really the sort of thing I want to discuss while we're eating. Let's talk about something else.'

* * *

By the time the waiter appeared with their food, he was starting to feel better. As he watched the young man setting down the white plates and deftly replacing their cutlery, Harland wondered why steak knives weren't provided by default — he couldn't imagine anyone coming here and ordering anything else.

'So,' he said, once he'd swallowed the first mouthful, 'you busy at the moment?'

'Yes,' Mendel said with a nod, then shot him a warning glance. 'And *don't* sound so surprised, thank you.'

Harland recalled how they used to joke about

graffiti and missing cats — the perception of more provincial policing — but he knew from experience that very bad things could occur in out-of-the-way places.

'You remember that container storage depot, up by the Oil Basin in Avonmouth?' The big man leaned forward, speaking quietly now. 'You know, behind the railway line?'

'Yeah, I remember it.'

'Well, last Sunday night, someone drove a JCB down there and made themselves a new door in the side of the main warehouse.'

Harland put his cutlery down.

'Really?'

'Really,' Mendel said. 'But that's not the best bit. Whoever these jokers were, they definitely weren't joyriders. They left the JCB and drove two articulated lorries out of there, two lorries that were fully loaded with machine parts worth . . . guess how much?'

'I don't know.' Harland shrugged. 'Hundred grand?'

Mendel sat back and smiled.

'Three and a half million,' he said softly.

Harland whistled.

'All that in two trucks?'

'Two big trucks, yes.' Mendel cut a piece of steak, then looked up again. 'A lot of very dull, very specialised, *very* expensive kit.'

'Insurance job, maybe?'

'Perhaps. Or an insurance ransom.'

Harland nodded as he savoured another mouthful. Sometimes the insurance companies would pay to get stolen property back, if they could do it cheaply and quietly enough. It was rare, but not as rare as it once was, and times were tough all over just now.

'Any idea where they went with the trucks?' he asked.

'No sightings so far,' the big man replied. 'But just think how many quiet little industrial units there are between Avonmouth and the M4.'

'A lot of door-to-door work for you to organise,' Harland smiled.

'I've got Firth on it,' Mendel explained, taking a sip of his beer.

Harland's smile faltered. He glanced at his friend but, mercifully, Mendel's eyes were on the glass, not on him. PC Sue Firth was one his biggest regrets from his time at Portishead. After Alice died, he'd lurched back and forth between feelings of lust and guilt when it came to women. Then, when he finally started to level out, he'd told himself Sue couldn't possibly be interested. By the time he got his head together enough to see that she really had been, she was dating someone else.

'Firth's more organised than the two of us put together,' he managed.

She was a good police officer. It would have hurt both of their careers if they'd been caught seeing each other while working out of the same station. He didn't much care about his own reputation, but he was glad he hadn't messed things up for her. She deserved better than that.

He reached for his beer, taking a deep draught. It was a sunny evening, and more people were gathering at the tables outside.

Looking at them through the windows, Harland felt a sudden urge to go out and smoke. He patted his pocket to make sure he'd brought his cigarettes from the car . . . yes, they were there. Maybe once they'd finished eating . . .

'And how about you?' Mendel was asking him. 'Big city copper now, eh?'

'Something like that.'

'Is Pearce keeping you busy?'

'Haven't seen much of him lately,' Harland replied. The chief had been focused on the recent shootings in Easton. 'He's been keeping *himself* busy.'

Eating the last of his chips, he sat back in his chair, munching silently.

Mendel waited until he had finished, then gave him an innocent smile.

'And how's life with dear brother Pope?' he asked.

Harland grimaced.

'Pope . . . ' He reached for his glass and drained it. 'If we're going to talk about him, I think I want another beer.'

'You're not driving?'

'I'm parked round the back of the square,' Harland said with a shrug. 'I can walk home, pick up the car in the morning.'

'OK, but I think we should sit outside.'

'Sure. Why?'

Mendel pushed his chair back from the table and stood up.

'Because you've been sitting there, fidgeting with that damned fag packet for the last twenty minutes,' he growled.

Harland nodded and got slowly to his feet.
'You Portishead boys don't miss a thing, do you?' he smiled.

5

Harland turned right and followed the access road until it emerged into the car park. The morning sun was already painfully bright, glaring through the windscreen as he manoeuvred into his space and killed the engine. He got out, yawning as he locked the car, then walked across the tarmac, squinting against the light until he reached the cooling shadow of the building. Even in silhouette, it was an ugly structure. The department had moved here a decade ago, abandoning the sturdy civic grandeur of the old Bridewell Station where his father had once worked. That was an arts and entertainment venue now, the fortress-thick walls slowly blossoming with graffiti, an overspill from the nearby Stokes Croft.

There was no graffiti here, though. Set a long way back from the road, fenced in and surrounded by a huge car park, CID headquarters was a lonely outpost, far from the heart of the city. Bristol had become too expensive for the police — his generation were out in the hinterland, with the builders' merchants and the haulage depots. Sighing, he walked up the steps and pushed through the glass double doors.

Emerging from the canteen with a coffee, he climbed the stairs, being careful not to spill his drink, then made his way along the corridor. As he passed the glass-fronted offices, he saw the familiar figure of DCI Raymond Pearce waving to him from behind a desk, beckoning him in. Curious, he opened the door and leaned inside.

'Sir?'

'Morning, Graham,' Pearce greeted him. He was a solid-looking man in his late forties, with dark grey hair and an East End accent that sounded tough amid the voices of his West Country colleagues. His eyes often had a mischievous twinkle, but not today, and there was an old scar that ran down his left cheek, hinting at the serious streak beneath his easy-going nature. 'How's things with you?'

'Fine thanks.'

'Good. Look, I need a word.' He inclined his head towards an empty chair in front of his desk. 'Come in and close the door.'

Harland stepped into the office and sat down, leaning forward to put his cup on the desk.

'What are you up to at the moment?' Pearce asked.

'We're working on that nightclub murder in Stokes Croft,' Harland replied. 'Arnaud Durand?'

'Oh yeah, the French Connection bloke?'

'That's him.'

Pearce sat back in his chair. There were framed photos of a police football team on top of the filing cabinet behind him, and a collection of small plastic trophies.

'Well, I reckon the world can manage with one less drug dealer,' he mused. 'Think the others could struggle on without you for a bit?'

'I suppose . . . ' Harland frowned. He was still finding his footing here in Bristol, but he didn't think he'd done anything wrong. Why was he being taken off the investigation?

'And before you start worrying, this has nothing to do with your work on that case.' Pearce held up a warning finger, as if he'd read his thoughts. 'It's just that something else has come up, and I reckon we could do with having you in on it. Right?'

Harland lowered his eyes and nodded. 'Yes, sir.'

Pearce had always been able to see straight through him.

'Good man. Now, did you hear about Laura Hirsch?'

Harland looked up.

'I don't think so,' he replied. 'Who is she?'

Pearce leaned forward, his face serious.

'Twenty-four-year-old school teacher from Totterdown, last seen on Friday night. Hasn't been home, hasn't shown up for work . . . ' He shook his head. 'Neighbourhood unit made the usual enquiries, risk assessment looked bad, so the case was escalated to us. We've checked for activity on her bank cards and her phone, but it's like she suddenly fell off the map.'

'I see.' Harland looked at him, unsure what to say. People went missing all the time. Sometimes they showed up alive, sometimes dead, sometimes not at all. Missing persons were a concern, naturally, but certainly not unusual. Why was Pearce telling *him* all this?

'There's more,' Pearce continued. 'When she was last seen, Laura was on her way to visit her boyfriend, or ex-boyfriend, whatever the hell he is. Anyway, *he* says she never got there.'

Harland caught the emphasis.

'But?' he asked.

Pearce gave him a grim smile.

'We pinged her phone,' he explained. 'No response, but the last place the network registered it was in his street, late on Friday night. So if something *has* happened to her . . . '

' . . . then he's a good bet for it,' Harland said thoughtfully. 'What do we know about him?'

Pearce folded his arms. 'That's where you come in.'

'Sir?'

'Remember when you first got here from Portishead, and you were filling in for Marley?'

Harland remembered. Burglaries . . . vandalism . . . all sorts of daft calls. *A chance to get to know your new patch*, Pope had said with a smirk.

'Well,' Pearce continued, '*you* interviewed the bloke.'

Harland stared at him.

'The boyfriend?'

'That's right. Does the name Matt Garrick ring any bells? There was some kind of break-in at his flat, and as far as he's concerned, you were the friendly face of Avon and Somerset.'

Harland frowned, thinking back.

'In Cotham?' he asked. 'Up by the Arches at the top of Stokes Croft?'

'That's him,' Pearce said, nodding.

Harland settled back into his chair, trying to recall, the man he'd met, but it had been a while now.

'What makes you think he'll tell me anything?' he asked.

Pearce shrugged. 'Because he asked for you.'

* * *

They made their way along the corridor, towards the main office, Harland carrying his coffee.

'So what happens about the Arnaud murder?' he asked. They'd been making progress on that one but there was still a long way to go.

'You had Linwood working it with you, right?'

'Yes. Oh, and Pope.'

'They make a lovely couple,' Pearce grimaced. He pushed the door and held it open. 'Let 'em run with it for a bit. We're short on bodies just now, and I'm up to my eyes with that shooting over in Easton. I need you on this.'

Harland nodded. Resources *were* stretched at the moment.

'Of course, I just . . . ' He shook his head and smiled. *Time to stop talking*. 'Thank you, sir.'

'Good.' Pearce clapped his hands together with an air of finality. 'Now, I want to introduce you to someone.'

They walked out into the open-plan area. As they approached his own group of desks, Harland saw an unfamiliar woman in a dark tailored jacket unpacking a cardboard box.

'Settling in all right?' Pearce asked her brightly.

Turning to face them, the woman straightened up, and nodded with a slight smile.

'I'm fine thanks, sir.' She was almost as tall as

Harland, with straight brown hair that swung just above the shoulder, piercing dark eyes and a low voice.

''Course you are.' Pearce turned to him. 'Graham, this is DS Imogen Gower. Imogen, meet DI Graham Harland.'

'Imogen,' Harland repeated, committing the name to memory. Not unattractive, but not his type — probably a good thing. 'Nice to meet you.'

'Glad to meet you too, sir.' She inclined her head very slightly, then gave a polite smile as he extended a hand. Her movements seemed careful, controlled, as though she were constantly reining herself in — maybe she was self-conscious about her height.

Pearce gave them an approving look.

'Imogen was helping out on some of the cold cases, but obviously this takes priority.' He glanced at his watch. 'I'll let you two get acquainted, then Fuller can bring you up to speed — he's coordinating for me. I want the pair of you to go and speak to Garrick this morning, OK?'

'OK,' Harland replied.

Pearce gave him a long look, then his expression softened slightly.

'Chin up, Graham. Everything'll get done.' He shot a meaningful glance at Linwood and Pope's desks, then turned back to Harland. 'And we'll keep an eye on the dynamic duo for you, all right?'

Harland gave him a wry smile.

'Yes, sir.'

6

Imogen drove quickly but smoothly. Leaning back in his seat, Harland glanced across, studying her as they made their way through the city. There was a quiet confidence about his new colleague, shifting down to overtake a bus that was pulling over, then sweeping back on to their own side of the road to avoid an oncoming car, her expression calm and impassive throughout.

Circling the Bearpit roundabout and sweeping beneath the grey edifice of the old Avon House complex, they emerged on to Stokes Croft — a long drag of crumbling brick buildings, reclaimed by eclectic shops and tiny cafés, and all wreathed in murals. As they passed the turning that led down to the nightclub, he found himself staring out through the window, trying to catch a glimpse of the old converted warehouse. It niggled him, leaving an investigation like that, just as they'd been starting to make some progress . . .

. . . but he had other things to think about now. A young woman had disappeared and it was down to him to find out what had happened to her.

Harland rubbed his eyes, picturing the photograph that Fuller had shown them in the briefing — a sunlit snapshot of Laura that looked as though it was taken on a walking holiday — long, blonde hair framing an honest, youthful face, with blue-green eyes and an easy, laughing smile.

She looked so *alive* in the photo, but nobody had seen or heard from Laura all weekend, and that was out of character for her. By all accounts she was a sociable person, definitely *not* the type to suddenly go quiet. A planned meeting with a friend had been missed without any explanation and then, much more worrying, Saturday had seen her sister's birthday pass with no phone call, no text, no nothing . . .

He wondered what she'd look like when they found her.

'It's just off Zetland Road, isn't it?'

Imogen's voice snapped him back from his reverie and he turned to face her again.

'Yeah, a little way up the hill,' he said, nodding. 'There's quite a few little garages and workshops round here . . . I'll tell you where to turn.'

They passed under the Arches — a towering brick viaduct with its central iron span that carried the railway high above the traffic — and swung left at the junction.

'Up here somewhere . . . ' Harland peered ahead, searching for the entrance. 'Yes, there it is.'

Imogen slowed, then turned on to a narrow access road that ran down the side of a kitchen showroom. They emerged into a small yard, paved in uneven concrete and surrounded by low, whitewashed buildings. Ahead of them, two sets of broad blue doors stood open, revealing a pair of old garage workshops. In one, a silver Renault sat with its bonnet up, while the other housed a blue Ford lifted up on a yellow hydraulic platform.

Switching off the ignition, Imogen undid her seat belt and glanced across at him.

'So . . . how do you want to work this?'

Harland leaned back against the headrest and drew a hand across his chin.

'Nothing too dramatic. Not yet anyway,' he mused. They didn't have anything definite on Matt Garrick at the moment, and to go blundering in with accusations might be dangerous if he *was* involved. But it would be good to get a sense of the man, see how he responded to some questions. 'For now, I think we just nudge him gently, see if he wobbles.'

'OK.'

* * *

As they got out, a young man in blue overalls emerged from the shadows beneath the jacked-up Ford and started towards them, pushing an untidy mop of black hair away from his eyes. He straightened up as he walked, unfolding into a tall figure — lean but muscular, judging by the way the overalls moved. Harland recognised the familiar jawline, the slightly prominent teeth, and nodded to him.

'Hello, Matt. Long time, no see.'

'All right, Mr Harland.' He seemed edgy, pale blue eyes flickering occasionally towards Imogen, but that was normal enough when the police came calling unannounced. He rubbed his palms on the front of his overalls, as though expecting to shake hands, but then seemed to think better of it and fixed Harland with a steady gaze. 'They sent some bloke round asking questions about Laura, but the way he was talking . . . it was like he was accusing me of something . . . '

'So you asked to speak to me?' Harland said.

'Well, at least you know me,' Matt replied. 'You came to my flat when I had that break-in.'

'I remember, yes.' He became aware of Imogen standing beside him, and glanced across at her, feeling relief as he managed to recall her surname. 'This is DS Gower, by the way.'

'All right,' Matt acknowledged her, then regarded them both warily. 'So is there any word on Laura yet?'

Harland looked past him to where a couple of workmen were leaning against a wall, watching them.

'Is there somewhere we can talk?' he asked.

Matt hesitated, then took a languid step backwards, pivoting slowly on one heel.

'Yeah, of course,' he replied. 'Come on through.'

* * *

They followed him as he led them into the gloom of the garage, where the air tasted of petrol, and the thin echo of music crackled from an old radio. Picking their way between the engine parts and tools that littered the oily floor, they edged around behind the silver car, where he unbolted a small door in the rear wall. Daylight and fresh air flooded in as it opened, and they emerged on to a narrow alley that ran along the back of the buildings, enclosed by a high wooden fence topped with barbed wire. Stacks of old tyres rose in lopsided piles, shoulder high on either side of the doorway, and Harland glanced up at the sheets of corrugated plastic that extended out from the roof to form a primitive lean-to — once transparent but now muddy green, choked with leaves and moss.

'So . . . ' Matt had stopped beside an old metal bucket, filled with cigarette ends. For a moment, Harland thought he was going to light up, and involuntarily started to reach for his own packet, but the young mechanic leaned back to slouch against the whitewashed wall, jamming his hands into his pockets. 'What's going on with Laura? Hasn't anyone heard from her?'

It was the right sort of thing to say. An innocent person would probably assume she was still alive. They'd be anxious — or at least curious — for news from the police. They'd want to ask questions, rather than answer them, be more demanding than defensive because they had nothing to hide . . .

So it was the right sort of thing to say.

Unless Matt was smart. Harland considered him, weighing up whether he was genuine, or whether he'd just figured out what sort of things they'd be expecting to hear.

'We're still looking for her,' he replied. 'Part of that involves building up a picture of where she went, who she saw . . . '

He left it hanging, an awkward pause that stretched out between them, inviting Matt to volunteer something, to start talking.

The young mechanic shifted his weight from

one foot to the other.

'Well, I haven't seen her since the week before last,' he frowned. 'I told that other copper, we'd kind of finished.'

'Kind of?'

'We'd had . . . ' Matt's brows came down and he took a deep breath. 'We had a couple of rows. And I just didn't want the hassle, you know?'

The young man's eyes flickered up, searching their faces, but Harland kept his expression blank.

'What did you row about?' He asked the question casually, but it was always going to provoke some sort of reaction.

'Just . . . stuff, nothing important.' Matt was frowning now, suddenly wary. 'Why, what are you getting at?'

Again, the right sort of response, if he was innocent.

'I just want to get a sense of how things were,' Harland explained. He kept his own voice quiet, slow, trying to prevent the tone of the conversation from escalating too quickly. Matt looked as though he was about to clam up and that would be no good to anyone.

Imogen took a step forward, her shoe crunching on the gravel.

'So you finished with her the week before last?' She said it well — no clumsy attempt to placate him, just calm and matter-of-fact, but with a subtle nod to his ego: *he'd* finished with *her*.

'That's right.' Matt's expression eased just a little as he turned to address Imogen. 'And Laura seemed OK about it, you know? I mean, we had a laugh together, but I don't reckon she thought it was any more serious than I did. Not really.'

'Were you still talking, calling her, that sort of thing?'

'Nah, what's the point of all that? If something's not going anywhere, no sense dragging it out.'

Imogen nodded, as though she agreed with him.

'So she gave you back her keys and that was that?'

Matt shook his head.

'She didn't have keys,' he corrected her. 'We never got *that* far.'

Harland suppressed a smile. Imogen was going to be a breath of fresh air after the artless approach that Linwood sometimes employed to question people. And anything was an improvement on working with Pope.

'Have you still got any of her stuff at your flat?' she asked him. 'Or has she taken it all?'

Matt shook his head and looked down.

'She only stayed over a few times so there wasn't much, and I don't think she left anything.' He lifted his head, suspicion dawning. 'Why?'

Imogen shrugged.

'Just wondering if she might come back to collect anything.'

Matt pushed himself up off the wall to stand up straight, scowling at them now.

'I mean, why are you asking me all these questions?' he demanded. 'We're not together any more. You should be speaking to her housemates, or whoever saw her last, not wasting your time with me . . . '

'What were you doing on Friday evening?' Harland interrupted him. 'This Friday just gone by?'

'Eh?' Matt stared at him, caught off guard by the question.

'Friday evening. What were you doing?'

'I . . . I stayed home. Why?'

'All night?' Imogen asked. 'You didn't go out at all?'

'I think I was tired . . . fell asleep or something . . . '

'Anyone with you?' she pressed.

'No, I . . . ' He stopped, a flicker of panic in his eyes. 'What are you not telling me? What's this really about?'

Harland stared at him, holding his gaze, letting him get uncomfortable. He leaned forward, opening his mouth as if he was about to say something, then drawing back slightly, letting Matt know there was something, but not revealing what it was.

An older man, with a tangle of salt-and-pepper curls, appeared at the doorway. He wore an ancient set of overalls, open at the front to reveal a crumpled check shirt — pretty elderly to be a mechanic, but maybe he was the garage owner. He looked at Harland and Imogen, assessing them, then turned to Matt.

'Everything all right here?' he rasped.

Matt took a deep breath.

'Yeah, it's fine,' he said, waving his colleague

away. 'On you go, I'll be there in a minute.'

The older man stared at them for a moment longer, then turned around and shuffled back inside.

Matt swore under his breath, clearly agitated now.

Harland waited for him to look up, then allowed his own face to relax into a neutral expression.

'So you've had no contact with her since the week before last . . . ' He said it lightly, as if drawing a line under it. 'Well, I suppose that's that.'

He shot Imogen a quick glance then turned back to smile at Matt, who looked confused.

'Anyway, sorry to have bothered you at work.'

Matt, realising that they were leaving, seemed to relax a little.

'That's OK,' he muttered, his shoulders dropping. 'I wanna help out. For Laura, you know?'

'Of course.' Harland turned as if to go, then looked back at him. 'What time do you finish here? Just in case we have anything else we need to ask you . . . '

Matt hesitated, just a fraction, then shrugged. 'We're open from eight till five.'

Harland looked at him for a moment longer, then smiled again.

'Then I think we're done for now.' He looked at Imogen, expectant.

'Thanks for your time, Mr Garrick,' she said.

They turned and made their way back through the garage. Harland could feel Matt's eyes following him as he walked across the concrete to the car, and he raised one hand in a backwards wave without looking round.

Imogen slid into the driving seat and started the engine, as he climbed in and shut his door.

'Well?' she asked him.

Harland glanced back towards the garages thoughtfully.

'I don't know about you,' he mused, 'but I need something to eat.'

7

The café interior seemed almost dark after the bright sunlight of the street. Harland picked up a bottle of iced tea from the chiller cabinet and placed it on the counter, next to Imogen's Diet Coke.

'And this, please.'

The man behind the till was young — late teens or early twenties — with a thin beard and carefully styled hair. He wore a skinny blue T-shirt with the café logo on it, and had some kind of porcelain spike jammed through one of his earlobes.

'Paying together?' he asked.

Imogen had her purse in her hand and was pulling out some money, but Harland waved her away.

'It's OK,' he said, taking a twenty from his wallet. 'Let me get this one.'

She looked at him, then gave a slight shrug.

'Thank you, sir. My turn next time.'

The man with the spike handed Harland his change, and placed their drinks on a small tray, along with a metal table marker labelled '12'.

'Where will you be sitting?' He gave them an expectant look. 'You know, for the food?'

Harland glanced around. A flight of narrow wooden steps led upstairs but there was a garden area at the back, with ashtrays on the tables . . .

He looked at Imogen, who seemed content to follow his lead.

'It's a nice day,' he said. 'We'll be outside.'

* * *

They made their way out through the back of the building, emerging into a walled garden area, under a square of brilliant blue sky. The space was crowded with metal tables beneath the shade of large square parasols, and little patches of glaring white burned on the old paving, where sunlight shafted down between the dark canopies. Two women were sitting in the far corner, talking quietly, and a serious-looking man was tapping away at his laptop, but otherwise they had the place to themselves.

Harland chose a table by the wall, putting the tray down and dropping into a chair.

'Well,' he sighed, raising his drink. 'Cheers.'

Imogen pulled her chair around, scraping it across the stone slabs, then lifted her own drink.

'Cheers.'

The iced tea tasted good and he took a long, cool sip. Then, settling back into his seat, he looked across at his new colleague.

'So. What did you think of him?' he asked.

'Matt Garrick?' Imogen put her drink down, then shrugged. 'Hard to say. He came across as a pretty normal guy — didn't seem particularly nervous, didn't seem particularly anything really.'

'For a man with absolutely no alibi, he did seem fairly calm,' Harland agreed.

'You think he's involved?'

'He *was* involved with her, and the ping on her phone puts her at his place on Friday evening . . . but whether he's *done* anything to her?' He paused, then shook his head slowly. 'Not sure yet.'

They sat in silence for a moment.

Missing persons cases bothered him — too much uncertainty, too many possibilities. Without a body you couldn't launch into a full-scale murder investigation, but the longer you waited to see whether the person would turn up safe, the greater the chances were that they wouldn't.

'I just wish we knew what we were dealing with,' he murmured to himself.

'You think she's dead?' Imogen spoke softly, without emotion.

Harland glanced across, studying her for a moment, then looked away.

'It shouldn't matter,' he said.

'Sir?' She was frowning at him, puzzled.

Harland reached up to rub the back of his head.

'We have to assume she's alive until we hear otherwise,' he explained. 'We have to try.'

Imogen nodded slowly, then reached into her bag to retrieve her phone, which was buzzing.

Harland twisted in his chair, looking over his shoulder, back towards the café door, then reached into his jacket and drew out his cigarettes and lighter.

'Do you mind?' He turned to Imogen, then shot a guilty glance at the packet. 'We've probably got a few minutes before the food comes . . . '

Imogen, staring at her phone, gave a non-committal shrug. 'It's your health.'

Harland hesitated, then frowned and closed the packet.

'Oh no, I didn't mean . . . ' Imogen looked up at him, eyes suddenly widening. 'I was just kidding. Really.'

He gave her a wary look, then jammed the cigarettes back into his jacket pocket.

'I'll have one after we eat,' he muttered. 'Trying to cut down anyway.'

She stared at him, then put a hand across her mouth to stifle a snort of laughter.

'I'm sorry, sir . . . ' She managed an embarrassed smile.

Was she laughing at him now?

'What's so funny?' he asked, suddenly feeling foolish.

'It's not you, it's just . . . ' Imogen shook her head, taking a deep breath to settle herself. 'My first day working with someone new, and I *promised* myself I wouldn't put my foot in it . . . ' She glanced down at her watch, then looked up at him with a wry smile. 'Didn't even make it past two o'clock.'

A nervous laugh. It was the first chink in that guarded exterior, the first glimpse of who she really was.

'I take it you're a non-smoker?' he asked dryly.

She nodded, putting her phone away.

'Yes. My partner . . . ' A flicker of hesitation. ' . . . used to smoke. But not now.'

'My wife never liked it,' Harland mused.

For a moment, he was somewhere else, years

ago, promising he'd quit sometime, while Alice looked at him and nodded and didn't believe a word of it. But he didn't want those thoughts, not now, not today. He looked at Imogen. The mask seemed to have snapped back into place again.

'Anyway,' he said, leaning forward to rest his elbows on the table. 'When we're done here, I want to go and speak to Matt's neighbours.'

'I thought Uniform had already been round there. You think there's more to come?'

Harland shrugged.

'I think it might rattle him a little, when he gets home and hears that we've been round asking questions. We'll see.'

Imogen was looking over his shoulder towards the door.

'Food's coming,' she said.

* * *

Harland had the all-day breakfast, while Imogen had a chorizo salad. The sun grew warmer as they ate, drawing a few more people out to occupy the tables around them.

'So before the cold cases, you were working with Burgess?' he asked.

'Briefly, yes. You know him?'

'Only to say hello to,' Harland replied. 'He was on that murder over in Durdham Down — a woman who was asphyxiated or something?'

Imogen held up a hand as she finished a mouthful of food, then swallowed.

'With a plastic bag,' she agreed after a

moment. 'And it was three women, actually.'

'Really? I hadn't heard that.'

Imogen nodded.

'He linked it with two other similar killings, one in Gloucester, one in Swindon. All three woman were elaborately tied up, then raped. Sometimes, the killer used bleach to . . . ' She took a breath. ' . . . clean them out, post-mortem.'

He watched her as she took another sip of her drink. She spoke dispassionately; the mask was firmly back in place now. He didn't blame her; you couldn't allow yourself to care too much about the people you were protecting, not in this job.

'And that was what you were working on before moving on to this?' he asked.

'I get loaned out to all sorts of investigations.' She toyed with her fork as she looked across at him. 'You were working with Linwood and Pope?'

'A murder at a nightclub in Stokes Croft, yes.'

Her eyes narrowed slightly.

'Victim sealed up with superglue?'

Harland took a mouthful of food, then looked across at her, nodding as he chewed.

'I know Andy Reed,' she explained. 'He was driving the area car that night.'

Harland swallowed.

'It wasn't pretty,' he told her.

* * *

The sun had crept round, lighting up one side of the table. Harland moved his chair slightly to stay in the shade, but Imogen appeared happy to bask in the rays. There was something familiar about her, a vague feeling that grew as they ate, but he couldn't quite place where he'd seen her before. Not at Portishead, certainly.

'How long have you been with CID?' he asked her.

'Nearly two years,' she replied.

Harland frowned.

'Did they bring you in on the Redland murder?'

She looked up at him, that faint smile again.

'For a little while, yes.'

'That must be where I know you from.'

She nodded, taking a last forkful of salad from her plate.

* * *

Harland finished his meal and pushed the plate away, sitting back in his chair. The sun was warm, and the air still within the walls of the garden. He took out his cigarettes and placed the packet on the table. Imogen set down her knife and fork.

'That was very good,' she sighed. 'Thank you, sir.'

'You're welcome,' he told her.

A harried young woman emerged from the doorway behind them, and sat down a couple of tables away, holding a grumbling baby on her knee.

Harland toyed with his lighter as he looked across at them, then turned to Imogen.

'You don't have kids, do you?' he asked absently.

'No. Perhaps one day, but . . . ' She looked as if she was about to say something, then shook her head. 'There's a lot to think about.'

She was smiling now, but he recognised another carefully guarded response.

Across from them, the baby seemed to be quietening down. Harland put a cigarette in his mouth.

'Do you have children, sir?'

He paused, lighter in hand.

'No, we didn't . . . '

He thought about Alice, about how he always assumed there was plenty of time — all those plans, all those things they'd discussed and looked forward to — just another part of his life that was lost . . .

Imogen was looking at him. It wasn't her fault — she couldn't have known — but the sunlit table had lost its charm and he was suddenly impatient to get back to work.

'You're very easy to talk to,' he told her. *Too easy, in fact.*

'Sir?'

Harland put the cigarette back in the packet and scraped his chair back.

'Come on,' he frowned, getting to his feet. 'Let's go and see what you can coax out of Matt's neighbours.'

8

Harland sat back with his eyes closed, listening to the steady tick-tick of the indicator, while Imogen waited for a break in the traffic. After a moment, the engine note rose and he felt the car swing round to the right.

'Whereabouts?' she asked.

He opened his eyes, blinking as he focused on the familiar view of Eastfield Road, a long terrace of flat-faced town houses, now carved up into a warren of flats. Cars lined the narrow pavement on the right-hand side, while the left was a mish-mash of driveways, and the backs of low industrial buildings. At the far end, the road angled round sharply, where a tall railway embankment cut across the skyline.

'Park anywhere you can,' he murmured. 'It's just there on the right.'

They found a space halfway down the road, and Imogen eased the car in tight to the kerb.

'So you were here before?' she asked, switching the engine off.

'A little while ago,' Harland said, rubbing his eyes. 'Matt reported a burglary, and we thought it might be connected with a run of violent break-ins but it wasn't. Bit of a non-event, really — don't think there was very much taken, so we just gave him the usual tea and sympathy.'

He opened the door and got out. On the other side of the car, Imogen stood looking up at the house. Sharply pointed gables formed a jagged zigzag, like a serrated edge against the sky. The upper two floors were rendered in a grey plaster, while the ground floor was fronted by sandstone blocks, stained brown where water had spilled from the guttering. A basement flat peeped out above some overgrown bushes, with a faded *To Let* sign in front of it.

'Who are the neighbours?' she asked.

'Hang on . . . ' Harland took out his notebook to refresh his memory on the names. 'There's a Mrs Hamilton on the ground floor — I think I met her before — then there's Matt in the one above her, and a Nigel Reynolds at the top.'

'And who do you want to speak to first?'

'I don't mind.' He pushed the car door shut. 'Let's start with the old lady.'

A cracked concrete path led from the gate to a short flight of steps. At the top, Harland tried the door just in case, but it wouldn't open. He leaned forward to study the three bell-pushes, set one below the other. Only the bottom one was labelled — 'Hamilton' — and he pressed it.

On the steps behind him, Imogen had turned to look across the street, where a high brick wall enclosed a small yard.

'What's down there?' she asked, pointing at the narrow lane that led away round the side of the yard.

'Backs of people's gardens, some derelict garages.' Harland shrugged. 'It doesn't lead anywhere.'

They turned around as the door clicked and a buzzer sounded. Harland's eye caught the subtle movement in the net curtains of the ground-floor window and he smiled to himself.

Mrs Hamilton, I presume.

Twitching curtains were often a good sign. With luck, she'd be the sort of person who made it her business to know about the comings and goings in the street.

Opening the door, he stepped over the threshold into the cool stillness of a small entrance hallway. Ahead of him, a straight flight of stairs ascended to the upper storeys, while a narrow passageway cut through to the back of the building. The floor tiles were worn enough to be original, but they were spotlessly clean.

On his right, beside a four-panel door, painted in an old-fashioned shade of green, a slim storage unit hung on the wall with pigeonholes for letters, and a small wooden table below supported a stack of free newspapers, neatly folded.

They walked over to the door, and Harland knocked. A moment later, there was a muffled rattling, before the door opened as far as the safety chain would allow.

'Yes?' A thin strip of the old lady peered out at them through the gap.

'Mrs Hamilton?' Harland took out his warrant card and held it up for inspection. 'It's Detective Harland. Do you remember, I came to see you once before?'

'Yes, of course. Just a minute.' The door quickly shut as the chain was removed, then it swung open to reveal Mrs Hamilton's full width. 'Come in, both of you.'

She was a very large woman — late sixties or early seventies, it was impossible to say for certain — with oddly tinted grey hair, and thick-framed glasses which she peered over the top of. On the floor behind her, a small white and brown dog stared up at them anxiously.

'This is Detective Gower,' Harland said, introducing Imogen as he stepped inside.

'Pleased to meet you.' The old lady closed the door behind them. 'You're here about the missing girl?'

'That's right.' Harland nodded as they all stood in the awkward closeness of the inner hallway. 'We just have a few questions, if that's all right.'

'Certainly.' She smiled, apparently very pleased at the idea of questions. 'Do go through to the lounge. Can I offer you a cup of tea? It's no trouble . . . '

'I'm fine, thank you,' Imogen replied.

'Not for me, thanks.' Harland smiled. He walked into a large front room that smelled of furniture polish. Two mismatched pairs of high-backed armchairs faced each other across the patterned rug, each topped by a delicate antimacassar. Antique cabinets and occasional tables interspersed the chairs and every flat surface was dressed with some sort of lace napkin.

He paused, wondering where he should sit, then noted the small television set, and the two chairs angled to face it.

One for her, one for the dog.

He took a seat on the other side of the room, and Imogen took the one beside him. They watched as Mrs Hamilton settled down opposite them, both her and the chair groaning as she lowered herself into position.

'Oh, that's better,' she grimaced, then patted the chair on her right. 'Come on, Gordon.'

The little dog, which had been lurking in the hallway, scampered across the rug and jumped up onto the empty seat beside her.

'Good boy,' she cooed.

'He's a fox terrier, isn't he?' Imogen asked, leaning forward slightly.

'That's right,' Mrs Hamilton beamed. 'Say hello to the nice policewoman, Gordon.'

Gordon peered across at them doubtfully.

'My aunt had one,' Imogen smiled. Harland wondered whether that was true, or whether she'd just said it to put the old lady at ease. In any event, it seemed to have had the desired effect.

'I know you've already spoken to one of my colleagues,' he began.

'Yes, that pleasant young officer who came round yesterday.' Mrs Hamilton nodded gravely. 'He asked me about all the times Laura had visited. I take it there's no news on her . . . ?'

'We're still making enquiries,' Harland replied.

'Oh.' Her expression darkened, but she rallied hopefully. 'Well, sometimes no news is good news. How can I help?'

'I'd like to know about the last time Laura was here,' Harland explained. Best to start with some general things, and see what came up. They could drop in a few subtle questions about Matt along the way. 'That would have been on Friday, yes?'

'That's the last time I saw her,' Mrs Hamilton said.

'You were in all evening?'

The old woman drew herself up in her chair, which creaked alarmingly as she shifted her weight.

'Well,' she said. 'As I told that nice uniformed officer, we were watching *Doc Martin* that evening . . . '

We? Harland glanced at Imogen, but she gave him the faintest of smiles and looked at the dog. *Of course . . . 'we'*.

' . . . they're repeating the first series just now and I think it's marvellous — that Martin Clunes is *such* a talented actor. Anyway, it finished at eleven, because we were watching it on the Plus One channel, and I had just popped through to put the kettle on for a final cup of tea. I won't drink coffee, not any more — the caffeine, you see . . . '

Harland gritted his teeth and nodded encouragingly.

' . . . anyway,' Mrs Hamilton leaned forward and lowered her voice. 'That's when I saw them.'

'Saw who?' he asked.

Mrs Hamilton frowned, as though greatly inconvenienced by details.

'Matt and his young lady friend, of course.' Her expression became a little haughty and she glanced towards the net curtains. 'I heard the front door slam, and I just happened to look out of the window. I did tell your colleague all about this, you know.'

'Of course.' Harland forced himself to smile

patiently. From her vantage point at the window she probably saw everyone who came and went. Except when there was something she liked on TV. 'And they got into his car?'

'The little red one, yes.'

'Right.'

Matt claimed not to have seen Laura since the week before last. What was he playing at? Did he honestly not think they'd check up on that?

'Do you know if they'd been here all evening?' Imogen asked.

Mrs Hamilton paused, her face lined in thought.

'I can't be certain,' she said after a moment. 'I don't *think* so. I'm fairly sure I heard Matt come in around six — that's his usual time — but I didn't hear anyone with him. And I definitely didn't see *her* arrive.'

Imogen appeared to consider this.

'Do you happen to remember what either of them was wearing?' she asked. 'When they left?'

Harland nodded to himself. It was a good question.

'She was wearing a *very* short skirt and some sort of cream-coloured top,' Mrs Hamilton replied. 'I'm afraid I couldn't see the front of it because they were going down the steps and he had his arm around her.'

'And Matt?'

'Oh, he had on that leather jacket of his — the one with the big embroidered eagle on the back . . .' She paused, eyes turning to the window again as she tried to remember. ' . . . and I think some sort of cap or hat? It was difficult to see.'

'His car was parked right outside?' Imogen asked.

'Yes.' Mrs Hamilton attempted to turn around and point, then thought better of it and waved one hand vaguely over her shoulder. 'Just out there on the left.'

'Did you see which direction they went when they drove away?' Harland interjected. 'Up or down the street?'

The old lady closed her eyes for a moment, remembering, then pointed to her left.

'Down the street,' she said firmly. 'They went towards the railway, I'm certain of it.'

Harland nodded thoughtfully.

'And that was the last time you saw either of them that evening?' he pressed. 'You didn't see or hear Matt coming home that night?'

'Oh no, I would have been in bed,' Mrs Hamilton assured him. She turned to Imogen and confided, 'I always go through before midnight; beauty sleep, you know.'

Imogen smiled back, then affected a concerned frown.

'How's he taking it?' she asked, leaning forward a little. 'Matt, I mean. Is he holding up all right?'

Very nicely done. Harland settled back in his chair as the old lady's reservations seemed to evaporate.

'Well,' she sighed heavily, reaching out a hand to give the dog a reassuring pat. 'He's always struck me as a pleasant enough young man. Not without his faults, of course, and he seems quite determined to misunderstand the recycling bin rota, but nice enough . . . '

She paused, as though weighing up how best to broach a delicate subject, then continued, 'Now, I'm not one to pry, but I do think he and Laura have a . . . *close* relationship. I don't know what sort of girl she is — Matt hasn't introduced us, so there's never more than a passing 'Hello' in the hallway — but I *have* seen her leaving the house in the morning, *wearing last night's clothes*, if you know what I mean.'

Imogen maintained a straight face.

'So Laura stayed over here quite a few times?' she enquired.

'Well, I couldn't say for certain,' Mrs Hamilton allowed herself a disapproving look up at the ceiling, 'but sometimes one hears things . . . noises, if you know what I mean.'

Harland smiled to himself, imagining her straining to hear the creaking of the bed from upstairs.

'And on the Friday evening, did you hear anything then?' he asked. 'Anything out of the ordinary?'

Mrs Hamilton's face fell.

'I'm sorry.' She shook her head, rippling the folds of skin around her neck. 'The first I knew was when I heard the front door close.'

She looked sad now. He wondered whether she was sorry that she was unable to help the enquiry, or disappointed that she didn't have more information to prolong the interview. It must be lonely living here, with only the dog for company.

'That's all right,' he reassured her. 'You're

being very helpful. We just have to ask a lot of different questions to make sure we don't miss anything important.'

He saw her face brighten a little.

'Are you sure I can't get you a cup of tea?' she asked hopefully.

Harland rubbed the back of his neck.

'That would be lovely,' he lied.

* * *

They waited until the green door clicked shut behind them, then turned and made their way over to the stairs. Harland gripped the banister and looked at Imogen. She knew they'd spent longer than necessary with the old lady, but she was smart enough not to mention it. Good.

'Let's see if the Reynolds guy is in,' he said.

'OK.'

The first-floor landing was still and gloomy, with indirect light reflected up from the hallway below, and a faint glow from the floor above. Harland paused, then consulted his notebook again.

'Nigel Reynolds, twenty-six years old . . . ' He paused, frowning slightly. ' . . . digital artist, whatever that is.'

Beside him, Imogen nodded silently, her eyes already turned upward towards the next floor. There was something a little unnerving about her, but at least he didn't have to worry about her blurting things out and being overheard by others in the house . . . something he'd needed to remind Pope of more than once. He glanced at Matt's pale blue door, then began to climb the second flight of stairs.

The top-floor landing was brighter, lit by a small skylight. There was one door, painted white, and Harland knocked on it sharply. They stood there, waiting, listening, but there was no sound from beyond the door. Imogen glanced at her watch.

'Out at work?' she suggested.

'Maybe,' Harland said, knocking once more. He should have rung the bell downstairs, saved them coming all the way up here, but he hadn't wanted to announce their arrival unnecessarily — you could often learn more when you surprised people. 'Looks like we'll have to come back.'

The glare of the sun seemed very bright after the dim interior of the house. At the foot of the front steps, Harland paused, then wandered slowly round to look down at the basement flat. The curtains were half drawn, and a drift of dust and debris had blown up against the sunken front door.

'Want me to find out who's got the keys to the place?' Imogen asked. He nodded, pleased by her anticipation. It didn't look as though anyone had been in there for a while, but the thought of a bloodstained body, bound and gagged and a few feet away, flared suddenly in his mind. *Better safe than sorry*.

'Make sure it's been searched.' He turned and followed her back down the concrete path. 'Good work in there, by the way.'

Imogen hesitated and smiled at him across the

roof of the car, unguarded again for a moment.

'Thank you, sir.'

They got in and she reversed the car back into the narrow lane to turn around. Harland gazed out through the windscreen at the building.

'Well, someone's not telling the truth,' he sighed.

Imogen nodded.

'Matt said he hadn't seen Laura for a couple of weeks but Mrs Hamilton says they were here the night she disappeared.'

'Exactly.' The tiny flame of hope he'd held — that Laura might simply turn up, alive and well — flickered and went out. 'And that makes me a lot less optimistic about her chances.'

Imogen tapped the steering wheel thoughtfully.

'Maybe Nigel Reynolds will know something,' she frowned.

THREE MONTHS EARLIER

9

There was something . . . *different* about the man who was moving into the empty flat downstairs. Nigel noticed things like that. Not *wrong*, just different.

The place had been vacant for less than a month, silent and still, ever since Linda and Eric had moved out. They'd been nice. Nigel had liked them both, and often spoke to Linda when he'd passed her in the hallway — but with a baby on the way they needed more space and fewer stairs. They'd boxed up their lives and gone, leaving the middle floor quiet and empty. Now, Matt Garrick would be living there.

Mrs Hamilton, the enormous old lady who occupied the ground floor with her tiny white dog, had told him the name. 'About your age,' she'd said, nodding encouragingly, as though describing a distant cousin who might join them on a family holiday. But age didn't tell him anything. And there had been no other clues as to what Matt might be like until this morning, when the old Volvo estate had pulled up in the street below.

Nigel leaned closer to the window, staring down through the bright gap in the dark curtains, watching his new neighbour lifting cardboard boxes from the back of the car. As far as he could see, Matt was indeed about the same age as him, tall and slim with a mop of black hair that bounced as he straightened up and slammed the hatchback shut. From here, he looked like one of the mannequins in the cool shops, with his jeans and a red T-shirt beneath a crumpled check shirt, faded Converse All Stars on his feet — that 'nothing special' style that looked so effortless but was so difficult to pull off.

And he was confident. Nigel watched him carrying a large, taped-up box towards the gate, then balancing it on the garden wall as he stopped to speak with the quiet coloured woman who lived two doors down. They were too far away to hear what was being said, but he saw the smiles, a moment of shared laughter, the friendly goodbye as they parted. Matt seemed to be the sort of person that got on with everybody.

Lucky him.

Nigel lowered his hand, letting the gap in the curtains fall shut, then turned away, walking back to his desk and the restful glow of his screen.

* * *

They didn't actually meet that week.

Nigel had heard the muffled noise of the TV late at night, and found there was something reassuring about it. Since Eric and Linda left, the only sounds had been the creak of the floorboards as he moved around, and the rattle of the old sash windows that always shook when a train rumbled across the Arches and along the tall embankment at the end of the road. Working largely from home meant he spent a lot of time here, and he welcomed the echoes of habitation from the floor below — comforting, familiar sounds to banish the lonely atmosphere that had been gathering over the previous weeks.

The first letters started appearing a couple of days after Matt moved in. There was a small wooden storage unit on the wall of the downstairs hallway, with open pigeonholes, one for each of the flats. Early one morning, Nigel went down to find that someone — presumably Mrs Hamilton — had gathered up the bundles of circulars that still arrived for Eric and Linda, and moved them to the small parcel table below the unit. There was something rather sad, rather final, about that. But the middle pigeonhole still contained a single letter — from a broadband supplier, judging from the logo on the back. Nigel eased the envelope into the light so that he could read the name *Matthew S Garrick* on the address label. He wondered what the S stood for, as he pushed the envelope back into its hole and gathered up his own mail.

There were no further sightings of the Volvo that week. Walking back from the takeaway, late on Wednesday night, he wondered whether it had been borrowed for the move. After all, it was an old man's sort of vehicle and didn't really fit the image of his new neighbour. Turning right into Eastfield Road, he paused for a moment. There were plenty of spaces to park but only one strange car — a red Mini, which he'd noticed yesterday, farther along the road. And Matt was definitely home — the middle flat was still without curtains and light shone out from the windows. Nigel walked along the pavement, glancing down as he drew level with the Mini, but it was too dark to see anything inside.

Must be Matt's.

It wasn't a particularly sporty model but somehow it seemed cooler than his own car — a black Peugeot turbo that he'd soon regretted buying and which now languished in one of the old garages down the narrow lane opposite. He frowned and walked back to the gate, fumbling for his keys as he climbed the steps to the front door. Once inside the downstairs hallway, he heard faint music — not the sort of thing he listened to, but the kind of music they played on the radio — and it grew steadily clearer as he climbed the stairs to the first-floor landing. A few feet away, he could see the old, four-panel door, with its layers of sky-blue gloss and the shiny number 2 screwed to it. Should he go over and knock? Introduce himself?

Hi, I'm Nigel Reynolds, your neighbour from upstairs . . .

No, not unless he wanted to come across as a complete homo. What would he look like, standing there in the hallway with takeaway-for-one in his hand, knocking on the door late at night? He was such an idiot. Shaking his head, he turned back to the stairs and continued his climb to the top floor. This was a chance to make a friend — he wasn't going to screw it up.

* * *

It happened on Sunday night, as he trudged slowly down the stairs with two black plastic sacks of rubbish. He'd been working some long hours recently, and the normally tiresome chore of tidying up had actually been a welcome relief from staring at the screen. Rounding the first-floor landing, he heard the front door latch snap shut below him and, as he made his way down to the hallway, came face to face with his new neighbour at the foot of the stairs.

'All right.' Matt's voice was low and smooth, and his face broke into an easy smile. 'I'm the new guy; Matt. You must be . . . top floor?'

'That's right. Oh, and the name's Nigel.'

'Good to know you, Nigel.' He extended his hand, then noticed the rubbish sacks and withdrew it with a grin. It triggered a memory of being at school, where other kids would offer him their hands then jerk them away and jeer as he reached for them, but Matt wasn't teasing, only smiling.

His teeth were slightly too large and, up close, he looked rakishly thin, but broad shoulders and a strong jawline compensated for that. Thoughtful blue eyes gazed out beneath the untidy black hair that was long enough at the front to touch his eyebrows. His leather jacket looked old, but good.

'Er, likewise,' Nigel managed, trying to adjust his grip on the knots that held the sacks shut.

'Sorry, fella.' Matt stepped smoothly to one side. 'Let me get out of your way.'

'Thanks . . . ' The black plastic twisted awkwardly around his fingers as he moved. 'The bins get collected tomorrow.'

'Yeah?' Matt's eyes had flickered towards the

stairs, as though his mind had already moved on, but he turned back and smiled again, appearing interested. 'You'll need to come up — or down, I suppose — once I've got the flat straight. Then you can tell me all the stuff I need to know, like the bins, and who's who in the street.'

'Great.' Nigel smiled at him, though part of him suspected it wouldn't be long before his new neighbour knew more people round here than he did himself. 'That'd be . . . great.'

He had the curious sense of being welcomed to his own building.

'Nice one.' Matt started up the stairs, then paused, turning to lean over the banister and inclining his head along the hall. 'Manage the back door OK?'

Nigel did his best to shrug with the rubbish bags.

'It's fine,' he said. 'No problem.'

'OK. Later.'

'Later,' Nigel replied.

Later?

He *never* said 'later'. It was a bit like the times he'd used a different way of speaking when faced with a plumber or a repairman — nothing too proper, trying to sound more like them, so they wouldn't overcharge him or sell him something he didn't need. Why was he doing it now?

He frowned, opening his mouth to say something else, but Matt had already turned away, and was taking the stairs two at a time. Nigel watched him disappear, until the weight of the rubbish bags became uncomfortable. Bowing his head, he made his way outside to the bins.

Back upstairs, he used his elbow to ease the door shut behind him. He worried about germs from touching the bins, and there were still dishes in the kitchen sink, so he went into the bathroom to wash his hands.

At least they'd finally met. And he'd got through the encounter without saying anything stupid or putting his foot in it — that was *something*, yes. But what about the next time? And the time after that? He wished he knew more about his new neighbour, so he could make sure he didn't say the wrong thing.

He straightened up from the basin and reached for a towel, staring at his reflection in the mirror as he dried his hands.

They *were* about the same age. Similar height, too. But his own hair wasn't black, it was a mass of dreary brown. His brows were too prominent, his nose too pointed. He looked down at the slight tummy bulge in his black *Inception* T-shirt, the spotless trainers with their expensive shock-absorbing soles, and sighed.

The same age, but really quite different.

Once, when he was growing up, his mother had regarded him with obvious disappointment and asked why he couldn't be more like Declan Boyle, the sporty kid who lived across the street from them. Tonight, he stared into the mirror and asked himself why he couldn't be more like Matt.

10

Nigel trudged up the slope with his head down and his hands jammed into his pockets. The pharmacy had been full of old people and he hated that. The infirmity, the slow movements, the timid expressions. For some reason it bothered him more today. He waited for a break in the traffic and hurried across the road.

There was no answer from Mrs Hamilton's door, so he left the bag with her prescriptions on the small parcel table where she'd see it, then went upstairs. The fresh air had given him an appetite, though it was too early for lunch. He promised himself a small snack before he got back to his work. Reaching the top-floor landing, he drew out the small silver key and let himself in, but his attention was immediately caught by a scrap of paper on the hall carpet. Someone had slipped a note under his door, and he stooped to pick it up.

Watching the game tonite if U want 2 swing by. Matt.

Nigel stood for a moment, then pushed the door closed behind him. He was aware of the foolish grin on his face but that didn't matter. Nobody could see him. And this evening, he'd be downstairs watching the game — football presumably — with Matt. It was short notice, of course, but it'd be OK. Clutching the note in his hand, he walked through to his computer and began searching for information on which teams might be playing tonight.

It was some time past his usual lunch hour when the rumbling in his stomach finally pulled him away from the screen. Standing up, he stretched his arms out wide, then wandered through to the kitchen. There were four meatball pasta meals stacked in the fridge, the one with the shortest sell-by date on top. He took it out, removed the cardboard sleeve, and placed the container in the microwave. While it was cooking, he opened a new bottle of Fanta and poured himself a glass, then paused.

Should he take something with him tonight?

People often took a bottle of something when they visited someone. It was polite, friendly. And Matt had just moved in, so it would be kind of like a house-warming thing as well, wouldn't it? Yes, he ought to take something with him. But what?

Not a bottle of Fanta. That would be lame. Wine? He knew nothing about wine and anyway, it might come across as a bit gay. He scratched the back of his neck, wondering what Matt drank.

Behind him, the microwave beeped. Frowning, he took out the hot plastic tray, holding it carefully by the edges, then carried it through to his desk.

* * *

Kick-off was scheduled for 7.45 — he'd checked on the BBC website — so he locked up and made his way downstairs at 7.30. Walking along to the light blue door, he halted, took a breath, then knocked smartly, the four-pack of beer tucked under one awkward arm.

In the end, it had been obvious what to bring. He felt sure he'd seen bottles in the recycling bin that belonged to the middle flat, and had popped outside to check. Sure enough, there were several green bottles and Nigel had lifted one out carefully, not wanting to draw attention to himself with the clinking of glass, and checked the label . . .

Now there were footsteps approaching. The door opened and Matt stood there. He smiled as he noticed the beer.

'Ah, someone else who drinks Becks,' he grinned, pulling the door wider and beckoning Nigel inside. 'Man after my own heart.'

Nigel smiled and stepped into the hallway. His little bit of research had paid off — it was going to be a good evening.

'Come on through.' Matt walked ahead of him. 'Living room's this way.'

It was the strangest feeling. He'd often spoken to Linda and Eric in the hallway, but he hadn't seen inside the flat before — for some reason they'd never invited him in. Now, though, as he stepped into the large front room, he was struck by the similarity in the layout. Just like his own flat — the same wood panel door opening on to the same high-ceilinged room, with two tall windows in the far wall. Just like his own flat, and yet completely different. The position of the two comfy sofas, the TV on a glass-topped stand, the coffee table and the big piles of DVDs stacked against the wall — it was as if he'd come home to find someone had replaced all his furnishings.

'Nigel?'

He turned round to see Matt watching him expectantly, one hand outstretched. For a moment, he didn't understand why, then realised it was the beer his neighbour was looking at. He held the bottles out.

'Sorry. There you are.'

'Ta.' Matt took the four-pack from him. 'I'll get you a cold one — these could do with some time in the fridge.'

Shit. Forgot to chill them.

Nigel was suddenly annoyed with himself for making such a silly mistake, betraying the fact that beer and football weren't the sort of things he normally did, but Matt didn't seem to mind. He turned to enter the kitchen.

'Grab a seat,' he called through. 'Make yourself at home.'

The TV was already on, snarling out a succession of brash adverts for razor blades and car tyres, but as Nigel sank into the sofa his eyes were sweeping around the room, noting all the little details and differences from his own living room; the glossy magazines on the table, the framed black-and-white print of a New York street, the huge cylindrical floor lamp that stood in the corner of the room. Cool things that girls would be impressed by.

Matt appeared in the doorway with two cold bottles and a huge bag of crisps.

'Catch,' he said, tossing the packet across the room.

Nigel lunged forward, almost bursting the crisps open in his determination not to drop the bag.

'Thanks,' he said, sinking back into his seat.

'No worries.'

Matt moved round to the table, took a bottle opener from under one arm, and expertly flipped the tops from the two bottles onto the floor. He handed one to Nigel, then flopped down into his chair.

'Barça or Madrid?'

Nigel looked up from his bottle and blinked at him, momentarily confused.

'Pardon?'

'Barcelona or Real Madrid — who do you reckon will win?'

Of course — the game.

The man on the BBC website had suggested that Real Madrid would probably struggle with two of their star players unavailable through injury. Nigel frowned, as though considering the two teams.

'I've got a feeling Barcelona might do it,' he said.

'Hope so,' Matt replied. 'Never been that keen on Madrid.'

He put his feet up on the coffee table and took a long pull on the beer bottle.

Nigel smiled, pleased with himself.

'So,' he said, eager not to allow any awkward silences, 'how are you settling in?'

'Yeah, it's all good.' Matt nodded, then gave a

little chuckle. 'But I reckon I've already screwed up with old Mrs Battleaxe downstairs.'

'Really?' Nigel leaned forward. 'What happened?'

'Oh, nothing happened. It's just the old biddy getting herself all worked up.' He stared at his bottle, turning it in his hand. For a moment it seemed as though that was all he would say on the subject, but then he shook his head and smiled. 'She started banging on about how I had put some stuff in the *wrong bin*. You know, like I put some of my recycling into one of *her* container things. Like *that* even matters.'

He gave a short laugh and took another drink.

'Yeah, well, she has a thing about the recycling,' Nigel said. 'She doesn't like the wrong things in the wrong containers.'

And neither did he, but he wasn't about to say anything to alienate his new friend.

'Yeah, well, *I've* got a thing about stupid little yappy dogs,' Matt scowled, 'but do I *recycle* her stupid little rat mongrel in one of the bins?'

Nigel gaped at him, aghast.

Surely he wouldn't . . .

'Nah,' Matt winked at him. 'I make *allowances*.'

He leaned forward, and clinked the neck of his bottle against Nigel's.

'Cheers.'

'Cheers.' Nigel nodded at him uncertainly, then raised his bottle and took a long swig.

Matt grinned, then leaned across to take the remote control from the arm of the sofa. Aiming it at the TV, he began turning up the volume so that the roar of the crowd filled the room.

'Here we go,' he said brightly.

* * *

Conversation contracted to football once the match kicked off. At first, Nigel was concerned that his limited knowledge would let him down — he'd never been interested in sport, and there was too much to learn in a single afternoon. But if Matt sensed the inexperience, he didn't seem to mind — indeed, his enthusiasm for the game was infectious and, when Barça took the lead with a looping volley into the top corner, they both cheered.

'See that?' Matt beamed, passing Nigel another bottle of beer. 'Pure class.'

'Brilliant,' Nigel agreed, genuinely excited.

They clinked bottles together and settled back to watch the screen.

* * *

Half-time came quickly, with another hail of adverts. Returning from the bathroom, Matt dropped into his chair and gave a satisfied sigh.

'So,' Nigel picked up the bag of crisps and offered them to Matt, 'what do you do for a living?'

He'd been curious, looking round the room for clues, but there was nothing to suggest what his neighbour did.

'I'm a mechanic.' Matt took a handful of crisps. 'Cars mostly, but we do a bit on vans and all that. Nothing special, but it pays the bills.'

Of course.

Nigel knew his neighbour kept regular hours, and had seen him leaving the building early on weekday mornings. He'd been unable to guess what he did from his clothing, but Matt would wear overalls, and he probably kept them at work.

'I'm not much good with cars,' he smiled. 'Broke down once, went to lift the bonnet up and then I thought, *Why did I do that?* I mean, it's not as if there's anything under there that I know how to fix.'

Matt laughed.

'Ah, it's not just you, mate.' He spoke through a mouthful of crisps. 'Most modern cars, you just plug 'em into the computer and it tells you what needs replacing.'

Mate.

Nigel smiled to himself and took another drink. He was doing well, and determined to keep the conversation going.

'So what do you drive?' he asked, quietly pleased that he already knew.

'I've got a Mini,' Matt replied.

'The red one, parked outside?'

Matt looked at him curiously, then shrugged.

'That's right,' he said. 'Mate in the trade did me a really good deal.'

Nigel nodded. A sudden idea came to him — an opportunity to make himself look good and do something for his new neighbour.

'There are some empty garages down the lane opposite,' he explained. 'I took one when I bought the flat upstairs. I can probably dig out the details if you're interested?'

It had been his research that had tracked down the owner of the garages. The man didn't live in Bristol any more so they were just sitting there. Another 'good deal', and one which would surely ingratiate him.

But Matt was shaking his head.

'I don't really have any spare cash at the moment. Getting this place was tough enough.' He seemed to dismiss the idea, then reached forward for the remote control and started tapping the volume up again. 'Aye aye, here we go.'

* * *

The second half seemed to unfold at a slower pace. Nigel found himself watching the clock in the top left corner of the screen, aware of the growing need to pee. He shifted positions once or twice, but he knew he would never make it through to full time.

Eventually, he sat forward on the sofa and turned to Matt.

'Mind if I use your bathroom?'

'Sure.' Matt's eyes never left the screen, but he gestured vaguely towards the door. 'It's straight down the hall.'

Nigel smiled. Just like the layout upstairs.

He got to his feet, feeling a little unsteady. How many beers had he had? Then again, he didn't usually drink at all.

The sound of the TV diminished as he walked

down the hallway. The bathroom door was painted in the same white gloss as his own. He pushed it open and instinctively reached for the light switch, an oddly familiar motion for a different place, then pushed the door closed behind him.

Moving forward, he planted his feet apart and hurriedly unzipped himself, then sighed as the relief spread up through his body. He was surprised how badly he'd needed to go, had forgotten how beer went straight through him.

Flushing the toilet, he turned to wash his hands. Bending over the basin, his eyes were drawn to the different products arranged on the shelf below the mirror. Toothpaste, shaving gel, moisturiser, a small plastic container that seemed to contain some sort of pills, and a sculptured glass bottle of aftershave.

He leaned forward, bringing his nose to the top of the bottle so that he could smell it.

Very nice. Women must love that.

He made a mental note of the name, and determined to look for it among the sprawling department store perfume counters next time he was in town.

Straightening up, he turned to the towel rail, but was momentarily thrown to find there wasn't one — just a blank space on the wall. He glanced around, suddenly at a loss, until he spotted a dark blue towel draped over the shower curtain. With a faint smile, he dried his hands, then went back out into the hallway.

He walked slowly, pausing as he passed the bedroom. The door was ajar, and it was oddly tempting to look inside, but a crescendo of noise from the TV and a whoop from Matt spooked him, and he hurried back through to the front room.

'Two nil!' Matt was pointing at the screen, where action replays were showing the second goal from a succession of different angles. 'Whoa! Just imagine how it must feel to score like that.'

He shook his head slowly, an expression of wonder on his face as he watched the Barcelona striker punch the air in exultant slow motion.

'Incredible,' Nigel agreed.

⋆ ⋆ ⋆

Barcelona won the game, and Matt was in a good mood, bounding through to the kitchen as the adverts started, and returning with the four-pack of beer bottles.

'Here we go,' he grinned. 'They should be cold enough now.'

'Thanks.' Nigel had been about to lever himself out of the sagging sofa and struggle to his feet, but the evening didn't seem to be ending quite yet. He accepted another bottle from Matt and slumped back into his seat, feeling warm and mellow.

'So I meant to ask before,' Matt dropped into his chair and reached for the crisp packet, then crumpled it when he found it was empty, 'what do *you* do?'

Nigel smiled, letting his head sink back against the upholstery.

'I'm a Photoshop artist,' he replied.

'You what?'

'Photoshop. You know?' He sat forward with some effort. 'I retouch digital photographs on the computer.'

'Oh . . . like, airbrushing pictures of people to make them look better?'

'Yeah, like that.'

'Wow.' Matt seemed impressed. 'Where'd you learn to do that?'

Nigel shrugged.

'Dunno really, just picked it up. Been doing it for years and just got more and more into it.'

'So you spend all day making women look thinner and that?'

'Well, it's not really like that,' Nigel laughed, 'but yeah, sometimes.'

'Lucky so-and-so.' Matt took another swig of beer. 'Work in town, do you?'

'Depends.' Nigel rubbed his eyes, stifling a yawn. 'I work with an agency at the Watershed, so I go down there sometimes. But mostly I work at home.'

Matt shook his head and grinned at him.

'Sitting at home, looking at photos of women all day? And they *pay* you for that?' He raised his bottle in salute. 'You really are a lucky, lucky guy!'

* * *

Back upstairs, Nigel pushed his front door closed, then allowed himself to lean against it, a foolish grin spreading across his face. It had been a great evening, and Matt was a great guy. Just being around him filled Nigel with a tingle of unfamiliar confidence.

He pushed himself upright and started through to the front room, but halted as he realised that he needed something. Frowning, he stood swaying in the hallway, trying to concentrate.

What was it? Oh yes . . .

He turned and lurched towards the bathroom.

Standing at the toilet, he gave out a long, happy sigh. This was how evenings should be, enjoying yourself and relaxing. He flushed, pressing the lever with an extravagant flourish, then turned to wash his hands. Drinking a few beers and watching the game with a mate. He nodded to himself as he dried his hands, then paused for a moment. Taking the towel, he draped it carefully over the shower curtain, and smiled to himself.

It had been a great evening.

11

Nigel leaned forward, his face close enough to the screen that he could feel its warmth. A set of tiny Lego figures were arranged along the top edge of the monitor, silhouetted in the gloom, and a stylised rubber Guy Fawkes mask — just like the kind the Anonymous hackers wore — leered out from its resting place among the other collectibles that crowded his desk. With one hand resting on the keyboard, and the other lightly holding the mouse, he panned easily around the photograph, following the natural line down from the woman's eye to the side of her nose. There was a little discolouration on her upper lip — a tiny red-brown mark below her nostril — and he zoomed in until it was magnified in the centre of his screen. Choosing a soft airbrush mode, he selected a nearby area of her face that caught the light in the same way, then began copying it across, gently stroking the blemish away beneath a veneer of perfect skin. It was delicate work, and he didn't blink until the mark was gone. Then, rubbing his eyes, he sat back and zoomed the photograph out again, studying the face for any telltale trace of his correction, but there was none. The upper lip was flawless.

People assumed that photo editing was all about giving models longer legs and narrower waists, but that was just a minor part of what he did. So much of the work went into correcting the little things — spots, stray eyebrow hairs, open pores, wrinkles. A typical face might have a hundred tiny blemishes, none of them important on their own, but it made a real difference when you compared the 'before' and 'after' versions and saw them all suddenly fixed.

There was always a host of things to put right — fly-away hair to tidy, skin colouration to smooth, eyes that needed to catch the light better so they'd sparkle — and each image required grading and toning, so that it would look its best in print or on-screen.

Nigel gazed at the woman in the photograph. She was in her thirties, wearing a bright red cardigan, looking over her shoulder and smiling with teeth that (thanks to him) were beautifully even. The agency had told him this job was for a dental firm, so he'd paid particular attention to the mouth. He wondered whether he should give her larger breasts, but decided against it. The photographer had caught her well enough, and the image showed off her shape nicely. Better not to overdo it.

Leaning right back in his chair, he yawned and rubbed his eyes again, then peered down at his watch. It was later than he'd thought — almost eight o'clock. He clicked to save his work, then pushed himself away from the screen. It had been a long day.

Getting to his feet, he wandered over to the window and drew back the curtain to peer down. The street below was deserted and he lifted his gaze to look out across the low buildings and the untidy grey-green foliage, where the railway embankment swept round in a long, lazy arc. From childhood, he'd felt a curious excitement when he looked at a railway track — continuous parallel lines of steel, curving into the distance. There was a sense of potential in those rails — of being connected to faraway places and people, even if he never visited any of them. As a boy he'd stared at the track, hoping that wherever his father was, he was living near those same rails, because it seemed to bring his memory closer.

Sighing, he let the curtain fall closed, and turned away. Walking through to his small kitchen, he moved slowly along the short counter, opening the cupboards even though he knew he wasn't hungry. He briefly reached in and withdrew a packet of crackers, unfolding the wrapper a little, then thrusting it back onto the shelf.

Snacking wouldn't do any good.

He closed the cupboard and wandered back into the front room. The TV was flickering away in the corner. He hadn't been watching it, but having it on in the background made the flat seem less lonely. As he looked, the screen began showing one of those awful charity adverts — sick people, bravely trying to guilt him into giving more money to fight cancer. He shuddered, and moved quickly to pick up the remote control, muting the plaintive voices, and vowing never to donate a penny to any cause that used that sort of advert.

Click, silence.

He put down the remote and exhaled slowly,

turning to look across the empty living room.

Not quite silence.

He stood still, listening for a moment. Stilling his breathing, he could make out the sound of voices, indistinct yet close. He glanced towards the door, but it wasn't coming from the hallway . . .

. . . and then lowered his eyes to stare at the floor.

Of course.

It must be coming from the downstairs flat. This sounded like a TV show, but it was difficult to be sure. Linda and Eric never seemed to have their TV on loud and they'd been gone for a while.

Nigel listened, inclining his head. He found himself wondering what Matt was watching. From what he could tell, it seemed to be a woman's voice talking. He squatted down, straining to hear better, then placed his palms on the floor and knelt forward so his ear was just above the carpet.

He could nearly make it out now, but it was still very faint.

Raising his head, he looked up at the front room, seeing it from a low, unfamiliar angle. His own place, yet . . . different. He found himself recalling the room downstairs.

How did Matt have his things laid out?

Staying on his knees, he shuffled across to the side of living room where he would be directly above Matt's TV, and leaned forward to listen again. The voice was louder now, and he could almost hear what it was saying . . .

As he concentrated, his eye settled on the edge

of the carpet, slightly curled up where it stopped at the wall. Frowning, he reached out a hand and worked his fingers down between the frayed edge and the skirting board, wriggling them down until he could feel the rough underside against his fingertips. Then, very slowly, he began to pull, working the loose edge towards him, curling the carpet back a little more to reveal the old floorboards beneath.

The sound was clearer now. Moving forward, he lowered his ear to a gap between the age-blackened boards, smiling as he made out snatches of conversation clearly. The female voice had been joined by a male one, and he caught the phrase 'to make sure it doesn't burn'.

He glanced back across the room, frowning, then got up on to his knees and leaned across to retrieve the remote control from the arm of his chair. Returning to the exposed floorboards, he switched his TV on again and muted the volume. Then, listening carefully, he worked his way up the channels, eyes on the screen, until he found the programme that Matt was watching.

A cooking show.

Nigel smiled to himself. There was a curious thrill as the images in his flat synchronised with the sounds from downstairs. Lowering himself down, he stretched out on the floor and watched the screen, not bothering to turn the sound up, happy to share the audio from downstairs.

Matt and he were watching the same show.

If they passed on the stairs, this would be something to talk about. Something they had in common.

The idea pleased him.

At the end of the show, he heard Matt flipping through the channels, but managed to follow his selection and settled in to watch a show about Alaskan crab fishing. The floor was a little uncomfortable, but during the commercials he brought the cushion from his chair and found a better position so he could view the screen without craning his neck. It would be easier if his TV was on the same wall as Matt's but he couldn't do anything about that. Not tonight, anyway.

Matt's choice of viewing wasn't what he'd expected: a documentary about aircraft, a motoring show, and a bizarre programme about a man who went round America taking on challenges to eat enormous meals. Not the sort of thing that Nigel would usually watch but, now that he had an excuse, he didn't find them all that bad. Some were even pretty entertaining in their own way, especially the American food guy.

All in all, it had been an entertaining evening's viewing. And the thought that watching these shows made him more like his neighbour could only be a good thing.

When the downstairs TV finally fell silent, a little after midnight, Nigel felt an odd sense of loss. Pressing his ear down against the floorboards, he listened for a few moments, but was unable to discern anything. Perhaps Matt was still there, sitting on the sofa, reading. Or maybe he had already gone to bed. There was no way to tell.

Feeling a little gloomy, Nigel sat up, then got

stiffly to his feet. He'd think about it tomorrow. For now he needed some sleep. Frowning, he walked across to switch off the light, then closed the door.

12

Nigel stood up and worked his way down to the front of the bus, swaying from one grab-handle to the next as it slowed and pulled in at the Centre. Thanking the driver, he stepped down onto the pavement and adjusted the strap of his *X-Men* shoulder bag, checking to make sure he hadn't left anything behind. Satisfied, he turned and walked past the network of little fountains, making his way down towards the harbour, where a small ferry was nosing in alongside the large boat that had been converted into a floating restaurant.

The old brick warehouse buildings, on the right side of the inlet, now housed cafés and bars, as well as an art-house cinema. A covered walkway led along the front of them, and he threaded a path between the slow-moving people until he came to the door that led into the studio. Upstairs, he followed the quiet corridor along to the end, where he tapped in his entrance code on a small keypad and pushed the door open.

Sarah, the receptionist, was wearing a voluminous Gothic dress and had her black hair piled up in a chaos of shiny curls. She glanced up from her desk and gave him a brief nod of acknowledgement, but turned back to her screen before he could say anything to her. He sighed to himself.

Maybe next time.

Inside, the studio was a light and airy space, with an open-plan sprawl of desks and a lofty, pitched ceiling. Lots of different creative companies worked here, with an eclectic mix of people and desk decoration, and a constant buzz of conversations that gave the place a vibrant feel. Sometimes, Nigel thought it might be nice to actually work from here — he could, if he wanted to — but he worried about all the socialising that seemed to go on and whether he'd be able to fit in. Working from home was a lot less stressful.

He walked between the clusters of desks to where Angela and Bella were sitting, beneath a hand-made sign that read Feinman Images.

Angela Feinman was a slender woman in her forties, with short brown hair and quick, bird-like movements. She was always impeccably dressed, as though she were just about to attend something grand. He imagined she must live in a big house, with interiors like the ones he sometimes touched up for magazine spreads, but though he knew she often hosted what she called 'little soirees' he had never been invited to one.

'Nigel!' As usual she sounded very pleased to see him, but he could never be sure whether she really was, or why. 'So lovely of you to come in. We've got a new brief that we want to go through with you, but I just *know* you're going to make everything pop, like you always do.'

Despite himself, Nigel grinned sheepishly. Something about the way she talked made it impossible for him to object. Or get a word in edgeways.

'Come round here,' she beckoned, nodding towards her screen and swivelling it round a little. 'We've got sample shots, mood-boards and goodness only knows what to go through.'

Nigel stepped forward, into the haze of floral perfume that hung over Angela's desk. Glancing across, he noticed that Bella had lifted her head and was staring at him. He nodded to her and attempted a smile that wasn't quite returned.

Officially, Bella Ottram was still an intern, but she had been here for as long as Nigel could remember. These days she handled almost all the admin work for Angela, answered phones, took bookings and arranged photo-shoots. Her manner was routinely self-deprecating — she'd once joked that even her initials were unappealing, but Nigel hadn't laughed, and she'd been distant with him ever since. Today, she was wearing a shapeless knitted top and stripy leggings. A shock of scarlet hair framed a round face, and she gazed out through glasses with oddly asymmetrical frames. Nigel wondered whether she wore them to distract attention from her nose, which was large. It would be so simple to fix that, shape her nose into something pretty . . . but only in Photoshop.

'Hello Nige,' she said, regarding him as though he was something to be organised and filed.

'Hi Bella,' he replied, feeling suddenly awkward. Even women with big noses weren't impressed by him.

'Now then,' Angela took charge of the conversation and nodded towards the screen, 'this is what they've sent us.'

The client, a local corporate finance company, had supplied an unusually detailed brief. There were rough snapshots of the senior partners, photos lifted from the internet to show the sort of look they wanted, and even samples of their new online brochures.

'And they *love* the ads we did for Merentha Group last year, remember those? That low-vibrancy thing you did with the colours, and the filmic toning.' Angie might not have Photo-shopped a picture in her life, but she talked a good talk. He imagined the clients nodding in rapt agreement as she swept them along on a wave of enthusiasm and jargon.

'Who's doing the shoot?' he asked.

Angela smiled at him, as though she was giving him a treat.

'I'm going to pair you up with Frank again. He's a safe pair of hands for the creative . . . ' She made some show of consulting her delicate gold wristwatch. ' . . . though heaven knows where he's got to this afternoon — he was supposed to be here for all this, and I've not had a peep out of him.'

'OK,' Nigel said.

He had worked with Frank's images before. The man was an old pro — a decent photographer, but with seemingly no desire to embrace the technology of digital. Bella had once joked that he'd still be shooting on film if they'd let him, and Nigel suspected this might not be an exaggeration.

'Oh, and there's one more tiny thing.' Angela's infectious confidence sometimes trivialised aspects of a brief, but Nigel knew better than to take anything for granted.

'What is it?' he asked.

'Well, I spoke to one of the senior partners, Peter Garnock, and he was *very* sweet about it, but terribly keen that he and his colleagues' appearance should . . . how did he put it . . . *chime* with the newer generation of business leaders.'

Nigel frowned. How was he supposed to know what new businesses leaders wanted?

Bella, who was still staring at him, removed a pen from the corner of her mouth.

'He wants you to make them look young,' she explained, in a stage whisper.

'Well . . . ' Angela shot her a look of mild reproach, then sighed. ' . . . yes, I suppose that's the gist of it.'

She turned to Nigel.

'Nothing too obvious, but if you could just give them a *teensy* dip in your fountain of youth . . . ?'

Nigel smiled.

'No problem,' he told her.

* * *

Nigel was getting ready to leave when the studio doors swung wide and Frank walked in.

'Hullo darlin',' he greeted Sarah in a broad Scottish accent, breezing past reception and making his way across to Angela. He was a rangy man in his fifties, tall with spiky white hair, an untidy moustache and a ruddy complexion. As usual, he was wearing a pale grey anorak, with blue jeans and brown hiking trainers.

'Sorry I'm late, Ange.' He unslung his weathered old Lowepro rucksack and placed it on her desk. 'It's gettin' so you can't park anywhere round here.'

'There's always spaces in the one at Millennium Square,' Bella murmured, rolling her eyes.

'Aye, 'cause they charge you an arm and leg.' He clapped his large hands together, loud enough to make Bella jump, then made some show of rubbing them together as he turned back to Angela. 'So, what's my favourite boss got for me today?'

Angela gave him a stern look, then shook her head.

'I'll run you through the brief quickly.' She sighed, clicking her mouse to restart the presentation, then glanced up. 'No need for you to suffer this all again, Nigel. You can toddle off if you want to.'

'Thanks.' Nigel went to gather up his bag, but Frank paused, looking at him speculatively.

'You're not in a hurry, are you?' he asked.

'Well . . . ' Nigel hesitated, the bag half on his shoulder. 'I was about to go and catch my bus . . . '

Frank moved a little closer to him.

'Stick around for five minutes.' He gave Nigel a friendly pat on the back, then lowered his voice. 'I want a wee word with you, but not in front of the ladies, eh?'

Nigel looked at him, then shrugged. There

would be other buses, that was no problem . . . but why did Frank want to talk to him alone?

'Five minutes,' Frank grinned, holding up his hand with the fingers extended. 'Come on, I'll even run you home after, save you the bus fare.'

He winked, then turned and walked over to Angela, who was tapping her fingers impatiently on the edge of her keyboard. Nigel stood for a few moments, then took his bag off again and perched on the corner of a neighbouring desk. It was going to be a long five minutes.

He watched as Angela hurried through the brief while Frank stood behind her, staring over her shoulder at the screen.

' . . . and we'll need some head-and-shoulders shots for the senior partners,' she was telling him.

'That's no bother,' he said. 'Have you got dates?'

'I'll try and get us some options. Obviously it'd be simpler if you could do them all in one visit.'

'Shooting at their offices?'

'If we can.'

Frank jerked a thumb towards Nigel.

'Well, in that case you should get the boy wonder here to punch up the lighting an' all that.'

'That's the idea,' Angela agreed.

As the discussion continued, Nigel looked around the room, his eye eventually settling on Bella. She was sitting at her desk, arms folded, staring warily at Frank. Nigel watched her, wondering what she was thinking, but she seemed to sense his eyes on her. Glancing round, she caught his eye and gave him a half-smile, and the moment passed.

* * *

A breeze had blown up, squalling along the narrow service road that ran behind the Watershed, and the cry of gulls filled the air, as Nigel followed Frank between the brick buildings to emerge on Anchor Road. They waited for a break in the traffic, then hurried across to the pavement on the far side, where Nigel's curiosity finally got the better of him.

'So, what did you want to talk to me about?' he asked.

'Yeah . . . ' Frank slowed down a little, falling in step beside Nigel. 'I wanted to ask you about that computer airbrushing stuff you do.'

'Photoshopping?'

'Aye, that.' The older man raised his voice to be heard over the noise of a passing lorry. 'See, I'm doing a bit of portfolio work just now, but you know me — I'm no whizz-kid. I know what I'm doing with the camera but I don't have a clue about Photoshopping and all that.'

'OK . . . ' Nigel glanced across at him, not quite sure what he was getting at.

'Ah, but you see, it's *not* OK.' Frank scowled at the parade of modern glass buildings on the opposite side of the road, then turned to Nigel. 'More and more these days I'm getting asked to deliver images that have had a bit of work done on them. You know, like different processing, punching up the contrast in certain bits of the frame . . . '

'Yeah, that's straightforward . . . '

Post-processing effects and selective tone adjustments were easy. Nigel always felt slightly guilty that people seemed so impressed by the results.

'And what about spots?'

'What?'

'Zits, pimples, whatever you want to call them,' Frank frowned. 'I know this one girl — absolutely beautiful, right? But her skin's always letting her down. Can never get a shot of her face without a bloomin' zit. Can you do that thing where you . . . ' He waved his hand theatrically. ' . . . paint them out?'

'Of course,' Nigel said, shrugging. 'That's easy to do.'

'Amazing,' Frank said, shaking his head. 'And it works on scars? Stretch marks?'

'Oh yes.' He couldn't help feeling a little bit pleased with himself now, explaining how he could work his own little miracles on other people's pictures, even though he knew how simple they were to achieve. 'I can fix all kinds of blemishes, or smooth skin, or make people taller, thinner, whatever.'

Frank was looking at him with what was surely admiration.

'That's magic,' the older man smiled. 'Just what I'm after.'

'Well,' Nigel adopted what he hoped was a nonchalant tone, 'if there's anything you need, just drop the raw files with Bella and she can — '

Frank slowed suddenly, placing a strong hand on Nigel's shoulder.

'I'm not sure we want to bother the ladies with this.'

Nigel looked at him, puzzled. Angela and Bella booked almost all of his work now. It made his taxes and accounting so much easier.

'Why?' he asked.

Frank grinned and gave a little chuckle.

'Some of the material is a bit more . . . ' He stroked his chin thoughtfully. ' . . . artistic. Glamour stuff. And you know how women can get all silly about that kind of thing.'

'Oh.' Now he understood why Frank hadn't wanted to discuss it back at the studio.

'But you're a man,' Frank was saying. 'You'll no' mind looking at some desirable female forms?'

He gave Nigel a wink.

'It's not that, it's just that Angela handles all my invoicing . . . ' As soon as he said it, he realised how lame he must have sounded, but Frank was undeterred.

'Cash in hand, pal. Cash. In. Hand.' He picked up his pace a little, moving in front of Nigel so he could make eye contact. 'Come on, you're no' a queer, are ya?'

'No!' Nigel was actually a little excited about the thought of doing some glamour editing. It would make a welcome change from food or fashion photography. And he *certainly* wasn't gay. 'No, I'd be happy to take a look at some images for you.'

' 'Course you would,' Frank cackled, that hand

on the shoulder again, squeezing. ‘’Course you would.’

They turned right, down a narrow lane that angled back between two tall buildings, leaving the traffic noise of the main road behind them.

‘Now, just so we’re clear,’ Frank told him, his voice echoing back off the walls. ‘We keep this between ourselves, right? I own the images, and you’re the invisible man, OK?’

‘Sure. That’s fine.’

‘Good man.’

At the top of the alley, they rounded a corner to find an abrupt dead end — space enough to turn a car, walled in on three sides. Frank’s silver Mercedes was tucked in at the very back, straddling the double yellow lines.

‘It’s a good place, this is,’ he told Nigel. ‘You can’t see it from the road. And what bloody traffic warden’s gonna come all the way up here, just on the off-chance, eh?’

He laughed to himself, and unlocked the doors.

Nigel got in, tentatively shifting the pasty wrappers that lined the passenger footwell with his shoe. The car smelled of fast food and cigarettes.

‘Right.’ Frank started the engine, then gave him a long look. ‘Where do you live?’

13

There was a leaflet lying on the hallway floor, and the word POLICE caught his attention. He stooped to pick it up, but it was just a note appealing for information about some burglaries in the area. He put it on the table for Mrs Hamilton to read, then turned and ran lightly up the stairs.

He was in a good mood as he reached the top landing, keys already in hand as he approached his front door. Once inside, he walked through to the front room, pausing to admire his handiwork with a smile of satisfaction. The place looked so much better since he'd rearranged the furniture.

He'd started with the TV, moving it across to the other wall. That had made it necessary to reposition the chairs and generally shift things around, but it had all fallen into place quite naturally, with a table in front of the sofa, and his DVDs piled up against the wall.

Just like Matt's flat downstairs.

He'd rolled back a short fold of carpet along two edges of the room, so it was easier to hear what Matt was watching on TV. And yet, far from being satisfied, his curiosity about his neighbour was growing.

Where was Matt right now? What was he doing? What was he eating, drinking, wearing?

A succession of questions flickered in his mind, each one increasing his need to know more about the man who lived just a few feet below him. What about the flat itself? He'd seen the front room and the bathroom — but what was the rest of the place like?

The questions nagged at him, but he felt a kind of confident calm as he sat down on the repositioned sofa and looked around the room. This must be how Matt felt all the time. He only wished he could experience it more deeply.

They'd spoken on the stairs several times now, and their shared interest in the same TV programmes had made the encounters easier. A bond of sorts was forming between them — Matt had even suggested that they go out clubbing sometime — but he hadn't asked him in again since that evening when they'd watched the football. Nigel had done everything he could to engineer another invitation, but all he'd been able to glean from Matt was that he'd been 'busy'.

He had certainly been out a lot recently. Clearly, there was much still to learn about his neighbour. Just a few feet below him, tantalisingly close, but out of his reach . . .

. . . and that was when he had the idea.

How difficult would it be to gain entry to Matt's flat?

The hair stood up on the back of his neck as he imagined it. How cool would that be? And he wouldn't be doing anything wrong. Not *really*. After all, Matt had invited him in before, hadn't he? This would be just like extending his previous visit. He wouldn't steal anything, or disturb anything, just look around.

His first thought was to try to pick the lock. Matt kept regular hours and was out during the day. Nobody else used the stairs to the upper floors, so he would be able to take some time over it without having to worry about being disturbed. Excited, he searched online, looking for information on lock-picking technique, but the more web pages he read, the more dejected he became. It clearly wasn't as easy as it looked on TV.

He was on the point of giving up, when he stumbled on a site about lock-*bumping*. On some properties, especially older ones like his, cylinder locks could be opened using a key that had been filed down to a particular shape. With a bit of skill, it was possible to partially insert the key and, by bumping it with something heavy while twisting it, spring the tumblers and open the lock.

It would still require practice, but it was vastly simpler — and quicker — than picking a lock.

The main drawback seemed to be that you needed a key of the right type to begin with, so that you could then file it down. Getting Matt's key would be impossible, and he could hardly visit a locksmith and ask for a blank.

But he did have one advantage; all the front doors in the building were old, with similar fittings. And that clinched it — if his door had the same type of lock as Matt's, then getting a blank key would be easier.

* * *

The gnomish little man in the key-cutting shop hadn't even looked up at him when he'd asked for a couple of spares.

'I need them for my neighbour,' Nigel explained. He'd constructed an elaborate story about someone feeding his cat while he was away on holiday, but the little man wasn't interested in chatting. With a grunt of acknowledgement, he'd hunched down at his workbench, revealing a hair-cream comb-over, and started up the lathe.

Back at home, Nigel had consulted his web pages again, then spent a couple of hours with a file, carefully rasping down the points on the key until he had the 'blank' shape he needed. He wondered about going out on to the landing, and practising on his own front door, but decided against it. There was no guarantee that the locks would respond in the same way, and besides, it was getting late. He didn't want to disturb his neighbours with any banging tonight.

⋆ ⋆ ⋆

The following morning, he was up early, watching from behind the curtain as Matt ambled down the steps and set off for work. He forced himself to wait there for a moment, staring down at the street to make sure he wasn't coming back. Then, with a rising sense of excitement, he gathered up the blank keys, made his way out into the hallway and crept down to the middle floor.

He moved quietly along the landing. Mrs Hamilton would be occupied, watching one of ‘those dreadful morning television programmes’ from which she hated being disturbed, but he was determined to be careful.

Approaching the light blue door, he took out one of the blank keys, and his hardback copy of *Harry Potter and the Goblet of Fire*. The websites he’d read recommended using a block of wood or something similar to bang the key in quickly, but the book was heavy and ought to do just as well.

He knelt down, bending forward so the door handle was at eye level, and positioned the tip of the key into the lock, keeping it in place with two fingers. Then, licking his dry lips, he hefted the book and smashed it against the key.

Thud.

The key shot partway in, but jammed. For a moment, Nigel panicked, fearing that it might become stuck in the lock, but he was able to pull it free without any real problem. Kneeling by the door, he held his breath, listening for any sounds from downstairs over the thumping of his pulse in his ears.

Nothing. And it was OK. He wasn’t really doing anything wrong. Not really.

His hand was trembling, but he lined the key up and tried again.

Thud.

The key slid all the way home. He went to turn it, then grimaced as he remembered he had to twist it as it went in. *What an idiot*. He drew they key out and adjusted his grip, ready to try again.

Thud.

He banged and twisted simultaneously, but nothing happened. The key refused to turn.

Thud.

Again, twisting as it slid home, but nothing.

Thud.

Thud.

Thud.

His fingers were sore, from the effort of trying to force the key, and he paused to shake some of the discomfort out of his hand. After a moment, he turned his head to look back along the landing, listening for anyone approaching, but the stairwell was silent.

Good.

He returned his attention to the door, lining the key up, ready to try again.

Thud.

He continued for ten minutes or so. Once, swinging the book hard in frustration, he worried he might snap the key off in the lock but, to his surprise, there was a tiny click. It was the slightest of things, felt more than heard, but as he twisted the key it seemed to give just a little. Excited, he exerted more pressure, trying to turn it farther, but it wouldn't move. In desperation he tried wrenching it back and forth, then cursed and shook his head as he felt the lock pins reset.

Mustn't twist it back on itself.

Sighing, he leaned forward and rested his forehead against the door for a moment. This was going to be difficult. He took a breath, then reached down for the book and the key once more.

* * *

After thirty minutes, his knees were beginning to hurt. Scowling at the lock, he got stiffly to his feet, and made his way back upstairs. Walking through to the front room, he stood in the silence and tried not to feel disappointed with himself. It wasn't that he'd expected it to work first time — that was never going to happen. But he'd come so very close, sensing that little click beneath his fingers . . . and then screwed it up again.

He tried to get on with some work, waking his computer and loading in the image file he'd been working on. It was a view of a rural English street, but Angela's client wanted something a little more idyllic. Nigel spent an hour or so, carefully painting out an unsightly electricity pylon, and removing a clutter of repetitive road signs, to restore some of the village's natural charm. He loaded up the original image and compared it with the new one — before, after, before, after — smiling as the ugly elements appeared and disappeared again. But it wasn't long before his thoughts returned to the lock. Saving his work, he pulled up the websites again, reading through the comments. He *was* doing everything right, it was just a matter of practice.

Getting to his feet, he wandered through to the kitchen to get a drink. Taking a glass down from the cupboard, he went to the sink to fill it, then hesitated, and left it on the counter. Turning, he hurried out into the front room, swept up the blank key and the book, and went back downstairs.

Kneeling down at the door, he closed his eyes for a moment, trying to visualise the levers inside the lock. He knew he had to bang and turn in one fluid movement, twisting the key before the pins could drop back into place.

He positioned the key, ready to twist it, and lined up the book, determined not to hold back this time . . .

Thud.

The key turned.

He dropped the book and it tumbled to the floor, but he had the presence of mind not to let go of the key. Holding his breath, he twisted it round as hard as he could, trembling as the lock snicked and the door gave way before him.

Fuck!

He pushed it a little wider, revealing the interior hallway, a glimpse of what was now his to explore. Leaning forward on his knees, he peered inside, his pulse racing. He could look everywhere now. Withdrawing the key from the lock, he stooped to retrieve the book, then got to his feet and stepped across the threshold.

He considered closing the door, then decided against it. Mrs Hamilton never came upstairs, and if Matt should come home unexpectedly, he could say he found the door open and had simply come in to investigate. That would probably work. And he wasn't doing anything bad. Not really. Just looking around.

He crept along the hallway, one stealthy footstep after another on the thin carpet. What if there was a creaking floorboard? He imagined Mrs Hamilton just beneath him, staring up at the ceiling, her eyes following him as he blundered around . . . What if she called the police?

No!

She wouldn't hear anything. He'd be quiet and she'd be watching TV and it would be fine. This was his chance to see everything, to really know Matt properly.

* * *

He moved into the front room. It looked different in daylight, but the sense of his neighbour was everywhere. The rugby shirt draped over the arm of the sofa, cool men's magazines on the floor beside it, the Bristol Rovers mug with half an inch of cold coffee still inside.

Nigel stood in the centre of the room, turning slowly to sweep his eyes across everything — the tall bookcase, the framed art prints, the stylish floor lamp — committing it all to memory.

On a whim, he reached into his pocket and drew out his phone. Tapping the camera button, he shuffled through 360 degrees, snapping shot after shot, capturing a panoramic view of the whole space.

The kitchen area opened off the side of the room and he walked in, glancing around before reaching out and opening one of the cupboards. Plates, bowls and cups, neatly stacked, and heavy glass tumblers like the ones you got in American restaurants — even his crockery was cool. The other cupboards revealed an interesting range of foodstuffs. Matt ate a lot more healthy things like fruit, and there was juice in the fridge. Perhaps his diet was how he stayed so thin? Drawing out his phone again, Nigel snapped a couple more photos, then closed up the cupboards and went back through to the front room. He stood for a moment, taking another look round, noting the blinking red light of the broadband router beside the bookcase, then moved silently into the hall. He slowed as he came to the open front door, listening for any sound of movement outside, but there was nothing.

This was it.

Up until now, he could probably claim that he'd just walked in when he found the front door open. But he had to see the rest of the place and Matt wouldn't be back for hours. There was very little chance of being discovered.

He stole farther along the corridor, ignoring the bathroom for now — he'd seen it before. The other door drew him forward, slightly ajar, and he reached out to brush it with his fingertips before gently pushing it open.

Stepping into the bedroom, he picked up a vague scent in the still air, like talc, faint but pleasant. The bed was in the same position as his own, but it was on a low, wooden base, with a crumpled, dark blue duvet and matching pillows. An iPhone charging cable hung from the wall socket, and a tall wardrobe stood in the far corner, with several pairs of shoes lined up beside it. On the other side of the bed, a low storage unit doubled up as a table, littered with grooming products. There was also an open laptop, with a pile of DVDs stacked up beside it. Nigel moved closer, bending down to look at the titles, then lifted his phone and photographed the pile. He straightened up and turned, snapping more shots of the room, then went to the wardrobe and examined the clothes inside.

Jeans and trousers, shirts and jackets, a couple of jumpers and a hooded fleece top — Nigel worked his way along the rail, studying the different garments, noting the names on the labels. Matt was a little slimmer than him, but only by a couple of inches. He could dress like this if he wanted to. He could look cool.

Pushing the wardrobe door shut, he walked round the bed and opened the drawers in the storage unit, browsing through the T-shirts, committing the brand of underwear to memory. Then, closing the drawers quietly, he made his way back out into the hallway.

He stopped just inside the doorway, listening to reassure himself that there was nobody around, before stepping out on to the landing, and pulling the light blue door gently shut behind him.

Click.

He'd been clever, leaving everything as it was before, with nothing to indicate he'd ever been there. Breathing a sigh of relief, he moved quickly up the stairs, excited and pleased at his success.

He knew more about Matt now. And he was only looking, after all. It wasn't as if he'd done anything wrong.

14

The phone startled him when it rang, a harsh trill that filled the room. Nigel rubbed his eyes then sat up and pushed his chair back from the desk a little. Reaching for the handset, he picked it up, annoyed at his work being disturbed.

'Hello?'

'All right, pal. It's me.'

It took him a moment to place the voice.

'Oh, hi Frank.'

'Yeah, hi.' He sounded as though he was somewhere outdoors. 'Look, are you at home just now?'

Nigel turned in his chair slightly, eyes adjusting to the dim room after the glare of the screen.

'Yes,' he said. 'Why?'

''Cos I'm downstairs with a hard drive full of pictures for you.'

Nigel stiffened.

'Didn't know which doorbell was you, so I rang Bella and she gave me your number,' Frank continued. 'So are you gonna let me in or what?'

'I'll . . . be there in a moment.'

Nigel ended the call and got to his feet, his eyes hunting round the room. Did he need to tidy up a bit? Was there anything he should hide? On his desk there were a couple of letters addressed to Matt that he'd picked up by accident — probably nothing important, and he fully intended to return them — but not the sort of thing he should leave lying around. Then there was the expensive new underwear he'd bought yesterday, still sitting in its stylish shopping bag on the sofa. Snatching up the bag, he dropped the letters inside and took it through to his bedroom, feeling curious pangs of guilt. But why should he? And anyway, it would be all right . . . he hadn't buzzed Frank in, and certainly *wouldn't* be inviting him up here.

⋆ ⋆ ⋆

At the bottom of the stairs, he hesitated for a second, attempting to settle his features into a calm expression, before walking over and opening the communal front door.

'You took your time,' Frank grinned at him from the steps, seeming to loom even taller as he moved up to stand on the outside mat.

'Sorry . . . ' Nigel held out his hand, trying to accept the hard drive on the doorstep, but the tall photographer was already so close that he found himself taking an involuntary step backwards.

'I'll show you which ones I want done.' Frank moved forward to stand in the threshold, his eyes glancing round the entrance hallway before settling on Nigel again. 'Lead the way, pal.'

⋆ ⋆ ⋆

The big man was right behind him all the way up the stairs, boots scuffing uncomfortably loud and close as they reached the top-floor landing. Nigel hesitated at his front door, then reluctantly pushed it open. He turned, unable to say 'Come in', but Frank was already stepping inside.

'Which way?' The big man leered at him, holding up a portable hard drive and waggling it.

Nigel glanced along the hallway. 'Through here.'

They went into the front room, where Nigel's screen was still bright, bathing the room in a pink glow from a soft-focus image of a Japanese woman surrounded by cherry blossoms. Frank glanced at the Lego figures on top of the monitor, then turned to look around the room, a slight sneer on his face.

'What is it?' Nigel frowned at him, suddenly defensive.

'Nothin'.' Frank handed him a portable hard drive. There was a Café del Mar sticker on it and the smooth black surface was touched with sweat. 'Here you go, I'll let you plug it in.'

Moving over to the desk, Nigel reached around to connect the cable and a green light on the front of the drive winked into life. Lowering himself into his chair, he watched the screen, until a new icon appeared.

'OK,' he said.

'It's workin'?'

'Yes.'

Frank stepped closer.

'There's all sorts on there, but I've made a list . . . ' He twisted around, fumbling in the back pocket of his jeans before drawing out a folded sheet of paper. 'Here we are. These are the ones I want worked over.'

'Thanks.' Nigel took the paper, then moved the mouse to click the icon, opening a new window.

Frank was right beside him now, uncomfortably close, leaning over and pointing, even *touching his spotless screen*. 'There, in the DSC folder . . . '

He smelled of stale smoke and bad aftershave.

Shrinking into his chair, Nigel clicked on the folder and a series of mini thumbnail images appeared. Glancing at the handwritten list, he located the first filename and selected it.

At his shoulder, Frank said, 'Yeah, open that one.'

The pointer changed to a loading spinner, then the screen refreshed to display a young woman. She was pale and naked, perched on the edge of a marble kitchen worktop, legs deliberately parted. Long red hair tumbled down over her slender shoulders and she stared out at them with a challenging pout.

Despite himself, Nigel leaned forward a little.

'Lovely, isn't she?' Frank hissed. 'Her name's Megan.'

'Megan.' Nigel swallowed. 'OK.'

Suddenly there was something shockingly intimate about the picture. Perhaps it was because this was a real person, someone who'd posed for a photographer he knew. She might live right here in Bristol . . .

'Zoom in on her chest for me.' Frank was leaning on the back of his chair. 'I'll show you what I need doing.'

Nigel tapped the keyboard to magnify the

image, then panned it across with the mouse, until Megan's breasts filled the screen.

'Up a bit, you pervert,' Frank cackled. 'There, just below her throat.'

Nigel repositioned the image, noticing what appeared to be a birthmark above her collarbone.

'You want me to paint that out?' he asked.

'Aye,' Frank said. 'And can you do anything about her freckles? She's a babe but she'd be incredible if you could clean up her up a bit.'

Nigel leaned forward, studying the pale skin.

'Yeah, that should be fine,' he replied. It would take a bit of time, but he could do it. He glanced at the list of filenames. 'What about the others?'

'Same deal,' Frank told him. 'Clean skin — no spots, no scars, and no bloody stretch marks, right?'

'OK.'

'And you'll do what you normally do with the contrast and stuff, yeah?'

'Sure.' Nigel clicked the mouse and dismissed the image of Megan from the screen. 'Want me to email you the first one when I've done it?'

'Good idea.' Frank reached into his pocket and drew out a crumpled business card. 'The address is on there, down at the bottom.'

Nigel took it from him.

'I should have something for you in a week or two,' he said, placing the card on his desk.

'Great.' Frank straightened up and grinned down at him. 'Well, I'd better leave you to it. You're probably keen to get wanking over the photos, eh?'

'What? No!' Nigel felt himself blushing.

'It's all right,' Frank cackled. 'That's what they're for, pal.'

* * *

It was an hour since he'd left, but the whole flat still seemed to resonate with his presence. Even with Frank gone, an unwholesome echo of him remained, clinging to everything.

Nigel shifted uncomfortably in his chair. He'd tried to continue his work on the cherry blossom scene, but somehow he just couldn't concentrate. He sighed and leaned forward, resting his elbows on the desk.

On the front of the black drive, the little green light winked at him.

Nigel slouched back in his chair, head tilted back as he rubbed his eyes. Then, with a sigh, he sat up and put his hand on the mouse. Closing the file he'd been working on, he located the DSC folder and opened it. A window appeared, filling with thumbnail images, and he moved the mouse then clicked Preview.

A naked blonde suddenly filled the screen. She looked a little older than Megan, with a fuller figure and tanned skin. Photographed in front of a crimson wall, she stood with her feet planted apart and her hands behind her head, mouth slightly open as though she were about to speak. Nigel's eye moved across her body, noting the faint creases below her stomach, the slight rash where she'd shaved herself.

He could fix that for her.

Clicking, he loaded the next picture. It was the same blonde, looking back over her shoulder as she bent forward to lean against the wall.

He clicked again.

Another shot of the blonde leaning on the wall, but cropped tighter so that her bottom took up most of the frame, with everything else deliberately out of focus.

Nigel squirmed a little, moving in his chair as his arousal grew, reaching a hand down to adjust the front of his jeans.

That's what they're for, pal.

The memory of Frank jolted him upright in his chair and he moved the mouse quickly to close the Preview window.

He would look at it later.

* * *

In the bedroom, he lifted the shopping bag and tipped the contents out onto the bed. His new underwear was so cool — he'd made sure to buy the same brand and style as Matt wore, even the same colours. He considered them for a moment, pleased by the way they looked, then folded them away in his top drawer, infused by a strange new confidence. He'd look good in them.

As he turned to go out of the room, his eye settled on the two envelopes lying on the duvet. He really ought to return them to the pigeonhole downstairs, but there was no hurry. Post was often delayed, wasn't it? He picked them up, turning each one over to study the sealed flap on the back, running his thumb under the edge where the glue didn't quite reach, curious about their contents.

How difficult could it be?

Taking the post, he made his way through to the kitchen. As always, the internet proved invaluable. A quick search on his phone yielded numerous articles about steaming envelopes open, and the consensus seemed to be that a pan of boiling water worked much better than steam from a kettle. Switching on the hob, he took a frying pan from the cupboard and held it under the tap.

While waiting for the water to heat, he went through to the front room and dug out some of his own unopened junk mail — better to practise on them until he knew what he was doing — then returned to the kitchen.

Holding each envelope over the bubbling water, he turned his hand this way and that, directing the steam along the flap. As the paper grew hot and started to deform, he eased a finger into the gap at the edge, slowly separating the glue as it softened, working his way along. At last, the flap popped open and he withdrew the envelope from the steam to look at it.

Not bad. He could easily reseal this without anyone noticing what he'd done. Satisfied, he put his envelope down on the counter, then lifted one of Matt's and held it over the steam.

There was a curious thrill as he slipped the letter out, unfolding the warm paper and turning to study it in the light from the front room window. Although it was just a gym membership letter, he felt a renewed closeness to his neighbour that pleased him. The other envelope contained a letter about local council elections — again, not exciting in itself, but strangely satisfying to read.

Setting the mail down on the counter, he smiled to himself. Tomorrow morning, he'd replace these in Matt's pigeonhole downstairs. There would be no sign that anyone had tampered with the letters, no harm done — just another way to know his neighbour better.

* * *

Evening was drawing in before he went back to his desk again. Tapping the keyboard to wake the computer, he dropped into his chair and frowned as the screen lit up. No sense putting it off, he'd have to look sometime.

Bringing up the DSC folder, he unfolded the handwritten piece of paper and studied it. There were fifty images on the list — quite a few for him to work through, but there were many more than that on the hard drive.

Scrolling past the thumbnail images of the blonde woman, he selected another file and clicked Preview.

This time it was a wavy-haired brunette, delicately slim with a girlish grin that suggested an air of innocence. She was looking up at the camera, one hand positioned to cover her breasts, the other placed modestly between her legs. It was a brilliant photo, and Nigel admired it for a moment before zooming in and panning the magnified view around. There seemed to be almost nothing wrong with it — maybe a little toning and contrast here and there would help make the colours pop a bit more, but otherwise it was fine.

He selected the next file.

A second shot of the brunette filled the screen. In this one, she wore a more bashful expression, lowering her eyes behind long, dark lashes as she dropped her hands to her sides, exposing herself more fully to the camera. Again, the lighting and focus looked good — a little work on the contrast and it'd be perfect.

Leaning forward to prop his chin on his hand, he began idly clicking the Next button, watching the photo-shoot unfold through the sequence of images. The poses became more daring, the camera getting closer and more intimate. Nigel undid the front of his jeans to make room for his growing erection, clicking the mouse with his other hand.

There were lots of other images in between the ones that Frank had chosen. That was quite usual — shots where the model had blinked, or her pose wasn't right, or a flashgun hadn't fired properly. For the brunette, there were over a hundred photographs — number 79 was the last one marked on the list, but Nigel carried on clicking. *Next . . . next . . . next . . .*

There was something different in her expression now. The early shots had been naughty, eager, a blend of teasing and desire, but there was something else now . . .

He stopped and zoomed in tight on her face.

She looked unhappy.

He paged back to the earlier images where she had been OK. Or at least *looked* OK.

Frowning, he returned to the later shots again, studying her face intently. It was in her eyes — a sort of emptiness, as though that spark had gone out. Her mouth was still smiling, pouting seductively, but her eyes seemed lost. He tapped the keyboard, zooming out from the magnified view to reveal the whole image, her sudden nakedness catching him unawares.

Adjusting his jeans in guilty arousal, he clicked forward to the next photograph, zooming in until her face filled the screen. Tapping to open a menu, he chose a Soft Selection tool and began to gently tease up the corners of her mouth. With great care, he lifted the blush of her cheekbones just a fraction, trying to elicit the sense of a smile.

But it was no use. The same empty eyes stared out at him.

He sagged back into his chair. For some reason, the brunette's expression bothered him. There were hundreds of files on the hard drive but he wasn't so eager to explore them any more. Perhaps he should just stick to the images Frank had listed.

Closing Photoshop, Nigel moved the mouse pointer and clicked his Mac into Sleep mode. But as the screen dimmed then went dark, it revealed an ugly fingerprint on the polished black glass.

15

It was easier to get in now. With practice, he'd steadily improved his technique until he could bump the lock open after just a few attempts. He'd felt an odd sense of satisfaction in this, mastery of a skill that few people could claim, a skill that allowed him to go somewhere that would otherwise be beyond his reach. And then, one morning as he'd been idly browsing round in Matt's kitchen, he'd pulled open a drawer beside the sink and found a spare set of keys. It was too good an opportunity to pass up, and he'd taken a bus into the city centre to get them copied, returning the original set to the drawer before Matt got home. Now, there were no more barriers to entry. He could come and go as he pleased.

This morning, he'd waited for half an hour after Matt left for work, then crept downstairs and quietly let himself in. The middle flat was silent, but there was a lingering smell of toast and coffee, welcoming him, as he eased the front door shut behind him with a faint click. He stood for a moment, head titled back, eyes half shut, then smiled.

This was how it felt to be home.

He looked along the inner hallway, to the light streaming in from the front room window, then turned to face the other way. Treading softly, he moved to stand at the bedroom door, then reached out a hand and gently pushed it wide open. He took in the now familiar view, noting a couple of shopping bags on the floor beside the wardrobe. He'd come to have a poke around on Matt's laptop, but perhaps there was something new to look at?

Moving around the bed, he peered down into the bags, but they were empty, save for some swing tags and a couple of receipts. Raising his head, he reached out and opened the wardrobe door. It took him a moment to recognise what was new, but yes — there, at the end of the rail, were a pair of jeans and a casual shirt, both brand new. Stretching out a hand, he carefully lifted each one by the hanger, unhooking them from the rail and draping them softly on the rumpled bed.

They looked good. Somehow his neighbour always knew just what to buy. Nigel felt sure that he could go into the same shops and find nothing — he didn't have an eye for clothes, but Matt did.

He sighed, about to return the garments to their place in the wardrobe, then hesitated. These were fashionable things, fashionable *now*. They hadn't even been worn yet. He stood still, taking a slow, deep breath.

It was almost like finding a gift. As if Matt had bought them for *him*.

He looked across to the laptop, then glanced at his watch. He had time. Plenty of time. And they'd never been worn. He could be *first*.

Taking another breath, he held it, listening intently. The dull mumble of voices from Mrs

Hamilton's TV bled up through the floor, otherwise there was nothing. He *had* to.

Working quickly, he gripped the bottom of his T-shirt, pulling it up and over his head, feeling the cool air on his bare torso. It was oddly scary, with his face covered, until he pulled it up past his ears, and he could see and hear again. He gulped down another breath, listening, but still nothing. OK.

He fumbled with his belt, undoing it as quickly as he could, then undid the top button and tugged the zip down. Kicking off his trainers, he slid his jeans down, then froze as he glimpsed his reflection in the mirror — naked apart from his trunks. It was an oddly unsettling image, and he turned away as he stepped out of his jeans and reached over to lift the new pair from the bed.

They felt different, unfamiliar and rough against his skin, as he pulled them up and struggled to fasten them. A little tight, yes, but he sucked his stomach in and managed to button the fly. The shirt was easier, a baggier fit that felt more comfortable, and he smoothed the material down before turning back to face the mirror.

He saw the bashful smile fade almost immediately, struck by how different he looked — how different he *felt* — in these clothes. Matt had made him look good. He stood for a moment, studying the image before him, turning slightly, allowing himself to stand up straight rather than slouch.

'All right,' he greeted his reflection, then cleared his throat, lowering the pitch of his voice to sound more like his neighbour. 'All right.'

His daydream was disturbed by the rumble of a train, passing along the embankment, and he lowered his eyes, embarrassed at himself.

Dressing up in someone else's clothes? Really?

And yet, he looked so much better, so . . . cool.

He picked up his own jeans from the floor, searching in the pocket until he found his phone, then held it up and tapped the Camera icon. Pointing it at the mirror, he lined himself up, then stared straight forward, the way Matt would, a confident expression on his face.

Click.

He tapped the button a few times, taking a series of photos in case some of them were blurred.

'All right . . . I'm the new guy.' He half-turned, affecting an easy smile as he savoured the unfamiliar way of speaking. 'Good to know you . . . make yourself at home . . . '

For one perfect moment, he was a different person . . .

'Later.'

And then, with some reluctance, he turned away, slowly stripping off the shirt and the jeans, and returning them to the wardrobe.

His own clothes felt baggy and wrong as he pulled them on, as though he was dressing himself in disappointment, but he determined not to dwell on it, focusing his attention on the laptop that lay waiting for him on the other side of the room. That was the purpose of his visit today — something that he'd repeatedly overlooked, but which would surely help him learn more about his new friend.

Moving back around the bed, he sat down on the edge of the duvet, then leaned forward to open the lid and power up the computer. He'd been worried about it being password protected but, as the machine whirred and the screen came to life, he noticed a small scrap of paper sticking out from under the side of the keyboard. Drawing it out, he noted the handwriting — 'MattG1985' scrawled in blue biro — then glanced up at the login screen.

This might be easier than he'd imagined.

He tapped in the sequence and pressed the Enter key. It was a terribly unsecure password — his own involved various clever combinations of numbers and letters that could never be guessed — then watched as the screen was replaced by a desktop image of Matt and some friends, standing at a beach bar, somewhere warm and exotic. They all looked so happy, holding up beer bottles and laughing at some joke. He wondered where the photo had been taken.

He sat on the edge of the bed and waited for Windows to start up. Though the laptop was quite new it ran terribly slowly, and he was tempted to take a look through the settings, maybe optimise the boot process . . . but of course, he knew he mustn't. Everything had to be left as it was — there could be no trace of his visit, not even a helpful tweak to Matt's computer.

Eventually, the hard-drive light stopped

blinking, and Windows seemed to settle. Placing a finger on the trackpad, Nigel moved the pointer to click on Internet Explorer and went straight to the History view to see what websites Matt had been looking at. BBC Football, Sky Sports News and the Bristol Rovers home page — no surprises there, he knew his neighbour was a football fan. His eye scanned farther down the list, past a couple of porn sites he recognised, an online car price guide, then Facebook and YouTube . . .

He paused, then moved the pointer back up to click on the Facebook link. The computer seemed to think about it for a moment, then the screen updated to display the news feed of Matt's Facebook page. Nigel smiled to himself.

Already logged in — perfect.

He scrolled down the page, looking at the posts from Matt's friends, stopping now and again to click on interesting messages, enlarging the profile pictures for some of the prettier girls to get a better look at them. Matt knew an awful lot of people — it would take a long time to go through all this.

He sighed and sat back, elbows sinking into the duvet. It would be so much better if he could do this at his leisure, but he'd need the account details for that . . .

Account details.

Frowning, he leaned forward again. There was a good chance that Matt was unimaginative about *all* his passwords, but he'd need the login email address too . . .

* * *

A few minutes later, he had everything he needed. Opening a different browser, he brought up the Facebook login page, tapped a few keys, and pressed Enter. The screen refreshed successfully and he lay back into the duvet with a smile of satisfaction. Now, he could access Matt's Facebook account from anywhere — he'd know more about Matt than anyone else.

Pleased with himself, he sprawled out on the bed and stared up at the white plaster ceiling, imagining how it might look if it was suddenly made of glass. He pictured his own bed directly above him, tried to visualise himself standing up there, looking down. Smiling at the thought, he splayed his arms out wide, stretching, then yawned.

He should really take a quick look through Matt's email while he was here.

Sighing, he forced himself to sit up, then reached forward and clicked the Mail icon. The screen filled with messages but almost all of it was junk — Nigel opened a couple of order confirmations from online retailers and read about ticket details for a gig later in the year, but there seemed to be little else of interest. After a moment, he scrolled back through the list of emails he'd looked at, carefully marking each one as 'Unread' again, so there would be no trace of what he'd done . . .

. . . then paused, frowning. He should really take some precautions before accessing Matt's websites from his own computer upstairs. Every connection left a digital trace for those who knew where to look — an IP address that could be traced back to an individual's broadband account.

Broadband.

Nigel nodded to himself. Leaning forward, he powered the laptop down, then pulled the lid closed to leave it exactly as he'd found it. Then, getting up, he gave the duvet a quick shake to remove the impression he'd left, and set off in search of the wireless router. He recalled seeing something in the front room, near the bookcase, and made his way along the hallway to check.

Yes, there is was. He squatted down, studying it — a little black plastic monolith with a couple of flashing lights, one of the standard boxes that cable TV companies gave away free with their basic broadband. He reached out and picked up the router, being careful of the trailing wires as he turned it over and peered at the base. There was a tiny sticker on the underside, with a sixteen-character pass code printed on it. Nigel smiled. Resting the unit on its side, he took out his phone and snapped a photograph of the sticker. Now, he'd be able to access Matt's websites from upstairs using the broadband down here — and it would appear as though Matt was doing it! Very pleased with himself, Nigel set the router upright again, then stood up and turned around.

He felt it before he heard it — a faint resistance, the pull of his shirt, then a dreadful dawning of realisation as everything seemed to slow down . . .

. . . and then the smash.

In the quiet stillness of the flat, it seemed deafening — a whole bottle of Jack Daniel's, pulled from the bookshelf to break on the edge of the TV stand, bursting into pieces. Bits of glass danced, skittering across the floor, and an explosion of dark brown spirit spattered out over the rug.

Oh shit!

Nigel held his breath, frozen to the spot, not knowing what to do.

Mrs Hamilton would have heard that, surely. And she knew Matt was at work. He imagined her downstairs, staring up at the ceiling, prising herself from her chair to call the police. He stood absolutely still, listening, but the silence continued.

After an eternity of waiting, a dreadful curiosity overtook him. Breathing quickly, he stepped around the wreckage on the floor, and crept down the hallway to Matt's front door. Opening it as quietly as he could, he tiptoed out on to the landing, hardly daring to lean over the banister and look down.

What would he do if she was down there looking up at him?

But there was nothing. The hallway was empty and there was no indication of activity — the only sound was the muffled echo of a morning TV show. He swallowed, trying to calm himself enough to think, then moved quickly back inside Matt's flat.

The aroma of alcohol hung thick in the air, and the front room floor was a mess. Glass glittered everywhere and a sticky brown stain had bled out across the rug. How the hell was he going to clear this lot up? Crouching down, he reached out, hesitating as he wondered how to pick up the pieces without cutting his fingers. And then he stopped.

He couldn't clear it up.

Slowly, very slowly, he rolled back on the balls of his feet and stood up, glancing round the room.

If there had been a break-in, a burglar wouldn't clear up, would he?

Frowning, he moved over to the window, his eyes darting around the frame. No, not here. Even if they managed to climb up this far, nobody could get in here without being seen from the street.

Shaking his head, he paced nervously down the hall. The door was a possibility, but that would lead to questions . . . and with Mrs Hamilton unlikely to manage the stairs, he'd probably be the prime suspect. No, the door was a bad idea.

He carried on, striding into the bedroom, moving around the bed to the smaller back window. Leaning forward, he peered down on to the low roof of the porch that extended out into the garden below. This was better, much more likely, and weren't there some sturdy old drainpipes running down the back wall? He craned his neck to see, but they were out of sight.

It didn't matter.

This was clearly the best option. Glancing

down, he noticed an old security bolt on the window, but it was one of the kind you could turn by hand. The situation could be salvaged. He just had to make it look convincing, and that would mean breaking the window from the outside.

⋆ ⋆ ⋆

A few moments later, he was standing on the porch roof. He'd opened a few drawers and taken some money from the stash beside Matt's bed to further the idea of a robbery, then carefully wiped down all the surfaces he might have touched using a tea towel from the kitchen. Once satisfied, he'd lifted an old Stephen King paperback from the shelf in the front room, unbolted the window and opened it. Lowering himself down onto the porch was easier than he'd feared, and he turned around to slide the window shut . . .

. . . just as it would be when a burglar found it.

He wrapped the book in the tea towel, which he hoped would reduce the noise, hefting it in his hand. Fortunately, the back of the property wasn't really overlooked, but he was determined to get this over with quickly.

Taking a deep breath, Nigel swung the book against the centre of the glass. He hadn't expected it to break first time, but it did, shattering inwards and sending long shards clattering into the flat. Again, the noise seemed too loud, startling him, but somehow he managed to get a hold of himself. Pulse racing, he worked quickly to knock out a few more fragments, just as a burglar would do if he wanted to reach the security bolt. Then, he reached in through the hole he'd made, brushing pieces of glass off the sill, and opened the window using the tea towel.

So far, so good.

He was about to turn away and let himself down into the garden when his gaze caught the flat pale reflection of sky on a large section of glass, lying on the bedroom floor. He paused, staring at it, knowing that it wouldn't look right.

Damn.

With a hurried glance over his shoulder to make sure nobody was watching, he pulled the window farther open, then swung one leg over the sill, placing his shoe on the large piece of glass. Straining, he forced his weight onto it until he heard it snap and felt the fragments being ground into the carpet.

Better.

He withdrew his leg and took a breath. It was all coming together now. He was smart enough to do this, to make it work, and to get away with it. Crouching, he moved cautiously to the edge of the porch, twisted himself around, and steadied himself on the drainpipe as he lowered himself over the edge. Then he let himself drop down, landing quietly on the paved area at the back door. Thankfully the basement flat was empty just now, otherwise he'd have been seen, but the place had been on the market for months now.

He took a moment to get his breathing under control, experiencing an odd flicker of elation, and scuffed his shoes a few times to make sure he'd got rid of any glass. Then, climbing the concrete steps, he made his way up to the back door and quietly let himself in. Shutting the door behind him, he crept along the ground-floor hallway, pausing outside Mrs Hamilton's door to listen.

From inside, a ripple of applause and canned studio laughter reached him — she was still watching TV.

Perfect.

Stepping back, he was about to make his way upstairs when he stopped and looked towards the front door. Treading softly, he moved over to it, twisting the handle and opening it without making a sound. Then, he waited for a lull in the noise of the TV show, and slammed the door hard, just the way that Mrs Hamilton was always asking him not to. Coughing, he walked back along the hall and mounted the stairs, treading heavily as he went up. If anyone asked, he'd say he'd been down at the shops. And hopefully, Mrs Hamilton would be annoyed enough to remember, and back him up.

His heart was racing as he stepped back into his own flat. Shutting the door and leaning back against it, he noticed he was trembling, and felt the clamminess in his palms . . .

. . . but he'd been man enough to tidy up his mistake, and the thought sent a curious thrill through him. With a bit of luck, he might just get away with it.

16

There was considerable excitement at Eastfield Road in the period following the 'break-in'. Matt actually came upstairs and knocked on his door that first evening. The sound gave Nigel a shock — nobody ever came up to the top floor, at least, not without the warning of the outside doorbell — and when he saw his neighbour his first instinct was to blurt out an apology, to explain that it was all just an accident, that he hadn't meant any harm . . .

. . . but Matt didn't seem to be angry at him.

'Mate, have you heard?' He leaned up against the door frame, and pushed his dark hair back out of his eyes. 'Someone's broken into my bloody flat!'

Nigel stared at him blankly, struggling to think what he should say.

'Sorry . . . ' he croaked.

'I know,' Matt shook his head. 'I couldn't believe it either.'

Nigel took a breath. It was OK. He wasn't in trouble here, he was Matt's *friend*. What would a friend say in this situation?

'Have you called the police?' he managed.

'Oh yeah,' Matt scowled, kicking at the skirting board lightly with his shoe. 'Had a couple of coppers round here already.'

Nigel swallowed. He'd watched *CSI*. He knew that every contact with every surface left a trace

— evidence, fingerprints, maybe even DNA. Sure, Matt had invited him down to watch the football, but what if he'd made a mistake, overlooked something?

'What did they say?' he asked.

Matt folded his arms and stared right at him.

'They gave me a leaflet,' he said, his voice suddenly tight with anger. 'A *bloody* leaflet.'

'What?'

'Some stupid Victim of Crime thing,' Matt fumed. 'Fat lot of good that is.'

He looked so angry, standing in the doorway, but Nigel could already feel himself relaxing a little. It would be OK. With so many other burglaries recently, what was one more? The police had to go after the big cases — they wouldn't spend a lot of time on something like this.

'What did the burglars take?' he asked. It was a great question, and he felt pleased with himself for thinking of it. As well as demonstrating that he didn't know anything about the break-in, it suggested there may have been more than one burglar, maybe even a gang.

'I'm still checking.' Matt gazed up at the ceiling. 'But there's a couple of hundred quid in cash that's gone.'

Nigel stared at him. It hadn't been *that* much. He knew — he'd counted it.

'I reckon the window will cost me more, though.' Matt frowned. 'Glass is really expensive . . . '

'Is that how they got in?'

'Plod seems to think so,' Matt muttered. He

turned to Nigel and gave him a wry smile. 'My door was still locked when I got home, so that's something, I suppose. Couldn't afford to change the bloody locks on top of everything else.'

'Are you not insured?'

'Yeah, I am,' Matt said, letting out a long, weary sigh. 'But with the excess payments and losing my no-claims discount it'll probably end up costing me more. You know how those bastards work.'

Nigel nodded sympathetically, feeling genuinely bad for him. It was such a shame . . .

'Are you OK for money?' he asked suddenly. 'I could lend you some if you need . . . '

Matt stared at him, taken aback.

'Mate . . . ' He shook his head, a broad grin lighting up his face — the first proper smile since he'd come to the door. 'That is *so* decent of you. I'm OK for cash, really, but I *seriously* appreciate the offer, you know?'

Nigel shrugged to hide his stupid smirk.

'It's only money,' he mumbled. 'You'd do the same for me.'

'Well, I owe you one,' Matt replied. He took a step back on to the landing, then gave an apologetic shrug. 'I'd invite you down for a drink but the bastards even smashed my bottle of JD. Can you bloody believe it? I mean, if they'd *nicked* it, fair enough, but they just . . . '

He mimed throwing a bottle on the floor.

Nigel saw his opportunity.

'I could bring some beers down,' he offered. Bottles he'd bought on the off-chance, just in case he got invited down again. And he'd learned his lesson — he'd kept them in the fridge. 'They're cold.'

Matt's grin widened.

'You're a top bloke, you know that?'

⋆ ⋆ ⋆

The next morning Nigel woke late, with a fuzzy feeling in his head and a bad taste in his mouth. He was unusually hungry but a quick inspection of the kitchen cupboards revealed nothing that really appealed as breakfast. He decided to get dressed and go out.

Mrs Hamilton must have been listening out for him. There was no way she could have got to her door quickly enough, but it swung open just as he reached the bottom of the stairs.

'Nigel, dear?'

He put on the cheeriest face he could muster and turned to face her.

'Morning, Mrs Hamilton.'

'Did you hear about the break-in?' she blustered. There was no time for pleasantries this morning, she had something big to gossip about. 'Poor Matt's been burgled!'

Nigel nodded wearily.

'Yes, he popped upstairs and told me last night. He said the police gave him a leaflet.'

Mrs Hamilton looked a tiny bit crestfallen to find that Matt had stolen her thunder, but she rallied valiantly.

'Ah,' she said. 'But did you know the police came back?'

'What?'

'Oh yes.' She looked happier, now she had something that would be news to him. 'A thin-looking man, but not in uniform — *plain clothes*.'

Nigel ground his teeth together silently as a hundred different worries flickered in his imagination.

'Do you know what he wanted?' he asked.

'Well, I just happened to see Matt as he was leaving for work this morning, and he says it was a *proper* detective this time.' She paused, leaning forward and lowering her voice as though she were suddenly worried that the burglars might overhear her. Which, when Nigel thought about it, was rather ironic. 'He said they wanted to check a few things, to see if this was connected to those other burglaries in the area, or if it was just a random break-in.'

'And?'

Mrs Hamilton frowned.

'Matt didn't say whether they thought it was or not,' she admitted, then brightened. 'Still, it's all *terribly* exciting, isn't it?'

* * *

It was early evening, and the police had come and gone now. A pair of uniformed officers, one male, one female — they'd sat on his sofa, one looking round, one asking questions.

Had he been at home between eight and five yesterday?

Had he heard anything out of the ordinary?

Had he seen anyone acting suspiciously,

yesterday or over the past weeks?

The words sounded formulaic, stripped of their meaning by too much repetition. How many different doors did they have to knock on, reciting the same questions? He felt a certain sympathy towards them, listened attentively, explained how sorry he was that he couldn't help them more. The policewoman had smiled at him as they'd left, thanked him for his time.

And that was that. There was no sign of the thin detective. No visits by forensic teams in their special overalls. By the following day, things were back to normal. The world had lost interest in Eastfield Road.

⋆ ⋆ ⋆

A week passed. Nigel had refrained from making any further visits to the flat downstairs — it was just too soon — but the self-imposed exile saddened him. He'd busied himself by stitching together the photographs he'd taken, making one long, seamless image that he could pan around, zooming in and out to study everything. All of his own furniture was now positioned to echo that of the flat below him, but it wasn't the same. All too often, he found himself returning to stare at the lifeless pictures, wondering, wanting more.

Maybe that was where the idea came from.

⋆ ⋆ ⋆

The equipment had been easy enough to get hold of. There was a large electronics shop at the bottom of Gloucester Road, and he stopped in there frequently — it was his kind of place. This week, they'd had a new window display, with a tiny video camera relaying images to a small monitor screen, and he'd stopped to smile at his own image. But it was the printed sign below the camera that caught his attention.

Wireless.

He paused, gazing at the clear image of himself, his face now thoughtful. Then he went inside and made his way across to the far corner of the store where they kept the cameras. He knew he couldn't ask for what he wanted directly. But as he stood there, before several shelves of different security camera kits, he turned and noticed the remote control planes in the next aisle.

Yes. That would sound better.

He went to find a member of staff.

* * *

'Well, if you're going to attach it to a balloon or a remote control plane, it'll need to be light and small.' The sales assistant was pale, with curly brown hair and thick, gold-framed glasses. 'These ones are just the job.'

'The cameras can broadcast directly to the internet?' Nigel asked.

'Not directly, you need a receiver, but it's all included in the kit.' He patted the box with a moist-looking hand, the fingernails bitten short. 'That connects to your laptop or router, then you can access the feed from anywhere. A lot of people use them for home security — you can log in and check your house is OK from work, that sort of thing.'

'Does the receiver need to be very close to the camera?'

'No. It has a decent range — maybe a hundred feet, or farther if you're outdoors.' The man looked up at him. 'So, what do you think? Will it do what you want?'

Nigel paid in cash.

Back at home, he'd unpacked one of the kits and tried it out in his living room. The set-up was fairly straightforward, and before long he was able to turn the tiny video camera in his hand and watch the swaying images relayed wirelessly to his iPad screen. Everything was ready.

* * *

There had been some guilt as he sat there, packing everything up into a carrier bag, but also a tangible sense of excitement. And it wasn't as if he was doing anything particularly wrong, not really. After the close call with his previous break-in, he knew it was too risky to keep visiting Matt's flat. This would address that problem.

It was mid-afternoon when he made his way quietly down to the first floor. He knew that, despite his good intentions, actions like this were likely to be misunderstood, so he'd vowed to be careful. He was even wearing gloves — ridiculous yellow ones, the kind you wore for washing up — but a little extra caution wouldn't hurt him.

He waited for a long time on the middle landing, holding the carrier bag tight against his chest to prevent it rustling as he listened, but there was no sound — the coast was clear. Letting himself in with his duplicate key, he pulled the sky-blue door until it snicked shut behind him, then moved silently through to the front room. He'd spent a lot of time studying the photos, considering sight-lines and viewing angles; he knew exactly where he wanted to place the cameras.

In the top right-hand corner of the bookcase, a forgotten copy of some football manager's autobiography stood propped up against the end of the shelf. Standing on tiptoe, Nigel shoved the book slightly to the left, and slotted the tiny camera into the gap he'd opened. He'd stuck a little ball of Blu-tack under it, so he could angle it down into the room and, once he was satisfied with its position, he tipped the football book over slightly, shadowing it from view.

Stepping back into the middle of the room, he looked up and nodded to himself.

Perfect. Unless you knew it was there, you'd never spot it.

Satisfied with his work, he turned and walked across to the TV on its glass-topped stand. Kneeling down beside it, he craned his neck to peer around the back. There was a tangle of cables on the floor behind it. Very carefully, he took the receiver boxes and placed them in the shadow behind the DVD player, plugging them into one of the four-bar power sockets where the cables would blend in and go unnoticed.

He was particularly pleased by this part of his plan. Even if they were discovered, there would be nothing to link the cameras to him. The receivers would remain down here, and be connected to Matt's own wifi. To all intents and purposes, Matt would be spying on himself.

He was almost finished. There was just one more camera to place. Getting to his feet, he picked up the carrier bag and made his way through to the bedroom.

* * *

The ventilation grille was set high on the wall, opposite the bed. Nigel had to stand on a small chair to reach it, but the two screws that held it in place were easy to undo. He used another lump of Blu-tack to secure the camera to the inside of the grille, angling it to look down through one of the narrow slats. After replacing the grille and screwing it back firmly, he stepped down and returned the chair to its spot beside the wardrobe.

All done. But would it work?

Reaching into the carrier bag, he drew out his iPad and powered it on. Tingling with anticipation, he connected to the web feed for the front room. The screen flickered and there it was — Matt's living room! Grinning, he connected to the second feed, and saw himself, standing in the bedroom, holding the iPad.

It was so cool.

He waved to the hidden camera, delighting as the small figure on the screen waved too. Then, conscious that he really shouldn't spend any longer in his friend's flat than he had to, he switched the iPad off and put it back in the bag, ready to go. He took one last look around to make sure he hadn't dropped anything . . .

. . . and that's when he saw it.

There, on the floor at the far side of the bed, almost hidden by the draping edge of the duvet, was a tiny deodorant container. But this wasn't Matt's usual brand, this was a small, pastel-green deodorant with a leafy design flowing around the base.

Nigel stooped and picked it up, twisting off the cap, inhaling the delicate citrus scent.

It was a *woman's* deodorant.

He frowned to himself. Was this why Matt had been so 'busy' recently? Because he had a girlfriend now? And, much more troubling, why hadn't he mentioned her?

PRESENT

17

Eastfield Road looked less welcoming in the rain. It was a summer shower, sudden and torrential, large drops spattering heavily on the windscreen and blackening the dusty tarmac of the street. Imogen switched the engine off and they sat for a moment, listening to the rain drumming down on the roof, waiting for it to ease a little. A police van was parked farther along the street, with uniformed officers going from door to door, trying to galvanise the community into remembering something useful.

'At least we know he'll be there this time,' Harland observed. Now that the wipers were off, the view through the glass had dissolved into a rippling montage of amorphous shapes. He could barely make out anything of the building that loomed before them.

'You called ahead?' Imogen asked him.

'Yes.'

They waited for a couple of minutes longer, until the noise abated a little, then got out of the car. The rain was passing as suddenly as it had arrived, with the last drops falling and sunlight breaking through to glitter on grass, as they made their way up the path and mounted the steps to the front door.

Harland leaned forward to push the bell for the top floor, then stood back, breathing in that clean, fresh smell that always followed summer rain. There were no twitching curtains this time; Mrs Hamilton must be otherwise engaged.

The door buzzed and clicked; Harland pushed it open and stepped into the empty hallway. Motioning for Imogen to follow him, he climbed the long flight of stairs in silence, emerging on to the first-floor landing, where he paused by the sky-blue door.

What had happened to Laura after she left with Matt that night? Why had Matt lied? *But perhaps he didn't know that he'd been seen*. And there was no reason to enlighten him about that just yet; better to wait and see what other mistakes he might make first . . .

'He'll be at work just now, won't he?' Imogen mused.

'Yeah.' Harland nodded, then glanced over the banister, down towards Mrs Hamilton's flat. 'But maybe someone will tell him we popped round.'

They moved on, climbing the second flight of stairs to the top floor. The single door stood before them and Harland walked forward and knocked.

It opened almost immediately, to reveal a pale young man with untidy brown hair — Nigel must have been waiting for them. He was wearing jeans and a fashionable-looking T-shirt, with an open shirt over the top. His Converse trainers looked new.

'Detective Harland and Detective Gower.' Harland held up his warrant card. 'You're Nigel Reynolds, yes?'

'That's right.' Nigel took a moment to study the identification before stepping back and opening the door farther. 'Come in.'

They followed him into a narrow inner hallway and through to the large front room. Sunlight spilled in from the two tall windows in the far wall. There was a desk by the window, with an enormous computer screen, but the rest of the space seemed to be a normal living room — sofa and easy chairs, a large TV on a glass-topped stand, a low coffee table, and DVDs stacked up against the wall.

Nigel gestured towards the sofa. 'Have a seat.'

'Thanks.'

Harland and Imogen sat down as Nigel dropped into a chair opposite them.

'This is about the missing girl, right?' He looked at them expectantly. 'Mrs Hamilton told me you came to see her yesterday.'

'That's right,' Harland said, nodding. 'We knocked on your door too, but you must have been out.'

'Probably,' Nigel said. 'So how can I help you?'

He looked a little uncomfortable, but that was normal enough with a visit from the police . . . and there was a slight shyness about him that suggested he might not get many visitors here at all.

'We believe Laura Hirsch may have been coming to see your neighbour, Matt Garrick, when she went missing,' Harland explained. 'That was last Friday night, probably some time after eleven p.m. We want to know if you remember anything about that night, if you saw or heard anything . . . '

Nigel lowered his eyes.

'Last Friday . . . ' He considered for a moment, then shook his head. 'I'm sorry. Mrs Hamilton said you'd probably ask about that, but I don't remember much about that night . . . '

He looked at them apologetically, then sat back in his chair.

'Were you here on Friday evening?' Imogen asked him.

'Oh yes, I was in.' He answered a little too quickly, then looked at her, embarrassed. 'I don't usually go out that much . . . on Fridays, I mean.'

Imogen smoothly ignored his admission. 'So you would have been in, but you didn't hear anything?'

'I . . . ' Nigel hesitated, then frowned, as though conflicted about something. 'It's just that I'm not sure about which day it was . . . '

'Which day what was?'

Nigel glanced up at her, his face wretched, then looked away.

'I heard them,' he mumbled. 'I heard them fighting.'

There was a strange reluctance in his voice, reminiscent of the way family members eventually gave up a loved one under interrogation. But that didn't make sense here. Why was Nigel so unhappy about incriminating his neighbour? After all, Matt had only moved here a couple of months ago — it wasn't like they'd had time to become particularly close.

Harland leaned forward on the sofa.

'Fighting?' he asked.

'Well, arguing.' Nigel had his arms and legs crossed in front of his body now. He was certainly uncomfortable about something.

'Can you remember when that was?'

'No, sorry.' He thought for a moment, then shook his head sadly. 'They'd had a few rows but I didn't think anything of it. Linda and Eric, the couple who used to live downstairs, they argued all the time. You get used to it, you know?'

Imogen steered him back on to the subject.

'Could it have been the Friday night?' she pressed.

Nigel looked at her, crestfallen.

'I'm sorry. I've been racking my brains but . . . ' He held his hands out apologetically. 'I just don't remember.'

'It's OK, don't worry about it.' Harland did his best to hide his frustration. Another vague witness who wouldn't last five minutes in front of the CPS. Great, just great.

Imogen appeared to have read his mood and was wisely moving the conversation on.

'Did you ever see Matt and Laura together?' she asked.

'No, sorry.' Nigel unfolded his arms. 'I never actually met her at all. I'm usually stuck up here, working.'

Harland rubbed his eyes. If he'd never met Laura, his statement that he'd heard her arguing with Matt became even less credible.

'What is it that you do exactly?' he asked, as pleasantly as he could manage.

'Oh, I'm a Photoshop artist.' Nigel twisted

around in his chair and gestured towards the computer on the desk. 'I freelance a bit but mostly I work for Feinman Images, down at the Watershed?'

'So you take photographs and doctor them? Make people thinner, that sort of thing?'

Nigel gave a sheepish little smile.

'That's what everyone seems to think it is.' He was warming up a little, now that he was allowed to talk about something that he felt good about. 'Most of what I do is really boring stuff — removing blemishes if it's a person, or painting out unwanted cars and bystanders if it's a picture of a place. Often I get asked to put in a better sky . . . you know, if the weather wasn't right when the photo was taken.'

Harland nodded, keen to keep him talking.

'You can do all that on the computer there?'

'That's right. It's simple really . . . ' Nigel wore a bashful grin, his eyes flickering to Imogen, then back again. 'Well, maybe not *that* simple . . . '

'And do you take the pictures as well?'

'No, they usually come via the agency, or direct from the photographer.' Nigel tapped a portable hard drive on his desk, then turned back to face them as he relaxed into his subject. 'I get what they call *raw* images of a person or a product, or whatever the subject is, then *I* make the changes that are needed and send them back the finished shots.'

'Still, very impressive . . . '

'Well . . . ' He gave a modest shake of his head. 'It's not nearly as exciting as it sounds.'

But he was clearly very pleased — time to ask

some more real questions while he was feeling talkative.

'I was wondering,' Harland's smile never faltered, so Nigel had no warning, 'how well do you know Matt?'

'Er . . . I'm not sure.' The young man shrugged. 'Well enough, I suppose. We watched the football together sometimes.'

'Really?' Harland was pretending to be interested now. 'Bristol City? Down at Ashton Gate?'

'No, just whatever game was on the TV . . . ' He paused, smiling to himself. 'We'd sit and have a beer and watch the odd match, you know?'

Harland nodded. He had no trouble believing that Nigel would be more comfortable in front of a screen.

'Do you get on well with Matt?' he asked.

'He's a nice enough guy, yes.' Nigel blinked at him, somewhat puzzled. 'Why?'

Harland ignored the question.

'Have you noticed any change in his behaviour?' he pressed. 'Especially since last Friday?'

Nigel stared at him, a look of dread spreading over his face.

'Oh shit,' he whispered. 'You think he did something to her, don't you?'

* * *

Imogen reversed the car into the little dead-end lane on the opposite side of the terrace, then drove up to the end of the street.

'Well, he was worth speaking to,' she noted, peering out for a gap in the traffic.

'Yeah, he was.' Harland fiddled idly with his wedding ring, turning it slowly round and round with his thumb.

A van rattled past, and Imogen pulled out behind it, coasting smoothly down the road towards the Arches.

'And we know there was an argument,' she added, braking as they came to the junction at the bottom of the hill. 'Several arguments, in fact.'

'We knew that already,' he reminded her. 'Matt volunteered that when we saw him.'

'True,' Imogen frowned. 'But if they had a row on the *Friday* night, that could be significant.'

'That would make a difference,' Harland agreed. 'But we can't be sure it was on the Friday, not yet. Nigel doesn't seem to grasp his days of the week, and Mrs Hamilton — who seems much more reliable — said nothing about raised voices, even though that's the sort of thing she'd love to have told us.'

Imogen turned right, leaving the Arches behind them as they drove back down towards Stokes Croft.

'Probably too busy watching TV,' she mused. 'With the volume right up.'

Harland glanced across at her, then nodded.

'Matt's definitely in the frame,' he admitted, relaxing back into his seat. 'But I think we've still got a way to go before we bring him in.'

'Nigel gets us a bit closer.'

'Does he?' Harland frowned. 'He thinks he heard Laura having an argument, but he can't be sure when it was. Then it turns out he's never even met her. No, I reckon Pearce will want a lot more than that.'

'What are you going to tell him?'

'Damn.' Harland rubbed his eyes wearily. There was a case review with Pearce scheduled for the afternoon — he'd forgotten, and there wasn't a lot of progress to report.

'Sir?'

'I'll tell him we've got a lot of people still to speak to.'

He looked across at Imogen.

'Find out when Laura's housemates are likely to be home this evening,' he told her. 'I want to have a word with them and we can take a look over her place at the same time.'

Imogen shrugged.

'Sure,' she said, slowing as a bus pulled out in front of them.

Harland nodded to himself, then stopped and glanced across at her.

'Sorry,' he said. 'Unless you have something happening this evening. I can go myself, if you had plans . . . '

He'd grown used to being unreasonable while working with Pope, but Imogen was more than pulling her weight. There was no reason for him to mess things up if she had an evening planned with her boyfriend.

'It's fine.' Imogen turned her head to give him a brief look. 'Really.'

Harland nodded awkwardly.

'Well, let me know if I'm taking things for granted or . . . ' He trailed off and shook his head. 'Oh, you know what I mean.'

Imogen's eyes stayed on the road, but she was smiling now. A genuine, unguarded smile.

'Yes, sir,' she said softly, then added, 'And thanks.'

18

He was early. The case review wasn't scheduled until two, so Harland wandered into the canteen. He glanced around, scanning the tables, but thankfully there was no sign of Pearce. Whenever they bumped into each other down here, the chief inspector seemed to be eating something healthy, which always made Harland feel guilty about whatever was on his own plate.

He ordered sausages and chips, then carried his tray across to a vacant table. The canteen was quiet today — most of the lunchtime crowd had gone — so he sat and stared out of the window at the sea of parked cars beyond.

He wasn't looking forward to the review. Hopefully someone else would have made some progress. His own enquiries weren't that encouraging; clearly there was a discrepancy between Mrs Hamilton's account of Friday night and Matt's version but that wouldn't be enough, not on its own.

He sighed. This was the thing he hated most about missing persons cases — the dead-end frustration, the terrible sense of sand draining from an hourglass. With a murder, it was simpler, clearer; the victim was already dead — you couldn't save them, only give them justice. Was Laura Hirsch already dead? He hoped she wasn't, but the thought that she might still be out there somewhere, alive and afraid and relying on him to find her, was troubling.

He pushed his plate aside, the meal half finished, and looked up to see the familiar figure of Linwood approaching.

'All right, Jack,' he called out. 'How's it going?'

Linwood noticed him and slowed.

'Hello, sir. Um . . . you got a minute if I just . . . ?' He gestured towards the counter.

'Sure.' Harland waved him on. 'Go ahead.'

* * *

Linwood returned a few moments later with a laden tray — jacket potato and beans.

'I reckon you were right about that club owner.' He sat down opposite Harland and started organising his cutlery and condiments. 'Jones is a difficult bloke to get hold of, as it turns out.'

'Yeah?'

'Well, he *was* . . . ' Linwood smiled brightly, waving his knife for emphasis. 'But we caught up with him this morning.'

'Keeping a low profile, was he?'

'You know the type; a different pay-as-you-go mobile every week, and nobody can remember the new number . . . '

'Yeah,' Harland shook his head wearily, ' 'cos there's *never* anything dodgy about that.'

'Exactly.' Linwood shovelled in a mouthful of potato and chewed until he was able to talk round it. 'Anyway, we found his car parked outside an address in Fishponds — girlfriend presumably — and this morning a couple of uniforms knocked on the door. Jones *claims* he didn't know we were looking for him, says he wants to help in any way he can, then clams up when we ask about the missing CCTV footage and the bouncer outside the Gents.'

Harland allowed himself a grim little smile.

'Is he here now?' he asked.

'Chatting to his lawyer,' Linwood replied.

'Anyone we know?'

'Grantham.'

'Really?' Harland raised an eyebrow. Grantham had a reputation for getting people out of trouble but he was expensive and Jones didn't strike him as being a big spender. 'He must be worried. Maybe we've touched a nerve.'

'That's what I thought.' Linwood nodded. 'You should have seen his face when I offered to show him the missing footage.'

Harland chuckled. 'Surprised, was he?'

'Yeah. I don't think Kevin fully explained the nature of our visit.'

Harland sat back, rubbing his chin thoughtfully.

'Good,' he murmured. 'Hopefully, with a bit of pressure, he'll tell us if Arnaud had any competition for his patch . . . *and* whether there'd been any trouble recently.'

Linwood nodded and took another mouthful of potato and beans. Harland watched the food disappearing and felt the last of his own appetite going with it.

'What about the bouncer?' he asked.

'Conspicuously absent,' Linwood replied from behind a paper napkin.

'OK. Keep looking.'

Linwood nodded and swallowed, then wiped his mouth.

'How about your missing woman? Any progress?' He resumed eating.

Harland closed his eyes, massaging the bridge of his nose between finger and thumb.

'Nothing definite,' he sighed. 'Not yet, anyway. You know how these things go.'

Linwood nodded silently. He didn't say anything, but he didn't need to; the longer they took to find her, the more likely she was dead. Harland was glad that the little man had the decency to keep his mouth shut.

'Anyway, I'm going to have a cigarette before I see Pearce.' He pushed his chair back. 'Enjoy your lunch, Jack.'

Linwood watched him stand up from the table.

'Good luck, sir,' he murmured.

* * *

Pearce was late, which was unusual. Harland leaned back in his chair and looked around the glass-partitioned meeting room, an island of eerie quiet in the middle of the open-plan CID offices. Sitting on the opposite side of the table, DS Michaela Thomson was reading something on her phone. To her right, DI Martin Fuller was leafing through a printed report, the pages held together by a single staple in the top corner.

The door opened suddenly, and Pearce swept into the room, bringing a surge of office noise from outside.

'Sorry, people.' He raised a hand in apology as he shut the door behind him. 'Caroline can't make it this afternoon, so we're not waiting on anyone else.'

Everyone leaned in around the table, attentive, as Pearce dropped into his chair.

'Right,' he said, looking round at each of them. 'Before we get going, I just wanted to bring everyone up to speed on where we are. As you know, Laura was in the city centre on Friday evening with a couple of friends, and we've confirmed that she was wearing a tan leather jacket, light-coloured top and dark skirt, and carrying a small black handbag. At half-eight she gets a text message on her phone and tells her friends that she's going to see her ex-boyfriend Matt Garrick, who lives in Eastfield Road. At the moment, that's the last *definite* sighting, but the ping on her phone suggests that she got there. Seeing as she doesn't own a car, we're working with the bus company and taxi drivers to try and trace her movements — no joy from them as yet.'

He paused and looked at Harland.

'Now then, Graham's been over to Eastfield Road and spoken with the neighbours. One of them *thinks* they saw Laura — or someone answering her description — leaving the place with Garrick, and driving away in his car. This would be around eleven o'clock, but Garrick denies ever going out — says he stayed in all evening.'

'Garrick's lying, then,' Fuller suggested, in his deep Welsh voice. He was a stocky man in his forties, not quite fat but definitely heading that way, bald on top with the rest of his hair clippered short to compensate.

'He probably is,' Pearce countered, 'but I reckon we need a bit more before we haul him in and start taking him apart. It's not a murder investigation yet — Laura could just turn up, alive and well.'

Fuller shrugged.

'I can think of worse outcomes,' he murmured.

'We all can,' Pearce sighed. 'Anyway, you've been doing some digging, what have you got for us?'

Fuller put his hand on the report in front of him.

'I've been to see her parents, down in Southampton,' he explained. 'Hampshire Police are supporting us locally and their Family Liaison team are looking after things.'

'Did the parents shed any light?' Pearce asked.

'Not really, sir,' Fuller replied. 'As far as they knew, Laura was doing fine. She phoned them earlier in the week and they said she sounded happy enough, everything completely normal. I'm not sure how much she confided in them — they're a fairly strait-laced couple, to tell you the truth — but there's also an older sister, Suzanne. She *did* seem to know how Laura was getting on — she certainly knew about the boyfriend, Matt — but she was adamant there was nothing the matter, nothing that would explain why her sister would disappear.'

'Are the parents doing an appeal?' Harland asked.

'It's arranged for this afternoon,' Pearce told

him. 'Might just be in time to catch the evening news tonight.'

'I reckon they'll come across well,' Fuller noted. 'Get the mother to do the talking if you can — she's more articulate.'

'Fingers crossed it gets some decent coverage,' Pearce sighed. 'I hate dangling the parents in front of the cameras . . . '

Harland glanced across at him. The chief inspector had taken a lot of unfair criticism in the media during the Redland murder investigation last year, but now he had to go back to them and act as though none of that persecution had happened. It was the price of getting the appeal out there — that was just the way the game worked.

'Anyway,' Pearce leaned forward, folding his arms on the table, 'back to Laura. What about colleagues at her school?'

'We've spoken to the headmistress,' Fuller replied. 'Same story there — no problems that she was aware of, no recent changes in behaviour or anything like that. There's more staff to speak to but nothing to report so far.'

Pearce shook his head.

'OK,' he said. 'Michaela, how are the tech team doing?'

Harland liked Michaela. She'd coordinated the CCTV work on the Redland murder the previous year, and had a cool, methodical approach that seemed impervious to pressure.

'They've only just started going through Laura's laptop, so it may be a while before we hear back on that.' Her short, blonde hair was swept back today and she spoke calmly as she addressed them. 'Initial focus has been on email and social media — I've got people going through those looking for anything untoward but nothing out of the ordinary so far.'

'Any interesting Facebook activity between her and Matt Garrick?' Harland asked.

'Some messages, a few photos of them together, the usual,' Michaela replied. 'For what it's worth, there'd been less of him on her timeline in the last few weeks, but I wouldn't read too much into that.'

'That ties in with what Matt said,' Harland mused. 'He reckons they'd kind of drifted apart.'

'And yet he was one of the last people to contact her,' Michaela noted. 'And the last ping on her phone placed her at his address.'

'Hang on, we're jumping about a bit here.' Pearce turned to Harland. 'Graham, you've spoken to Matt . . . what did you make of him?'

Harland sat back in his chair. There was a discrepancy between Matt's account of the evening and Mrs Hamilton's, and yet . . .

'Honestly? Not sure, sir,' he replied. 'We spoke to the neighbours, and we *do* have one report that suggests he drove off with a woman — presumably Laura — late on Friday night.'

'But?' Pearce pressed him.

Harland shook his head.

'Matt's reactions are just . . . wrong,' he replied. 'His girlfriend goes missing, he has no alibi, and yet he doesn't seem rattled when we show up to question him? I don't know, maybe he's just got a brilliant poker face, but if he *has* got something to hide, he's hiding it very well.'

'Let's get a full ANPR check on his car,' Pearce decided. 'See if his plates showed up on traffic cameras, garage forecourts, whatever. CCTV sweep as well please, Michaela. We need to know if he *was* driving that evening and, if so, where.'

'Are you not going to bring him in, sir?' Fuller asked.

Pearce drummed his fingers on the table for a moment, then slowly shook his head.

'Not just yet,' he decided. 'ANPR check first, before we show our hand. In the meantime, we've got people going door to door around his neighbourhood, and you can finish up interviewing the other teachers at Laura's school. Maybe we'll get lucky.'

'Right you are,' Fuller said, shrugging.

'What about you, Graham?' Pearce asked.

'Imogen and I were going to have a word with her housemates in a bit,' Harland replied. 'See if there's anything that uniform missed.'

'Fair enough.' Pearce pushed his chair back. 'I'll keep you all posted and we can regroup once we get an answer on Matt's car. Thanks, everyone.'

* * *

They walked back along the corridor together.

'How's it going with Imogen?' Pearce asked as they approached his office.

'Fine,' Harland said. 'She's good. And she's very clever.'

Pearce nodded.

'Everyone I've spoken to has been really impressed by her,' he confided, opening his door. 'But don't tell her I said that, OK?'

'Said what?' Harland replied with a faint smile.

'Exactly.' Pearce clapped him on the shoulder. 'Let me know if you turn up anything with the housemates . . . '

He went to step into his office.

'Sir?'

'Yes?'

'Any more news on the Arnaud Durand investigation?' Harland asked. 'I spoke to Linwood downstairs and . . . '

He tailed off as he saw the smile fading from Pearce's face. He'd been here before.

'Blimey, Graham, what's the matter — one case not enough for you?' Pearce shook his head and placed a heavy hand on Harland's shoulder. 'Seriously, don't get distracted, not right now. There's nothing bringing Durand back, but Laura may still be alive, OK?'

19

The sun had dropped lower in the evening sky now, its golden glare flickering in at them between the trees and buildings as they drove. Parking near the end of William Street, they walked back up the slight rise, counting down the house numbers as they went. It was a narrow street, tucked away in a crowded warren on the hill south of the railway lines — an endless terrace of flat-fronted two-storey dwellings that pressed in close to the road, blocking any hope of a view.

Harland glanced at the succession of smartly painted front doors, noted the value of the cars parked tight against the pavement. Not the most expensive place to live, but not cheap either, especially on a schoolteacher's salary. Fuller's report said Laura shared a house with two other people — Georgina Carlisle and Oliver Ross. That must be how she managed it.

Their place was one of the neatest in the road, with new-looking double glazing and a line of paving stones traversing the tiny gravel-patch garden.

Laura, Georgina, Olly . . .

Harland approached the door, wondering about the interplay between the housemates. He reached up to push the bell, then stepped back down on to the path to wait.

'Two women, one man . . . '

'Sir?' Imogen was beside him, an enquiring look on her face.

Harland glanced across at her, then shrugged.

'Two's company, but three's a triangle,' he smiled.

Imogen looked away.

'Not necessarily,' she murmured.

There was something about her reaction, but before he could question it, they heard the sound of a lock turning and the door was opened by a young woman with wavy brown hair.

'Yes?' Wearing tight jeans and a short-sleeve top, she looked down at them with curiosity from the doorstep.

'DI Harland and DS Gower from Avon and Somerset Police . . . ' He held up his identification for her to study. 'You must be Georgina Carlisle?'

'Yes.' She seemed to brighten, starting to open the door, then stopped and stared at them in horror. 'Oh God, you're not here to . . . it's not bad news, is it?'

Harland quickly held up his hand.

'No, nothing like that,' he reassured her. 'Just some questions.'

'Oh, thank goodness.' She placed her palm to her chest and offered them a weak smile. 'I suddenly thought . . . anyway, do please come in.'

She sounded as though she came from money; well educated and with no trace of the usual West Country accent in her voice. Standing back, she held the door wide open for them as they stepped into the hallway. Their footsteps echoed noisily on the laminate wood flooring that extended in a continuous swathe from the hall into the front room.

'Through there.' She ushered them towards an archway. 'Would you like me to call Olly down too?'

Harland considered this. It might be worth speaking to them together at first — he could always split them up later if necessary.

'If you would,' he agreed.

Georgina turned back into the hallway and looked up the stairs.

'Olly,' she called, then again, louder. 'Olly?'

'Uh-huh?' An indistinct answer from somewhere above.

'Olly, it's the police. Can you come down?'

She turned back, following them into the front room and gesturing for them to sit.

'Olly will be right down,' she smiled. 'Can I offer you tea or coffee?'

'We're fine for the moment.' Harland shook his head, declining for both of them; he could take her up on the offer later if he wanted to get her out of the room.

Georgina hovered in the doorway, waiting for Olly.

'So *is* there any news?' she asked suddenly. 'About Laura, I mean. Any . . . developments or anything?'

'Well, there's a televised appeal going out this evening, but we're still making enquiries,' Harland told her. He eased himself down onto one end of a low sofa, next to Imogen. 'These things take time, and we have to be thorough.'

'Of course.' Georgina nodded gravely. She turned her head at the sound of footsteps descending from upstairs. 'Ah, here he is.'

Oliver Ross appeared in the doorway and halted to stare at them. He was thin, with a deep mauve shirt and skinny jeans worn low on the waist. His dark hair was short and shiny, fashionably clippered at the sides.

Harland got to his feet and held out a hand. 'I'm Detective Harland, this is Detective Gower.'

'Hello,' Olly replied. *Had he seemed a little reluctant to make eye contact? There was certainly no enthusiasm in his handshake* . . .

They sat down, Olly taking a spot beside Georgina on the opposite side of a low coffee table.

'So, as I was saying, I'm afraid we don't have any definite news on Laura yet,' Harland began. 'I know you've both spoken to some of my colleagues, but we'd just like to ask a few more questions, if that's all right?'

Olly frowned, but Georgina was already leaning forward, nodding earnestly. She was probably going to be the more cooperative of the two.

'How long has Laura been here?' Harland asked. 'Living here, I mean.'

Georgina thought about this.

'About two years,' she replied after a moment. 'I bought the place almost two years ago, and Laura moved in a couple of weeks after I did . . . ' She turned to Olly, 'And you were a few days after her, I think?'

'That's right,' Olly said, nodding. His accent

was from up north somewhere, but it was difficult to place.

'So it's been the three of you together since then,' Harland mused. 'Does Laura usually spend a lot of time at home?'

'I'm not really sure . . . ' Georgina hesitated, then shrugged. 'She's here as much as any of us, I suppose.'

'When she isn't round at *Matt's*,' Olly added quietly.

'That would be Matt Garrick?' Imogen asked him.

'That's right.'

'How would you describe their relationship?' Imogen said, leaning forward. 'Friends? More serious?'

The question seemed to catch Georgina off balance, but Olly frowned to himself.

'I suppose she's *quite* into him,' he conceded after a moment. 'She certainly seemed keen at first, and I guess he *is* fairly good looking . . . but she said he could be a right pain as well.'

'Pain?' Imogen enquired.

'Well . . . unreliable,' Olly explained. 'You know, forgetting to call, standing her up, that sort of thing. I don't know if they were ever going to be properly serious about each other, 'cause she wasn't really like that — but she said they usually had a laugh and I suppose she liked that about him.'

Harland studied Georgina's expression while Olly talked. You could learn a lot watching a person's face as they listened to someone else being questioned. Did they agree with the person speaking? Which questions bothered them? The look on Georgina's face suggested she was hearing some details about Laura's relationship for the first time. Perhaps she didn't know her housemate as well as she thought.

'Was he round here much?' Imogen asked.

'Every now and then,' Olly shrugged. 'But not too often.'

Harland glanced around the room. The furniture looked expensive, coordinated — the house was in Georgina's name so all of this stuff was probably hers. His gaze rested on a framed photo on the bookcase — there she was, smiling in a summer dress, standing beside a bearded young man who had his arm around her.

'Who else spends time here?' he asked her.

'I'm sorry?' She looked at him, confused.

'Close friends? A boyfriend maybe?' He turned to Olly. 'Girlfriend? Anyone that Laura might have spoken to, or confided in?'

'Well, there's Ben,' Georgina replied. 'He and I have been seeing each other for a few months now, but I don't think he's met Laura more than a couple of times . . . '

She tailed off, looking across at Olly, who folded his arms and shook his head. He suddenly seemed defensive about something. Was he jealous of Ben perhaps? *Or maybe he was jealous of Matt . . .*

'Anyone else who's round here regularly?' Imogen enquired.

'Just friends,' Olly said quietly. Georgina glanced at him, but said nothing. Was she waiting for him to tell them something? Something he didn't want the police involved with? Maybe he had a little stash of weed in his room and one of his friends supplied him . . . Harland decided to move on and return to that later.

'Do you both work?' he asked.

'Yes, we do.' Georgina seemed relieved to have a question she was able to answer. 'I work in a gallery on Whiteladies Road. Contemporary stuff — the most frightful rubbish, actually — but the owner is a real sweetie and you get to meet some lovely people.'

'I work for the council,' Olly said, sitting up slightly. He looked less sullen now. 'Planning department, dealing with building applications.'

Harland nodded thoughtfully.

'And what sort of hours do you keep?' he continued. 'Nine to five?'

'Most of the time,' Georgina said.

'And Laura?'

'She's normally the first one home.'

'She does her marking and prep work at the kitchen table,' Olly added. 'She's often still at it when I get home.'

'But neither of you saw her after work on Friday?'

'No.' Georgina shook her head.

'Was it unusual for her to spend the night away?' Imogen directed her question to Olly. Harland smiled to himself. She'd figured out that he knew Laura better and, now that he had started talking, she wanted to keep him going.

'I dunno. She stayed round Matt's a few times, but not that often,' Olly mused. 'Mostly she'd get a taxi back — I think she preferred her own bed.'

'Did she stay over with anyone else recently?' Imogen pressed.

'No,' Olly frowned, then paused. 'Well, I'd have been *very* surprised . . . '

'So when she was away for the whole weekend, you both assumed she was with Matt?' Harland asked.

'Of course,' Georgina replied, then frowned. 'It was only when Mandy phoned that we started to get worried.'

'Mandy . . . ?' Harland asked.

'Mandy Hilton,' Olly explained. 'One of her old school-teacher friends.'

'Of course, thanks.'

'And how had Laura seemed recently?' Imogen asked them. 'Any changes in her behaviour?'

'She was fine . . . ' Georgina said, then looked to Olly for reassurance. 'Well, she *seemed* OK, didn't she?'

Olly nodded slowly.

'Nothing worrying her?' Imogen continued. 'No mention of anything that might lead to her spending time away?'

Olly shook his head, clearly at a loss. Georgina looked at them, then sank back into her seat, an anxious hand in front of her throat.

'I wish we . . . knew *more*,' she said.

You wish you'd known her better, Harland thought to himself.

* * *

They climbed the stairs in silence. Georgina waited for them at the top, then led them along the hallway to a closed white door.

'We haven't been in, not since the other officers went through her things,' she said, standing back as Harland reached for the handle and turned it.

'Thanks,' he said, stepping inside.

Laura's room was large and airy. A broad window, framed by cheerful yellow curtains, looked out over the back garden and on to the rear of the houses that formed the next terrace. There was a line of blue-glass bottles and jars, arranged along the sill, with an old photo of Laura and another girl — her sister, judging by the resemblance — in a plastic frame shaped like a sunflower.

Imogen had walked around to the far side of the unmade bed, her cool gaze already sweeping across the bedside table, but Harland glanced back at Georgina, who had halted, paralysed in the doorway, her hand across her mouth, eyes starting to glisten.

It would be better for everyone if she were downstairs.

'Georgina?' He repeated her name so that she would focus on him, meeting her look with a reassuring nod.

'We won't be long,' he promised, then held her gaze as he gently dismissed her. 'I don't suppose that offer of coffee is still valid, is it?'

'Coffee?' Georgina blinked at him, spared her moment of private grief. 'Sorry, yes, of course. I'll go and put the kettle on.'

Seeming relieved to be sent away, she disappeared back down the hallway. Harland pushed the door shut behind her, then turned to Imogen.

'Alone at last,' he sighed, reaching up to rub the back of his neck and stretching the tension out of his shoulder. 'That coffee should buy us a few minutes.'

'Uniform have already been over the place,' Imogen said, surveying the room. 'What are we looking for?'

'Nothing specific . . . ' He walked over to the bedside table and pointed to the phone charger cable plugged into the wall beside it. 'You noticed?'

'First thing I saw,' Imogen replied. 'I suppose she might have had a spare, but if I was *planning* to be away for a while, I'd make sure I took my charger.'

'Exactly,' Harland mused. He looked across to the desk by the window. 'Her laptop's back at CID — tech services are working on it now.'

'There wasn't a diary, was there?'

'Sadly not.' Harland shook his head. 'That might have been useful but you younger people prefer your Facebook and Twitter, don't you?'

Imogen looked over at him, a slight smile playing at the corners of her mouth.

'Are you on Twitter, sir?' she asked.

'I've got an account,' he told her, then sighed, 'I just never know what to say.'

* * *

There were ribbons tied to the white metal bed frame — decorative rather than functional. The rest of the furniture was an odd mix of mismatched pieces that appeared to have been restored — a wardrobe, chest of drawers and writing desk — all painted in a pale blue matte and decorated with stencilled plants and birds. It looked as though it had been finished by hand — perhaps Laura had done it herself. A three-panel dressing screen stood in one corner of the room, genuinely old, with Chinese patterns set into the dark wood.

'What do you think of the interplay between the housemates?' Harland asked as he opened the wardrobe, looking at the rail of neatly hung clothes.

'Pretty normal,' Imogen replied. She sat on the crumpled duvet and leaned forward, pulling a storage box from under the bed frame. 'Georgina seemed a bit lost, didn't she?'

'Yeah, she did,' he mused. 'But it's Olly I'm interested in. He was very guarded, I thought.'

'Sir?'

'The way he got defensive when we were talking to him . . . something's up there. Maybe he and Laura were more than just friends. Or at least, he wanted them to be.'

Imogen looked up from the storage box.

'I doubt that, sir.'

'Why do you say that?'

'Well . . . I'm pretty sure Olly's gay.'

Harland glanced at her.

'What?'

'His manner . . . the way he went quiet when you started asking about girlfriends.' She shrugged. 'Didn't you notice?'

Harland stared for a moment, then scowled and turned away. He hadn't noticed, but now that she'd pointed it out . . .

'I don't know why he didn't just tell us,' he grumbled. 'I don't care who he dates — makes no difference to me either way.'

'Maybe he doesn't feel it's something he needs to explain to people.'

'Maybe he doesn't, but that's not the point . . . '

'I mean, it's not as if his sexuality has a huge bearing on the case.'

'Of course not, but . . . ' Harland shook his head, marshalling his thoughts. 'Look, if he comes across as having something to hide, *that* gets my attention . . . and wastes everyone's time.'

Imogen pushed the box back under the bed and stood up.

'I'm not sure you can expect everyone to see things from your perspective, sir.'

'I *don't* expect that,' Harland told her. 'But we're trying to find out what happened to his housemate, and unless he has some sinister reason not to, I expect him to cooperate with us.'

Imogen stared at him for a moment, then turned away and busied herself with an examination of the drawers.

Harland frowned. Didn't she see what he was saying? Surely she understood how misunderstandings and false suspicions could delay an investigation . . .

'Hello?' Georgina's voice came to them from downstairs. 'Coffee's ready.'

Harland took a last look round the room, then moved to the door.

'Come on,' he said. 'Let's get out of here.'

* * *

They sat in the car at the bottom of the hill, waiting for the traffic lights to change.

'So?' Harland asked. 'What did you make of them?'

Imogen stared out through the windscreen, frowning slightly.

'On probability, I'd say I believed them,' she replied. 'I liked him more than her. How about you?'

Harland shrugged.

'Well, you know what I think about Olly . . . ' He shook his head, annoyed at his earlier mistake. 'Not quite sure about Georgina, but I think perhaps she's feeling a bit embarrassed.'

'Embarrassed? In what way?'

'Well, she didn't really know Laura that well — maybe neither of them did. I'm not sure she even noticed her dear housemate was missing until that other woman phoned up. And even then, she wasn't the one who called it in — again, that was her friend, Mandy.'

'So all that concern in there, you think that was just crocodile tears?'

'Not sure she's quite *that* fake,' Harland frowned, 'but I think there's an element of *doing what's expected* when it comes to her emotional responses.' He paused, then imitated Georgina's accent. 'She's *terribly* worried for poor Laura because she feels she *ought* to be terribly worried for poor Laura.'

Imogen nodded thoughtfully.

'So, what now?' she asked.

Harland rubbed his eyes wearily.

'Drop me off at CID. Then go home, and forget all about this till the morning.' He glanced up, then looked across at her expectantly. 'The light's green, by the way.'

* * *

It was late when he finally left his desk, waved goodnight to Pearce, and made his way downstairs. The car park was well lit but deserted now, and his own vehicle stood alone, surrounded by a sea of empty spaces. He paused on the tarmac, listening to the dull rumble of traffic from the overpass, and wondered about Laura; what had happened to her, where she was now, out there in the darkness of the city somewhere . . .

The lights of the big twenty-four-hour supermarket twinkled between the trees as he drove along Coronation Road, and he pulled in rather than going straight home. *Milk, bread, time to think* . . .

Passing between the sliding doors, he shrugged off the smothering caress of the warm-air blowers, and picked up a garish green basket. The place was quiet — just the shift workers and the insomniacs, lonely souls drifting up and down the long aisles. Ahead of him, there was an older man with a trolley. As Harland passed him, he glanced up briefly from the packet he'd been studying, his face pale and drawn under the harsh fluorescent lights . . .

. . . like Laura's family, their faces pale and drawn under the harsh TV lights as they were led in to face the eager gaze of the press.

The appeal had gone out on the evening news. Pearce had said a few words, then sat like a guard dog beside the parents, his jaw set with grim defiance, while the mother choked out a faltering plea for information. She looked so terribly ordinary — a small woman in her fifties, with short, grey-blonde hair, and a beige cardigan draped round her narrow shoulders — but her expression was a mask of torment. The father was taller, older. He'd sat there like a statue, distinguished and grey, unable to let go in front of the cameras, helplessly stroking his wife's hand as she grieved for both of them, desperately begging for the return of their little girl.

Somehow, the families always seemed to look like that. Tired faces, fighting to contain the storm of emotions within — broken men, struggling to appear stoic because they didn't know what else to do, brave women stripped bare of their make-up by the tears.

The mother read from a piece of folded paper, clutched in her shaking hand. Her voice was thin but clear, every pause punctuated by the insistent clicking of the cameras.

'Laura always stays in touch with her family and her friends, and that is why we are all so worried. She cannot have simply vanished. Someone somewhere must know something that can help the police to find her . . .'

The wording had, no doubt, been carefully vetted, yet it was hard to hear it as anything other than a plea for the return of the body. Harland wondered whether they really believed Laura was still alive. Perhaps they flickered back and forth between anguish and hope — embracing the pain and steeling themselves for the worst, before guilt drove them to torture themselves with new hope . . . and the awful possibility that their little girl might still be suffering somewhere while they did nothing.

'My daughter is a bright and good-hearted young woman . . . ' The mother's eyes stayed on the paper, but she raised her chin a little, and there was a determined pride in her voice. 'She is at the heart of our lives, and the heart of our family. If anyone knows anything . . . '

And then she'd cracked, her face twisting into an awful expression of anguish as she began to sob. 'Please, oh God, *please*, I want my baby . . . '

It couldn't have been better, but Harland hated himself for thinking that.

The father had sat there, lost, not knowing how to comfort his wife as she clung to him, and the cameras had drunk it all in greedily, until one of the Family Liaison officers had drawn things to a close and helped Laura's mother away.

Harland sighed, reaching up to get a microwave meal from the chilled cabinet in front of him. He wondered what the Family Liaison people said in situations like that, whether there was any measure of comfort in their words. Did it really make things any easier, more bearable?

There had been no team of specialists when Alice died, no soothing words or support; just him, alone in an empty house, making the reluctant decision to carry on . . .

He rubbed his tired eyes, and took a breath. No, there was nothing anyone could have done for him. But there *was* something he could do for this family. He could find out what had happened to Laura.

20

'You want to talk to Mandy.' That was the one thing that everyone at William Street seemed to agree on. But Mandy didn't seem particularly keen to talk to them. She'd sounded odd on the phone — not nervous as such, but something didn't sit right. After all, if your best friend went missing you'd want to do all you could to help the police, wouldn't you? In fairness, she *had* been the one who reported Laura missing in the first place. And yet now, Harland had got a sense of reluctance from Mandy Hilton — nothing specific, just a feeling.

They'd arranged to meet her after work, in a quiet café round the corner from the school where she taught, and she was uneasy from the moment she walked in. Wearing a shapeless grey cardigan over a dark blue dress, she looked older than in her photograph — five foot six with short dark hair, a round face and narrow glasses with white plastic frames.

'Hello, Mandy.' Harland stood up and smiled politely, then gestured towards the empty chair on the other side of the table. 'We spoke on the phone earlier. I'm Detective Harland and this,' he inclined his head towards Imogen, 'is Detective Gower.'

'Hi,' Mandy said, with a brief smile. She twisted herself into the chair rather than pulling it out, and settled back, gathering a large suede bag onto her lap. 'Sorry I'm a bit late. There was a thing with one of the parents.'

'That's OK,' Harland said smoothly. 'Can I get you anything before we start?'

She shook her head. 'I'm fine, thanks.'

Already in a hurry to leave. And they hadn't even asked her any questions yet.

'OK. Now, I know you've already spoken to one of my colleagues about Laura, so I'll try not to cover too much of the same ground.' He tried to make his voice friendly, reassuring. 'DS Gower and I are trying to build up a better picture of Laura's day-to-day routine, her work, her friends, her interests . . . anything that might help us find out where she is.'

'Our priority is to make sure that she's safe,' Imogen explained, leaning forward. 'That's why everything you can tell us is really important.'

Mandy nodded.

Harland looked at her, hiding behind her bag. Better let her settle down a bit first. He decided to start with something safe, something easy that would let her talk a little.

'So, you've known Laura for a while?'

'Yeah,' Mandy replied. 'I met her at uni. We just hit it off, you know?'

Harland gave her a rueful grin.

'My recollections of uni are a bit . . . foggy.' He said it to put her at ease and she did manage a very slight smile. 'So you've been friends for a few years now?'

Mandy nodded slowly.

'Yeah, we have.'

Behind his smile, Harland groaned to himself.

She wasn't much of a talker. He had to get her to loosen up a little — an open question, something that would draw the words from her. He leaned forward and said softly, 'Tell me about her . . . '

Mandy looked down, eyes focusing on the empty tabletop before her.

'She's . . . she's just like a really fun person . . . ' For a moment, it looked as though she might dry up again, but then her brow crinkled into a slight frown as she decided to continue. ' . . . and she's really bubbly but she's got a good heart, you know? Some people, they're all smiles on the outside but deep down they're just out for themselves. Not Laura, though. She's a really genuine person.'

At least she was talking now. And speaking about Laura in the present tense — that was an encouraging sign. He nodded for her to go on, but Mandy glanced up, self-conscious again.

'That's kind of it,' she said, shrugging. 'She's a . . . good person.'

Harland fed her another safe question.

'What about work?' He smiled. 'She likes being a teacher?'

'Oh yeah, it's what she always wanted to do, which is great really.' Mandy looked down, a wistful smile touching her lips. 'I was a bit jealous at first . . . I sort of ended up in it . . . something to do, you know? But Laura's always been dead keen on the idea. And she adores her kids.'

'She's over at St Edith's Junior?'

'That's right.'

'Is it a good school to teach at?'

'I guess so.' Mandy paused, then shrugged. 'Some people think that you're better off in more affluent areas but it comes down to the kids really. If they're a bunch of spoilt little brats, it doesn't matter how much money their parents have.'

'What about the staff there?'

A deliberately vague question, to see whether there was anyone significant they should be looking at, but Mandy just shrugged again.

'Yeah,' she said. 'The rest of the staff sound nice enough from what I've heard.'

Harland leaned back in his chair, deciding to try something else.

'So what does she get up to when she's not working?' he asked.

'Um . . .' It was very subtle, but Mandy seemed to stiffen a little; he wondered whether Imogen had picked up on it too. 'Well, we go into town together quite a lot — shopping sometimes, or maybe clubbing at the weekend. And we go to the gym together, but not as often as we should.'

She trailed off with an apologetic smile. There was nothing untoward about her answer, but Mandy had narrowed it down from the broader question he'd asked.

Harland smiled at her. Was she was one of those slightly possessive women who didn't like their friends getting too close to the opposite sex?

'What about men in her life?' he asked.

Mandy eased back in her chair a little, her shoulders dropping.

'Well, she's been seeing a bloke called Matt — you know about him, right? The mechanic? They're kind of an item, on and off.'

She didn't seem troubled by Laura's choice of men.

'On and off?' Imogen interjected.

'Yeah, for a while I got the feeling they might be splitting up, but she was going to see him on that Friday, last time I heard from her . . . '

Mandy suddenly looked as though she might become upset, but Imogen was there quickly, steering her away from distress with a different question.

'Had she been seeing him long?'

Past tense. Harland sighed to himself, but let the mistake pass.

'A few months, I think,' Mandy said. 'She met him at a party but it was a while before they started going out together.'

'Was there anyone special before him?' Imogen asked.

'She always had a lot of interest, but the last one who she saw regularly was Gary . . . ' Mandy frowned, then shook her head. 'Gary something-or-other, sorry, I don't remember his name, but that was finished months ago. He moved away just after Christmas, I think . . . '

Harland watched her as she spoke. He wanted to take his notebook out, but he didn't want to risk spooking her. Hopefully Imogen would keep him right on any details.

'Anyone else on the horizon?' he asked.

Mandy looked at him, her expression defensive.

'It's OK,' Imogen reassured her. 'We just want to get a picture of things, that's all.'

'No,' Mandy said firmly. 'I think she was still quite keen on Matt . . . '

She tailed off as a young man brought over a tray and set two cups of coffee down on the table.

'Sure I can't get you anything?' Harland asked her.

Mandy shook her head. 'I'm fine, really.'

'OK, then.' Harland thanked the young man, then lifted his coffee and took a tentative sip. 'So, you were the one who reported Laura missing . . . ?'

Mandy nodded slowly.

'I just got worried,' she explained. 'I hadn't heard from her and she wasn't answering her phone or replying to texts or anything.'

Her voice was almost apologetic, as though she felt bad about involving the police for nothing. A normal, honest response from someone who had no idea where their friend was, but it could also mean that she wasn't yet worried enough to tell them everything.

'So you got in touch with her housemates?' Imogen took up the questioning.

'Yeah, I called Georgina on the Monday,' Mandy replied. 'She said Laura hadn't been home all weekend.'

Imogen sat back a little, a thoughtful expression on her face.

'Laura could have been staying with someone else . . . ' she suggested.

'Yeah, but she'd have called or sent me a text.'

Imogen appeared to consider this for a moment.

'Even if she was . . . ' A pause, then tentatively,' . . . maybe spending the weekend with someone she felt she shouldn't be?'

'No.' Mandy sat forward, eager to contradict her. 'We told each other *everything*. I knew all her secrets.'

Harland saw the opportunity and decided to push it.

'But she didn't *have* any secrets, did she?' He leaned forward, forcing Mandy to look at him. 'Mandy?'

Mandy stared at him for a moment, her face unhappy.

'Is there anything that we should know?' Harland pressed. 'Come on, Mandy.'

She seemed to shrink behind her bag, her eyes flickering across to Imogen for support, but there was no way out now.

'I know this puts you in a difficult position but it really is important,' Imogen insisted. 'We're going to find out everything anyway, but you can help us get there sooner. Don't hold back, please.'

Mandy looked down, toying with the fastener on the front of her bag.

'It's silly really,' she murmured. 'I mean, it's not like she was doing anything wrong or anything . . . '

'Go on . . . ' Harland told her.

She glanced up at him, then turned her head more towards Imogen. *Easier to talk to*.

'She was doing some modelling work. You

know, the odd evening or weekend. There's nothing wrong with that.'

She sounded as if she was trying to justify something to herself.

'OK,' Imogen said. 'And had she been doing this long?'

'A month or so.' Mandy sounded relieved to have an easier question to answer. 'She was kind of funny about it at first but everything was OK after a while.'

'Funny about it?'

'You know, like a bit embarrassed maybe?'

Imogen nodded sympathetically.

'Was it glamour work?' she asked.

'Yeah, but nothing . . . you know . . . ' She rolled her eyes, embarrassed. 'Nothing *dodgy* or anything.'

Imogen regarded her calmly.

'And this was to make a bit of extra money?' she prompted.

Mandy hesitated.

'I don't know. Maybe.' She stared down at the table and shook her head slightly. 'Sometimes I thought Laura got a buzz out of it . . . maybe it made her feel good about herself.'

Harland watched her. Was she projecting herself into that position? Wishing she felt good about herself? Wishing she had her friend's confidence?

'Well,' Imogen said, 'if you've got a good body, then why not?'

'Yes.' Mandy sat up, pleased that someone understood. 'That's exactly what I said to her.'

'But still, not something that you'd want

everyone to know about,' Harland mused. He had already guessed why.

'Well, no. Not if you're a primary school-teacher,' Mandy admitted. 'Not that it should make any difference, but people can get silly about stuff like that.'

She was right, of course. And some people might react very badly to that sort of information.

'What about Matt?' he asked her. 'Do you think he knew?'

'No idea,' Mandy replied, 'but I reckon most blokes might have a tough time getting their head around it. They can be *so* hypocritical . . . ' She broke off, looking at Harland. 'No offence.'

'None taken.' He gave her a faint smile, then took another sip of coffee. 'Did she say who she was modelling for?'

'Some dodgy old Scottish photographer in town.' Mandy turned to address Imogen. 'She said he was always trying to get into her knickers — well, *you'll* know how it is — but he was pretty harmless.'

Imogen smiled but said nothing.

'You don't have a name for him, do you?' Harland asked.

Mandy frowned, then shook her head.

'Sorry. I just remember her talking about an old Scottish guy. She said something about a studio over in St Paul's but I don't know where.'

'It's OK,' he told her, noting that she'd relaxed the grip on her bag.

'Did you ever see any of the photos?' Imogen asked.

Mandy turned to her. 'Yes, why?'

Imogen shrugged. 'Were they any good?'

'Actually, yeah.' Mandy smiled. 'Really professional looking. And she's always been very photogenic.'

'Were these prints?' Imogen asked. 'Like *photograph* photos, or was it all digital?'

'The ones I saw were on her phone,' Mandy replied.

Harland put his coffee cup down.

'I feel bad that you're not having anything,' he told her. 'Are you sure you wouldn't like a coffee or anything?'

Mandy half-turned to look round at the counter, considering.

Harland smiled. It must have been the glamour work that had been worrying her. Now that was out in the open, she was more relaxed.

'Maybe just a Coke?' Mandy smiled.

'No problem.'

He stood up and made his way across to the counter.

Glamour photos. That's why they hadn't come across them yet. No physical prints sitting in a drawer, and not exactly the sort of material you'd want to post on your Facebook page. They'd have to go through her laptop, and get into her email, but that'd take time . . .

He stared along the counter at the street beyond the window. Perhaps there was a quicker way.

21

It was almost six by the time they returned to CID. Harland wanted to make a few calls about the photographer Mandy had mentioned, and Imogen said she needed to get something from her desk, so they climbed the stairs together.

'How did you like your last job?' he asked. 'You know, working with Burgess?'

'Fine,' Imogen replied. 'He's a good man, taught me a lot.'

'Not an easy case to be on, by the sound of it . . . '

'I don't know . . . ' She slowed a little, her brows tightening slightly as she considered something. 'It was certainly disturbing, but in a way that made it . . . even more important . . . does that make sense?'

'Yeah, I can understand that,' he said as they reached the top of the stairs and turned right on to the corridor. 'Getting that kind of monster off the streets really matters.'

She seemed slightly withdrawn, and he wondered whether he'd said the wrong thing. Perhaps it gnawed at her that she'd been unable to get a conviction . . .

'Did Burgess have a favourite suspect for it?' he asked.

'Not really, no.' Imogen shook her head, gazing down at the floor as she walked by his side. 'We did all the usual stuff — looked at people with relevant form, tried to find a common factor that would link the victims — but there was nothing. It was like he was taking women at random . . . '

'Tough to catch someone when the victims are random,' Harland agreed, as they walked through into the office. He knew from experience just how tough it could be but that wasn't something he could share with her. 'So what happened? Did he just . . . stop?'

'Not sure,' Imogen replied. 'Killers like that are supposed to escalate, not just . . . finish. My guess is something changed. At one point, I actually wondered if he'd maybe become ill and gone into hospital, or lost his job, or something like that had disrupted him.'

'Maybe.' Harland watched her as she made her way round to her desk. She was imaginative in her thinking. That was a useful trait to have.

'Or maybe his method evolved somehow,' Imogen continued. 'Maybe he's still active and we're just not connecting his new crimes with his old ones.'

She reached under her desk and pulled out a plastic carrier bag. Harland glimpsed a loaf of artisan bread, and one of those expensive bottles of olive oil — the kind that only people who really knew about food would appreciate.

Must be cooking him a special meal tonight.

He moved around to his own desk, pausing as he put his hand on the back of his chair.

'How did you link the ones you knew about?' he asked. 'You said something about bleach?'

'What? Oh, no. It was the knots. He only used

bleach with two of the women but all of them were restrained using these really odd, really intricate knots.'

'Interesting,' Harland mused. 'You searched nationally? Looked for any sex cases where the victim was restrained?'

Imogen straightened up and put her hands on her hips.

'I'm *still* looking,' she said, her voice cold and quiet. 'Spent a lot of hours, hunched over the computer, looking at pictures and wishing I hadn't.'

Harland felt a new sympathy for her.

'You'll get him.' He managed an awkward smile. 'Anyway, I'd better let you get on. See you tomorrow . . . '

She paused, resting the carrier bag on her desk.

'You're not finishing yet?'

'In a while,' he told her. 'I'm going to phone a couple of people, see if I can get a line on who this photographer is.'

'You think there's something in that?'

'You never know.' Harland shrugged. 'It won't do any harm to ask around, see what turns up.'

'Want me to stay?'

'Not tonight, you've got plans.'

Imogen frowned at him.

'How did you . . . ?' She followed his gaze to the shopping bag on her desk, then her eyes narrowed. 'Ah! For a moment, I thought you'd done something clever.'

'Everything becomes commonplace by explanation,' Harland smiled.

Imogen grinned.

'Is that a quotation?'

'A loose one, yes.' He pointed at the bag. 'So is your other half a foodie too?'

'Yeah, she is . . . '

She? Harland looked up in surprise.

A number of different emotions flickered across Imogen's face, before she got control of herself, adopted her neutral expression, put the barriers back up.

'I'd better go,' she said, quickly gathering up the bag. 'I'll see you tomorrow, sir.'

'OK . . . '

But she was already away, striding across the office and disappearing down the corridor.

Harland watched her go, then shook his head, slowly pulling his chair out and sitting down.

She. How had he read his new partner so wrongly?

ONE MONTH AGO

22

Nigel stared at the screen. The girl's name was Laura Hirsch. Sifting through the entries on Matt's Facebook account, he'd patiently studied all the messages from female friends until he'd found her. It had started several months ago, with flirty exchanges that made him smile as he read them.

Matt: Good 2 see U ystdy
Laura: Yeah. Been ages.
Matt: Still go 2 the club in SC?
Laura: Only went cpl times with mate. Prefer city cntr now
Matt: Shame. U look good on dancefloor
Laura: Thx hun X

Laura: HiHi
Matt: Hey
Laura: U broke up with Susi?
Matt: Ages ago. Who told U?
Laura: Bradley. R U OK?
Matt: Yeah. Bit down but its cool
Laura: Hugs babe X

Laura: Saw Susi last nite
Matt: Yeah?
Laura: She was being such a cow to Daryl. U R better off without her
Matt: Thanks :)

Laura: Still single?
Matt: Why? U asking? ;-)
Laura: LOL. U wish :-)
Matt: :-)
Laura: X

She was funny, but her sense of humour was never cruel. As time had gone on, their chat had become more suggestive, more intimate, and their friendship had developed into something sexual.

Laura: Hows things?
Matt: Bored :-(
Laura: Few of us going 2 club tonite. Fancy it?
Matt: I fancy something ;-)
Laura: LOL Want to come over?
Matt: Over what? :oO
Laura: LOL UR a v bad man
Matt: U know it

Laura: Get 2 work on time?
Matt: 10mins late but was OK
Laura: Soz babe
Matt: NP. Totally worth it ;-)
Laura: Yeah. Georgie asked me what noise was LOL
Matt: U tell her?
Laura: No!!!! Anyway she wd only B jealous
Matt: Why? She got a bf
Laura: Not like U babe X

It made fascinating reading. There were hundreds of photos on her profile page — charting several years of her life — and Nigel took the time to download them all, magnifying each one, staring and studying. She was beautiful. Not like some of the models he saw — all make-up and carefully constructed poses — but naturally beautiful, with bright eyes, and a warm smile. How amazing it must feel to be the *object* of that smile, to gaze into those eyes as they gazed back. Matt was so *bloody* lucky.

Nigel charted the course of their relationship, reading it from the very beginning, living every word. Kind words, eager words, *from a woman*. It was as if a glorious new landscape had opened up before him and he felt his heart soar within him. Before, he'd known only snide comments and cold put-downs; women were to be desired and feared. But Laura was different. She was beautiful and good and unlike any other woman he knew.

⋆ ⋆ ⋆

The sun was shining, sparkling on the spray from the fountains, and glaring bright on the water in the harbour. Nigel strode across the cobbled plaza and down the steps towards the Watershed. He'd thought about bringing his bag but finally decided against it. He didn't need to carry his laptop *everywhere*, and besides the *X-Men* bag didn't really go with his new clothes. They felt different, but in a good way, and he smiled at the glimpses of his reflection as he walked past the bars and restaurants.

Just like Matt.

He ran lightly up the stairs and walked along the corridor into the studio. Sarah was at the reception desk and she looked up from her screen as he walked in.

'Morning, Sarah,' he greeted her.

'Oh, hi.' She smiled back at him, an unfamiliar smile that suggested she'd noticed the change, that she was re-evaluating her opinion of him. 'How's it going?'

'Good, thanks,' he replied. 'Angela's expecting me . . . catch you later.'

He turned away from her, and smiled to himself as he heard her awkward reply, 'Later.'

The meeting was scheduled for eleven and it was already a few minutes after that. Bella was standing by the desks and hurried over when she spotted him.

'There you are,' she said, a note of relief in her voice. 'The client's already arrived, and Angela's taken him through to the meeting room. They're waiting for you.'

Nigel nodded. There was something rather satisfying about being the one who others waited for. 'I'll go on through.'

'Thanks,' Bella smiled. She paused. 'Would you like me to get you a drink of anything?'

'Oh . . . a Diet Coke. Thanks.'

'I'll bring it in.' She paused, looking at him. 'That's a new jacket, isn't it?'

'Yes. Why?'

'Looks good,' she said, then gave him a shy smile. 'Go on, they're waiting for you.'

* * *

The meeting went well and Nigel found himself enjoying it. Angela gushed about his abilities and the client, a rather wet-looking man with greying hair who worked for a regional development group, seemed very impressed with the preliminary mock-ups he'd done. They finished just after twelve, and the man even made a point of shaking him rather limply by the hand before leaving, something that didn't go unnoticed by the watchful Angela.

'Well *done*, darling,' she said afterwards, giving him a long, steady look. 'That inadequate little man is going to give us a *lot* of business and you did a super job with him today.'

'Thanks,' Nigel smiled. There was something different in her voice, and it took him a moment to recognise what it was.

She was being genuine. For as long as he'd known her, she'd always seemed to drift around in an endless haze of compliments, but this? This was the real thing: *actual approval*.

'Indeed,' Angela mused. 'I think this is going to be the start of something rather exciting.'

23

Nigel leaned over his desk, running a careful line of school adhesive along the inside flaps of the envelopes, just where the original gum had been. He'd developed a routine now, opening the mail in the morning, and resealing it in the evenings when the paper had dried out again. Tomorrow morning, he'd go downstairs and put today's letters back in Matt's pigeonhole, and collect any new mail — a short delay for the post, but one which helped him to understand his neighbour that little bit better.

It was mostly junk mail — promotions from a supermarket or the local gym, and countless offers of credit cards — but every now and then he'd learn something. A mobile phone bill had given him Matt's number, and the numbers of several people he'd called as well as how often he called them. A bank statement showed his wages, how much money he had tucked away, and where he withdrew cash. Credit card bills were the most interesting, though — itemised details of each purchase, where and when, and how much. It was his friend's whole life, presented as an ongoing jigsaw puzzle — all he had to do was collect the pieces and put them together. And the more he understood Matt, the more alike they'd be, the *closer* they'd be.

Sealing the last envelope, he sat up stiffly, leaning back and stretching as he glanced at the clock in the corner of his screen. It was getting late and he was tired. Yawning, he got to his feet, and wandered through to the kitchen to get himself a drink.

A faint sound from the floor below halted him. Matt must be home. He stood still for a moment. At first, he thought it was the TV but there was something different about the voices. He leaned forward, straining to hear, then stepped lightly back to the front room and picked up his iPad. Connecting to the downstairs wifi, he entered the address of the web feed and stared at the screen.

Yes, there was Matt now, emerging from his kitchen, walking over to put a wine bottle down on the coffee table. He was wearing a smart-looking shirt, one that Nigel hadn't seen before.

Must be new.

On-screen, his movements looked purposeful, gathering up a couple of magazines and tossing them behind the sofa . . .

And then he heard the muffled rushing sound of water — a toilet flushing in the bathroom downstairs? Nigel saw Matt look towards the doorway and felt his own pulse quicken.

It must be her!

Gripping the iPad tightly, he watched as she entered the room, as elegant and lovely as he'd imagined her. She was wearing a tiny dark jacket over a pale dress, her long blonde hair bouncing as she walked over to the sofa and sat down, twelve feet below him. He couldn't quite make out what she was saying, but Matt asked her something, and she nodded before reaching out for the bottle on the table. A moment later, he was beside her with a couple of glasses and they were laughing and drinking.

Nigel's mouth was dry. Staring at the iPad, he went through to the kitchen and propped the screen up where he could see it, while he took a dusty bottle of wine from his cupboard, opened it, and poured himself a glass.

It was late. They'd obviously been out for the evening, but she didn't appear to be in any hurry to leave. Matt had got up from the sofa and walked through to the kitchen, reappearing at the doorway with a packet of something in his hand. He bowed extravagantly and Laura laughed as he placed tortilla chips and some sort of dip on the table, then dropped onto the sofa beside her.

They looked comfortable together, relaxed and happy. Nigel held the screen up close to his face, staring at the scene downstairs, imagining how it would feel to be on that sofa, to have her beside him. He went and sat on his own sofa, taking the same side as Matt occupied directly below him. If only he could hear what they were saying . . . but the words were indistinct, difficult to make out. He imagined the conversation, guessing what he should say to her, then responding for her as she spoke. He knew that Matt didn't have a lot of money, especially this month, but she wouldn't mind about that. She was a *good* person, just happy to be having a quiet drink at the end of their evening.

She was a keeper.

He sat there, staring at the iPad, enthralled. Their TV was showing a stand-up comedy show, and he had his own TV showing the same channel with the sound down low, but none of them was really watching it. When Matt put his arm around Laura, Nigel stretched out an arm to surround a cushion, mirroring the action. As the programme continued, she cuddled in closer to him, leaning her head against his chest, and Nigel leaned back a little to accommodate her, just as Matt did.

There was a synchronicity to their movements now. Matt leaned forward, pouring more wine for them, while above him Nigel did likewise. When Laura slipped her shoes off and tucked her feet under herself on the sofa, both men bowed to kiss her hair, both men smiling . . .

. . . but now, there was a change, a subtle sense of urgency.

Matt had his arm around Laura's waist, lifting a hand to gently cup her breast as Nigel sighed, his hand raised, imagining how good it must feel. Laura tipped her head back with laughing abandon, and he could hear her as she asked, 'What's the hurry? We've got all night . . . '

All night.

He was already aroused, but her words made him stiffen with eagerness.

'Is someone getting a bit excited?' she teased, staring up at him as she reached a hand down between his legs, playfully grabbing his crotch through the denim. 'Wow, you *are* keen tonight.'

Nigel nodded quietly, a bashful smile on his face.

‘Poor thing.’ Laura had turned her head to watch something on the TV screen, but her hands were busy undoing Matt’s belt, dragging down his zipper. Directly above them, Nigel unzipped himself.

Matt leaned in close, kissing Laura’s neck until she was no longer able to concentrate on the TV. Upstairs, Nigel was breathing fast. They were going to do it. He was going to have sex with Laura!

Matt’s movements were becoming more eager now, and it looked as though he might be about to take her right there on the sofa, but she managed to disentangle herself from him, dragging his hand out from beneath her skirt as she kissed him. Then, getting unsteadily to her feet, she pulled him up and led him towards the hallway.

Nigel stared at the iPad, then switched views to the bedroom camera as he followed them down the hallway to his own bedroom. On the screen, Matt walked into view and began kicking his shoes off. But where was Laura? Had she gone to the bathroom again? No, he could hear them talking, and Matt was pulling his shirt off now.

It was really going to happen!

Propping the iPad up on his pillow, Nigel began taking his own shirt off. When he pulled it over his head and looked back, Laura was in view again. She walked slowly over to the bed, putting her arms around Matt’s neck and drawing him down for a kiss. His hands roamed across her back, slipping her top off her shoulders and letting it fall to the floor, undoing the back of her bra. They kissed again, turning slightly as her hands snaked in between their bodies to free him. Pulse racing, Nigel pulled his own shorts down, imagining her touch between his legs as he stared at the screen. For a moment he couldn't quite see, as she was obscured behind Matt, but then she stepped out from behind him, and he saw her naked body for the first time — a small, pixelated view, but perfection nevertheless. Full breasts, a gorgeous little tummy that led his eye down to that dark little triangle and those long, slender legs.

And then, she was climbing onto the bed, lying back and pulling Matt down on top of her. Directly above them, Nigel crawled onto his own mattress, lowering himself down into the yielding softness of the duvet. His face was inches from the screen now, staring down into it as though it were a hole in the floor. He began to move, following Matt's lead, learning what she liked. Below him, he could see Laura's face, see her expression change as her body responded to his movements.

It felt as though it would last for ever.

This was what he'd wanted — the pure, exultant joy as he made love to this beautiful, responsive woman; watching as each wave of pleasure broke over her, pleasure that came as they moved together. He had no sense of how long it continued, but after a time he noticed a change in their rhythm, a heightened urgency. Gasping now, he matched the new pace, thrusting his body down hard into the soft duvet, down towards her, faster and faster . . .

. . . and then he saw her eyes squeeze shut in a desperate moment of ecstasy, as Matt's body stiffened, and Nigel felt his own inevitable climax beginning. Eyes wide, he stared down, seeing Laura's mouth fall open, hearing her cry out, feeling her hands on his back, as they clung to that moment, clung to each other . . .

* * *

Afterwards, Nigel lay in a haze of warm emotions. He turned to look at the iPad on the pillow beside him, watching his beloved as she slept, taking in every detail . . . the sheen of perspiration on her pale skin, the way her hair spread out across the pillow. Part of him wanted to pull the duvet up to cover her exposed shoulder-blades, but he knew he mustn't disturb her, not just now. Reaching out a hand towards the image on the screen, he let his eyes close and drifted away into a peaceful sleep.

24

In the morning, she was gone. Nigel woke up late, momentarily puzzled to find himself naked, before remembering the excitement of the night before. He sat up and reached for the iPad, fumbling to switch it on, but the views of the downstairs flat were still and empty — there was nobody home. A pity, but it didn't dampen his spirits, and he sank back into the pillows with a satisfied sigh.

* * *

A week passed. There had been no sign of Laura, but Nigel was confident that it wouldn't be long before she returned. He'd spent a lot of time sitting at the front room window, hoping to see her walking up the path, so he could hurry downstairs for a chance meeting in the corridor, but she hadn't appeared.

He wondered whether she would smile at him, perhaps even pause and chat for a moment or two . . .

Gazing down into the early evening street, he leaned his forehead against the cold glass, then jolted upright as he heard a loud rapping on his door. Getting quickly to his feet, he hurried down the hallway and opened the door to find Matt there, leaning back against the banister.

'All right, mate,' his neighbour greeted him. 'You busy this evening?'

Confused, Nigel stared at him for a moment, then shook his head.

'No,' he managed. 'Why?'

'Well, I was thinking about how decent you were to me after the break-in,' Matt grinned at him. 'And I reckon it's about time you and I had a boys' night out.'

* * *

The club was uncomfortably hot and the music relentless, pounding out with an intensity that seemed to reverberate inside his chest cavity. There was no air, only a confusion of sweat and aftershave, and the smoky taste of dry ice. He followed Matt, fighting to keep close to him, as they pushed their way through the press of revellers, squeezing between the warm bodies of women and men. There was no way to maintain any kind of personal space — passing between two groups of dancers, a pretty redhead in skimpy shorts backed into him, her bottom brushing his groin, but she just smiled and laughed as he blushed. Apparently it was no big deal.

He still wasn't quite sure why Matt had brought him here. There had been some talk about being his 'wingman', whatever that meant. Maybe it was just that they knew each other better now. In any case, it was an exciting invitation and he'd said yes without thinking.

Now that he was here, it was a little more daunting. Matt turned round to face him, shouting something, but he couldn't hear over the music.

‘What?’

‘I *said*, what d’you think?’

Nigel forced a smile, nodding at the sea of people moving all around them.

‘Great.’

Matt gave him a quizzical look, then laughed and leaned in closer.

‘Mate, you need to lighten up,’ he shouted. ‘Come on, let’s get a drink, then I’ll see if we can sort you out.’

They struggled across the floor to a starkly illuminated bar area, besieged by a dense jam of people. There seemed to be no hope of reaching the counter, but Matt pushed and grinned his way through, emerging triumphant a few moments later, and pressing a cold, wet beer bottle into Nigel’s hand. The label felt sticky and bore a name he’d never heard of.

‘Get that down you,’ he laughed.

‘Cheers,’ Nigel smiled. Chinking the neck of his bottle against Matt’s, he lifted it to his lips, shutting his eyes against the strobing lights, turning away and enjoying the cold sensation inside as he swallowed. When he looked again, he found that two women were dancing right in front of him, slender arms twisting above their heads, lost in the music. Both had stripped down to their bras, shoulder blades glistening with sweat, hair whipping from side to side. There was a sense of joyful abandon in their movements and he gazed at them for a moment until a firm hand on his shoulder startled him and he looked round.

‘You would, wouldn’t you?’ Matt grinned, his

face suddenly very close.

'What?' It took him a second to understand. 'Oh, yeah. Definitely.'

'Which one?'

Nigel turned back to stare at the two women. One of them had dark brown hair in dreadlocks, with an exotic floral tattoo below her navel, but her friend was blonde, and looked a bit like Laura.

'The blonde . . . ' he replied.

'Not both?' Matt joked. 'Be a shame to break up the set.'

'That's greedy!' Nigel laughed. 'Anyway, I thought you *had* a girlfriend already?'

'So what if I do?' Matt snorted. He glanced at Nigel, then shook his head sadly. 'Man, we *really* need to get you laid.'

Stupid! He'd said the wrong bloody thing.

But Matt was smiling again.

'Anyway, that's a bigger project.' He adopted a mock-serious expression and wagged a finger. 'Tonight is just about us having a good time.'

'Sorry.' Nigel lowered his eyes. 'I didn't mean to . . . '

'Hey, forget about it.' Matt placed his hands on Nigel's shoulders, bending down so he could look up into his face. 'I reckon I know *exactly* what you need.'

* * *

The crowd seemed to give way for Matt as he threaded a path across the floor. Nigel kept close, but slowed when he realised his friend was making for the scuffed metal door that led to the Gents.

'C'mon,' Matt beckoned, pushing the door and holding it open.

Nigel hesitated. There was a sign that said *Men Only*. He knew that women went to the bathroom in pairs but would it not look a bit queer for him to follow another man into the toilets?

'I think I'm all right for a bit,' he said. It was one of his hang-ups. He always found it difficult to go if someone he knew was standing next to him, and impossible if they talked to him.

Matt rolled his eyes slightly.

'Not for *that*.' He held the door wider. 'Just get in here.'

Feeling slightly confused, Nigel followed him inside.

It was a horrible old toilet, buried in the base of the building like a white-tiled dungeon. A torrent of graffiti chased along the walls to engulf a line of cubicles at the far end. Nigel glanced around nervously, his nostrils burning with bleach, while Matt walked across to the mirror by the sinks and made some show of pushing his hair back. In the reflection, he briefly caught Nigel's eye, warning him with a look to say nothing, then nodded very slightly towards an athletic man with a black vest and a ponytail who was relieving himself at the urinals.

Nigel waited, suddenly feeling very self-conscious. In the mirror, Matt's eyes followed the man as he zipped up and left. Then, as the door to the club swung closed, he straightened up from the sink and motioned for Nigel to follow him.

They made their way along the line of toilet stalls. The door of the last one was closed and Matt leaned in close to it.

'Hey.' He spoke in an oddly quiet voice. 'It's Matt . . . you know, from two weeks back?'

For a moment, nothing happened. Then there was movement, the snap of a bolt being drawn back, and the door opened very slightly. Something glinted in the shadow beyond — an eye — looking first at Matt, then at Nigel, then back to Matt again. The door closed a little.

'It's OK,' Matt explained. 'He's my friend, he's legit.'

There was a pause, and then the cubicle door opened wider to reveal a thin man with a red zipper top and brilliant white trainers. He tilted his shaven head back a little, as if peering down his nose at them, then shrugged and took a step backwards.

'Inside, please.' Only two words, but he clearly had a strong foreign accent.

Glancing round nervously, Nigel followed Matt into the stall. The bald man moved towards the toilet bowl to allow them in, then stretched out an arm along the side of the cubicle to push the door shut. Straightening up, he studied Nigel for a moment, deliberately looking him up and down, then seemed to lose interest.

'So?' He turned to Matt and gave him a chilly little smile.

'Want to score a couple of love-hearts,' Matt replied. 'Got twenty quid with your name on it.'

The bald man pursed his lips thoughtfully.

'That's not a lot of money,' he said, a slight sneer in his voice. 'Maybe you can buy yourself a beer?'

'Come on, don't mess about, Arnaud,' Matt frowned. 'Can you do it or not?'

Arnaud seemed to stiffen at the use of his name. Folding his arms, he leaned back against the side of the cubicle.

'For twenty? No. Thirty? Yes.'

Matt drew himself up, anger gathering in his face.

'Thirty?' he hissed. 'Since *fucking* when?'

Arnaud shrugged again.

'Since you bring strangers to see me, that's when.'

Standing in such a confined space, Nigel was dreadfully aware of the rising tension and felt a sudden desperate need to smooth things out.

'Here.' He jammed a hand into the pocket of his jeans and drew out a twenty-pound note. 'Let me chip in a bit.'

Arnaud regarded him with a raised eyebrow, then reached out a slender hand and took the offered note. Amusement glittering in his eyes, he turned back to Matt.

'And you?' he asked. 'Will you also *chip in?*'

Matt seemed oddly put out, but he sighed deeply and handed over a tenner of his own.

Taking the payment, Arnaud bowed his head slightly, then turned away from them, lifting one white trainer onto the edge of the toilet bowl so he could jam the money inside his sock.

'Can I help you guys with anything else?' he

asked, pulling something from a hiding place inside his clothes.

'No, we're good,' Matt replied.

'What about a little GHB for your friend?' Arnaud turned to face Nigel. 'You want to make some girl an offer she can't refuse, eh?'

'I *said*, we're good,' Matt snapped.

Arnaud raised his hands, apologetically.

'Chill, man, I only ask.' He held out a shiny palm with two violet-coloured tablets on it. 'Here, these will put the smile back on your face.'

* * *

Nigel's heart was racing as they emerged from the cubicle. He'd never bought drugs before. Glancing over his shoulder, he caught a glimpse of Arnaud grinning at him before the stall door closed and the bolt slid across.

Matt moved across to the far side of the room and stood by the sinks. As Nigel approached him, he looked up and held out one of the tablets. At first, it looked like one of those cheap, powdery sweets that you got in tiny cellophane tubes, but there was a crude dancing stick man inscribed on it. He looked up at Matt.

'Are you sure this is OK?'

'Of course. I'm taking one, aren't I?'

And that was that. There mustn't be anywhere that Matt could go where he wouldn't follow. He *had* to take it.

'You'll love it,' Matt reassured him. 'Just remember to drink plenty of water, OK?'

'OK.' Nigel took the tablet, placed it on his tongue, and swallowed it.

'Nice one,' Matt grinned, knocking back his own. 'Come on, let's go and see if those girls are still outside.'

* * *

He couldn't really tell when it happened.

At first, and for quite a while, there was no effect; maybe a slight tingle, though that could have been the heat, or the beer. But as time passed, a subtle change seemed to have occurred. They were in the middle of the dance floor now. Matt had started dancing with a group of people that he didn't know, but everyone appeared to be having a good time.

And so was he.

Part of him dimly felt that he ought to stick close to Matt, but the music became better and better, and he found himself tilting his head back as he moved, staring up at the coloured paper butterfly shapes as he let the beat wash over him and through him.

He was hot and tired but he knew he could do this all night.

Matt was smiling at him from a few yards away — smiling, indicating with his eyebrows that he should look to his left. He did, and found that there was a girl dancing right next to him. She was shorter than him, with mousy brown hair and a crop top that showed some glistening cleavage.

Matt nodded encouragingly and turned back to the people he was with, as Nigel let himself relax into the beat. Watching the girl as she danced, he began to respond to her, anticipating her moves. She looked up at him, flashing a brief, dreamy smile, then tilted her head back as she began to spin around. Nigel did the same, gazing up at the ceiling of coloured flowers, drinking it all in; the sound, the sensation, the pure *joy* of it.

Her hands were on his arms now, touching him, moving with him, dancing with him. He wasn't sure what to do, but it didn't matter. Nothing mattered just now. He could just go with it, let it all happen, because even though he'd never heard it before, they were playing his new favourite track.

He was lighter now, as if he could almost float above the dance floor, mind and body ready to drift upwards. He felt her hands on his face, tilting his head forward, and then the warmth of her breath as her tongue pushed into his mouth. A wave of pure pleasure rippled up through his body, and he opened his eyes at the same moment she did.

'I have a girlfriend.' He heard the words, unsure why he'd said them, but it seemed vaguely important somehow.

The girl smiled at him. 'She'll understand.'

And then she was dancing again, now turning her back to him, now facing him again.

And Nigel knew she was right. He didn't want to cheat on Laura. The kiss was an accident but it felt so good, and anyway this wasn't cheating, it was just two people dancing. Laura would understand.

He glanced across to see Matt grinning at him, thumbs up. They both laughed, a moment of connection across the dance floor, before Nigel surrendered himself to the sensation. The music and the coloured lights bled into each other to form something that he breathed, and he raised his arms above his head, dissolving into the crowd that surrounded him. He wished tonight would never end.

25

Nigel woke up, aching and shivery, in an uncomfortable sprawl. His head and limbs were as heavy as lead, and it was an effort to sit up. Groggy, he took a moment to try to steady himself, arms out behind him, hands gripping the duvet weakly. He was in his bed . . . or at least *on* his bed. And he was still wearing the clothes he'd had on last night.

Last night.

He had no idea how he got home. His recollections of the evening were confused, tapering off into a haze of smiling faces, coloured lights and pounding bass . . .

. . . then nothingness.

The bedside clock read 11.27 a.m. How could he have slept so late? He tried to get up, swinging his legs over the edge of the bed, groaning as the muscles responded with a wave of deep dull pain. What the hell had happened to him?

Getting to his feet was a struggle and he had to place a hand on the wall, fingers spread as he tried to stop himself swaying. He was remembering now: the ecstasy, Matt telling him to drink more, the heat of the dance floor. Could dehydration really feel this bad? Desperate for anything that might aid his recovery, he staggered out of the bedroom to get himself a glass of water.

In the hallway, he wobbled to a stop. His front door was open. Not wide open, but certainly ajar. How out of it must he have been, not to lock up? He stood staring at it for a moment, then pushed it shut, and stumbled on towards the kitchen.

Standing at the sink, he downed two glasses of water from the tap, which didn't make him feel any better, but did remind him that his bladder was very full. Groaning, he put the glass down and made his way carefully to the bathroom. Next time, he would drink gallons of water, not that he actually thought there'd *be* a next time. Unzipping himself, he planted his feet wide apart and put a hand on the wall to prevent himself swaying. It was good of Matt to invite him along, but he should have warned him about this, about how absolutely awful his head and his limbs might feel if he didn't drink enough.

He flushed the toilet, wincing slightly from the effort of leaning forward, then turned very slowly to face the basin. Turning on the hot tap, he glanced up at his reflection . . .

. . . and paused.

He looked terrible — hair matted and sticking up, dark circles around his eyes, stubble on his pale skin; all that was to be expected — but there was something else, something different. Ignoring the aches and the waves of nausea, he leaned forward to stare at his mouth.

Lipstick?

He drew back slowly from the mirror, trying to understand, struggling to remember. There were indistinct images of a mousy-haired woman, grinding and swaying under the coloured lights, hot hands on his face and her small tongue teasing his as they kissed. He felt his unwanted erection stiffening and screwed up his eyes, as the room began to spin around him.

What had he done?

He forced his eyes open and his wretched reflection stared back at him, those guilty red smears around his mouth. And now, he remembered the open front door. Had she come back here? Had they . . . ? Surely he wouldn't have . . .

Oh shit, no!

Breathing quickly, he turned and stumbled through to the bedroom, snatching up his phone from the folds of the duvet, head thumping as he searched for the number. It was too much. He had to know.

He managed to tap the name and pressed the phone to his ear, listening as the number started to ring. It seemed to take forever, but then there was a click.

'Hello?'

'Hi . . . it's Nigel.'

'Ah, it's my *mate in a state*.' He heard Matt give a friendly chuckle. 'You're alive, then?'

'Only just.' He sank down onto the bed, then tipped over until his head was resting on the pillow. 'I feel really . . . ill.'

'I warned you, fella. You need to drink water, keep yourself hydrated,' Matt reminded him. 'And the way you were going for it last night . . . well, I'm not surprised you feel rough this morning.'

Nigel frowned, then put his free hand over his eyes to shield them from the daylight.

'Going for it?' he asked. Had he ruined himself with the mousy girl?

'Yeah, man. I practically had to drag you off the dance floor.'

'Dance floor?' A flicker of hope kindled in the fog. 'So you took me out of there?'

'Yeah.'

'And we came back here together?'

'That's right. You paid for the taxi and I left you on the stairs, remember?'

Nigel felt some of the cold dread in his stomach melt into relief. He moved his fingers down his face, tracing around his lips. The mousy girl had been pretty enough, and his vague recollection of her kiss was pleasant, but it wouldn't have been right to go farther. Not with his feelings for Laura. Not with the way things were developing between them.

'I . . . I thought I might have come home with someone else,' he sighed, embarrassed.

'Hey, you can't win 'em all.' Matt seemed to have misunderstood, mistaking his relief for regret. 'But for what it's worth, you did seem to be getting on OK with that girl you met.'

'Yeah, I suppose so.'

He *had* done well. He'd followed Matt's lead and things had worked out for him in a way he'd never believed possible. Now that it was clear he hadn't done anything stupid, he found that he was rather pleased with his progress.

'So did you get her number?' Matt pushed him.

'What? Oh, no. Well, I don't think so . . . ' He had no memory of asking her anything.

'Shame . . . ' Matt gave a wicked laugh. 'I got mine.'

Nigel's brow furrowed and he struggled to roll himself up into a sitting position.

'What do you mean?' he asked.

'The girl I was dancing with,' Matt explained. 'I got her phone number. Might have got more, but someone had to make sure you made it home in one piece.'

'Um . . . thanks.' Nigel rubbed his eyes, trying to think. His friend wasn't actually thinking of calling this other girl, was he?

'No worries,' Matt replied. 'Guessed it was your first time doing E. And anyway, I've got stuff to do today, so I couldn't really have managed a proper all-nighter, though she *was* tempting . . . '

His laugh sounded oddly sinister.

'Well, I'm glad you're OK, but I've got to go.' There were voices in the background but it was impossible to make out what they were saying. 'Catch you later.'

There was a click and then silence.

The phone felt hot against his face, and Nigel let his hand drop down onto the duvet. The idea of Matt calling this other woman was troubling. What would it mean for Laura . . . and for himself?

26

It had been a bad fight, he could tell. Not that he'd had a lot of experience with turbulent relationships — or any kind of relationships — but the volume alone had been enough to persuade him that things were serious.

It was the raised voices that had first alerted him. From his last check via the cameras, he'd imagined that Matt was going to spend the rest of the evening watching the film on Channel 4, and had settled down upstairs to watch it with him. But when he heard the noise from below, he muted the TV and picked up his iPad again.

The screen resolved into the familiar view of the front room downstairs. Matt was standing by the coffee table, with Laura on the other side of it, and neither of them looked happy. Whatever they were arguing about, it was enough to make them shout, and he could actually pick out snatches of what they were saying. Laura was swearing, calling him names.

Gripping the iPad, he took it over to the edge of the room and set it down on the floor. Squatting, he set about working his fingers in between the skirting boards and the carpet, prising the edge up and rolling it back under his knees. Then, lying down so his head was close to the gaps between the exposed floorboards, he listened intently as he watched the action unfold on the screen.

' . . . so I just want to know what the hell you think you're playing at.'

That was Laura's voice, but there was steel in it. He'd never even imagined her angry before, but she sounded furious now. On the iPad, he could see her gesticulating, jabbing a finger at Matt to punctuate her shouting.

'And I've *told* you, I don't *know*.' Matt was bobbing forward to emphasise certain words, his arms spread wide. Under other circumstances, Nigel might have thought it funny, but not here, not with her. 'I don't know what the hell you're on about.'

'Yeah?' Laura snapped back. 'Well, I think you do. I can't believe you thought I wouldn't find out.'

'Find out what?'

'About you and your *bloody* girlfriend!'

On the screen, Matt took a step back from the table.

'What are you talking about?' he managed, but his voice sounded different.

'Jenny saw you.' Laura's hands were on her hips, her posture defiant. 'She *saw* you, snogging your slutty little friend up at Jahanna the other night.'

'You what?'

The tone was derisive, but he had turned away from her now, folding his arms to hide behind them. He knew he was caught.

Laura stared at him for a moment, then bowed her head, one hand rising to massage her temple. When she spoke again, her voice was quieter, and Nigel had to press his ear to the floorboards to make out her words.

'Matt, we've been through this before. If you want to be just friends, that's fine by me . . . ' She left it hanging for a moment, waiting to see whether he would respond, then continued in a more dangerous tone. 'But if we're going to sleep together, then you *don't* fuck around behind my back.'

Matt whirled around to face her.

'I'm *not* fucking around . . . ' His arms were still folded, trying to tough it out, but Laura was already shaking her head.

'Oh, give it a rest.' She reached down and picked up her bag. 'If you aren't even man enough to apologise then what's the bloody point?'

'I don't . . . ' He broke off as he saw she was leaving. 'Aw, come on, Laura. You know Jenny's always had it in for me . . . '

But she was already in the doorway.

'Call me when you're ready to grow up,' she snapped, then turned on her heel.

Nigel watched in horror as she left the room. He felt the clammy chill spread across his palms . . . What was the *matter* with Matt? Why wasn't he running after her? Why wasn't he stopping her?

But maddeningly, his neighbour didn't seem that bothered, turning away from the hallway, and dropping down to slump in the corner of the sofa. Nigel felt the ominous slam of the front door through the floorboards, yet a moment later the sound of Matt's TV drifted up to him — the same film as before, as though nothing had happened.

That was four dreadful days ago. Four days of helpless frustration and four nights of troubled sleep . . .

Then yesterday, as he'd been sifting through Matt's Facebook messages, he'd had a glimmer of hope. There, in his neighbour's inbox, was a message from Laura.

Laura: Hi. I just wanted you to know that I meant what I said the other night. I do care about you and I am your friend, but you can't treat a friend like this. I need to know you understand that X

Nigel leaned back in his chair and sighed with relief. Thank goodness — a chance for them to make up. She'd taken the risk, she'd reached out to him, and all she needed was an apology. Everything would be all right again.

He moved his mouse so that the pointer was hovering over the Reply button. It was so very tempting to answer her message himself — he could do it and he knew in his heart exactly what to say . . .

. . . but then Matt would know. He'd realise that he'd been hacked, and he'd change his passwords, and that would be that — shut out once more.

No, he couldn't answer the message — Matt would have to reply to it himself. And that was OK, because it would be better coming from him — more honest, even if he had been a little stubborn over things.

But there was no reply.

Today, when he opened Facebook, there was a new message from her.

Laura: Don't bother calling me again until you're ready to be my friend.

There was no kiss on the end of this one, just a cold full stop. Things were bad. *Surely* Matt would apologise as soon as he saw this . . .

. . . but then he spotted another message. This one was from Matt, and it was newer, which meant he must have seen Laura's messages. But this one was for someone else.

Matt: Hey. Top nite at Jahanna. Thanks 4 making it so much fun. Let me know if U want 2 meet up sumtime ;-)

He'd sent it to someone called Libbi. Nigel clicked on her name, brought up her profile page. She was a new friend, added in the last week. He stared at her picture, squinting, trying to remember. Was she the girl Matt had been dancing with at the club? She must be.

Nigel slumped back in his chair. Cupping his hands together over his nose and mouth, he stared at the screen, trying to imagine some positive outcome to the situation . . . but it seemed hopeless. Matt wasn't going to apologise.

They were losing Laura.

He got up and walked over to the window. It was so unfair. How could his friend be so thoughtless, so cruel? And after things had been going so well between them . . .

Leaning forward, he rested his forehead against the cold glass, screwing his eyes tight shut, tensing the muscles in his shoulders.

How *could* Matt put him in this position?

* * *

He spent the rest of the afternoon on the sofa, staring blindly at the TV. The closer he'd come to Matt, the better things had become for him . . . acceptance, friendship, and finally the girl he'd always hoped he'd find. But now Matt was pushing her away. And if Matt pushed her too far, how could *he* continue his relationship with Laura?

Sighing, he clicked the TV off, and got slowly to his feet. Perhaps he just needed to take his mind off things, keep himself busy. Walking over to the desk, he dropped down into his chair and clicked the mouse. In front of him, the screen lit up, and he was just about to close the internet browser when he noticed an alert — *2 New Messages*.

Refreshing the page, he leaned in close and stared at the screen.

> *Libbi:* Going 2 the Red Lion on Friday. CU there? Was yr mate OK?

His heart sank as he read Libbi's message. But Matt had already replied.

> *Matt:* Not my mate. Just a guy I felt sorry for. Don't worry, won't bring him on Fri :-)

Nigel swallowed hard, his stomach tightening in an icy knot.

Not my mate.

For a moment he was back at school, the needy kid who'd finally pushed his luck too far, as Declan shoved him away with a snort of contempt.

'Piss off, Nigel. You're not my mate.'

He'd tried so hard to be like Declan, to look like him and act like him, but as he'd slunk away like a coward, he'd felt the eyes of the whole class on his back, and they'd all seen through him.

Not my mate.

Leaning back from his desk, he suddenly felt as if he was going to be sick, and twisted in his chair, leaning down to grab the wastepaper bin. But as he sat there, hunched over the rubbish, he felt a cold anger growing inside him. Slowly lifting his head, he sat up straight.

No.

He wasn't going to let it end like this.

PRESENT

27

Harland took his change and thanked the barmaid. Then, lifting the two pint glasses, he turned and made his way across the room, stooping as he passed beneath the old wooden beams studded with horse-brasses. It was quiet in here tonight — mostly locals, rather than the weekend crowd. Two red-faced old men were hunched over a game of dominoes, locked in silent concentration. And then there was the young couple sat side by side in the far corner, each of them dressed as though they'd made an effort for the other, holding hands as they spoke.

Good luck to them . . .

Setting the glasses down on a small table by the window, he eased back into his seat and looked across at Mendel.

'There you go.'

'Cheers, Graham.' The big man took a sip of his drink, then leaned back, making his chair creak. 'So . . . what do you reckon now?'

Harland put one finger on the corner of a beer mat, turning it gently as he stared down at the table.

'Well, I suppose Matt Garrick is still everyone's favourite,' he mused. 'We'll see what the ANPR check turns up tomorrow.'

Mendel watched him thoughtfully, then shook his head.

'You don't sound convinced,' he rumbled.

Harland glanced up at him, then lowered his eyes again.

'I don't know,' he said. 'That's the trouble, really . . . too many things we just don't know.'

He sighed and began turning the beer mat again. On the other side of the room, the young couple got up from their table and made their way towards the door. Harland watched them go, still holding hands.

At least someone was going to have a good evening.

He took another sip of his drink, wincing as he felt the tension in his shoulder.

'So you're going to try and track down this photographer?' Mendel asked him.

'It might lead to something.' Harland stretched, trying to ease the discomfort. 'Laura kept the whole glamour thing quiet — understandable given her job — but it's something to look into. Maybe she kept other things quiet too.'

'You don't have a name for the guy?'

'Not yet, but I know he used a studio in St Paul's and I've put the word around. Shouldn't be too hard to track him down.'

He lapsed into silence, wondering what he'd do if the photographer turned out to be a dead end. The chances of finding Laura alive were already fairly slim, and the longer things dragged on, the more likely it was to end up as a murder investigation.

Mendel seemed to sense his mood, and changed the subject.

'How's it going with your new recruit?' he asked. 'Imogen, isn't it?'

'That's right.'

'Bet you wish you were still working with me,' Mendel winked. 'The old dream team, eh?'

'Dream team,' Harland chuckled as he stared down at the table . . .

It *had* been an awkward moment, though. He pictured her face, earlier that evening; the brief, distressed expression as she'd slipped up and told him . . .

'What is it?' the big man pressed him.

Harland shook his head.

'Nothing really . . . ' He frowned. It troubled him that he'd misread her.

'Graham?' Mendel leaned forward in his chair.

Harland looked at his friend.

'She's a lesbian,' he murmured. 'I had absolutely no idea.'

Mendel stared at him for a long moment, waiting for him to continue, then started to laugh.

'What does it matter if she's into women?' He tapped his chest with a large finger. '*I'm* into women and *that* never bothered you. Why should this?'

'It doesn't bother me . . . ' Harland gave him an awkward look. 'I just don't want to say the wrong thing, you know . . . '

'It's not like she's got a terminal illness,' Mendel grinned. 'I'm pretty sure it's all right for you to have normal conversations with her.'

Harland drummed his fingers on the table, wondering how to explain.

'I know all that,' he frowned. 'It's just . . . well, she seemed kind of . . . *tense* when it came out.'

'That's her problem, not yours. You said she was good, right?'

'Oh, yes. She's good.'

'And you get on OK with her?'

'I think so,' Harland reflected. He was beginning to understand his new partner now. There was still a long way to go, but she was already an improvement on Linwood, and anyone was better than Pope . . .

Mendel, raising his glass, paused and gave him a serious look.

'You don't fancy her, do you?' he asked, warily.

'What? No.' He honestly hadn't thought of her that way, though he could see that a lot of men would. 'I mean . . . well, I suppose she's attractive enough but . . . no, not my type.'

'Thank goodness for that!' Mendel appeared relieved and took a mouthful of beer. Relaxing back into his chair, he put the glass down on the table. 'So what's she like, then?'

'I'm not really sure,' Harland replied. Perhaps that was the problem. It was certainly a huge asset having someone who had a natural ability to get information out of people, but it made him uneasy that he couldn't read her. *And* she'd managed to get him talking about Alice.

He gave his friend a wry smile. 'Maybe she's just smarter than me.'

Mendel looked at him thoughtfully, then grinned.

'Well then,' he said. 'In that case she ought to keep you on your toes.'

* * *

The light was failing when they stepped out on to the harbour-side cobbles, a fiery red glow throwing the city skyline into deep silhouette. Harland yawned and lit a cigarette, blowing a pale cloud of smoke up into the gloom.

'How's Firth getting on with those Avonmouth trucks?' he asked, slipping his lighter into a pocket. 'Any progress?'

'She's getting it done,' Mendel replied. 'Nothing definite on our trucks yet, but she did turn up a trailer full of stolen cigarettes, so that's a bonus.'

'Good for her,' Harland smiled. He missed being around her, missed talking to her, seeing her smile . . . but it was probably for the best. 'She's doing OK?'

Mendel nodded, then slowed and gave him a sly look.

'She finished with that bloke she was seeing, if that's what you're asking.'

Harland turned sharply.

'That's not what I . . . ' He faltered, then looked away over the water with a sigh. 'Sorry to hear it.'

Mendel shook his head.

'No you're not,' he chuckled. 'I'll tell her you said hi.'

Harland was about to protest, but there was no point pretending to his old friend.

'Thanks, James.'

'Don't worry about it.'

They made their way along to the corner of the quayside.

'You OK getting home?' Harland asked. 'You can always crash at mine if you want.'

The house wouldn't seem so empty with Mendel there, but the big man was shaking his head.

'Thanks, but I reckon I'll find a cab,' he rumbled. 'Besides, my back's still recovering from the last time I tried sleeping on that sofa of yours.'

Harland shrugged and smiled.

They walked along the old waterfront towards the swing bridge, music and laughter echoing across the harbour from an open-air bar on the far side.

'See much of Pope these days?' Mendel asked.

'He's working with Linwood just now . . . ' Harland felt his phone vibrate, and reached for his pocket. 'You know, on that nightclub murder.'

'Poor old Linwood,' the big man chuckled.

Harland drew out his phone and slowed to a standstill as he gazed at the screen, glowing bright in the evening dusk. Mendel halted, then moved back to stand beside him.

'What is it?' he asked.

'Looks like one of the studios returned my call.'

'And?'

'They left a message with the switchboard,' Harland smiled. 'Our photographer's name is Frank Guthrie.'

He slid the phone back into his pocket. They'd pay Frank a visit in the morning.

28

Harland leaned back in his chair and yawned. He'd found it difficult to wake up this morning. It wasn't as though he'd been particularly late last night — just a few drinks with Mendel — but he'd slept badly, disturbed by dreams about something he couldn't quite remember . . .

He shook his head and sighed.

Sitting at her desk opposite him, Imogen was typing something, leaning forward so that only the top of her head was visible over the screen. She'd been a little quiet when she came in but otherwise everything seemed normal enough between them. On hearing about Frank, she'd brightened and started digging up some background on him before they went to interview him later that morning. There was no reason to suspect him of any involvement in Laura's disappearance, but nobody else had spoken to him yet, and Harland wanted to be sure they were prepared.

'He's got a website.' Imogen's face appeared at the side of her screen as she leaned over to look at him. 'Frank Guthrie Photographic Services — seems quite professional.'

'Have a look through it,' Harland replied. 'See if there's any pictures of Laura on there, especially anything recent.'

'OK.' She glanced at something on her screen, then frowned. 'It looks like mostly corporate stuff on here. I think I'll see if his photos show up on any other portfolio sites as well.'

'Good idea.' Harland nodded as he turned back to his own screen and carried on reading.

Frank had a record. Nothing too serious — drunk and disorderly a few times, assaulting someone in a pub fight — and nothing particularly recent. But there had been a number of complaints filed against him for sexual harassment too. None of those had ever led to anything other than a caution, though that didn't mean there hadn't been more behind them — offences like that were always difficult to prosecute.

Harland leaned back in his chair and gazed up at the ceiling, letting his mind wander . . .

There must be a lot of temptation when you're looking through the camera at a naked woman, especially if it's just the two of you, alone in the studio. With all that sexual tension in the air, a lot of thoughts must come to mind, and if you're the kind of person who enjoys taking liberties with women, you might find those thoughts difficult to resist. But what happens if you try it on with someone who won't let you do what you want? What happens when things get out of control?

Harland glanced down at the screen again. Yes, they definitely needed to have a closer look at Frank.

Stifling another yawn, he sat up and stretched his shoulders, then got to his feet. There was time for a coffee before they set off. Grabbing his mug, he started towards the kitchen, then turned round to where Imogen was sitting.

'I'm going to get a drink. Want anything?'

She glanced back at him, shaking her head.

'I'm all right, thanks, sir.'

He looked past her, to the website of Frank's images on her screen. There were several enlarged photos — artfully lit studio shots of two women, naked, kissing. There was an erotic intensity to them that held his attention for a moment. Then he caught Imogen's eye and nodded awkwardly to her, before turning away towards the kitchen again.

* * *

It was a small house, part of an uneven terrace in a dip on Filton Avenue. The properties on either side had been renovated, with fresh, painted exteriors and clean roof tiles, but this one still sported its original brown pebbledash and the roof was black with old moss. There was a creosoted gate in the bare brick wall, with a tiny cement garden beyond.

Harland walked up to the front door, but there was no sign of a bell. He shrugged to Imogen, then rapped smartly on the frosted glass and stood back to wait. A moment later a shape appeared. They heard a chain being drawn back and the door was opened by a red-faced man with spiky white hair and a moustache. He stood there, dressed in a grey sweatshirt and black tracksuit bottoms, squinting at them.

'Frank Guthrie?' Harland asked.

'Aye, that's me.' The man had a strong

Scottish accent and his blue eyes lingered on Imogen for a moment, before he continued. 'You're the one who called up this morning?'

'That's right. Detective Harland and Detective Gower.'

Frank nodded to himself, then stood back abruptly and opened the door farther.

'Come on in,' he muttered. 'Sorry, I was out earlier. Jobs to do.'

'No problem,' Harland said, as they stepped into the cramped hallway. There was a faint, lingering smell about the place, like burnt fat. 'Early start?'

'All part of being a humble snapper,' Frank replied. He stood, blocking the hallway and the stairs, one arm outstretched to guide them into the front room. 'Go on through, sit wherever you like.'

'Thanks.'

The room seemed small, overpowered by two huge cream leather sofas that faced each other over a low, smoked-glass coffee table. Hardly any of the deep pile carpet was visible. A large plasma TV hung above the fireplace, while the other walls were littered with photographic prints in tasteless, eighties-style clip frames.

Harland sank down onto the creaking leather, Imogen sitting beside him, and looked up at the pictures. Most were of women — artistically lit nudes with muted skin tones and scarlet lips — but there were two shots of idyllic beaches, with white sand and palm trees, and clear blue water.

They heard the front door shut, and Frank

strode in, dropping down onto the sofa opposite, and regarding them cautiously.

'So what's this all about?' he asked.

'I think you know what it's about,' Harland frowned.

'I only know what you told me on the phone this morning, pal.'

'You don't follow the news?' Imogen cut in.

Frank seemed amused by her interruption.

'No, darlin', I most certainly do not,' he replied. 'I've worked with plenty of old hacks over the years, and you soon figure out that the 'news' is all just a game to sell papers.'

Harland glanced across at her. If she was annoyed, she wasn't showing it.

Good for her.

Taking a deep breath for patience, he began again, determined not to let himself become riled.

'Right, then, as I said on the phone, we're investigating the disappearance of a young woman.' He paused for effect, sitting forward slightly. 'Does the name Laura Hirsch mean anything to you?'

Frank leaned slowly back in his chair, and folded his arms.

'Aye, I know Laura.' Was he a little more wary now perhaps? 'Is it her that's missing?'

Harland nodded.

'As part of our investigation, we're trying to get as much information as we can about her — what she did, who she knew — and your name came up.'

Frank's face remained impassive.

'So?' he responded after a moment.

'So, where were you last Friday evening?' Imogen interrupted.

Frank turned to look at her, his gaze working its way up to her face.

'I was in Brighton on Friday,' he told her. 'Got there around lunchtime, and didn't get back here until Sunday afternoon.'

'Can anyone confirm that?'

'About two hundred people,' he grinned. 'I was doing a wedding at the Hilton — Mr and Mrs Sherwood. I'll get you the details before you leave.'

'And you slept at the hotel?' Harland prompted him.

'That's right.' He narrowed his eyes. 'So Laura's been missing since then, has she?'

He shook his head slowly and settled back into his chair.

'How did you know her?' Imogen asked. There was an edge to her voice — nothing obvious, but Harland picked it up.

Frank sighed.

'You do know I'm a photographer, right, *Detective*?' He waved a hand, gesturing to the prints on the wall behind him, his eyes never leaving hers. 'Well, I took *photographs* of her.'

Imogen ignored the patronising tone, holding his stare.

'When did you see her last?' she pressed.

Frank gave her a yellow-toothed smile, turning slightly so he could address his answer to Harland.

'A month ago, maybe longer. I don't

remember exactly.' He looked mildly irritated by the questions, but not anxious. Not yet, anyway.

'Had you photographed her before?' Harland asked.

'Yeah,' Frank said with a nod. 'We did a couple of shoots a wee while ago, and I asked her back to do some more.'

'What sort of photos?'

'Mainly glamour stuff, portfolio work, you know.'

Harland glanced across at one of the nude prints, then back again.

'By glamour, you mean nudity?' he asked.

'Well, she wasn't modelling the latest Paris fashions, if that's what you're asking,' Frank chuckled.

'Where did these shoots take place?' Imogen enquired.

Frank turned to her, his eyes still twinkling.

'There's a private-hire studio down in St Paul's that I use,' he replied.

'The one on Brigstocke Road?'

Frank hesitated, looking from her to Harland and back again.

'You've been checking up on me,' he said, softly.

Imogen gave him a blank look, and said nothing.

'All right.' Frank turned to Harland, palms up in mock surrender. 'I got her in to do a shoot . . . must have been three or four weeks ago, something like that? She showed up, I took some pictures, she left — that's all I know.'

'And that's the last time you saw her?'

'Yes.'

Harland nodded thoughtfully. There was a tone of annoyance in the answers now.

'Were the pictures good?' Imogen asked suddenly.

'Eh?' Frank glanced across, wrong-footed by her question. 'Yeah, they were fine. Why?'

'Can we see them?' she continued.

Frank scowled at her, wary now. 'Why?'

'I'm just curious . . . ' Imogen inclined her head to one side. 'Is there a problem?'

He stared at her for a moment, then shrugged. 'No. No problem.'

Leaning forward, he reached for the laptop on the coffee table, setting it on his knees and opening it up.

'I'll have copies on here somewhere,' he muttered, clicking on the trackpad. 'Just give me a minute . . . '

Watching him hunched over the laptop, Harland was about to ask how he'd met Laura but a covert look from Imogen warned him not to. With a slight nod, he settled back in his chair.

'Ah, here we are.' Frank clicked the trackpad again, then turned the laptop around so it was facing Imogen. On the screen, a slideshow of images began playing — a striking shot of Laura's naked upper body, her skin glowing against the dark backdrop, eyes lowered demurely. The next picture was cropped tighter, highlighting her pouting lips while the light caught her hair tumbling down towards her exposed breasts.

'Well?' Frank leaned forward, leering at her. 'Do you like them?'

Imogen calmly lifted her eyes from the screen and stared back at him.

'Did Laura like them?' she countered.

Frank seemed disappointed at her lack of reaction.

'Yeah,' he said, after a moment. 'She did actually. Told me she liked the way I made her look in these.'

Imogen nodded thoughtfully, then affected a puzzled expression.

'Then I don't quite understand,' she mused. 'You *said* you hadn't seen her since the shoot, but if you know she liked these photos then you must have spoken to her *since* they were taken.'

Harland looked across at Frank, but the older man was shaking his head.

'She saw the preview images while she was still at the studio,' he explained. 'I always go through them at the end of each set, just to check the lighting's all right. And it helps the models feel sexy . . . '

He trailed off, as it dawned on him what Imogen had been trying to do, then gave her a mirthless smile. 'Nice try.'

She gave him a cold look in return.

Leaning on the arm of the sofa, Harland rubbed his eyes and sighed.

'Do you usually send people copies of their photos after the shoot?' he asked wearily.

Frank shrugged.

'Sometimes.' He gave Imogen a withering look. 'Which is why I show them the preview images . . . so they can choose the ones they want.'

'OK,' Harland said. 'You put them in the post to her?'
Frank shook his head.
'No way,' he replied. 'Have you any idea how much prints cost? Nah, I just email the images.'
Harland stared at him. Frank might not have known Laura's address, might not have known much about her at all.
'You paid her in cash?'
'The last time, aye . . . before that it was all TFP.'
Harland shot a sidelong glance at Imogen.
'TFP?'
Frank grinned at them, much amused.
'Time. For. Photos. You never heard of that?'
'No.'
The older man shook his head, as though it was a term everyone ought to know.
'All right. Say someone wants to try their luck at a modelling career. They aren't going to get very far with some crappy shots off a camera phone, are they? They need good-quality portfolio images, so they come to a pro.' He tapped his chest. 'Now, either they can pay me for my valuable time, in which case they get to own the photos and keep all the copies, or they can . . . do something else for me.'
He winked at Imogen, then continued.
'TFP means we both put in our time rather than any money changing hands. I get pictures for *my* portfolio without paying for the model, and she gets pictures for *her* portfolio without paying for the photographer. Make sense?'
Harland sat back in his chair. He could

understand the principle, but why anyone would offer to pose for a dirty old man like this was beyond him.

'You get a lot of people doing this?' he asked. 'Modelling for free?'

'Of course,' Frank replied. 'Come on, just watch the TV or look at a celebrity magazine. If you're a young woman, real success means being shagged by a footballer, or being a model.'

Imogen shook her head in disgust.

'Hey, don't blame me, darlin'.' Frank spread his palms wide. 'The media makes the rules, I just help the poor girls out.'

Harland could feel his temper rising, but managed to keep his voice calm.

'So tell me, Frank,' he asked. 'Do you *fuck* the women you photograph?'

A cold smile spread across the older man's face.

'Not all of them,' he replied.

'How about Laura?'

Frank tilted his head to one side and adopted a mocking tone.

'What's the matter?' he laughed. 'Did her boyfriend get jealous?'

'Did he have reason to be jealous?' Imogen interjected.

'A gentleman never tells,' Frank sneered at her.

Harland brought his open palm down hard on the arm of the sofa, striking the leather with a loud smack.

'*Don't* mess us about,' he hissed.

Frank gave him a long stare, then shrugged and looked away.

'No,' he muttered. 'I don't believe we had the pleasure. All right?'

They sat there in a moment of uneasy silence. Imogen frowned and sat forward.

'How do you know her boyfriend?' she said.

'I didn't know him,' Frank replied, his tone sullen now. He closed the laptop and put it down at the side of the sofa. 'I just knew she had one.'

'She spoke about him?' Harland asked.

'Now and then.' The older man shrugged. 'I think he'd dented her confidence a bit, and the modelling helped her feel better about herself. No really, that's how it starts for some of them.'

'And he knew about you photographing her?'

'I doubt it,' Frank sighed. 'She was always very careful, wanting to know where the pictures would be used, that sort of thing. And she got all funny about taking her knickers off for me.'

Imogen looked at Harland and shook her head.

'I can't imagine why,' she murmured.

* * *

Neither of them spoke as they walked back to the car.

Once inside, Harland fastened his seat belt and stared out at the traffic on Filton Avenue.

'Well,' he sighed. 'What a charming man Frank is.'

Beside him, Imogen gripped the steering wheel and shuddered violently.

'Ugh! I just wanted to . . . ' She thumped the wheel with the heel of her hand, then shook her head.

Harland glanced across at her. 'I know.'

Imogen stared out through the windscreen and took a deep breath.

'Sorry,' she said. 'About interrupting you back there, I mean. It's just . . . I thought we might catch him out.'

Harland nodded slowly.

'It's OK,' he told her. 'And Frank was right — it *was* a nice try.'

He gave her a slight smile, which he hoped was encouraging. Her expression softened a little.

'Anyway,' Harland continued. 'I think we can see why she was keeping quiet about this.'

'Yeah.' Imogen started the car, then frowned. 'Doesn't help us much, though, does it?'

Harland leaned back into his seat, recalling Frank's words.

What's the matter? Did her boyfriend get jealous?

There was nothing to suggest that Matt knew about Laura's modelling, but what if he did? Pearce had warned him about overlooking the obvious — but even if Matt *had* found out, he wasn't the jealous type . . . he wouldn't have done anything stupid . . . would he?

29

Harland leaned back from the desk, tapping a biro against his teeth, trying not to think about cigarettes. Pope was talking, which always set him on edge, but it was his own fault for asking while they were both around — he should have waited until Linwood was on his own.

' . . . and you'll be glad to hear that we've successfully tracked down our missing bouncer from the club. In lovely Blackpool of all places.' Pope was pleased with himself, head tilted back a little in that self-satisfied way that made his nose seem even more snout-like. 'His full name is Jason Patrick Kerr and it turns out he'd been given a few weeks off — a nice little holiday, considerately paid for by his employer Mr Jones.'

Harland sat back in his chair, glancing across to the adjacent desk, where Imogen was still on the phone.

'Very generous of Jones,' he mused. 'And very convenient.'

'Indeed.' Pope adopted a knowing smile. 'Naturally Jones denies this has anything to do with Arnaud's death or our investigation.'

'Perish the thought,' Harland agreed, his tone weary with sarcasm. They were dealing with idiots here — people who seemed too inept to cover their tracks. And yet, the manner of Arnaud's death had been so elaborate, so creative. 'What did Kerr have to say for himself when you finally tracked him down?'

'Well, he was a bit cagey at first,' Linwood cut in, eager to answer. 'You know how they can be . . . '

'Yeah,' Pope agreed. 'He actually thought we were going after *him* for the murder.'

'Don't know how he got that idea,' Linwood muttered. There was a momentary flicker of awkwardness in his expression — just enough for Harland to notice — before he continued. 'Anyway, he finally started talking. Seems he was told to turn a blind eye to Arnaud's 'business' dealings, and just watch his back for him. Any *other* dealers in the club, he was to come down hard on them. Like, *properly* hard.'

Harland sat up slightly.

'Told by who?' he asked.

'The club owner, Jones.'

'Kerr actually named him?'

'Eventually, yes.'

'Good.' Harland smiled to himself. 'Let's throw Jones to the Vice Squad. Kerr too, unless he can come up with the name of anyone who might have wanted Arnaud dead.'

'Fair enough,' Linwood said. 'Anything else?'

'Maybe ask Vice if they know any up-and-coming dealers in the area — anyone with enough ambition to kill. Oh, and tell them to keep this quiet — we don't want any other suspects taking sudden holidays to the North.'

Beside him, Imogen had finished her call and was putting the phone down.

'Frank's alibi checks out,' she sighed. 'He was there Friday to Sunday. I've asked Sussex to double-check but I think he's out of the picture . . . no pun intended.'

'Very good.' Harland grimaced at the joke.

'Oh, and DI Bensk said to tell you hello.'

Harland smiled. He'd never actually met Charlotte Bensk but their paths had crossed on a couple of cases now. He wondered what sort of person she was . . .

'Sir?'

He glanced back at Imogen, who was looking at him expectantly.

'Yes?'

'Well,' she mused. 'If we're ruling Frank out, where does that leave us?'

Harland gazed at her for a long moment, then shrugged.

'Matt Garrick, I suppose.'

It still didn't feel right, though. In fact, the more he thought about it, the less he liked the idea. Matt certainly didn't come across as the jealous type, and if it wasn't a jealousy thing then what possible reason could he have?

Pushing back his chair, he got stiffly to his feet.

'Lean on that bouncer,' he told Linwood, then turned to Imogen. 'Come on, let's get some lunch.'

* * *

The canteen was emptying out, as the earlier lunchtime rush dwindled, and there was nobody else at the counter when they reached the till. Harland put a chocolate bar next to the plate of chips on his tray and stood silently as the cashier started to ring the items up.

'Are you paying together?' she asked him, nodding towards Imogen.

'Sorry, no . . . ' He reached for his wallet, but Imogen spoke over him.

'Yes we are,' she confirmed, moving round to place her tray in front of his, then reaching for her bag. Glancing at Harland, she gave him a faint smile. 'It's my turn, after all, sir.'

They found a table near the windows, and sat down facing each other.

'Thanks for this,' Harland murmured, dusting his chips with black pepper.

'That's OK,' Imogen replied. She watched him shaking the pepper pot, then grinned and looked down at her salad. 'Anyway, it's cheaper here than the other place.'

Harland shot her a wry smile and picked, up the salt.

'So how was your meal last night?' he asked.

All the warmth went out of Imogen's grin.

'It was OK,' she said with a shrug. 'I could have worked later if you'd needed me to.'

'I just . . . ' Harland floundered for a moment, then looked away. He hadn't meant anything — it was just an attempt to get her talking, get to know her, but somehow his question had set her on edge. 'Thanks, but it was just a couple of calls. No need for us both to stay.'

'Well, you only have to ask.'

'Honestly, it's fine.' He shook his head and scowled down at his plate. 'Anyway, it's not like I had anything better to do.'

When he looked up again, Imogen's expression had softened a little.

'Sorry, sir,' she said quietly. 'I just really want to get a result on this one.'

'I know,' he replied. 'And I'm the same. I want to find her.'

They ate in silence for a few moments.

'I wish we could have nailed Frank for something,' Imogen frowned, reaching for her drink.

Harland stared into space, nodding gloomily.

'Yeah, it's a shame about him,' he said. 'Back to square one, now.'

'You thought he might have been involved?'

'I thought he might have told us . . . I don't know, *something* that would move us forward. The clock's ticking.'

Imogen sat back and regarded him thoughtfully.

'So you still think she's alive?'

Harland looked at her. The days were dragging on and they were no nearer to finding Laura. The longer it dragged on, the more likely it was that she'd turn up dead.

'What do you want me to say?' He laid his fork down and sighed. 'We both know the odds.'

Imogen lowered her eyes.

'Yes,' she murmured. 'We do.'

Harland frowned.

'Does it make it easier?' he asked her. 'Thinking that she's already dead?'

Imogen stopped eating and traced her knife along the edge of her plate.

'Honestly?' she mused. 'Yes, I think it does. For me, anyway.'

She took a long sip of her drink before she looked at him again.

'On that case last year, when I was working with Burgess . . . ' She hesitated, as though waiting for him to spare her, but he said nothing, forcing her to go on. 'One of the victims had been dead for less than a day when we found her. Just a few hours sooner, and she might have survived. If we'd put it together just a little bit quicker, if I'd . . . '

She trailed off, shaking her head slowly until she felt able to speak again.

'It's terrible, trying to pull a result out of the air, with that sort of pressure hanging over you. At least, if they're already dead, your job is simpler — to find the killer and deliver justice.'

Harland stared at her. Justice meant different things to different people. Closure. Revenge. Blindly following rules instead of doing what was right. Sometimes the thing they called justice was a mockery of the word. Sometimes there was no justice at all . . .

But that wasn't what she needed to hear.

'You can't let yourself think that way,' he told her. 'Losing someone isn't necessarily a failure. And it doesn't mean you're a bad cop.'

Imogen stiffened.

'I know that,' she bristled. 'I worked hard for my rank. And I'm here on merit, not because of any affirmative-action rubbish.'

'I . . . I don't doubt it.' Harland looked at her, taken aback by the change in her tone. Was it anger? Was that what she didn't want him to see, why she kept herself so tightly wound shut? 'All

I'm saying is that you can't win them all, nobody can. Some people just can't be saved.'

'Exactly.' Imogen gave him a bleak look. 'When they're dead, it's easier.'

She picked up her fork and started eating again.

Harland wanted to argue with her. He wanted to tell her how important it was that they maintained their hope and their confidence. He wanted to tell her that he believed Laura was still alive.

But he couldn't. His own doubts were growing and he was starting to fear the worst. They'd get a result — he felt sure of that — but it might not be the one they'd been hoping for.

* * *

On the far side of the canteen, the door swung open and Pearce strode in. Spying Harland and Imogen, he raised a hand in greeting and walked over to them.

'All right,' he said briskly. 'Where have you two been hiding yourselves?'

'We tracked down that photographer, the one that Laura posed for,' Harland explained. 'But it looks like he has an alibi for the weekend Laura vanished.'

Pearce leaned forward, his hands on the table between them.

'Never mind about him for now,' he told them, his voice eager. 'The ANPR check turned up a couple of hits on Matt's car — once on Gloucester Road, and once near Abbey Wood.

He was definitely out and about on Friday night.'

'After telling us he was in all evening,' Imogen said to herself.

'Exactly.' Pearce nodded. 'We're done with the softly-softly approach; I'm having him picked up. Might be good to have you sit in on the interview, Graham.'

'Of course.' Harland pushed his chair back, ready to get up, but Pearce waved him down.

'Finish your lunch,' he told them. 'I'll give you a shout when he gets here.'

Clasping his hands together in anticipation, he straightened up and made his way over to the counter.

Harland picked up a chip, but his food was cold. He pushed the plate to one side and sat back. He wasn't feeling so hungry now anyway.

'So the question is, why would Matt kill his girlfriend?' Imogen spoke around a mouthful of salad. 'Maybe jealousy . . . or perhaps it was an accident?'

Harland stared at her and shrugged.

'You spoke to him too,' he reminded her. 'That's one hell of a poker face for someone who just accidentally killed his girlfriend.'

'So it was premeditated?'

'I'm not convinced.'

Imogen frowned.

'You don't think he planned it?' she asked.

Harland folded his arms, then glanced across at the counter, where Pearce was lining up to pay.

'I don't think Matt's a killer,' he murmured.

TWO WEEKS AGO

30

He made his way along the corridor, conspicuously alone as he walked past the laughing couples and groups of friends. The insistent thump of the music swelled as he turned the corner and made his way down the steps into the club's basement room, sound and light and heat engulfing him as he stepped out on to the floor.

The place was alive. All around, people moving, dancing. To his left, a young man not so very different to himself, eyes closed in euphoria, swaying in unison with a skinny girl in a luminous crop top, her ponytail whipping back and forth, their hands touching, parting, touching again.

He felt an odd resentment, mingled with a vague sense of longing, as he watched them. Before, he'd have moved on, dismissing the scene as something for other people, but now a part of him yearned to fall into that rush again, to lose himself in the crowd and become one with them.

And, he realised, he could. He knew now just how easy it was. There was nothing to stop him from scoring one of the tablets he'd taken before, and surrendering himself to the heat and the music.

It was suddenly so very tempting . . . but it wasn't what he'd come for.

Turning away from the dancing couple, he

began to move across the room — one serious face among the sea of smiles, while sudden flashes of colour illuminated the huge canvas flowers above. The toilets were on the far side of the dance floor. He could see the metal door in front of him now and eased his way behind another knot of dancers, his mind made up. It was what he wanted. But before he could get there, a couple of younger men in open shirts barged in front of him, laughing at some joke as they pushed the door wide.

Damn.

Nigel veered left, changing course to walk along the wall, moving away from the Gents. He slowed when he got to the corner of the room, head bowed as he considered what to do.

He'd wait.

He checked the money in his pocket, fingertips brushing over the fold of notes. Still there. And he had more than he needed . . . He glanced across to the lights that burned bright above the bar area. Maybe he should get a drink first.

He moved over to join the press of people waiting to be served. It was even hotter here than it had been on the dance floor, sticky bodies and shouted conversations all around him. He tried to find a way through but the crowd seemed to ebb and flow before him — no matter how many people squeezed out holding bottles, he seemed to be no closer to the bar. After an eternity of struggle, in the heat and sweat, he turned away and untangled himself from the crush.

The drink could wait.

His clothes were sticking to him as he made his way back to the wall and glanced across towards the toilets again. The metal door was shut. He leaned back against the wall.

He could wait too.

He adopted what he hoped was a blissed-out expression, allowing his arms to fall limp at his sides, swaying and nodding his head to the music, while his eyes moved around the room, always returning to the door.

Ten minutes? No, five. If nobody came out in five minutes, it was probably safe to assume it was empty.

He leaned back, feeling the dampness of his shirt cold against the skin. Raising his chin, he rested his head on the wall as he stared up at the paper shapes suspended from the dark ceiling. Flowers and giant butterflies, crudely shaped but alive in the strobing lights, turning gently above the sea of heads and hands on the dance floor. And beyond them, a pair of security cameras looking down on the scene.

He glanced back to the door. *Still closed. Good*.

His eyes swept across the crowd, studying the faces of the people before him — laughter, concentration, rapture — all bathed in a succession of shifting colours. He wondered whether Laura ever came here, imagining how she would look, twisting and turning with her long hair catching the light. He pictured the expression of joy on her face and understood it — he knew now how good these moments could feel . . .

The door was still shut.

He glanced down at his watch. That must be five minutes by now. Pushing himself up off the wall, he turned and walked slowly towards the toilets.

* * *

The music receded as the door swung shut behind him, and he stood for a moment, glancing over at the mirror. His reflection looked nervous. He'd planned to go and wash his hands if there was anyone else in there, take his time until they left, but his vigil outside had been worthwhile — the toilets appeared to be empty.

Squaring his shoulders, he made his way along the stalls, treading softly on the wet floor. They were all open, except for the door at the end, which was closed, just as it had been last time. Halting outside it, he bent forward and spoke in a low voice.

'Hello?'

There was no response, no movement, so he leaned closer.

'I was here a couple of weeks ago . . . ' Something in his mind warned him not to give his name. 'You remember, Matt's friend?'

So close to his head, the snap of the bolt being drawn back startled him, and he jumped back as the door eased open a little.

'Hi.' He smiled hopefully at the figure within. 'You helped us out before?'

The door opened wider and Arnaud stepped into view, regarding him for a moment, then beckoning him forward.

'Inside.'

Glancing back over his shoulder, Nigel stepped into the cubicle. Arnaud backed up to give him space, then raised his hand and pointed a long finger at the door, indicating he wanted it locked again.

'Of course.' Nigel twisted round and fumbled the bolt into place. When he turned around again, the bald man was looking at him thoughtfully.

'Where is your friend?' he asked.

'It's just me tonight.'

Arnaud appeared to consider this, then shrugged.

'So, what's your pleasure?' he asked. 'Love hearts, yes?'

Nigel hesitated. He could hand over a twenty right now, then go outside and melt into the crowd. It would be so much easier . . .

Arnaud tilted his head to one side. 'Something else?'

Nigel met his eye reluctantly.

'Last time, you said something about . . . ' he looked down, 'about helping me get women?'

'Riiight . . . ' Arnaud leaned against the side of the stall, his face creasing into an unpleasant smile. 'A little GHB and you can get whatever you want, my friend.'

Nigel took a breath, nodded nervously.

'What . . . I mean, how does it work?' he asked.

Arnaud grinned, pushing himself away from the side of the cubicle.

'Just put it in her drink, man. You stay with her until her eyes go sleepy, then you take her home . . . ' One slender hand strayed to the crotch of his jeans. 'Then you do *a-ny-thing* you like.'

Nigel looked at him and suppressed a shudder.

'Will she remember?' he asked. 'You know, afterwards?'

'Not so much, no.' The smile faded from Arnaud's face and he shook his head, his tone impatient now. 'Look, man, if you wanna be a gentleman, dump her in a taxi when you've finished with her. Who cares, right?'

Nigel felt a cold knot tightening in his stomach.

'How much?' he murmured.

'For you?' The bald man stood back and looked at him speculatively. 'Thirty-five.'

Nigel swallowed.

'That seems . . . expensive.'

'You're kidding, right?' Arnaud spread his palms wide in a gesture of disbelief. 'You can have any girl you want, do anything you want to her, man. Thirty-five is fucking *cheap*!'

Nigel could feel his anger rising, and was suddenly determined to stand his ground.

'How about fifty for two lots?' he countered.

Arnaud pursed his lips for a moment, then folded his arms.

'Sixty,' he said with an air of finality.

Nigel frowned, then lowered his eyes and nodded. He reached into his pocket and drew out a handful of notes, counting the money as the bald man watched.

'There you are,' he said. 'Sixty.'

Arnaud took the notes and folded them before sliding them down the side of his sock. Then he reached behind him and drew something out of his back pocket.

'You're gonna have some *good* fun, I think.' He handed over two tiny plastic ampoules, a little clear liquid trembling inside each one. 'Maybe you got something *special* in mind . . . '

Nigel suddenly had an image of the bald dealer looming over an unconscious Laura — his leering smile, his long inquisitive fingers — and felt his stomach lurch. He jammed the ampoules down into the pocket of his jeans and turned to open the door, but Arnaud put a hand out, stopping him from leaving. He was close enough to smell now.

'We're done here.' Nigel felt his muscles tensing with anger and revulsion.

'Yeah, but I think you'll be back.' Arnaud gave him a sly smile. 'I tell you what — you take some photos of whatever you do to her, and if I like them maybe I let you pay fifty next time, OK?'

Slowly, deliberately, he licked his teeth, then stood back from the door. Trembling, Nigel jerked it open and almost sprang out of the cubicle.

'*Au revoir*.'

Behind him, he heard the bald man chuckle as the stall door bumped shut and the bolt slid back into place. Shaking, his fists clenched so that the nails dug into his palms, Nigel barged out on to the dance floor and made for the exit.

31

Nigel was restless. He knew what was troubling him but there was nothing he could do about it. Leaning back on the sofa, he rubbed his eyes, trying to drive the images from his mind.

He should never have gone there. It had been a stupid idea, and he'd acted without thinking. He needed to be more realistic . . .

. . . but he had to do something, didn't he? If he just waited, if he did nothing, Matt might push her away forever.

He couldn't even *think* about that.

Opening his eyes, he stared at the ceiling. He needed a distraction. Pushing himself up into a sitting position, he glanced across at his computer. Angela's corporate photos were waiting for him. Bella had uploaded the preferred images from the shoot, and they were now on his drive, ready to be enhanced. He really wasn't in the mood, but he knew he had to do something, had to stop thinking about it before it consumed him. And the work would have to be done some time — it might as well be now.

He got up and walked over to his desk, dropping into his chair and waking the computer with a tap on the mouse. The screen glowed into life, bathing him in its familiar glow, and he settled down, clicking the folder to open it.

There were a dozen images, standard corporate headshots, and he flipped through them in preview mode. Dreary-looking people, miserable-looking managers, scrubbed up and wearing their best fixed grins for the camera. He zoomed in on a couple of them, checking for image noise, colour distortion, blurring, but they were minimal. As usual, Frank had done a good job on the photography.

Nigel sighed.

The best job he could, given the subject matter.

Closing the previews, he selected the first image and loaded it into Photoshop. A portly man in a grey suit filled the screen. He was in his late forties or early fifties, with his brown hair carefully combed and his mauve silk tie done up too tightly.

Nigel rested his left hand on the keyboard, and flitted about the screen with the mouse. He added a temporary contrast boost that would make it easier to spot any blemishes, then magnified the image right up and started panning around it. There were a few errant strands of hair at the top of the head, but nothing difficult there. Sliding a finger over the top of the mouse, he pulled the image across to study the face. There was a small mole on one cheek, and a couple of tiny red blotches on the other — easy fixes, so he might as well do them straight away. Taking a spot-healing brush from the tool palette, he adjusted the size so that it was slightly larger than the worst of the blemishes, then dabbed it down over the top of each one. As if by magic, the marks disappeared, the texture of the surrounding skin filling over them. He zoomed out a little to make sure the tone of the repair was correct, then moved on to look for the next likely problem.

Eyebrows were often an issue. He centred the view on them, then magnified the image so they filled the screen. Leaning forward, he studied each brow carefully. Even zoomed up, they weren't too bad, but there were a couple of long, straggly hairs that jutted out. It was the sort of unnecessary thing that other people wouldn't notice, and he knew he should really be ignoring minor things like that, but he just couldn't help himself.

It had to be perfect.

Selecting a small clone brush, he lightly painted some skin texture over the errant hairs to tidy them back, then panned down to study the man's eyes. They were a deep blue-green, with nice glints of reflected light on them. Frank had captured the colour and lit them well, but Nigel knew that increasing the brightness of those glints would make the eyes shine even more. He tapped on a fine brightness tool and steadily worked each glint until the eyes seemed to sparkle.

Excellent.

There were certainly a lot of lines around the eyes. They weren't too bad, and the man was in reasonable condition for his age, but the brief from Angela had been clear.

Dip them in your fountain of youth.

Making people look younger wasn't usually difficult. He might want to work on the overall face shape, perhaps lift the slightly droopy jowls, but the first job was to improve the skin. Those lines around the eyes, the deep wrinkles, enlarged pores — the more pronounced these things were, the more they aged a person. He couldn't remove them completely — that would create an unnatural, airbrushed effect — but he *could* make them less distinct, giving the skin a smoother, more youthful appearance.

He spent some time tracing around the edge of the face, masking off the rest of the image, so that only the skin was exposed. Then, once he had the area isolated, he began building up a series of translucent layers on top of it, each one subtly softening the lines and wrinkles, melting them away.

Sitting back in his chair for a moment, he zoomed the image out to check it. Staring back at him from the screen, the man had a layer of perfectly smooth skin.

But it was a little too perfect.

Now, Nigel began to gently blend it with the original photo, lightly brushing away the overlay here and there so that the original facial texture shone through, hiding any edges so that it was impossible to tell which parts were enhanced and which were real.

When he was finished, he zoomed out to view the face as a whole. He tapped the mouse, and the overlay disappeared, leaving the older face visible, then tapped again to make it younger.

Older . . . younger . . . older . . . younger . . .

Satisfied, he saved a copy of the layered image, then leaned back in his chair, closing his eyes to rest them for a moment. He stretched his arms up above his head, then did the little up-and-round circles with his shoulders, trying to work out some of the tension. His neck was stiff too. They said it was bad posture, too much time in front of the screen . . .

Sighing, he leaned forward again, looking at the image in front of him.

Focus on the work.

He'd done a good job on the skin, so he might not need to reshape the cheeks, but he decided to have a quick play and see how they might look. Taking the new, younger face, he selected Liquefy — a toolset that allowed him to stretch and morph any part of the image, as though it were painted on an elastic gel.

He started with the cheekbones, gently edging them up a fraction — not so much that it would affect the eye area, but enough to let him tighten up the flesh below them. He narrowed the cheeks, bringing them in just a little, and nudged in the slight flabbiness around the chin.

Saving another copy of his work, he flipped between the before and after views, watching the face tighten, and slacken. You had to be careful you didn't overdo this bit, or it would cease to look like the subject of the original photo, but he'd been subtle and the effect was quite convincing.

He bowed his head for a moment, rubbing his eyes. He felt so tired, but it wasn't a lack of sleep. This was deeper, a profound weariness. He shook his head and scowled at the screen.

This picture was almost finished, but he found himself doodling now. Using a smaller brush, he feathered along the man's prominent lower lip, moving it up, making it thinner. On a whim, he brought the top lip down to meet it, easing them together until the ugly line of teeth was obscured.

He paused for a moment, looking at the overly distorted image, then clicked on the cloning tool again. Selecting a bit of clean skin texture as the source, he began painting across the lips, diminishing them even further, brushing away the mild redness until they disappeared and only a faint slit remained.

He knew exactly what was troubling him.

Taking the clone tool, he brushed a final line across the face, so the mouth disappeared completely.

He wouldn't allow it to trouble him any more.

32

He made his way down the sloping street, staying in the shadows, as the sound of traffic from the main road faded behind him. There were several old buildings on this side, pressed in close to the pavement — commercial units, converted offices, all empty — and he melted into one of the recessed doorways, leaning round the edge of the wall to stare out at the street-lit scene before him.

The club looked different tonight, the murals that danced around its old brickwork now menacing in the dark. He could hear the music from inside, the insistent bass that thumped out beneath the laughing voices of the people gathered at the entrance. There was no rush, so he waited until most of them had gone in, then emerged from his hiding place and strode across the tarmac. He kept his head down as he passed beneath the gaze of the security cameras, hands jammed down in the pockets of his new favourite jacket, as he joined up with the last of the group that were going inside.

He paid in cash — no words, no eye contact — then made his way along the black-walled corridor, his steps measured and calm despite the clamour of feelings that swirled within him. The music grew louder as he went down the stairs, rising to a wall of sound and heat as he emerged on to the basement dance floor. The familiar sea of bodies rose and fell below the coloured lights, and he stood for a moment, seeing the individual faces among the crowd. Was the mousy-haired girl in here somewhere, hands above her head, smiling and swaying? Would she even remember him if he she saw him?

No. Those kinds of thoughts weren't helpful just now. And he didn't want anyone to remember him . . . not tonight.

He walked around the edge of the room, moving slowly, looking for somewhere he could stand, somewhere he could watch from. Two girls were huddled together in a corner, gossiping, trying to make themselves heard over the music. As he approached, they turned to move on to the dance floor, and he slid into the spot they had vacated.

This was perfect. From here he could keep an eye on the door to the Gents without it being obvious what he was doing. Leaning back against the wall, he let his eyes sweep the room. The place wasn't as busy as it had been on his last visit, but there were still a lot of bodies, pressed together below the illuminated paper flowers. He glanced over to the security cameras, fortunately trained away from where he was standing, then looked back towards the metal door.

Still closed.

Across from it, standing motionless in a small alcove, a heavyset bouncer was watching a group of girls dancing together. It was nothing, but seeing the man, with his black T-shirt and his fluorescent identity armband, was enough to trigger a first sense of fear.

Was he really going to do this?

He bowed his head, forcing down the doubts. He'd made his mind up, and anyway, he was committed now. There was no option but to see the plan through.

The door was still closed. He turned to check that the bouncer was still focused on the girls. This was it. Pushing himself away from the wall, he walked quickly towards the toilets.

Inside, it was quieter. The music still thudded in from behind him, but it was subdued now. Part of him had hoped that there would be other people in here, somebody who'd look at him, force him to abort, but there wasn't. It was time.

He walked past the sinks and the urinals, stepping around the puddles on the floor, checking the line of graffiti-covered stalls. The doors were all open . . . all except the last one.

Steeling himself, overcoming the urge to turn and run, he swallowed, then knocked.

'Remember me?' His voice was little more than a whisper, but it seemed dreadfully loud in here. 'Matt's friend?'

Matt's friend. The words sent a jolt of anger coursing through him. He took a deep breath, tasting the harsh bite of citrus bleach that filled the air, then clenched his teeth as he heard the bolt being drawn across. The door opened just a crack, then swung wider.

'I said you'd be back,' Arnaud leered. Wearing a red zipper top, skinny dark jeans and brilliant white trainers, he held the door open, motioning Nigel inside. 'Come into my office.'

Swallowing his fear, Nigel stepped into the cubicle and locked the door behind him, his heart racing as he turned to face the dealer.

'I . . .' He had to get the words out but his mouth was so dry. 'I need . . . some more.'

An unpleasant smile spread across Arnaud's face.

'I *told* you so,' he said in an eerie, sing-song voice. 'Did you have some fun with a nice lady? Did you do those bad, bad things that you wanted to do to her?'

Nigel felt sick. Not trusting himself to speak, he drew out a handful of notes and thrust the money under Arnaud's nose.

'More,' he croaked.

'Of course.' Arnaud's long fingers closed around the money, his smile widening as he counted it. 'Plenty more.'

This was it.

Pulse racing, he watched as the dealer turned away from him slightly, reaching inside his clothing to find the merchandise.

Do it!

The bastard was still looking away.

Do it now!

He clenched his fist and slammed the heel of his hand into the side of Arnaud's head, catching him cold, knocking him back so that he stumbled over the toilet bowl and lost his footing. As the dealer fell, Nigel snarled and lunged forward, decades of hatred rushing to the surface, all directed at the collapsing figure in front of him. Both hands on that disgusting, sweaty scalp — one on each side — getting hold of his ugly, bald head, and slamming it backwards against the tiled rear wall.

Every taunt from Declan the bully . . .

He jerked the head towards him, then slammed it hard into the wall again.

Every disappointed look from his mother . . .

Panting with the effort, he wrenched forward once more, but this time there was no resistance as he slammed Arnaud's skull against the tiles.

Every lie that Matt had told him . . .

He paused, gasping, and looked down at the unmoving figure, then let go so that the body slumped back into the corner of the stall. It was done. Arnaud was dead.

He took a breath.

The difficult part was over.

* * *

He'd intended only to seal up the wicked, spiteful mouth, but now that he was here, alone with the body, he found himself staring down at the composition of the scene before him, imagining it as a photograph, thinking how it might be improved.

He drew the bottle of superglue from his pocket and twisted the nozzle open. Arnaud had slumped down between the porcelain bowl and the side of the stall. Nigel leaned forward, and took tentative hold of one of the hands. It felt unsettling — lifeless yet still warm. The arm was surprisingly heavy, but he turned the wrist around and squeezed a crisscross pattern of glue across the back of the hand. Then he carefully lifted the arm and pressed the hand firmly against the side of the stall, holding it in place for a few seconds, before slowly letting go.

The glue held.

Good.

He took hold of the other arm, lifting it and stretching it out, using his knee to keep Arnaud's body from slumping forward. It was difficult, but after a moment he had the other hand stuck to the tiled rear wall. Standing back, he studied the scene, pleased with the arrangement of the body, though it was a shame the bald head kept lolling forward.

It needed to be perfect.

Moving into the corner, he stood over the dead man and frowned. Then, leaning forward, he patted the back of Arnaud's head with his sleeve to ensure it was dry, before smearing it with glue. Once he'd used enough, he put a hand on top of Arnaud's head and pushed it gently back against the tiles, holding it in place until he was sure it had bonded.

This was more like it. The figure before him had an almost classical pose now — strange and compelling, not just a bundle of limbs at the side of a grimy toilet.

Pleased, he squatted down and looked at what remained of the dreadful man, that hideous, sneering face now gone slack in death. Taking up the glue bottle, he was positioning himself to apply it to Arnaud's ugly mouth when he paused, then smiled.

Of course. Why hadn't he thought of it before?

Leaning forward, he ran a thin line of glue

along each eyelid, watching the clear liquid soaking in between the black eyelashes, making them glisten.

'See no evil . . . '

He leaned to the left, dribbling a little glue into Arnaud's ear and squeezing the hole to seal it, then repeating the process for the right side.

'Hear no evil . . . '

And now, the finishing touch, the act that he'd come to perform. Arnaud's jaw was loose, his mouth slightly open. Shuffling in close, Nigel traced a thick line of glue along the bottom lip, then put the bottle down so that he could use both hands, pressing the lips together and holding them to ensure a good seal.

'Speak no evil,' he whispered. 'You sick, sick bastard.'

Job done.

Reaching down to retrieve the glue, he noticed that there was a little left in the bottle.

Shame to waste it.

Bending forward again, he slid the thin plastic nozzle up into Arnaud's left nostril, squeezing out a little blob of glue, then did the same for the right. Placing the bottle on the floor, he took the nose between forefinger and thumb, and pinched it closed . . .

. . . and then jerked backwards in horror as the dead man's cheeks bulged. The splayed arms tensed and the bald head began straining to pull itself free. Recoiling, Nigel stumbled and fell to the floor, stifling a cry as Arnaud's chest began to heave and his legs kicked out.

An awful sound came from the body, like a

muffled animal howl. Sealed up inside his own skin, Arnaud was trying to scream.

Nigel pushed himself back against the door as the thrashing legs kicked out at him, the white trainers squeaking and slithering across the floor, scuffing against his shins as he tried to pull away from the awful scene, but there was nowhere to go.

No! No! No!

He felt his stomach tightening, the wave of nausea rising, desperate for it all to *please just stop . . .*

But it *was* stopping. Arnaud's movements were slowing, weakening, as he ran out of oxygen and his limbs sagged. Unable to look away, Nigel stared at the body as it became still and silent, knees falling open, a dark stain blooming out across the denim between the legs.

* * *

He wasn't sure how long he sat there, but he became aware of the cold wet floor under his hand, the hard door against the back of his head. His shoulders felt as though they might go into spasm at any moment, but he pushed himself forward and got up onto his knees. He didn't want to look at the body, not after what had just happened. The rising smell told him Arnaud was really dead now, so he kept his eyes down, staring at the floor in front of him. Stooping to retrieve the bottle of superglue, he noticed something else, down by the base of the wall — a tiny polythene bag. He reached out a hand and picked it up, turning it to better see what was inside, but it took him a moment to recognise the contents.

GHB. A lot of it.

Snatching the bag and jamming it down into his pocket, Nigel got shakily to his feet. He felt cold now, shivery. How long had he been in here?

Get out. Get out now!

Turning towards the door, he listened intently, trying to hear over the pounding of his pulse in his ears. There didn't seem to be anyone else in the toilets — he had to go now.

Taking one final breath, he pulled the door open and looked outside.

Nobody around, thank goodness.

He turned, pulling the door quickly to hide the scene within, then made his way out into the club to disappear among the sea of dancing figures.

33

He'd expected to feel different in the days that came afterwards. Something like this ought to change a person, leave them disturbed or even traumatised . . . but it hadn't happened. Sitting here at his desk, staring deep into the screen, there had been several times when he'd actually forgotten about it, and the shiver of realisation when it all came back to him wasn't really so bad.

That leering mouth, sealed up and silenced forever.

Arnaud had been an evil, evil man — one who took profit and pleasure in the abuse of others — and nobody could possibly mourn his passing. There was nothing to be sorry for, no regrets, just a growing sense of pride that he'd had the strength to see it through. Yes, it had been scary at the time, and he'd felt his heart racing as he made his way home through the dark streets, but now he simply saw it as a necessary correction — editing, cutting out something ugly.

He'd read about his so-called crime in the local paper. The coverage was disappointingly small, just a few columns on page four, but they'd mentioned his clever use of glue and titled the piece *Toilet Death for Drug Dealer*, which struck him as oddly amusing.

At first, he'd resisted the temptation to scour

the internet for news — that sort of searching could leave a digital trail — until he remembered that he had full access to Matt's wifi. A bit of research on Google showed him several small-time blog sites that had picked up the story and were using it as an excuse to blame immigrants, or young people, or the Conservative Party — whatever the site's particular agenda was. But here and there, he found comments from people who genuinely seemed to agree with his actions — scum like Arnaud *should* be taken out of the picture.

Nigel leaned back in his chair and allowed himself a smile of satisfaction.

He had done the right thing.

It hadn't been easy, and of course it had involved terrible personal risk. Arnaud could have turned on him, maybe pulled a knife, or even a gun . . .

A gun! He hadn't considered the possibility that the dealer might be armed; would he have gone through with it if he had? There had been enough to worry about with the police.

In the hours after his return to the flat, he'd sat by the window, every room in darkness, waiting for the flashing blue lights, the heavy knock on the door. But it never came. Over the following days, he began to theorise that maybe the police weren't too worried about a dead drug dealer. Perhaps, from their point of view, this was no more serious than the break-in downstairs — a minor matter, to be logged and added to the statistics. He grinned, imagining a police officer questioning Arnaud's friends then offering them a leaflet about *Coping with Crime* . . .

No, the police weren't going to bother with this one. Not a dead dealer. Not *really*. They might go through the motions, but it would gradually be forgotten, dismissed as a dispute between criminals . . . and he would remain free. Maybe this was just how the universe worked — people who just *went for it* could get away with murder. Literally.

He shook his head and sat up.

All those wasted years of being nice, being polite, keeping himself to himself, getting *nowhere*. Decisive action — that was the key. Instead of being timid, he'd finally acted . . . and it had paid off. It was a huge milestone on his journey, a mark of his growing confidence, his transformation. He'd been proactive — seen a problem and done something about it. And the world hadn't ended — far from it, he'd actually made the world a slightly better place.

Pushing his chair back, he stood up and stretched.

He wondered whether it was wrong to feel so *pleased*, whether he ought to experience just a little bit of remorse for causing Arnaud's death . . .

No! He wasn't going to regret this. Everything he'd done had been necessary.

Turning, he walked through to the kitchen and opened the fridge. Reaching inside, he picked up a cold bottle of Becks, then hesitated.

Not tonight. Putting the beer back, he took out a can of Diet Coke and leaned back against the counter as he opened it. Taking a swig, he checked his watch. It was after five — Matt would be home soon. His two-faced neighbour *had* been a real help to him over the past months, and tonight he'd be helping again . . .

. . . even if he didn't know it.

Pulling the door of the fridge closed, he took his drink through to the front room and dropped down onto the sofa. Placing the can on the coffee table, he picked up his iPad and logged into the web feed. On the screen, Matt's front room appeared, and Nigel settled back to watch.

34

Laura made her way down to the front of the bus, swaying from one handrail to the next, and thanked the driver as she got off. Stepping down on to the street-lit pavement, she adjusted her bag and frowned at her reflection in the darkened glass of the bus shelter, as the doors hissed shut behind her.

She felt a little overdressed.

Tan leather jacket, silky top, short skirt and heels. She certainly didn't want him to think that she'd made all this effort for him — she hadn't — but time was getting on and she couldn't be bothered trailing all the way back to William Street just to change.

She turned and began to walk along the pavement as the lights of the bus disappeared under the arches.

Still, perhaps it wasn't such a bad thing that she looked good when he saw her. Though he could be infuriating, and unreliable, there was something she liked about Matt, and deep down she wanted them to patch things up. That was why she'd come, after all.

She smoothed her skirt down a little as she turned off the main road and started walking up the hill.

The text message he'd sent sounded genuinely apologetic — he was going to make it up to her. And if not, this outfit would remind the stupid sod what he was missing.

There was very little traffic here, and the click of her heels on the tarmac sounded loud as she crossed over to the opposite pavement. She paused at the corner of Eastfield Road as she felt her phone vibrating, but it was just a text from Mandy.

No probs. C U Sunday?

Thankfully, her friend didn't seem to mind the change in plans. Slipping the phone back into her bag, she started down Eastfield Road. Matt's red Mini was parked outside the gate and she looked up at the house as she walked up the path. The nosy old woman who lived on the ground floor was watching TV as usual — she could see the cold blue flicker of the screen, illuminating the net curtains — and there was a warm, yellow light on in the middle floor. She scampered up the steps and paused for a moment, finger over the bell button.

She would play it cool. Let him know that he couldn't mess her around.

Nodding to herself, she pushed the button. Almost immediately, she heard the click as the lock snapped back. He'd obviously been waiting for her. That was a good sign.

She stepped into the hallway, pushing the door shut behind her, then started up the stairs. Perhaps he really was going to make it up to her. It might be a good weekend after all.

There was no sign of Matt when she reached the first-floor landing, but he'd left the front door ajar for her. Licking her lips to make sure they would glisten, she smoothed the front of her top down and stepped inside.

As soon as she entered the hallway, she felt his hands over her eyes, the familiar scent of his aftershave. Smiling, she allowed him to move in close behind her, heard him bump the door with his foot and the latch snick shut.

Warm breath caressed the back of her neck as he whispered, 'Guess who . . . '

She wanted to be cross with him, to scold him for taking so long to apologise, but she found that she was giggling despite herself.

'Hello, Matt,' she murmured, leaning her weight back against him.

'No,' whispered the voice. 'Guess again.'

* * *

She remembered screaming, or trying to scream, but a strong hand clamped itself across her mouth, silencing her and jerking her head back. She felt something cold and metallic pressed against her throat.

'Don't scream.'

She swallowed, hopelessly off balance now, trying to pull her exposed neck away from whatever he was holding, even though it meant pressing herself back against him.

'Very still and very quiet, OK?'

She couldn't answer. Eyes wide, she stared up at the ceiling, arms outstretched, trying to get enough breath through her nose. There was something odd about his hand, a strange smell, like rubber.

‘*OK?*’

She nodded, very slightly.

‘Good.’

Gradually, the hand released its pressure on her mouth, hovering over her lips for a moment, ready to snap back, before slowly dropping away. The cold metal at her throat remained.

‘Very good.’

The muscles in her legs tightened, trying to keep her balanced against him as he moved behind her, doing something she couldn’t see. Was she allowed to speak now? Or would he hurt her if she did?

‘Here, drink some of this . . . ’ His whisper startled her, loud in her ear, and she swivelled her eyes down to where his hand had appeared, holding an open bottle of Coke. ‘It’ll help you relax.’

He moved it down, touching the plastic against her hand until she gripped it with uncertain fingers.

‘Drink.’

Trembling, she raised the bottle to her mouth, hesitating as it touched her lips.

‘Do as I say, Laura.’

How did he know her name? Unless . . .

‘Matt?’ she stammered.

But it wasn’t Matt. The metal pressed a little closer against her skin, and his other hand was on her shoulder, preventing her from moving. Fighting back sudden tears, she lifted the bottle and drank.

* * *

Afterwards, he made her kneel down, pressing her palms flat on the hallway carpet, the top of her head touching the closed door of the front room. That door was never closed, and she found herself wondering what was in there that he didn't want her to see. What could be so bad? What could be worse than this?

Matt! Had something happened to Matt? Was he lying there, covered in blood?

She was still scared, but her fear seemed more abstract now, more distant. As her pulse slowed, her thoughts seemed to drift between dread and detached curiosity. Was she going to die? Would it hurt? Her fingers were tired from gripping the carpet so she allowed them to relax, as the voice behind her murmured something that she could no longer make out. Her head felt strange, probably from leaning forward so long, though she'd lost track of how long it had been. She wished she could just lie down and rest for a moment.

'Laura?'

The whisper came from close behind her, like Matt's voice and yet not. She tried to turn her head, so she could see who it was, but the effort was too much and she felt herself slumping back against the door.

'My poor Laura . . . ' The voice seemed gentler now, tinged with regret. 'Don't worry, it won't be long now.'

35

As the screen went black and the credits appeared, Mrs Hamilton leaned back in her chair with a happy little sigh. *Doc Martin* was such a charming programme, with all that beautiful Cornish scenery. So much nicer than the dreadful things she was forced to watch in the daytime — those chat shows with the appalling families and their loose morals — all that shameful squabbling, airing their dirty linen in front of the nation. She couldn't imagine who that sort of rubbish appealed to.

As the theme music finished, an announcer's voice mentioned the ten o'clock news. For a moment, she was confused, thinking it felt later. Then, she remembered she'd been watching on the Plus One channel, where everything was an hour behind. It must be eleven, not ten, and she gave a little yawn as she sat up. Taking her glasses off, she placed them on the arm of the chair and rubbed her eyes.

On the seat beside her, dear little Gordon was watching her.

'That was delightful, wasn't it?' She beamed at him, loving the way his bright little face looked up at her. He was so attentive, so intelligent, he knew exactly what she was saying to him. 'Are you tired, my darling? It'll soon be time for bed, yes it will.'

She yawned again, tired now. It would be

bedtime soon, but she had a packet of ginger biscuits in the cupboard, and one last cup of tea might be nice.

'Come on, then, Gordon.' She grimaced, gripping the arms of the chair and beginning to rock herself forward and back, building momentum. 'Up we get.'

With some effort, she managed to heave herself upright, pausing to let the stiffness in her joints ease before turning towards the kitchen. Gordon jumped down onto the rug and dutifully followed her through.

The kettle felt light when she lifted it, so she removed it from its base and filled it up a little from the tap. Returning it to its place, she clicked the switch down and turned to smile at Gordon.

'Shall we have a nice cup of tea?' She leaned forward and clapped her hands together, making the little dog's ears prick up slightly. 'Shall we?'

Gordon emitted a single bark of enthusiasm, while she straightened up with some difficulty and turned away to the counter. Prising the lid off the jar, she took out a tea bag, and popped it into her cup. In front of her, the open cupboard revealed the half-packet of ginger biscuits, the wrapper folded over neatly and held in place with a clothes peg. She knew she really shouldn't, especially just before bed. What was it they said? Breakfast like a king, lunch like a lord, dine like a pauper? It was something like that, implying you shouldn't eat so much in the evening. But these particular biscuits were so very *thin*. There were only a handful of them left, and it would be a shame to let them get stale, but . . .

She half-closed the cupboard, paused, then opened it again.

Where would be the harm? There was practically nothing to these ones . . .

Reaching up, her fingers had just closed on the wrapper when she thought she heard something. Turning, she saw that Gordon's head had angled towards the hallway, and a moment later she heard a thud as the front door slammed shut.

Who could that be at this time of night?

Gathering up her bulk, she hurried through to the front room. Sensing her excitement, Gordon was running around in a little circle, but he got out of her way as she bore down on the bay window, steadying herself against the wall as the pain in her joints caught her. Drawing a deep breath, she gently pulled one corner of the curtain, very slightly so that the light wouldn't shine out — she wouldn't want anyone to think she was prying, after all — and peered outside.

There were two figures on the pathway, making their way out to the road. She recognised Matt immediately, that tall silhouette and, as the light caught him briefly, the distinctive leather jacket with that big embroidered crest emblazoned on the back. He seemed to be wearing some sort of hat, but she couldn't see it properly, and anyway she was looking at the other figure — his young lady friend.

When had she arrived? Unless it was earlier, while *Doc Martin* was on . . .

Matt's girlfriend was tottering along on her

heels, wearing a skirt that was really much too short. She looked a little unsteady — in fact, poor Matt was almost having to carry her down the path — the silly girl must have been drinking.

Mrs Hamilton squinted then shook her head.

At least she wasn't spending the night, getting up to goodness knows what. Some of the noises that girl made . . . it wasn't decent!

The two figures appeared to be getting into Matt's car. It was difficult to see much, now that they had reached the pavement, where they were obscured by bushes and the garden wall. There was the sound of a door closing, then another. A moment later, she saw the roof of the little red car pull away and disappear down the road.

He must be taking her home. And a good thing too!

From the kitchen, she heard the bubbling of the kettle, and the click as it switched itself off. She let go of the curtain and turned, almost knocking her glasses from the arm of the chair, and found Gordon in the centre of the rug staring up at her.

'Shall we go and have a drink and a biscuit, darling?' she asked him. 'Mummy's going to have a biscuit and you shall too, yes you shall.'

She leaned forward to pat the little dog, then groaned a little as she straightened up. Taking up her glasses, she put them on and smiled.

'That's much better,' she told him. 'Come on, then.'

Wagging his tail, Gordon followed her as she made her way through to the kitchen.

36

Her head hurt. At first, that was all she knew, but gradually she became aware that she was shivering, the movement firing an ache in her shoulder. She rolled over, trying to get comfortable, but as her hand extended beyond the edge of the fabric, everything was hard and cold and . . . damp?

Startled, she tried to sit up, eyes flickering open and blinking against the dim light beside her. Nausea welled up like an angry slick in her stomach, but her throat was dry and her head started to pound. Groaning through cracked lips, she sagged back, feeling the hard surface beneath the duvet she was lying on, and tried to bring her surroundings into focus.

For a moment, she thought she might be dead. It was a narrow space, with smooth stony walls, black like a burial chamber. But there was a light.

Moving slowly this time, carefully, she pushed herself up onto her elbows, squinting at the dim glow beyond her feet. It was some sort of lantern, small, like the kind of thing you might take on a camping trip. Struggling up into a sitting position, she bowed her head for a moment, waiting for the thumping to subside as she tried to remember what had happened.

Matt.

She'd gone to his flat to see him, but he hadn't

been there. She frowned, trying to marshal her thoughts. Someone else had been there, waiting for her. Not Matt . . . at least, she didn't think it was him. She remembered something at her throat and felt a flutter of panic, reaching up and brushing her fingers across her neck, searching for a wound.

But there was nothing there. Had she imagined it?

No, something must have happened, something that had brought her here. Wherever here was. Why the hell couldn't she remember? It was so difficult to think with such a sore head. Her body felt strange, numb and aching at the same time. She tried to swallow, finding it difficult, noticing the bad taste in her mouth. It was like a hangover, only much, much worse . . .

Drugged.

She took a sharp breath. There was a drink. She remembered a bottle of something being pressed into her hand as she stood in the hallway. But why would her attacker do that? Unless . . .

Oh please God, no!

Heart racing, she bent forward, hitching her skirt up and opening her legs as wide as her confinement would allow. Working a trembling hand inside her underwear, she examined herself for any soreness, any indication that she might have been violated . . .

. . . but there was nothing. Her clothing didn't feel as though it had been disturbed — even her shoes were still on. She took a deep breath.

There was a strange smell, very strong, like old

machinery. She twisted around, looking away from the lantern, trying to see what was behind her, but her own body was blocking any illumination. Panic surged up inside her and she turned back towards the lantern, fixing her eyes on it as she tried to get her breathing under control. Where the *fuck* was she?

* * *

She wasn't sure how long she sat there before she felt calm enough to move. Pulling her jacket around her against the chill of the stone floor, she rolled forward onto her knees and crawled towards the light. It gave out a dim glow, but the illuminated glass was warm to the touch and she hugged it close to her for a moment, closing her eyes against the sudden shadows that her fingers threw out across the walls.

It was going to be all right. Somehow she'd found her way in here, so there must be a way to get out. All she had to do was focus on that, fight the urge to panic, and start looking.

There was another smooth wall in front of her, sealing off the end of the long space she was in. Lifting the lantern, she glimpsed the ceiling of her enclosure for the first time — old metal, pitted and scored — so low that she doubted she would even be able to stand up without stooping. As she turned round, the light spilled past her to reveal two bulging black shapes — refuse sacks, with yellow drawstring handles — and beyond them . . . stairs?

Overcoming the stiffness in her limbs, Laura

crawled towards them, shuffling over the duvet, squeezing past the black bags that took up almost the whole width of the space. Reaching the far end, she put a trembling hand on the first step. It was grimy and made of stone — no, it was concrete. In fact, everything was old, pitted concrete. As she lifted the lantern, tilting it back to shine upward, her heart sank.

The stairs led nowhere.

The metal that covered her cramped little space continued on past the top step. There was a small gap between it and the top of the walls. No light came in, but the air seemed cleaner, colder, as she lifted her face to it.

And there was a sound.

Voices?

She pushed up against the metal but it wouldn't move.

'Hello?' She craned her neck so her mouth was closer to the gap, closer to the voices. 'Help! Somebody please help me!'

She took a breath, turning her head to listen for a response, but as she did so the voices subsided. Music swelled in their place — something heavy with electric guitars.

'Help me, please!'

She called out again and again. The music ended and the voices returned, quiet and indistinct. She screamed out louder, but they didn't hear her and before long the music started again, a different track this time.

Banging her fists on the metal made little noise, so she pressed her face into the gap and howled, shouting and screaming until her throat felt ragged, but there was no answer, and no one came. After a while, exhausted and numb, she crumpled down to sit on the useless stairs and bowed her head. Where was she?

Holding the lantern up she now saw that the whole space couldn't be more than fifteen feet long and three feet wide. It was so small, much too small. She shuddered and screwed her eyes shut, trying to think about something else, anything else, before the claustrophobia could claim her and drag her into screaming madness.

Think.

She had to get help, let someone know what had happened. But if they couldn't hear her when she shouted, what else could she do?

Her phone!

She opened her eyes and began frantically searching the pockets in her jacket. If she could just get in contact with someone . . .

But then she remembered; her phone was in her handbag. She'd put it in there after getting a text from Mandy and there was no sign of it now. She lifted the lantern and surveyed her narrow prison. There was nothing down here except the duvet she'd woken up on and the black plastic refuse sacks.

Perhaps there was something useful inside them, or something that might at least explain what was happening to her. She went to stand up, but the metal ceiling was too low, even when she got down from the steps. Stifling a little shriek of frustration, she moved forward, stooping, unwilling to crawl. The yellow drawstrings on the first sack were pulled tight but not actually tied. Taking the handle of the lantern between her teeth, she pulled the sack open and looked inside. There were several large bottles of spring water, packets of crisps, and a couple of bars of chocolate. She leaned forward so that the light could reach the bottom of the sack, revealing something else — batteries. They were the large, square kind, the sort you might use in a big torch . . .

. . . or a lantern.

Frowning, she turned to the other sack. This one bulged and the top came open as soon as she loosened the ties. Peering inside, she could see more bedding — two pillows and a couple of blankets — but there was something else too. She pulled out the pillows and tossed them onto the duvet, then lifted the blankets aside.

At the bottom of the sack, she found a strange container made of soft blue plastic. It was like a smoothly curved bowl, about eighteen inches across, with a close-fitting lid. Puzzled, she took it in both hands and drew it out so she could see it. What could it be?

She could feel something sliding around inside it, so she placed it on the floor and removed the plastic lid to reveal a sealed packet of wet-wipes and a tiny bottle of hand-sanitiser. It took her a moment before she realised what she was looking at.

The bowl was some sort of bedpan.

And then her blood ran cold as she realised what the items meant.

Somebody intended to keep her here for a long time.

PRESENT

37

There was a break in the clouds, and Nigel slowed his walk, closing his eyes as he enjoyed the welcome warmth of the sun on his shirt. To his left there were shallow ponds set in the cobblestones of the central plaza, each with an array of nozzles that created little arcing fountains of water. A young woman was laughing and squealing as her boyfriend carried her, struggling, to the middle of the ankle-deep water and threatened to put her down. Nigel smiled to himself. That sort of thing used to fill him with a jealous gloom, but not any more. Now he enjoyed seeing other couples in love.

He walked on, past the children with their splashing and their laughter, and made for the waterfront, where the benches were full of people eating chips and gazing out along the harbour inlet. Seagulls wheeled overhead, and he paused as he made his way down the quayside steps — it was a beautiful day, but he still had a lot of work to do. Swinging his plastic carrier bag, he turned towards the studio.

* * *

As soon as he opened the door, he noticed the little knot of people gathered around Angela's desk. Frank was there, his spiky white hair recognisable over the heads of the other people, who he seemed to be addressing. Angela was there too, listening intently — clearly something unusual had happened. Frowning, he made his way over towards the group. Bella was standing a little apart from the others, and he spoke softly to her as he approached.

'Hey there.'

Bella, who had been staring into the distance, turned sharply, before her expression softened.

'Oh, hi Nigel,' she said. 'Sorry, I was miles away.'

'That's OK.' He smiled at her, then nodded towards Frank and the others. 'What's going on?'

Bella's expression grew serious again.

'You know that girl that went missing?' she whispered. 'The one the police are looking for, Laura something-or-other?'

Nigel stared at her, his breathing suddenly short.

'Yes?'

'Well, Frank actually knew her,' she continued. 'He's been interviewed by the police and everything.'

Nigel swallowed.

'What did the police say?' he managed.

'Ask him yourself,' Bella said with a shrug as she turned away. 'He certainly enjoys talking about it.'

* * *

Frank was looking pleased with himself as Nigel approached him.

'Hey, pal,' he grinned. 'Didn't know you were here today. How's tricks?'

'I'm fine,' Nigel replied, fighting to keep his expression calm. 'Bella says you knew the missing girl?'

'Aye, that's right. Were you not here when I was telling everyone?'

'No, I just came in.'

'Ah, right.' The older man nodded, rubbing his hands together. 'Well, it's been mad, I can tell you. Had the police round my house, CID asking questions and everything.'

'What did the police say?' Nigel did his best to seem just politely interested. 'Do they know anything?'

'Nah.' Frank shook his head, then gave Nigel a cold smile. 'Bunch of amateurs. Wouldn't know a mass murderer if they tripped over one.'

He seemed to find their failings amusing.

'So what did they say?' Nigel pressed him.

Frank shrugged.

'All the usual crap,' he sighed. 'How did I know her, when did I last see her, that sort of thing. They haven't got a clue, any of 'em.'

Nigel nodded to himself, then frowned.

'So how *did* you know her?' he asked.

'Well . . . ' Frank glanced around, then gestured for Nigel to follow him. They walked away from the cluster of desks towards the relative privacy of the kitchen area before the photographer spoke again.

'It's really weird,' he confided quietly. 'She was actually one of my models.'

Nigel's stomach lurched.

'What?' he croaked. Not Laura. Not *his* Laura.

'Aye,' Frank grinned, lowering his voice still

further. 'She's pretty hot . . . great body, and lovely little titties.'

He raised his hands in a brief cupping gesture.

'I . . . ' Nigel choked back his protests; he couldn't let on that he knew her. 'She did . . . that sort of work?'

A succession of images flashed through his mind — exposed skin, pale and shivering, the haunted look in the models' eyes that spoke of something terrible . . .

'Oh yeah.' Frank leered at him. 'I had her in the studio more than once, if you know what I mean . . . '

Nigel felt cold. The thought of him touching her . . .

'You didn't . . . ' He felt sick, needing to know, but unable to finish asking the question.

Frank chuckled, then gave a wistful shake of his head.

'Nah, I hadn't shagged her yet,' he sighed. 'Some of them take more persuading than others, and this little tease kept her knickers on no matter what I tried.'

In his own private darkness, Nigel sensed a glimmer of relief. He took a breath and tried to keep his voice steady.

'Maybe she had a boyfriend,' he suggested.

'Oh, she did.' Frank gave him an evil smile. 'I think he was a bit of a jack-the-lad — you know, cheating on her and all that. So, when she needed something to boost her confidence, make her feel good about herself again? Well, that's where Uncle Frank came in.'

He laughed to himself.

'Then later, when she got back together with him . . . well, that just made me want it more.'

* * *

He made it through his meeting somehow, though he was only dimly aware of what Angela had been saying to him.

'Are you all right, Nigel?' she'd asked at one point. 'You seem a little distant.'

He'd shrugged it off, eager to be out of there, anxious to get away before his emotions got the better of him, betrayed him.

His beautiful Laura. What had Matt driven her to?

The thought grew in his mind until it threatened to drive out everything else, but he managed to nod his way through Angela's one-sided conversation. Afterwards, when he'd waved goodbye to Bella and was making his way down the stairs, it dawned on him that he still had Frank's hard drive, with those folders full of the photographer's private glamour images. He hadn't looked through them all yet . . .

What if there was a folder named Laura?

The bus journey back home seemed to take forever. He sat, hugging the carrier bag to his chest as he stared out of the window, helpless to prevent the nightmare visions that assaulted his imagination. What had happened between her and Frank? What had he tried to make her do? The uncertainty gnawed at him, and his only comfort was Frank's grudging admission that she'd resisted.

His pulse was racing as he ran up the stairs, fumbled his key into the lock and wrenched the door open. Rushing through to the front room, he woke his computer and clicked on the icon for Frank's drive. A window of folders appeared and he dragged down to the letter L, looking for her name . . .

Lana . . . Linda . . . Lisa . . .

But there was no Laura. She wasn't there.

He sank back into his chair and let his eyes close. In a way, he was relieved. He wasn't sure he could have borne the sight of her on his screen, exposing herself to that horrible man. She was too precious for that. Her life should be happy, joyful, not blighted by the unwelcome attentions of some filthy pervert.

Opening his eyes, he got to his feet and moved across to the sofa, where he dropped down, and picked up the remote control. He needed to clear his head, needed to shut out the storm of thoughts, just for a little while. Switching the TV on, he lay back, yawning as the weariness hit him. It had been a difficult day, and he decided he needed to put his feet up for a few minutes, stretching out lengthways and lying back to stare up at the ceiling.

A disgusting photographer who wanted to violate her, and a philandering boyfriend who'd practically driven her into his arms . . .

Laura deserved better than that.

38

Something loud woke him. He sat up too quickly, blinking and confused, until he realised it was just an advert on the TV. Sinking back against the armrest, he gave himself a moment, yawning deeply. His watch said it was almost nine o'clock. Pushing himself slowly into an upright position, he rubbed his eyes and stretched.

Must have nodded off.

His mouth was dry and he was thirsty, so he forced himself to get up and moved stiffly through to the kitchen in search of a drink. There was a new carton of orange juice in the fridge, and he poured himself a glass, wanting the cold sharpness of it to wake him up a bit.

Finishing his drink, he leaned back against the counter and frowned. He'd been putting it off, but he knew it was time, and the thought of what he had to do drove away the last of his drowsiness. Placing the glass in the sink, he stood up and went through to the front room. The carrier bag was where he'd left it, on the floor beside the desk, and he gathered it up, briefly checking its contents. Then, satisfied, he made his way down the hall to the bedroom.

There was no point in taking Matt's jacket — not tonight. He'd worn it before, but this evening he wasn't pretending to be anyone else. At least, not until he got there. Opening a drawer, he gazed down at the rubber Guy Fawkes mask, then lifted it and jammed it down into the bag.

He was ready.

Creeping down the stairs, he halted at the corner of the first-floor landing and leaned over the banister, listening. From below, he could hear the faint noise of Mrs Hamilton's TV. She must be watching something, and that was good.

Hurrying down the last flight of steps, he padded over to the front door and let himself out, pulling it behind him so that it shut with the faintest click. Then, with the carrier bag bundled under his jacket, he hurried away down the path and turned right towards the railway embankment, where there were fewer street lights and it was darker. He forced himself to walk slowly now, as though he had done nothing wrong, had nothing to hide. At the end of the street, rather than following it round the end of the terrace, he crossed over to the other side and came back along the opposite pavement. This was where he had to be vigilant. If there was anyone coming, anyone at a window, he'd have to walk straight on. His eyes swept the line of houses, looking for movement, or a silhouette, but there was nothing. He glanced over his shoulder, then on along the street. All clear.

Reaching the entrance to the dead-end lane, he turned off, melting into the shadows and leaving the street behind him.

The lane curved slightly, and he followed the wall round, past a couple of small brick buildings, and the entrance to a small builder's yard. From here, it grew darker, as unchecked foliage hung over the crumbling walls, covering the potholed tarmac with a carpet of mulch. Ahead of him, he could just make out the end of the lane, with the line of old garages — low, whitewashed brick, forgotten beneath the creeping green moss and ivy. The farthest of the garages had huge double doors, with ancient blue paint flaking from the wood, and there were rusty signs advertising old makes of tyre and oil brands — a throwback to when the former owner of Nigel's flat had his mechanic business. But nobody came down here now, and everything was grimy and corroded.

Except the padlock.

It hung from the old door latch, solid, and gleaming in the gloom. Nigel took a key from his pocket, and carefully fitted it into the base of the lock, twisting it until the steel hoop snapped open. With one final glance back up the lane, he opened the door and slipped inside.

* * *

There was music playing — something sad and unfamiliar with a haunting female vocal. He pushed the old door closed, letting it bump softly against the frame, then turned to his left, one arm outstretched in the darkness. His fingers recoiled from imaginary cobwebs before making contact with the smooth cold of the painted brickwork, and he fumbled around until he found the light switch.

The click echoed in the stillness and he

screwed up his eyes for a moment, opening them slowly as he waited to get used to the glare of the single bare bulb that hung down from the gloomy roof space. Placing his bag on the floor, he went over to the workbench and switched the radio off. This place was tucked away where nobody was likely to hear anything, but you never knew when some kids might come sneaking down here, and a radio left on was better than the sounds it might mask.

Now in the heavy silence, he walked quietly over to the car, pausing, listening . . . but he could hear nothing, even when he squatted down close to the floor.

That didn't mean anything.

He opened the driver's-side door, braced himself against the door pillar, and started to push the car, rocking it a little until it started to roll backwards, bumping down off the metal cover with a dull clang. Dropping quickly into the seat, he pulled up the handbrake to halt it, then climbed out and went back over to his bag. Drawing out the Fawkes mask, he stared at it for a moment, then pulled it over his head, tugging it down until he could see through the eyeholes. Then, taking a deep breath that smelled of rubber, he bent down to grasp the large iron ring, and started to pull the metal cover aside.

* * *

She was huddled in the corner, blinking up at the light, shielding her eyes with one slender outstretched hand. As he straightened up to look down into the old inspection pit, her voice rose up to him, hurried and urgent.

'Please, I don't know who you are, I don't want to know, just please let me out of here. I promise, if you just let me out I'll never say anything . . . ' She began coughing, choking slightly as her words raced ahead of her breathing. Other than the few words in his neighbour's hallway, this was the first time she'd ever spoken to him.

He watched her through the eyeholes of the mask. It broke his heart to see her like this, to know what he'd been forced to put her through . . . and after the appalling treatment she'd endured from Matt, poor thing.

'Please,' she gasped. 'Just please let me out.'

'I've brought you something,' he said, in a tone he hoped would be calming.

But Laura was already getting to her feet, her manner becoming more urgent, frantic.

'You have to let me out!' Her voice rose quickly to a terrible shriek. 'LET ME OUT!'

'Stop screaming,' he told her, as patiently as he could.

'No! YOU LET ME OUT!'

Behind the mask, Nigel sighed. Stooping, he grasped the ring and started to slide the metal cover back into place a little.

'Stop it, please.' He spoke firmly, but kindly. 'Or I'll have to cover you up again.'

Laura's eyes, still screwed up against the light, nevertheless widened in horror. Her fingers moved from the edge of the pit to try to hold the cover open.

'No, no please!' Her voice dropped to a desperate hiss. 'Don't cover me up, please!'

Nigel paused.

'Then no more screaming,' he warned her.

He hated to see the fear in her eyes but couldn't she understand that this wouldn't work if she became hysterical? He just wanted to make things as comfortable as possible for her. He was on her side, after all.

'I won't scream.' Her breathing was ragged now. 'Just tell me what it is you want.'

He let go of the metal ring and straightened up, seeing the slight relief in her eyes as he did so.

'I want you to be comfortable,' he told her in a soothing voice.

'But why am I here?' She squinted up at him. 'What have I done?'

Nigel moved to the edge of the pit and gazed down at her.

So lovely.

It pained him to see her in distress but it was a necessary stage, one they had to pass through together. And he would help her through it.

'You've not done anything,' he reassured her. Poor thing, she needed cheering up. He turned and reached for the carrier bag. 'Look, I brought you something . . . '

Turning back to her, he held up a cuddly toy. Her shoulders sagged a little.

'I don't understand,' she sobbed. 'Please. *Please* let me out of here.'

He knew she didn't understand — how could she? But it would be all right, in the end.

'Here.' He offered the teddy bear to her. 'I brought it for you.'

He stooped lower, holding it out for her until she slowly reached up a hand . . .

. . . and grabbed his wrist. The strength of her grip startled him as she hauled him forward, lifting her feet and putting all her weight into dragging him down. Caught off balance, he lost his footing and pitched forward, while she shrieked out a torrent of obscenities.

He almost went into the pit. For one sickening moment, it yawned before him, and he stared down into her snarling face, thinking that he was going to fall on her. But then, at the last moment, he pushed out hard with his feet. Laura lost her hold, dropping backwards with a scream of despair, while his outstretched hand slapped down on the concrete floor on the other side of the hole.

She was on her feet in a flash, clawing at him, trying to regain her hold and drag him down, but he was alert now, rolling away from her grasp and up onto his knees.

Her scream of rage filled the garage, echoing off the walls, but he already knew what he had to do. Grabbing the edge of the metal cover, he scrambled backwards across the floor, dragging it back into place.

As it moved, she let go of him, trying desperately to gain the edge of the pit, but it was too late, and her final howl of anguish was muted as the metal sealed her in again.

Nigel collapsed down onto the cover. For a couple of minutes, he felt her pounding on it from beneath, heard her muffled cries, but eventually she fell silent. He lay there for a while, catching his breath, then sat up and pulled his mask off, welcoming the cool air on his face, sweaty from the unexpected exertion.

Poor thing. He couldn't really blame her for that. It was only natural that she'd panic, try to escape. In time, she'd realise that it had all been necessary. She'd understand. And she'd apologise.

He rolled over onto his front, his face close to the edge of the cover. There was no sound, but he imagined he could feel her, pushing up against the metal he was lying on, their bodies just a few centimetres apart.

'I forgive you,' he whispered.

39

Nigel sat back in his chair and sighed. The place seemed so lonely now, even more than it had before. Just him, Mrs Hamilton and her stupid little dog again. He looked at the pair of tiny video cameras, sitting lifeless on the corner of his desk, and bowed his head.

It was a pity about them, but he'd known they would have to come out eventually. On Friday, while Matt lay unconscious on the sofa, sleeping off his spiked drink, Nigel had crept downstairs to text Laura from his neighbour's phone, and retrieved the two cameras. It wouldn't do for the police to find them, and he knew that the police would come eventually.

And now, they *had* come. Matt was gone, bundled away in a van to 'help the police with their enquiries' while the whole street watched from their windows in shock. Nigel almost felt sorry for him.

Almost.

Leaning forward, he returned his attention to the computer screen, which he'd split into two windows. On one side was a photo of Laura — taken at a Christmas party by the look of it. She was laughing into the camera, with her arm around another woman. Now that he had access to Matt's Facebook account, he also had access to all Matt's friends' pages too. He'd taken his time, going through all of Laura's photos until he'd found this one — *Laura and Mandy nite out*.

He'd studied the image, noting the tone and direction of the lighting, calculating how far away from the camera they'd been, and the angle of the shot . . .

Now he was looking towards the other side of the screen, at a series of photos of himself. He'd narrowed it down to three . . .

Frowning for a moment, he made his decision, dismissing two of the pictures so that only one remained.

OK . . .

He looked back to the Christmas photo. The first thing he had to do was to look after Laura. Picking up a selection tool, he began to trace around her, working carefully to create a protective mask. Locking the area within would ensure she remained untouched as he altered things around her. Switching to a clone brush, he clicked the mouse to pick up the texture from the background, then started to gently brush Mandy away. Working methodically, he slowly erased her, cloning from different areas of the image to avoid those telltale repeating patterns that would ruin the effect.

It needed to be right, if people were to believe it was real. It needed to be perfect.

When he was happy with his removal of Laura's friend, he turned his attention to the other photograph. Magnifying the image a little, he traced a quick selection area around himself, and pasted his cut out likeness beside Laura. Then, sitting back in his chair, he zoomed it out to get a feel for how it would look . . .

Yes, he could see it now. It would take a bit of effort — adjustments to the scale, and the tone of the lighting — but it was going to work. He'd need to refine the outline a bit, and blend it in a bit . . .

The door buzzer jolted him upright in his chair, and his head snapped round to look towards the hallway. He sat blinking for a moment, disoriented after staring so deeply into the screen.

Was it the police? He felt a momentary thrill of panic, then frowned, mastering himself.

So what if it *was* the police? It was only natural that they'd want to ask him questions about Matt. There was nothing to worry about.

He got to his feet, feeling slightly stiff from sitting hunched over, then cast a quick eye around. There were three envelopes — post from Matt's pigeonhole — lying on the coffee table. Not the sort of thing he wanted to leave lying around. Gathering them up, he walked through to the kitchen, placing them face down on the counter, where they wouldn't be noticed.

The door buzzer sounded again.

'Coming, Officers . . . ' he muttered to himself. 'Keep your hair on . . . '

Walking to the entryphone, he picked it up and did his best not to sound irritable.

'Hello?'

'All right, pal. It's me.'

For a moment, he couldn't place the voice. Then it dawned on him.

'Frank?'

‘Aye. Buzz me in, will ya?’

Wrong-footed, Nigel hesitated.

‘I . . . er . . . ’ He was trying to think. ‘What is it?’

‘Come on, mate.’ Frank’s voice was growing impatient. ‘I’m no’ a bloody Jehovah’s Witness. Buzz me in.’

Nigel pushed the door release button, then immediately swore at himself.

Idiot!

Why the hell had he let the disgusting man in? And what was he doing here anyway?

Shaking his head, he replaced the handset and trudged towards the front door. He’d see what Frank wanted, then get rid of him as quickly as possible. It was probably just something about his stupid glamour photos . . .

He stopped, remembering what was currently on his screen, the image that would be displayed as soon as he woke his computer up . . . then he froze at the loud sound of knocking on the door, right in front of him. Swallowing, he glanced over his shoulder towards the front room, then back at the door . . .

Do something!

‘Just a moment,’ he called out, then cursed himself for saying it so close to the door — Frank would wonder what he was up to — but there was no time to think. Sprinting through to his computer, he closed the images, leaving the screen clear. Then, calming his breathing, he walked back into the hall, fixing his smile as he opened the door. Frank was leaning right in against the frame, terribly close, regarding him with obvious suspicion.

'Did I come at a bad time?' he asked.

'No, no.' Nigel took a breath. 'It's fine. Everything's fine.'

Frank's eyes narrowed, and he looked past Nigel into the flat.

'Are you . . . entertaining someone?'

Nigel stared at him. *It was almost as if he knew!* But he couldn't know, nobody did. It was just a creepy old man being his usual, lecherous self.

'No.' It was important to keep his voice level, calm. 'There's nobody here. Only me.'

He realised he was holding the door ajar, just wide enough to peep through. Would that look suspicious? He pulled it a little farther open, but without making it too much of an invitation.

Frank stood away from the door frame.

'Good. I need to check some files on that hard drive I left with you.' He pushed past Nigel and stepped inside. 'I deleted the wrong folder on my laptop, some stuff I needed to keep. I just want to make sure I've still got a copy on the drive here.'

'Um . . . yeah, OK . . . ' Nigel stood, torn between closing the door and leaving it open. 'But you can only stay for a couple of minutes . . . '

Frank stopped suddenly in the hallway, turning to look at him.

Had that sounded like an insult? Quick, say something!

' . . . because I'm going out,' he added.

Frank's manner seemed to soften, just a little.

'Oh aye? What are you doing?'

'I'm . . . going to see someone.' Nigel lowered his eyes, dreadfully uncomfortable now. 'Look, it doesn't matter. Let me just get the drive for you.'

He pushed the front door closed, and they went through to the front room.

'So. You're seeing someone, eh?' Frank walked over to the window, pulling the curtains and peering down into the street. 'Gonna have a nice, romantic evening with him?'

Nigel bristled, but the photographer turned around, his moustache stretched over a broad, yellow-toothed grin.

'Just kidding, pal,' he cackled. 'I know you're not queer.'

Scowling, Nigel turned back to his desk, leaning round behind the screen to disconnect the cables. *Just give him the drive and get him out of here*. But Frank was talking again.

'So you've got a girlfriend, have you?'

'That's right.' Nigel didn't look round, just concentrated on pulling the drive cable out.

'Good for you, pal.' There was an unpleasant, mocking tone in the way he said it, but Nigel didn't care. Pulling the cable free, he stood up, and lifted the drive from the desk.

'Here you are.' He held out the unit. 'All your folders should still be on there.'

'But you haven't finished editing the other photos,' Frank said. 'How are you going to do that if I've got this drive?'

'It's OK,' Nigel told him. 'I copied the photos to my computer. I don't need this any more.'

Frank smiled.

'Of course, yeah.' He took the drive, and wrapped the cable around it neatly. 'Are the pictures comin' on all right?'

'Yes. Fine.' It was a little abrupt, but Frank just grinned at him and turned towards the door.

'OK, OK,' he chuckled. 'I won't keep you back, not if there's a potential shag at stake . . .'

Nigel stared, feeling his cheeks beginning to burn.

Frank's grin grew cold.

' . . . I certainly wouldn't allow anyone to stop *me* getting laid.'

Nigel suppressed a shudder.

'I'll give you a call when the edits are done,' he said, moving into the hallway.

'Aye, you do that.'

Frank opened the door, but paused on the threshold.

'Have a good night.' He grinned, then turned and walked away along the landing.

Nigel pushed the door shut and leaned against it, listening to the echo of footsteps receding down the stairs.

Such a horrible, sick man.

The photographer's visit had woken a vast feeling of revulsion in him, and he bowed his head for a moment, drawing a deep breath . . . but that wasn't the problem, not really.

It was the loneliness.

He glanced down at his watch. It was getting late, but he had to see her.

40

The street was quiet tonight. He pulled the door gently shut behind him and walked swiftly down the path, eyes flicking left and right, but there was nobody out here just now. Tucking his carrier bag under one arm, he turned right, hurrying towards the shadow of the railway embankment, where he paused, listening.

Nothing.

Satisfied, he crossed over, and came back along the opposite side of the road. He made it as far as the turning without seeing anyone, and ducked into the shadows of the lane. Already, his mood was lifting, the prospect of seeing her face driving out the unsettling memory of Frank's presence. His beautiful girl. Hopefully she was feeling a little more calm this evening, more settled. He'd already decided to give her another dose of GHB, partly to settle her and give her a good night's rest, partly because he wanted to check on conditions inside the pit.

Entering the darkest part of the lane, he walked with a hand held up in front of his face, brushing aside the strands of spiderwebs that trailed down to head height from the overhanging branches. Ahead of him, he saw the padlock, bright against the dark wood of the door.

He paused before unlocking it, turning around to gaze back up the lane, where the warm glow of the street lights bathed the tarmac. Had he heard voices? A woman's laughter?

He watched, studying the shadows, but there was no movement. He was alone.

Turning his back on the lane, he fitted the key into the padlock and unfastened it. Then, opening the door just a little, he slipped inside. Somewhere in front of him, he could hear the radio, the mellow voice of a DJ reading out a romantic dedication. He wondered whether Laura would like having a piece of music dedicated to her . . . once things were better between them, of course. Perhaps she might even phone up with a dedication for him . . .

Smiling at that thought, he moved across to stand beside the car. Placing his bag on the floor, he squatted down to listen, but there was no sound.

Perhaps she was sleeping.

Rummaging in the bag, he took out a small bottle of orange juice. It was cold in his hand, and he touched it against the side of his face, enjoying the chill on his skin. There was nothing worse than tepid orange juice, but this was just right.

Moving across to the back wall of the garage, he placed the bottle on the scratched surface of the old workbench and unscrewed the plastic top. Reaching into his pocket, he took out the folded polythene bag containing the ampoules, holding it up for a moment, watching how the clear liquid danced in the light.

So much power in such a tiny amount of fluid.

He didn't want to make her ill, but he couldn't risk her making a break for it again. She would trust him one day, but he understood that would take time, and he was prepared to wait. Breaking the seal on one of the ampoules, he tipped the liquid into the orange juice, before sealing the bottle again and shaking it. This was how things had to be for now.

He made his way over to the centre of the garage, placing the bottle of orange juice on the floor, before rolling the car out of the way. Returning to the bag, he drew out his Fawkes mask and grudgingly pulled it on — another necessary evil that he couldn't wait to dispense with.

Finally, with everything ready, he bent forward to grasp the metal ring and began to slide the heavy metal cover aside.

She was in the near corner of the pit, straining to look up through watering eyes that blinked against the sudden flood of light. Her hair was tousled and messy, but that didn't matter — he had brought a brush and would attend to it for her if necessary. The smell wasn't too bad — she'd obviously managed to use the bucket despite the darkness — and he nodded encouragingly at her as he squatted down by the edge of the pit.

'I brought you something to drink,' he said, placing the small bottle of orange juice where she could see it. 'Take some of it now, then I'll show you what else I've brought for you.'

'What's in it?' she asked, her eyes still squinting slightly as they flickered between him and the bottle.

'Nothing bad,' he assured her. 'But I need to see you drink it, Laura.'

She licked her lips, eyes hunting around for a

moment, before reaching out to take the bottle.

'That's good,' he soothed her, but she froze, holding the bottle in her hand as she stared up at him.

'I'll keep it for later,' she croaked, retreating back a little from him.

'No.' His voice was gentle but firm, a tone that brooked no nonsense. 'Drink it now, or I'll have to put the cover back over.'

He started to reach for the edge of the metal, but her eyes widened.

'Wait.' She was already fumbling with the top of the bottle. 'Don't close it up, I'll drink. I'll drink.'

He saw the moment of hesitation as she got the bottle open, the way her gaze lifted to meet his, and then the sag in her shoulders as she resigned herself to doing as he'd asked. Raising the bottle to her lips, she closed her eyes and drank it down, swallowing quickly, draining it completely before taking a breath and looking up at him again.

'OK?' she gasped.

'Very good.' He smiled at her, genuinely pleased. 'Thank you, Laura.'

Her hands were trembling slightly, and the empty plastic bottle slipped from them to bounce on the hard floor at her feet.

'What was in it?' she asked, leaning back against the smooth concrete wall of the pit.

'Why do you think there was something in it?' he asked her.

'It tasted funny. Bitter.'

She was so beautiful. And she was nobody's fool.

'Just something to help you relax,' he said softly. 'I know how difficult this must be for you, and I just want to try and make things a little easier.'

She lifted one hand to her chest, a nervous, defensive gesture, but it also pulled the fabric of her top tighter to reveal the beautiful shape of her breasts. Nigel sighed and smiled. He was so fortunate to have a girl like her.

'What are you going to do?' she asked, drawing away from him slightly, pressing herself further back against the wall.

He eased himself down into a more comfortable position, sitting where he could study her, enjoying her beauty, imagining the day when she would smile at him and welcome him to her with a kiss.

'You're drugging me with something.' She spoke more urgently now. 'What are you going to do to me?'

'Do?' He looked at her, saddened by the implication. Had she still not grasped how he felt about her? 'I'm not going to *do* anything to you. I'm here to care for you, to look after you.'

He shook his head and sighed. Of course it was difficult for her to appreciate at the moment, but he'd gone to so much trouble, had put himself at such risk. He just wished she could see that.

'Oh.' She peered up at him, seeming to discern something in his words, then lowered her eyes. 'I thought . . . '

He leaned over, waiting for her to continue, but she seemed to be lost in thought. It was all right. There would be plenty of time to talk, to understand each other properly.

Reaching around behind him, he drew the plastic bag to where she could see it.

'Want to see what else I brought you?' he asked her, brightly.

She looked up at him, her face unreadable, then nodded slightly.

He rummaged in the bag, considering what to show her first, then decided and drew out the hairbrush.

'I thought you might like to have this,' he said. 'I appreciate it's not very nice being stuck in here, but there's no reason why you can't have some basic . . . you know . . . comforts.'

He trailed off, placing the brush at the edge of the pit, annoyed at himself for sounding so lame. But if she noticed his awkwardness, she didn't say anything. Moving forward, she reached up and took the brush.

'You want me to brush my hair?' she asked, warily.

'I just thought you might like to,' he replied. 'To stop it getting too tangled.'

She stared at him, then nodded slightly. Keeping her eyes on him, she slowly raised the brush and began to pull it through her hair.

He watched her, noting the momentary flickers of discomfort in her expression as she worked out the snags in her long blonde hair, seeing her movements become smoother and easier as her hair began to move more freely.

She glanced up at him briefly, then lowered her eyes again.

'Thanks,' she said softly.

Thanks!

His heart leaped. Just a tiny glimmer, a promise of things to come, but she had glimpsed the kindness, the *care*, in his actions. He found himself grinning foolishly.

She had almost finished brushing her hair when he became aware of her movements slowing a little. She continued for a moment, then paused, swaying slightly as she raised her head to look at him.

'I . . . ' she began, then frowned to herself and resumed her brushing. Her hands seemed less coordinated and she soon slowed to a standstill.

'Something's not . . . ' She tried to look up at him but clearly had difficulty focusing. One hand snaked out along the wall to steady herself.

'It's all right,' he reassured her. 'Why don't you sit down for a moment?'

She nodded slowly, then slumped against the wall and slid down into a sitting position. All the fear and tension seemed to melt away from her, and she settled on the floor of the pit with her limbs splayed and a vacant expression on her face.

He sighed as he watched her muscles loosen, the pout of her lower lip as her mouth fell open, and the slow rise and fall of her chest as her breathing relaxed. Such a rare gift, and one that he would nurture and treasure. Until she loved him. And happily ever after.

'Relax now, Laura,' he whispered to her. 'Just relax.'

He gazed down at her for a few moments longer, smiling at his prize, before sitting up and loosening his shoulders a little. He'd need to empty her bucket and make sure she had enough water, but that wouldn't take too long. Then he might just sit with her for a while, maybe speak softly to her. He wondered whether it would be easier to explain his feelings while she was sedated, and whether her subconscious mind might take some of it in. He hoped that would be the case.

Smiling, he started to get to his feet, but a scuffing noise behind him made him stiffen. He tried to turn, but suddenly the sound became an explosion of pain in the back of his head and the world blinked out.

⋆ ⋆ ⋆

It was like waking up, only different. He became aware of himself lying on the floor, and his head felt . . . strange. He wasn't sure how long he lay there before a wave of pain washed over him, radiating out from the back of his skull, making him stiffen and gasp.

His thoughts wouldn't connect with his limbs, and his mind was sluggish, but then there was a sound. A scuffing sound, like footsteps, very close. It was a struggle to open his eyes and they took a moment to focus, but he saw something move in front of him. Everything was at a confusing angle and he tried to sit up and right himself, but his arms seemed unable to pull his hands around from behind his back.

The moving shapes resolved themselves into a pair of shoes, and a familiar voice far above him said, 'Wakey wakey.'

He struggled to look up, managing to make his arms work, but something bit into his wrists and he groggily realised that his hands were tied. Craning his neck, he managed to roll his body over a little and stare up at the figure towering over him.

'Careful now,' Frank told him, squatting down onto his haunches. 'Take it nice and slow.'

Nigel blinked at him in confusion, unable to think for a moment, until another wave of pain at the back of his head took his attention.

'What happened?' he asked, as the discomfort subsided.

'I think you banged your head,' Frank mused. Something about the way he spoke was odd, but Nigel's eyes glanced beyond him, seeing his discarded Fawkes mask, the partly uncovered inspection pit, remembering what he'd been doing . . .

Shit!

He stared quickly up at Frank, who nodded slowly.

'Yes,' he said slowly. 'I was very surprised with what you keep in your garage . . . '

Had Frank seen her? Was she even still in there? If he could only think . . .

'What do you mean?' He did his best not to give anything away.

Frank leaned a little closer, jabbing one thumb back over his shoulder.

'Your little girlfriend in the hole there.'

Nigel sagged, at a loss as what to say.

'Yeah,' Frank sighed, gravely. 'You told me you

were going to see your girlfriend, but I was still sitting in my car when you came out with your little bag, all suspicious and secretive. And when I saw you scurrying down this dead-end lane, I was curious and I thought I'd see what you were up to.'

He shook his head and tutted softly to himself.

'Dear dear, Nigel. What the bloody hell is going on here?'

He seemed so calm. Nigel stared up at the looming figure, desperately trying to read Frank's expression. What could he say to stop him from releasing Laura, going to the police, ruining everything?

'Please,' he begged. 'It's not what you think. She really *is* my girlfriend, it's just that . . . '

How could he explain his feelings, feelings so strong he could barely understand them himself? How could he make Frank see how much he cared for Laura, how deeply he loved her?

'The girl the police have been looking for . . . ' Frank said quietly. 'And you've had her tucked away in here the whole time.'

'Oh please, Frank . . . ' Nigel struggled to sit up again, but couldn't move with his hands bound. 'I love her — we love each other. Don't tell the police.'

Frank had been leaning forward. Now, he rolled back a little onto his heels, where he remained for a moment, staring at Nigel, his face thoughtful.

Surely he would understand . . . he *had* to.

Frank looked at the floor and shook his head. For a terrifying moment, Nigel thought he was going to report him, but when Frank glanced up at him there was the faintest of smiles.

'I was *this* close to turning you in,' he said gravely, pinching his thumb and forefinger together. 'But I won't call the police on you . . . '

Nigel's shoulders sagged in relief.

'Thank you, Frank,' he breathed. 'I promise you it's — '

'I *won't* call the police,' Frank interrupted him, 'because I am going to *fuck* your little girlfriend.'

Nigel's stomach lurched.

'What?' he croaked.

'You heard me.' Frank leaned in closer, his voice an oily whisper. 'I'm going to use her until I'm sore. And you're going to watch.'

'No! NO!'

But Frank was already standing up, moving over towards the inspection pit. Nigel struggled helplessly, thrashing his legs on the floor, unable to get his arms free.

'Don't touch her,' he screamed. 'You mustn't touch her!'

Frank turned around, his expression betraying irritation at the noise. Snatching up an old oil rag from the floor, he strode back to Nigel and bent over him.

'Open,' he commanded, pushing the rag towards Nigel's mouth.

'No!' Nigel twisted his head left and right, begging through gritted teeth, 'Leave her alone!'

Frank scowled at him, then snarled and stamped down hard on his instep.

Searing white pain stabbed up Nigel's leg and

he started to shriek but the rag was suddenly jammed into his mouth, making him gag as tears filled his eyes and he sucked in a polluted, choking breath.

'Better,' Frank said, nodding.

The agony in his leg was overwhelming, worse than the pain in his head, but it was the terror of not being able to breathe that distressed Nigel most. He tried to spit the rag out, desperately probing it with his tongue as he opened his teeth as far as he could, but that almost made him vomit — something that would certainly be fatal with his mouth blocked — and he ended up slumping faintly to the floor, gasping and sobbing, until his breathing settled a little.

'Stop your crying . . . ' The photographer's voice had a mocking tone to it. ' . . . or I'll give you something to cry about.'

Nigel struggled to roll over, craning his neck until he could see what was going on. Frank had moved back to the middle of the garage and was kneeling down beside the inspection pit, his head tilted over to one side. After a moment, he turned to Nigel.

'What are you drugging her with?' He spoke casually, as though it were a matter-of-fact situation. 'Roofies? GHB?'

Nigel's head felt heavy and he bowed it towards the floor.

He heard Frank getting up, coming back over, then there was a painful jerk as the photographer lifted his head by the hair.

'I *said*, have you given her roofies or GHB or something like that?' he hissed.

Blinking the tears from his eyes, Nigel struggled to reply, then managed to nod slightly.

'That's a pity.' Frank let go of his head and he rolled onto his side. 'I want her wide awake for what I'm going to do to her.'

His smile was unbearable, and Nigel howled at him through the gag, rocking violently as he tried to get to his feet.

'Oh, for fuck's sake,' Frank growled, standing up and aiming a vicious kick. His shoe swung down and connected with Nigel's jaw, blinding him with agony as his world winked out in a roar of pure pain.

* * *

He couldn't guess how much time had passed. He was moving. His T-shirt was riding up, and his back was being grazed, along with the back of his head, as he was dragged across the concrete floor. But it was the glaring white pain in his temples that magnified every bump and vibration into a nightmare of agony. He tried to scream, but his mouth wouldn't work properly, and a new panic gripped him as he felt his jaw moving in a way that he knew it couldn't. He could taste the blood now, reflexively swallowing it down before it clogged the rag and choked him. His feet had been raised, but they suddenly dropped to the ground as he stopped moving.

Something appeared against the dim blur of the ceiling above him, a face that might have been smiling.

'Bloody hell, pal.' Frank's voice drifted down

to him. 'If I *was* gonna let you live, you'd need some serious medical attention — there's something very wrong with your mouth.'

He chuckled, moving round to kneel in close at Nigel's side.

'But for now, I'll let you and Laura get some rest. That poor girl's gonna need *all* her strength.'

Nigel felt himself being rolled onto his side. Pain flared up from his jaw, and he didn't realise what was happening until he felt the edge of the concrete floor and then the sickening sensation of falling into the darkness.

PRESENT

41

Standing outside the interview room, Harland leaned back against the wall, and cast another sidelong glance down the corridor. He'd been early this morning, but it looked as though everyone else was running late. Bowing his head, he tapped the heel of his shoe against the skirting board.

They'd spent hours with Matt yesterday, patiently working their way through a long list of questions, building a detailed timeline for his movements. Today, unless Pearce had turned up anything new, they'd be asking the same questions again, looking for the slightest variation or inconsistency in Matt's answers. It was police work by attrition — the last refuge of an investigation with insufficient evidence. And time was against them in every sense.

Pearce appeared at the far end of the corridor and strode purposefully towards him.

'Morning, Graham.' He raised his hand briefly in greeting. 'Sorry I'm late — phone calls from those-who-must-not-be-ignored.'

Harland smiled. The chief inspector was always under pressure, but seemed to thrive on it.

'No worries, sir.' He pushed himself away from the wall and stood up straight. 'Matt's lawyer was delayed too, so we've not lost anything.'

'What do you call a hundred lawyers at the

bottom of the sea?' Pearce asked.

'A good start,' Harland smiled, giving the usual reply.

Pearce flashed him a brief grin, then glanced at his watch and frowned.

'We're gonna have to push him for something today,' he mused. 'I'll get him rattled early on, then we'll see if he's any more talkative.'

'OK . . . ' Harland waited for him to elaborate, but was met by an uncomfortable silence. 'Was there anything in particular that you wanted to focus on?'

Pearce shook his head.

'I don't care what it is,' he muttered. 'We just need one slip-up, one mistake. Something that we can use to hold him. Otherwise . . . '

Harland nodded. It was exactly as he'd thought.

'How long have we got?'

'Not long.' Pearce's expression was grim. 'The folk upstairs are getting nervous — can't afford another media circus at the moment. They're talking about cutting him loose this afternoon if we can't pull him up on anything.'

'No pressure, then,' Harland sighed.

Pearce gave him a bleak smile.

'Just another lazy day at Avon and Somerset.'

They stood in silence for a moment. Harland frowned to himself. He couldn't shake the feeling that Matt was innocent, but the mood around headquarters was eager for answers, not questions. Unless he had a better suspect to put forward, he knew his best bet was to keep his ears open and his mouth shut.

The doors at the end of the corridor swung open to reveal three figures. Flanked by a uniformed officer, Matt was wearing the clothes he'd been picked up in yesterday. His hair was untidier than usual and there were dark circles under his eyes — obviously a night in the cells had shaken him up a little.

Good.

Behind Matt, looking relaxed and perhaps even a tiny bit bored, came Enderby, a portly man in his late fifties, with thinning silver hair and rimless glasses. He wore a good suit and his shoes were mirror black. Tapping his client on the shoulder to slow him, he passed in front of Matt to come and greet Pearce.

'Chief Inspector,' he smiled, extending a hand. 'Sorry we're late — entirely my fault. Traffic.'

'You're not responsible for traffic,' Pearce replied, ignoring the offered hand.

'Quite so,' Enderby smiled. 'Shall we go in?'

'We wouldn't dream of starting without you.' Pearce's expression remained bleak as he gestured towards the door.

* * *

The interview rooms were deliberately bland, with blue-grey walls and a patterned vinyl floor — the sort that would hide scuff-marks from shoes and chair legs. The single table was small, and set to one side — leaving little room for legal representatives to spread out comfortably, and forcing their clients to sit in the open, with no barrier to hide their body language behind.

Enderby took his seat and placed a file folder and a notebook on the table, while Matt stared at the floor.

'Morning, Matt!' Pearce's voice was unnaturally bright and cheerful, as he dropped into the chair opposite. 'Sleep well, did you?'

Matt's head snapped up and he scowled angrily, but the warning hand of Enderby on his arm stopped him from saying anything.

'I'd really rather you *didn't* try to annoy my client, Chief Inspector.' The old lawyer sighed. 'He hasn't done anything wrong.'

'Must be nice to be so certain of things,' Pearce mused. 'But me? I'm not so sure.'

Enderby smiled kindly, as though patiently tolerating an unruly child.

'We spent yesterday — almost *all* of yesterday — in this room, fully cooperating with your investigation,' he reminded them. 'I just hope this isn't your only line of enquiry, for everyone's sake.'

As he spoke, Harland noticed Matt relax a little — his shoulders dropping and a faint smile touching his lips. That wasn't good — if he *was* hiding anything, they needed him to be on edge, not gaining in confidence.

Pearce seemed to have picked up on it too, sitting up straight and scraping his chair forward a little.

'Let's get started, then.'

He looked at Harland, who reached over and started the recorder, pressing the red button with a loud click.

'Interview resumed at 09.20 — present in the

room, DCI Raymond Pearce, DI Graham Harland, Matt Garrick plus legal representative Paul Enderby.'

He looked at Pearce, who turned to face Matt.

'I want to go back to last Friday,' he began.

Matt rolled his eyes.

'We've been *over* all this . . . ' His complaint faltered as Enderby nudged him.

Pearce gave him a brisk little smile to show he'd noticed.

'Last Friday, you'd been at work all afternoon, is that correct?'

Matt stared at him, sullen, until prompted by a nod from his lawyer.

'Yeah.'

'And after work, you walked home, via Kingsley Road, arriving some time around six o'clock?'

'Yeah.'

Pearce regarded him thoughtfully.

'You got home around six, and stayed in all evening, not leaving the flat until late on Saturday morning.'

'Yeah!' Matt gave him an exasperated look. 'I've told you all this.'

Ignoring the outburst, Pearce sat back in his chair, and rubbed his chin.

'So you spent Friday evening, all alone, in your flat. And you *never* opened your door . . . '

Matt frowned, trying to discern what he was driving at, but Pearce wasn't giving anything away.

'You never went out. And nobody came to see you. Right?'

'That's right.' Matt looked wary now.

Pearce gave him a smile, but there was nothing friendly or reassuring about it.

'What about the previous Friday?' he asked.

'What?' Matt and Enderby exchanged glances.

'Did you stay in all evening, Friday before last?' Pearce asked again.

'I don't think so. I think I went — '

Pearce interrupted him. 'How about the Friday before that?'

Perplexed, Matt turned to his lawyer. Enderby shifted in his seat, then regarded Pearce with a look of reproach.

'If there's something you're trying to ask my client . . . ' He left the statement hanging.

'I'm asking how often Matt stays tucked up at home on a Friday night,' Pearce told him.

'I fail to see why you'd concern yourself with that,' Enderby said, frowning.

Pearce shrugged.

'I suppose it depends what your client was doing.' He turned and fixed his gaze on Matt. 'Chilling out with a beer? Smoking some blow?'

'No.' Matt shook his head.

'No, you don't drink? Or no, you don't smoke cannabis?' Pearce asked pleasantly.

Enderby placed a warning hand on Matt's arm.

'Don't answer that,' he murmured.

Pearce leaned forward, holding Matt's gaze.

'What do you keep in that little tin?' he smiled. 'Behind the pile of DVDs in the front room?'

Matt's shoulders tensed, and he looked away, angry.

Enderby glanced at him, his face betraying a flicker of weary contempt, then turned to look at Pearce.

'I was under the impression we were concerned about a missing woman,' he said. 'Are you now abandoning that enquiry to pursue a possible minor infraction of the Controlled Substances Act?'

'Who said anything about minor?' Pearce countered.

Enderby turned towards Matt, who suddenly looked a lot less sure of himself, then sighed.

'I'd like a moment to confer with my client,' he said, casting a meaningful look towards the recorder.

Harland felt a strong urge to punch him, but refrained. Reaching across, he placed a finger on the red button.

'Interview suspended at 09.37.'

There was a click as the recorder stopped.

He scraped his chair back and got to his feet, turning towards the door. Standing beside him, Pearce gripped the door handle, then paused and waited for Matt to look up. Then he winked at him, and strode out of the room without another word. Harland frowned and followed him into the corridor.

42

Imogen sat at her desk and yawned. Harland was off with Pearce again, downstairs in the interview suite. She wondered how they were working Matt — who was good cop and who was bad? Harland wouldn't be the angry one, she decided. He was too careful, too self-aware, to play that role. She didn't know what kind of demons he kept caged inside, but she sensed that he couldn't afford to lose his temper, lose control, even if it was only done as an act.

And anyway, he didn't think Matt was their man.

They'd had him down there in the small room for much of yesterday, but Harland had looked even less convinced when she asked him how it was going this morning.

'Says he didn't do it.' He shrugged. 'Says he doesn't know anything about it.'

'And you believe him? she'd asked.

But Harland hadn't answered, just turned and walked away.

So now she sat, and stared at her screen and wondered. Leaning forward, she put her hand on the mouse and clicked to open an internet browser. She'd meant to look up the local papers, perhaps do a speculative search on Laura's school, but as she started to type, a list of previously visited websites appeared below the address bar. Absently, she selected the one at the bottom of the list, watching as the screen cleared to display one of Frank's portfolio websites. She was halfway through the gallery of photos when she stopped, and found herself tapping the cursor keys, idly scrolling through page after page of unseen images.

Frank was a pervert — there was no doubt about that. Though she could see that the pictures were technically well taken, there seemed to be an unpleasant undertone running through all of his work.

She clicked to view another page of thumbnails.

It was as though he wanted to portray women in a particularly vulnerable way, regardless of their pose or state of undress. She could feel the discomfort of the models, sense the revulsion behind their pouting expressions.

And then she paused, leaning forward to peer at the screen. Her hand moved the mouse, clicking to magnify the thumbnail image, and she stared at the picture until her eyes felt dry and she realised that she had stopped blinking.

It couldn't be . . .

She pushed her chair back and got to her feet. Then, her expression tightening into a serious frown, she headed for the stairs.

* * *

The interview suites were at the end of a short, white corridor — featureless apart from a couple of stacking plastic chairs. A uniformed officer that she vaguely recognised was sitting there waiting, and looked up as she approached.

'Ma'am.'

'Is DI Harland in there?' She pointed to the door beside him.

The officer sat up.

'Yes, with DCI Pearce.'

'Do you know how long they're going be?' she asked.

'Not sure,' he replied. 'They've just gone back in. You want me to knock for you?'

Imogen hesitated, then shook her head.

'No, it's OK. Just let DI Harland know that DS Gower was looking for him.'

'Will do, ma'am.'

She turned and made her way back towards the stairwell.

It was just a suspicion at this stage. She wanted to be sure.

* * *

She found a place to park on the wrong side of Filton Avenue, and pulled in beside a metal security fence at the end of a parade of small shops. Switching off the engine, she allowed the silence to surround her as she gazed out at the street. Above her, a telegraph pole jutted up, holding a taut spiderweb of dark wires against the grey sky. Her eye followed one of the wires across the road — a thin black line connecting the bare pole with the brown pebbledash house on the other side . . .

What would she say? She needed a plausible excuse for why she'd come back here, something that would help her decide whether she was right or not . . .

And then there was Harland.

She took her phone out and looked at the screen. No missed calls. Would she be making a mistake by calling him? Or by not calling him? He *seemed* to be on her side, but she'd been caught out before . . .

After a moment, she decided it was better to include him and dialled the number, but it went straight to answerphone. She listened to the recorded greeting, unsure what she was going to say, then heard the tone.

'Hi, it's me. I guess you must still be in with Matt . . . ' She hated speaking to a machine, even when she knew what she wanted to say. Now she floundered, not sure how to explain her idea without making a fool of herself. 'Anyway, there was just something I wanted to check up on with Frank Guthrie. I . . . I'll be back in a while.'

She ended the call and sat, shaking her head.

Smooth, Imogen. Really smooth.

But it was done now, and she was here. Taking a deep breath to compose herself, she got out of the car and locked it. Then, waiting for a blue van to pass, she walked across the road. Now that she knew him, Frank's house seemed even more unpleasant — the dirty roof, the desolate front garden, the peeling paint on the window frames. As she approached the door, she found herself hoping he wouldn't be in. Perhaps he was at work, in one of those sleazy studios. Anywhere but here.

She rang the bell and stood back, waiting, listening. At first, there was nothing — no sound, no movement — and she felt her hopes rising. But then she heard an indistinct voice from within and, a moment later, Frank opened the door.

Wearing blue jeans and a black sweatshirt, he seemed momentarily startled to see her, but his expression quickly settled into a wary smile.

'All right, darlin',' he said, softly. 'You can't keep away, can you?'

Imogen stared at him, determined to maintain her neutral expression, not allowing her distaste to break through. Frank's smile remained fixed, but his eyes were uneasy.

'So? What are you after?' he asked.

'We just wanted to get a bit more background on Laura, if that's OK?' She did her best to sound calm, even a little indifferent. Frank seemed to relax a little.

'Aye, if it doesn't take too long. I've got to go out in a while.' He leaned to one side, looking past her. 'Where's your boss? Did he get a better offer?'

Imogen flashed him her bleakest smile.

'DI Harland is interviewing a witness at the moment,' she replied. 'You'll have to make do with me.'

Frank chuckled, stepping back and opening the door wider.

'Ah, you'll do, darlin', you'll do. Come on in.'

Imogen suppressed a shudder and followed him inside.

* * *

He ushered her through to the front room, watching her more closely than was comfortable.

'Make yourself at home,' he said, gesturing towards the same leather sofa she'd occupied on her last visit. 'You want a coffee or anything?'

Imogen shook her head.

'No thanks,' she told him. The thought of drinking from one of his cups was enough to turn her stomach. 'I'm fine.'

'Sure?' Frank hovered in the doorway for a moment, then shrugged and sat down opposite her. 'Well, if you're here, I'm guessing you haven't found Laura yet.'

There was an unpleasant twinkle in his eye.

'No,' she admitted. 'Not yet.'

'So what are you after now?'

Imogen drew herself up, trying to make her voice sound official.

'Well, as part of our investigation, we're looking a little farther back . . . '

She trailed off, unsure how to proceed. Frank frowned at her.

'Sorry, darlin', I don't follow . . . '

She tried again.

'It would be a big help if you could give us details of your previous meetings with Laura,' she explained. 'Dates, times, that sort of thing . . . '

Frank sat back into his chair, and slowly shook his head.

'It's been a while,' he told her. 'How's anybody supposed to remember stuff like that?'

And that was the opening she needed.

'I thought maybe your photos would tell us?' She did her best to give him an encouraging smile. 'Aren't the files all stamped with the date and time that each picture was taken?'

Frank gazed at her for a moment, then shrugged.

'If you say so, but I'm not up on all that tech stuff,' he muttered. 'I wouldn't know how to find the dates and times.'

'It's quite simple,' she told him. 'I can show you how to do it if you like?'

Frank scowled, and glanced at his watch.

'Will it take long?' He seemed impatient but not particularly nervous. 'I'm wanting to go out soon . . . '

'Not long,' she assured him.

Sighing, Frank got to his feet.

'Let me go and grab my laptop, then,' he frowned.

Imogen watched him slouch out of the room, then forced herself to relax her shoulders. So far, so good, though she was feeling a lot less sure of her idea now . . .

. . . and that was all it was — an idea, a notion. What was she thinking of, coming all the way out here on a whim?

And on her own.

She bowed her head, annoyed with herself. It couldn't be helped. She was here now, so she might as well just do what she'd come to do, then get out.

She could hear Frank moving around upstairs. Did the same awful eighties decor run through the rest of the house? She shuddered as she imagined what his bedroom might be like.

Stop it! Stay focused.

Raising her head, she sat up straight as her eyes swept around the room. There was a blue sports holdall tucked in at the side of the chair where Frank had been sitting. It looked odd there, and she wondered what was in it, even considered reaching forward and taking a look, but then she heard him coming back down the stairs. As his footsteps approached, she shuffled herself to the centre of the sofa, so he wouldn't be able to sit next to her.

Frank appeared in the doorway.

Laptop in hand, he moved around to her side of the coffee table, paused, then settled for perching on the arm of the sofa.

'Just hang on a wee minute while I get it started . . . ' He tapped in his password, then frowned, balancing the computer on his knee as he dragged a finger over the trackpad. ' . . . ah yeah, here we are.'

He clicked and opened a folder, then turned the screen a little so she could see better.

'Is this the first set you did of Laura?' Imogen asked.

'Aye, this is the test shoot she did back in . . . ' He shook his head. 'Whenever the hell it was.'

'Do the image files not have dates on them?'

Frank pulled a weary hand across his eyes to rub them.

'I don't know,' he scowled at her. 'How would I find that on here?'

'You just . . . ' Imogen began to point at the

screen, then paused, glancing up at Frank with what she hoped was an innocent expression. 'Do you want me to do it for you?'

She held her breath, trying not to look too eager. He wouldn't really let her loose on his computer, would he?

But the old photographer appeared unconcerned.

'Aye, on you go,' he sighed, handing the laptop down to her. 'But mind you don't delete any of my files. I almost lost a load of stuff the other day.'

He leaned across, peering down over her shoulder to see what she was doing . . . or was he trying to see down the front of her top? Imogen felt her skin begin to crawl, but she had come this far.

'Don't worry,' she told him. 'I won't disturb anything.'

Clicking on one of the icons, she adjusted the folder view so that it displayed a time and date next to each filename, then studied the details.

'Yes, there we go . . . ' She tapped the screen. 'Your first shoot was on the tenth of March, around eight in the morning.'

Frank sat back, and appeared to mull this over.

'Aye,' he said after a moment. 'That sounds right enough.'

'Good.' Imogen casually moved the pointer and clicked so that the folder now showed a larger thumbnail preview of each picture, her eyes sweeping across them, searching. 'Are the other shots of Laura in another folder?'

Frank was glancing at his watch again.

'Aye. If you go up one, you'll see them numbered one, two, three . . . '

'I understand.' She clicked once, then twice, going up two folders rather than one. 'Sorry, I think I went too far . . . '

Her eyes were scanning the list of folders on the screen, each one a different girl's name — *Abby, Emma, Gina, Holly, Julie* . . .

But there was no sign of the names she was looking for. Perhaps she was mistaken after all.

Frowning, she moved the pointer back over the one labelled *Laura* and clicked to open it. There were several sub-folders inside it and she selected the number *Two*. The screen cleared, then filled with a new series of images.

'When were these taken?' she asked, slowly scrolling the pictures up the screen.

'About four weeks ago maybe?' Frank shifted on the arm of the sofa. 'I don't know, can't you see the date thing?'

'Of course, yes . . . '

Moving the pointer, she clicked on one photograph in particular, bringing up its details. She glanced at the date, but it was the image preview that caught her attention. Leaning forward, she stared at the picture, her mouth suddenly dry.

She hadn't imagined it.

'Well?'

Frank's voice made her jump and she turned to stare up at him, his red face looming large over her, the bushy moustache horribly close. For a moment, she didn't understand what he was asking her, but then she gathered her wits.

'You're quite right,' she stammered. 'About four weeks ago. Yes.'

She had to get out. Right now.

Pulling the screen towards her, she closed the laptop.

'Here you are.' She thrust it into his hands and began getting awkwardly to her feet. 'Thanks. You've been a big help.'

Frank stood up as well, looking puzzled as he moved around the coffee table.

'That's it?' he asked her, placing the laptop down on the arm of the chair opposite. 'That's all you came for?'

'For now, yes.'

Frank was taller than her. She felt fairly sure she could put him down if she had to, but this cramped room wasn't a good place to be, and he was standing between her and the door. Why on earth had she let this happen, put herself in such a vulnerable position?

He was staring at her.

'What's the matter, darlin'? You look like someone pissed on your chips . . . '

Imogen swallowed.

Shit! Could he read it in her face?

'It's nothing,' she said quickly. 'I just remembered something I had to do . . . '

Frank was peering at her, studying her.

'What are you not telling me?'

'Nothing.'

He stood up straight, putting a hand on the door frame. *Did he mean to block her exit?*

She tensed her muscles, trying to drive the

lethargy out of her legs and shoulders, getting ready.

Mustn't move first. Let him come forward, then grab his arm and twist him round, make his momentum work against him . . .

Frank wasn't smiling now.

'Why did you *really* come here?' he pressed.

This was it. Heightened senses, aware of everything, the distance between them, the amount of space behind her, making sure her feet were planted firmly, ready . . .

And then a shrill little tone cut across the awful silence.

Frank raised an eyebrow, as Imogen's hand went instinctively to her pocket.

'Sorry.' She took the opportunity to step back, just enough to subtly lessen the feeling that he was already on top of her. The ringtone swelled to fill the room as she drew out her phone, something mundane to break the tension. 'Just . . . one moment.'

She raised the phone to her ear, her eyes still locked on Frank. 'DS Gower . . . '

'Hi.' Harland's voice sounded very far away. 'You left a message on my voicemail while I was — '

'Yes,' she interrupted him. 'I'm with Mr Guthrie now.'

'What are you doing with him? I thought — '

'Thank you, sir.' Talking over him again.

'Imogen . . . ' He paused. ' . . . is everything all right?'

'No,' she smiled, as though discussing something trivial. 'I don't think so.'

'You're with Frank Guthrie?' There was urgency in Harland's tone now. 'At his house?'

'That's right. I'll be back in twenty minutes.' She hoped that wasn't tempting fate.

'Are you OK?' Harland asked. 'You want me to get some uniforms over to you?'

Frank's posture had slackened a little. He moved out of the doorway and eased himself down to perch on the arm of the sofa, though his gaze remained suspicious.

'It's OK,' Imogen breathed. 'We can sort that out when I see you.'

'Can you get out of there?'

'I think so, yes.'

'OK, walk out now, then call me from the car,' Harland insisted. 'If I don't hear from you in five minutes . . . '

'Thank you, sir.'

She ended the call, and slowly put the phone back into her pocket.

'That was your boss?' Frank asked her.

'Yes.' She stepped around the coffee table. 'I'm sorry, but I have to go. They need me back at CID.'

Frank gave her a long look, then gestured towards the doorway.

In the hallway, as her fingers gripped the deadlock and twisted it, he spoke again, his voice close behind her.

'Detective . . . *Gower*, yes?'

'That's right.' She turned to face him. 'Why?'

'Have we met before?' he asked. 'Before all this, I mean?'

'No,' she told him. 'No, I'd remember.'

Frank stared at her, a strange expression on his face.

'Yeah,' he said thoughtfully, 'I reckon you might . . . '

* * *

Her pulse was racing as she made the slow walk to the gate. She could feel his eyes on her, his cold gaze burning into the back of her head. It had been a stupid move, coming here on her own. Anything might have happened. But at least now she was sure.

She pulled the gate shut behind her, keeping her eyes down. Then she heard the bang of the front door slamming and looked up. It was closed — he'd gone back inside.

She breathed a quiet sigh of relief.

It seemed an eternity before there was a break in the traffic, and she hurried across to where she'd parked. Getting in, she locked all the doors then sank down into her seat.

Just take a moment, get it together.

She sat there, waiting until her breathing was under control. Then she took out her phone and dialled Harland's number.

43

When he opened his eyes, he couldn't see. Whimpering, he tried to move, but his body tightened with a vast, dull ache that threatened to overwhelm him. Collapsing onto his back, he gasped and stared up, wide eyed, into nothing.

Why couldn't he see?

And then there was the faintest sound — something moving, just beside him — and he stiffened, despite the sudden pains that shot up through his shoulder and hip. Trying to turn his head towards the noise, he almost blacked out from the surging agony in his jaw, but there was something there — a dim glow that drew his eye. Struggling to focus, he just managed to make out a silhouette, lit from behind, then squeezed his eyes shut as the light swung round towards him, bursting into a terrible, blinding flare.

He tried to curl up, tucking himself into a protective foetal ball against the blows he felt sure would follow. But as he sensed more movement, and saw the change of the light through his eyelids, there was no attack, just a sharp intake of breath.

'Hello?' Her voice drifted down to him, calling him back from the edge of terror. 'Are you OK? Who are you?'

She spoke softly, as though she was worried about being overheard. Something in her tone confused him, but he was too groggy to question why. A shadow passed over his face, and he felt something brush against his lips, then there was an awful moment of panic and pain as a sodden rag was drawn from his mouth. His whole body stiffened, spine arching up off the cold floor as a gurgling howl escaped him, before he collapsed in breathless exhaustion.

For a time, he could only lie there, trembling, then he became aware of the light moving away, and forced his eyes to open just a little.

It was Laura. She was bending over him, her long hair hanging down to veil her face in shadow, but it was definitely her. Catching the note of concern in her voice, he stared up at her, blinking stupidly.

'Thank God,' she murmured. 'I was worried you might . . . '

Her silhouette seemed to stiffen a little, and he watched her raise a cautious hand to the side of her head.

'Ow . . . ' she moaned, shoulders sagging, bowing her head as though it had become heavy. 'Sorry, but I don't feel quite . . . '

For a moment, he was afraid for her, wishing he could do something to help. Then he caught hold of a hazy memory — the orange juice he'd forced her to drink. Poor thing. She must be groggy, but she'd be all right in a while. His thoughts were confused, and he suddenly wondered why she wasn't angry with him. It was dark, but she'd shone the light on his face. Did she really not know who he was?

He struggled to sit up, faltering as the movement jarred his jaw and sent pains shooting up into his skull, making him whimper again.

Laura's head lifted, and she moved closer to him, despite her own obvious discomfort.

'Hey.' She placed a hand on his shoulder. 'I think you should lie still for a bit — you look as if he hurt you pretty badly.'

She eased him down into a more comfortable position, and he thought he glimpsed a weary smile of encouragement from her in the dim light, before she flopped down beside him with a groan.

'I'm Laura, by the way.' Her voice was soft, and he could feel her breath, warm on the side of his face. 'Just take it easy . . . '

Her kindness appalled him. He didn't deserve this, it wasn't right . . .

The mask! That was why she hadn't recognised him. Struggling, he fought to sit up, turning his face towards her through the waves of pain. He had to tell her, *had* to . . .

But as he tried to speak, his jaw shifted sideways, firing a cascade of blinding agony up and over his head. He cried out like an animal, and she was there, with a hand on his arm.

'Shhh . . . ' He could feel the sadness in her voice. 'Please, don't try to talk. I . . . I think your jaw's broken.'

Her movements were sluggish, as though it was an effort for her, but she wriggled closer to him and he felt her hand, hesitant at first, then gently rubbing him on the shoulder.

'It's OK . . . '

She was stroking his hair now, and it was finally too much for him. A dreadful shiver racked his body as the tears came at last, and he began sobbing uncontrollably into the darkness.

'Don't give up.' She was pulling him to her, cradling him gently now. 'We'll get out of here.'

He knew it was wrong, that he had no right to accept her comfort, but there was nothing else left for him. Surrendering, he allowed himself to lean back on her, letting go of his fear, letting go of his past, his pain. Then, closing his eyes, he welcomed her embrace, losing himself in the warmth that spread out through him from her touch.

44

Even over the phone, Harland could hear how erratic her breathing was, knew that she was struggling to get the words out.

'Sorry, Imogen.' He turned away from the window and pressed the handset to his ear. 'Say that again?'

'Remember I told you?' she repeated. 'About the murders in Gloucester and Swindon? How all the victims were bound?'

Harland lifted a hand to rub the back of his neck, trying to recall the details.

'Something about a particular type of knot?' he hazarded.

'Very particular, yes.' She took a breath that was loud enough for him to hear. 'Frank has photos of women tied in exactly the same way.'

Harland frowned to himself. *Was that it? Was that all she had?*

'OK,' he said slowly. 'But just because someone ties a similar knot, it doesn't mean — '

'NO!' Her voice rose to a shout, making the handset crackle before she got control of herself again. 'Not similar. I mean *exactly* the same. Honestly, it's *far* too intricate to be a coincidence.'

She sounded all over the place, almost as though she was in shock, and that worried him more than anything else; Imogen was too good, too smart, to spook easily.

'Where are you now?' he asked.

'Parked on Filton Avenue.'

'Outside Frank's?'

'Close enough,' she replied. 'I can see the front door in my mirror.'

'All right . . . ' He rubbed his eyes. Pearce would be expecting him back downstairs soon, but Imogen sounded so sure . . . and they were meant to be partners, weren't they? 'Stay where you are and watch the house. I'll get some uniforms over to you now, then let Burgess know.'

'OK.' She sounded as though she was keeping it together. Just.

'And you *call* me if he comes out,' Harland warned her. 'Do *not* try anything on your own, OK?'

'Right.'

Was she really listening to him?

'Detective Sergeant Gower?' Going formal on her made him feel bad, but he had to snap her out of this, had to make sure she understood.

'Sir?'

'Are we clear on that?'

'Yes, sir.'

He took a breath, shaking his head. Pearce wouldn't like it, but what else could he do?

'Imogen?'

'What?' The change in his tone seemed to throw her for a moment.

'Are *you* all right?' he asked.

'Uh . . . yeah. Yeah, I'm fine.'

'Good.' He picked up his jacket and paced towards the door. 'Just sit tight, OK?'

'Yes. Thanks, sir.'
'I'm on my way.'

* * *

The tyres squealed in protest as he flung the car round the roundabout and raced under the motorway bridge. A small blue Fiat was taking the same exit as him, but he managed to power past it, swerving back to his own side of the road as the driver beeped in protest. At another time, that might have annoyed him, but not now.

He glanced down at the dashboard clock. There was still no word from Burgess — he'd dialled repeatedly but the man wasn't answering his bloody phone. He overtook the line of traffic waiting to turn left into the superstore and veered right, accelerating up the hill.

Uniform ought to be on the scene by now. Dispatch had said there were two cars relatively close by, and he'd asked for both. He hoped they were there already, hoped Imogen was OK. She'd sounded bad on the call, really upset . . . but what the hell was she even doing there? And what possessed her to go there on her own? They were supposed to be looking for Laura Hirsch, not working her cold cases . . . and *he* was meant to be with Pearce, interviewing their only suspect. Scowling, he gripped the wheel and put his foot down.

* * *

He pulled up just before the house, bumping up hard onto the kerb. Getting out, he slammed the door and stalked along the pavement towards Imogen, who was running to meet him.

'Everything OK?' he asked, as she fell in beside him.

'Yes, sir.' She seemed steady, in control again. 'No sign of any movement at the house since we spoke. He's still in there.'

'Where are the others?'

Imogen turned, pointing back up the street.

'I sent two uniforms round to the back of the property,' she explained. 'There's one at the front with me, and another car on the way.'

Harland turned his eyes towards the house.

'If Frank's who you think he is . . . ' He left the sentence unfinished and shook his head. 'Come on.'

⋆ ⋆ ⋆

They made their way quickly up the slope to where another officer was waiting. Harland nodded to him.

'I'm going in with DS Gower,' he explained. 'Our man might try and run, but I need you to make sure nobody gets out. Let the others know, will you?'

'Yes, sir.' The officer unfastened his radio and began speaking into it.

Harland put his hand on the gate and turned to Imogen.

'Ready?' he asked her.

She stared up at the house, her face like stone.

'Ready.'

'Let's go.'

They strode up the path and Harland jammed his thumb against the bell for a moment, then started rapping hard on the door.

'Police,' he shouted. 'Open up.'

There was no answer.

Crouching down, he pushed open the letterbox and leaned forward to peer through.

'Open up, Frank,' he called, but the house stood in mocking silence. Imogen stepped back, looking up at the windows.

Getting to his feet, Harland inspected the door. It looked flimsy — old wood, with an upper half of frosted-glass panes — and it moved a little as he pushed on it. He turned to Imogen, wishing he could read her, wishing he didn't have to trust her.

'You're sure about this?'

'Absolutely sure,' she told him.

He stared at her for a long moment, then nodded grimly.

'Good enough.'

Standing back, he squared his shoulder against the edge of the frame, leaned back, then lunged forward. The door shuddered and gave a little. He drew back and lunged again. This time, there was a cracking sound. His shoulder was beginning to throb, but he took a breath, pulled back, and threw his whole weight forward. With a jarring impact, the lock broke free and the door splintered, bursting inwards so that Harland almost fell. Catching himself, he straightened up quickly, rubbing his shoulder as he stepped inside.

'Police . . . ' His voice echoed down the hallway. 'Come on, Frank. Give it up now.'

There was no response, and the silence swelled around them.

Frowning, Harland moved to the foot of the stairs. He turned and gestured to Imogen — pointing two fingers towards his eyes, then jabbing them upwards — *watch the upper floor*. She nodded.

'Frank?' Harland moved on, quietly, steadily. Approaching a doorway, he leaned inside, eyes sweeping the front room, but it was empty. Withdrawing, he made his way along the hallway towards the back of the house, yanking open the under-stair cupboard but finding it full of old boxes. Only the kitchen remained. He came at it slowly, treading silently as his gaze searched out the corners, but there was nothing.

A movement at the window caught his attention, and his muscles tensed in readiness before he recognised one of the uniformed officers standing outside.

Damn!

He caught his breath, annoyed at himself for being so jumpy, but glad to have someone else to watch his back. Stepping around the small kitchen table, he went to open the back door, reaching for the key to unlock it . . .

. . . but it was already unlocked.

Harland raised his head, staring out through the glass towards the open gate at the bottom of the small garden, then turned away and swore.

Frank was long gone.

* * *

There were two bedrooms upstairs, both a reasonable size. The master bedroom ran along the front of the house, dominated by a large, brushed-metal bedframe with charcoal-grey linen. Hanging on the wall behind it was a huge framed print, showing a naked woman on all fours, her wrists and ankles bound with intricate knots. A large, flat TV hung on the opposite wall and there were built-in wardrobes with mirrored doors. Harland made his way around the bed, peering into the small wastebasket that sat in the corner.

'Did you ever get any DNA from your man?' he asked.

'Some possible traces,' Imogen replied. 'Why?'

Harland nodded towards the crumpled tissues that lay inside, then shook his head. Imogen turned away in disgust. Faced with her own reflection, she reached out and grasped the handles of the wardrobe doors, pulling them open. Frank's clothes were all on hangers, squeezed in along a long chrome rail. The upper shelves of the wardrobe were filled with DVD cases.

'Anything?' Harland asked.

Imogen tilted her head to one side to read some of the titles.

'Porn,' she said, closing the door firmly.

* * *

The second bedroom was smaller — clearly used as a study. Harland walked in and stood in the centre of the brown carpet, looking around. There was a flimsy computer desk — with a pale wooden top and black metal frame — that ran along the far wall, piled up with junk. A monitor screen sat in the centre of it, with an expensive-looking laptop dock, but there was no sign of the laptop — just a space where it would have sat. Frank must have taken it with him.

On the landing, he could hear Imogen finishing her call. A moment later, she appeared in the doorway, her face pensive.

'That was Burgess.' She hefted her phone for a moment, then put it away. 'He's coming in. Should be here in an hour.'

'He'll be pleased,' Harland said, nodding thoughtfully. 'How long has he been after this bastard?'

'A long time,' Imogen murmured, looking down. 'I just wish I hadn't let him get away.'

'Don't be like that,' he told her. 'If it wasn't for you, we wouldn't even know who he was.'

She shook her head then gave him a thin smile.

'Thanks, sir.'

Harland turned back to look at the desk, and the shelves on the wall beside it.

'Think he knew you were on to him?' he asked.

'Frank? I suppose so. He ran, didn't he?'

'Maybe he just panicked.' Harland shrugged, wincing as the movement sent a pain through his shoulder. 'If he was sure you knew, he might have gone for you . . . '

'I could have taken him,' Imogen replied, her voice bleak.

But Harland was staring at something on the

desk. He pointed at the black hard drive, with a familiar Café del Mar sticker on it.

'Where have I seen that before?' he said, softly.

Imogen came over to stand beside him.

'What are you looking at?' she asked.

'This hard drive . . . ' Harland frowned, then turned to face her as it dawned on him what he was seeing. 'Eastfield Road! It was in his flat . . . you know, the digital artist guy . . . '

'Nigel?'

'Nigel . . . ' He stared at her. 'A digital artist, but he doesn't take his own photos.'

Imogen's eyes widened.

'You think they knew each other?'

Harland was already moving towards the door.

'I think we need to get over there now,' he told her.

45

Harland stared out through the windscreen as Imogen accelerated down Gloucester Road. He felt the buzz in his pocket and reached in to find his phone. There was one new text message, from Fuller at CID.

Had to release Garrick. Pearce wants to see you when you get back.

He sighed and leaned back against the headrest, letting his eyes close for a moment.

'Everything all right, sir?'

'No.' He willed his muscles to relax, but the pain in his shoulder was throbbing now. He turned his head to look at her. 'They've let Matt go.'

Imogen snatched a glance at him then returned her eyes to the road.

'OK.' She shrugged. 'You never thought he was responsible for Laura, though.'

'Other people did,' Harland murmured. He pointed to the approaching junction. 'Go straight on here, it's quicker.'

* * *

There was no answer from Nigel's bell. Harland kept the button pressed for a moment, then swore.

'For someone who works from home, he's never bloody here.' He jabbed Mrs Hamilton's bell instead.

A moment later, there was a buzzing sound and the lock snapped back. Harland pushed the door open and they stepped into the hallway. As they approached the stairs, they heard the inner door open and Mrs Hamilton appeared, with her little dog at her feet.

'Oh, it's you, Inspector,' she smiled.

'Hello, Mrs Hamilton.' He walked across to her door. 'I appreciate you letting us in but we're actually here to see Nigel.'

'Oh, thank goodness,' the old lady sighed. 'We've been so worried about him, haven't we, Gordon?'

She stooped to pick up the little dog, which was cowering beside her legs.

'Worried?' Harland paused. 'What do you mean?'

'Well, I've not seen hide nor hair of him for a day or two now,' she confided. 'It's most unlike him. I even called his mobile phone but it just rings and rings.'

Imogen stepped forward, smiling at Gordon.

'Perhaps he's staying with a friend,' she suggested.

'No, dear, I don't think so.' Mrs Hamilton looked vexed now. 'I mean that I can *hear* his phone ringing — you know, through the floors. It's upstairs, but I don't know where he is. I would have gone up to check, but not with my hip . . . '

'Let us go and take a look,' Harland told her,

rubbing his shoulder.

Imogen glanced at him, then turned back to the old lady.

'Mrs Hamilton?' she asked.

'Yes, dear?'

'Do you have a spare key for Nigel's flat?'

* * *

Harland stood in silence as Imogen leaned in close against the door, listening, then slid the key into the lock and twisted it.

'Police officers,' she called, pushing the door so that it swung wide open. 'Is there anyone here?'

They waited for a response, but there was none.

'Seems everybody's out today,' Harland scowled. 'But let's make sure.'

They stepped across the threshold and into the inner hallway. Imogen turned towards the bedroom but Harland touched her arm, then pointed towards the ceiling.

'The lights are on,' he noted. 'And it's the middle of the day.'

Imogen looked up.

'So . . . maybe it was dark when he left?'

'Exactly,' he said. 'Check the rooms at the back . . . I'll do the front.'

Turning away from her, he paused to rub his eyes, trying to see the bigger picture. *Nigel had clearly been gone for some time, so his disappearance wasn't connected to Imogen visiting Frank . . .*

He walked slowly into the front room, stopping for a moment to glance around — sofa, coffee table, everything as he remembered it. He moved over to the desk, his eyes searching out the various bits of high-tech equipment scattered around, satisfying himself that there weren't two hard drives, that Frank and Nigel really knew each other.

'Back rooms are clear,' Imogen's voice came to him from the hallway.

'OK,' he shouted back to her. 'With you in a minute.'

He wandered through into the small kitchen area, thinking how cramped it was. Out of habit, he opened the fridge, then took a look in a couple of cupboards, but there was nothing out of the ordinary. Turning around, he was about to go back through when he noticed the stack of envelopes, all neatly opened . . .

He looked closer.

Unsealed would be more accurate.

Idly, he turned them over, then frowned as he noticed the name on the front: Matt Garrick.

Nigel must have picked up one of his neighbour's letters by mistake . . . but it had been opened. And the other letters were all addressed to Matt too.

Harland put the mail down, and made his way quickly out into the hallway.

'Imogen?'

'In here, sir.'

He followed her voice into the bedroom.

'Something's really not right here,' he told her. 'I think Nigel's been opening Matt's mail. There's a whole stack of letters through in the kitchen . . . '

Standing by the wardrobe on the far side of the room, Imogen gave him a puzzled look.

'Why would he do that?' she asked.

'We'll ask him when we find him,' Harland replied, then shook his head. 'Come on, let's go and say goodbye to Mrs Hamilton.'

He turned to leave the room, but halted as something caught his eye. Retreating a couple of steps, he reached out and gently swung the bedroom door closed. Hanging on the back of it was a black leather jacket with a large, stylised eagle motif stitched onto the back.

'Ah,' he said slowly, as he turned to Imogen. 'That explains a lot.'

* * *

Mrs Hamilton was waiting at the bottom of the stairs for them. Gordon scurried back into her flat as they approached, turning to peer out from behind the door.

'No sign of Nigel?' the old lady asked.

Harland held up the leather jacket.

'Is this the jacket that Matt was wearing when you saw him leave with Laura on Friday night?'

Mrs Hamilton glanced at it, then nodded.

'That's right. I— '

'But you didn't see Matt's face,' Harland interrupted her. 'Did you?'

Puzzled, Mrs Hamilton shook her head.

'No, but I . . . ' She faltered, then looked at them, horrified as the alternative dawned on her. 'Oh dear God, no . . . '

46

Lying there, with his body aching and the chill concrete leaching the warmth from his skin, Nigel became aware of a strange, musical sound. At first, he wasn't sure what it was, but after a moment he realised that Laura was humming to herself in the darkness. He listened, trying to focus his waking mind so he could recognise the tune, but she stopped when she heard him moving.

'Watch your eyes,' she said, before there was a soft click and the lantern blazed up between them, throwing long shadows along the walls of the pit.

She was sitting opposite him, hugging her knees to her chest. Large eyes watched him, blinking as they caught the light, and her face softened into an expression of concern.

'Did I wake you?' she asked.

He started to nod, even smile, but the damage to his jaw was too painful, sucking the breath from him as he moved. Shakily raising a hand, he gave her a weak thumbs-up gesture, before letting his arm drop back to his side.

Laura nodded, lowering her eyes.

They sat there for a time, alone, with no sound except for each other's breathing. He stared across at her, noting the gentle rise and fall of her chest, the way her hair fell to frame her face, the tiny movements of her brow as she sat thinking.

So beautiful.

Weary with regret, he gazed at her until his eyelids felt heavy again but, just as they began to close, he noticed the corners of her mouth twitch into a faint smile, watched as she raised her chin a little to look at him.

'When we get out of here, I'm gonna have a long hot bath, and I'm gonna take a week off work.' She spoke slowly, deliberately, promising herself with every word. 'Duvet days and hot chocolate and bad TV . . . '

His poor, beautiful Laura. What the hell had he done to her? He'd never meant for anything like this to happen.

She gave a sad little smile and lowered her eyes again.

'You must think I'm silly, but it helps, thinking about better stuff . . . ' She shrugged to herself. 'I think it helps, anyway.'

He watched her idly tracing a shape on the concrete floor with her finger.

'How about you?' she asked. 'What are you most looking forward to?'

Nigel swallowed with some difficulty. He knew what he wanted most . . .

'Have you got a girlfriend?' she asked, glancing up at him. Her eyes were glistening.

Staring at her, he felt his own tears welling up again, blinked them away into a wet trickle down his cheek. Sniffing, he somehow managed to nod 'yes', despite the pain. *He had the best girlfriend in the world*.

'I bet she'll be glad to see you,' Laura smiled, a smile of kindness that broke his heart and dragged him up into a sitting position. He had to tell her, had to make her understand, but the sound that he forced out was unintelligible, hopeless. He clenched his fist in frustration, thumping the concrete.

'Shhh,' Laura soothed him. 'It's going to be all right. Just take it easy.'

He slumped back in defeat, tears streaming down his face as he closed his eyes. Beside him, Laura clicked the lantern off and went back to her tune, humming softly.

* * *

There was a noise, somewhere above them. He felt Laura stiffen beside him, then the lantern clicked on without warning.

She was facing him but her eyes were turned up towards the dark metal cover and, lit from below, her face seemed eerie.

'It's going to be OK,' she whispered, but her expression said otherwise. 'Just lie still, and keep quiet.'

There were crunching footsteps, then the sound of a car door opening. A moment later, he heard the scuffing of feet, and stared up at the metal cover, hearing it bend and flex.

The car was being rolled away.

They waited, frozen in a dreadful silence, until a sudden scraping noise filled the pit. Above and slightly behind them, a crack of glaring light expanded into a strip, then into a bright square of open space as the garage roof came into view. Nigel blinked as the inspection pit steps were dimly illuminated.

Frank — it had to be Frank! But he'd opened the other end of the cover — was he going to let them out?

Laura had dropped into a crouch on the floor beside him, her upturned face alert, her fingers clutching something dark and square in the shadows. Her gaze tracked the sounds of movement above, and she held up her free hand to shield her eyes, squinting against the light.

'Hello?' she called out.

From above, a familiar Scottish accent answered her.

'Hello, darlin'.'

Nigel saw the puzzled expression on her face, the hesitation as she realised this was someone different — not the masked man she'd expected.

'Who is it?' she frowned. 'Who's there?'

For a moment, there was no reply. Then the voice spoke again.

'Don't you remember me?'

Laura lowered her hand as the footsteps moved around, coming closer.

'Frank?' she asked.

'None other.'

'But . . . it wasn't you who . . . ' She trailed off, shoulders dropping as confusion gave way to relief and she started talking quickly. 'Frank, can you get us out? Someone's been keeping us prisoner down here . . . '

But Frank was laughing.

Laura's face fell, and she shrank back, pressing herself against the side of the pit.

'You're . . . part of this?' she called up to him.

'That's right.' Frank sounded pleased with

himself. 'I'm the final part.'

Deep in the shadows, Laura sagged down on her knees, slowly shaking her head in despair.

'Why are you doing this?' she cried. 'What do you want?'

There was more movement above them, and Frank's legs came into view, his heavy shoes on the edge of the pit. Laura backed away farther into the dark, staring up at him.

'Oh, darlin' . . . ' He tut-tutted her. 'Can't you guess?'

She gave a little squeal of horror, jerking her head away from the light. Nigel looked up to see the photographer's hand, steadily massaging the nasty bulge in the front of his jeans.

'You should have done as I asked, back in the studio,' he told her. 'I would have made it easy for you, you know? Just a nice wee fuck to show your appreciation . . . you should have taken it while you had the chance.'

Laura was trembling now. Looking up through her hair, she gave a little sob.

'Why?' she whispered, but Frank was still talking.

'See, I've never hurt the ones who put out. Well, not too much anyway. And I always let them live . . . ' He squatted down at the edge of the pit, his grinning moustache and his spiky hair coming into view. 'But then there's the ones who said no. Cock-teasing bitches who thought they were too fuckin' good for me . . . ' He shivered and smiled. 'That's when it gets interesting, watching them beg, watching them break.'

'Please Frank, no . . . '

'I'm gonna use you like a whore, darlin'. Long nights of sex and sodomy . . .'

'No!' Her voice was rising in desperation. 'NO!'

He looked down at her, laughing, then got to his feet and adjusted the bulge in his jeans.

'I just wanted you to understand what's going to happen to you,' he snarled. 'And it's gonna start happening right now.'

Moving round to the end of the pit, he placed one sturdy shoe against the edge of the metal cover and pushed it farther open. Then, taking them one at a time, he made his way down the steps, until he was standing on the concrete floor, one fist pounding rhythmically into his palm.

'Let's get your knickers off for starters.' He leaned forward, peering in under the cover. 'I want to see what I've been missing.'

'No!' Laura screamed. 'Get the fuck away from me. Get away!'

She was crouched low, staying back beneath the cover where it was harder for him to reach her. Nigel saw her hand, feeling blindly on the floor of the pit behind her. *What was she looking for?*

And then he saw the spare lantern battery — big, solid and heavy, with hard edges. Almost fainting from the pain in his jaw, he struggled to roll forward, stretching out to push the battery towards her hand.

'Come on, darlin', no point being shy now.' Frank had one hand on the cover and was leaning in towards her. 'I want a look between your legs.'

'No!' Laura's fingers closed over the battery,

knuckles tightening white. 'Fuck you!'

She sprang forward, swinging the battery around and up, slamming it hard into Frank's exposed groin. He doubled over, roaring in pain, and for a moment Nigel thought that he would topple, bring his head low enough for Laura to swing again and put him down for good.

But it was Frank who struck next. Braying with rage, he lashed out, one flailing fist catching Laura in the side of the head, knocking her backwards. The battery fell clattering to the floor as she banged hard into the wall and crumpled down on top of Nigel.

'Fucking bitch!' Frank gave a choking shriek. 'You're fucking dead, you bitch whore!'

But he was hurt. His breathing was fast, and he staggered backwards, one hand on the wall to steady himself, the other clutching his battered groin. Nigel watched him struggle up the steps and stumble out of sight.

The steps!

This was it — a way out, a chance to save them both! Desperate to get up, Nigel pushed with the last of his strength, trying to move Laura's unconscious body off him. The agony of his jaw grew maddening, but with a final shove, her arm flopped over and she rolled aside. Sobbing with pain, he forced himself up onto his knees, but it was already too late — above him, the cover shuddered and began to move, scraping and sliding back into place. He stared up in anguish as the square of light shrank, closing off any hope of escape . . .

But then it stopped, leaving a tiny gap in the

corner, and he heard Frank laughing, a rasping, mirthless laugh.

There was movement, indistinct and difficult to follow, before he heard the sound of the car being started, startlingly loud in the darkness. The engine ticked over for a moment, then the note changed as it dropped into gear, and the metal cover flexed and bowed as the wheels rolled into place, sealing them in.

Nigel listened, waiting for the engine to stop, but it didn't. He heard the car door open, and then there was movement at the edge of the pit — something sliding into the gap, obscuring the thin crack of light.

'Don't you worry, darlin'.' Frank's voice sounded laboured, still in pain. 'I'll be back again to shag you . . . whether you're breathing or not.'

And it was then that Nigel recognised the smell. Exhaust fumes — not just in the garage above, but close, and getting stronger. Panic gripped him and he shook Laura, trying to wake her. He knew he had to warn her, tell her of the danger, but he couldn't speak, only howl.

From above, he could make out Frank's laughter.

'Night night, kids,' he cackled. 'Sleep tight.'

47

The sudden rasp of a key, jammed hard into the lock, echoed across the hallway and they all turned to look at the front door. There was movement beyond the frosted glass — someone was coming in. Imogen took a step forward, but Harland raised a hand — *wait*.

As they watched, the latch turned and the door swung open. Pale and weary, Matt stepped inside, a bunch of keys in his hand. He hesitated when he saw them staring at him, then shook his head and swore under his breath, making for the stairs.

'Matt . . . ' Harland moved towards him, but the younger man whirled round and jabbed an accusing finger at him.

'No,' he snapped. 'You stay away from me. Just leave me alone!'

Harland held up his hands.

'Matt, wait . . . '

'My lawyer says you've got nothing, that you're just trying to pin this on me . . . '

'Oh, Matt,' Mrs Hamilton stepped forward. 'You just need to — '

'No!' Matt shouted, silencing her. 'I know what's been going on. I know all about the lies you've been telling, saying I was with Laura when I wasn't . . . '

'We *know* you weren't!' It was Imogen, her voice cutting him off mid-sentence.

Matt turned and stared at her.
'What?'
'We know it wasn't you,' Imogen explained. 'But someone wanted us to think it was.'
Matt regarded her with suspicion, then turned a baleful glance on Mrs Hamilton, who shrank backwards into her doorway. But Harland lifted up the leather jacket.
'Is this yours?' he asked.
Matt stared at it, his expression changing to one of puzzlement.
'Where did you get that?' he asked. 'I've been looking everywhere for it.'
'It was upstairs . . . ' Imogen told him. ' . . . in Nigel's flat.'

* * *

Matt was sitting on the stairs, hunched forward, shaking his head. Mrs Hamilton hovered nearby, her expression anxious, while Gordon looked up at her expectantly.
'We need to get hold of Nigel,' Harland muttered. It certainly looked as though their digital artist had left his flat in a hurry, but there was nothing to indicate where he might be going or how he was travelling. 'Does he have a car?'
'A car . . . ' Mrs Hamilton turned towards the front door, her face thoughtful. 'No, I don't believe so.'
'Yes he does,' Matt objected, raising his head. 'At least . . . yeah, he said it was a Peugeot, I think. Never seen it, though.'
Harland looked at him.

'Does he not park it outside?' he asked.

'No . . . but he was talking about a garage,' Matt said. 'Trying to get me to rent one, or something. Back when I first moved in.'

'Can you remember where?' Harland pressed him. They needed to know whether the car was still there.

'Sorry, no.'

'You wouldn't rent a garage unless it was close . . . ' Imogen mused.

Harland stared at the floor for a moment, thinking, then suddenly raised his head.

'Come on,' he said to Imogen. 'I think I know where he is.'

* * *

By the end of the garden path he was running, leaping from the pavement to sprint across the road. He looked back over his shoulder, making sure Imogen was with him as he pelted down the narrow lane.

'You said this was a dead end . . . ' she gasped, catching up with him.

'It is . . . ' Harland replied, breathing hard. 'Nothing down here but some old garages . . . '

He ran close to the wall as he rounded the bend, then skidded to a halt as he spotted a familiar figure coming back up the lane towards them.

But it wasn't Nigel.

It was a tall figure, stooping slightly, one hand holding his groin. Frank straightened as he saw them, the spiky white hair and red face rising up to greet them with an angry snarl as he suddenly lunged at Imogen. Fists clenched, he swung at her but she struck his flailing arm aside, twisting gracefully out of his path as he rushed forward.

And then Harland was on him, the tide of righteous anger momentarily unleashed, as he slammed into his quarry with an impact that forced the air from his lungs. Getting an arm around Frank's neck, he clung on, recklessly throwing his weight forward so that both men toppled over to crash, brawling on the ground. In the struggle, it seemed as though the older man might fight his way free, but Harland refused to let go, tightening his grip until Frank finally ceased thrashing around, and Imogen was able to drop down, pinning his arm behind his back.

Winded, Harland struggled to his feet. Everything ached, but he leaned forward, hands on his knees, and gave her a nod of acknowledgement while he caught his breath. Then he directed his attention to Frank.

'Where?' he gasped.

His head twisting round to one side, moustache brushing the ground, the photographer wheezed out a snarl. 'Go fuck yourself.'

Imogen brought her elbow down hard into his back, and he let out a choking cry.

'*Where?*' Harland shouted.

Frank struggled to look up at him, his red face smeared with mud, his mouth twisting into a grin as he began to laugh.

Harland straightened up and looked at his partner.

'You've got him?' he asked.

Imogen punched Frank again, making him bawl.

'Go!' she nodded.

* * *

Harland turned and ran on, swatting away the low-hanging branches, following the curve of the lane round until he saw the line of garages at the end. Breathing hard, he approached them, noticing a discarded padlock, gleaming on the ground. His eyes swept along the row of doors until he saw what he was looking for — an arc of exposed tarmac where the debris and mulch from the trees had been scraped away. Only one of these doors had been opened recently. Moving closer, he paused, becoming aware of a sound — was that a car engine, idling inside?

Reaching the door, he gripped the handle and hauled it open, leaning round to look inside.

'Police,' he called out. 'Anyone in here?'

The reek of exhaust fumes hit him and he hesitated, holding his arm across his face, using his sleeve to try to filter out the worst of it. In front of him, he could see the car — a Peugeot, just as Matt had said. It sat in the centre of the broad garage below a single bare bulb, the interior of the vehicle draped in shadow.

No!

Plunging forward, he went to the side of the car, bending to peer in through the window, half-expecting to see a figure slumped over the wheel . . . but it was empty. Relieved, he pulled the car door open, reached inside and switched off the engine. Then, struggling for breath against the sickening smell of the fumes, he turned and staggered back to the garage door, pushing it wide to let some air in . . .

. . . and froze.

Very slowly, he turned back to face the car, listening. There it was again — an insistent rapping sound, like something soft banging on metal.

Someone locked in the boot.

Eyes streaming, he stumbled round to the back of the car, fingers fumbling along the top of the number plate, searching for the release and wrenching the hatchback open . . .

. . . but there was nothing inside, just empty boot space.

Gasping, coughing, he stepped back, noticing for the first time the bit of old hose jammed into the exhaust pipe. But rather than feeding fumes back into the car, it bent round and down under the edge of a large metal sheet on the floor . . .

. . . and there was the sound again. He could feel it this time, as if something was banging beneath his feet. Crouching down, he placed his palm flat on the metal, and heard coughing — a woman coughing.

Laura!

'Hold on,' he yelled, springing to his feet. The driver's door was still open and he reached inside, releasing the handbrake, then braced himself against the front pillar to shove the car forward. Pain seared through his injured shoulder as he strained hard to get the vehicle moving — pushing it off the metal cover until it rolled away, crunching into the wall of the garage with a tinkling of broken glass — but he didn't care. Turning around, his hands were already scrabbling at the metal ring, gripping it and tugging the heavy steel cover aside.

The space it revealed was narrower than he'd imagined — an old inspection pit, yawning like an open grave, sunk five feet deep in the concrete floor — and as he leaned over the edge he saw Laura's face for the first time. She was staring up at him, eyes blinking red, neck muscles taut, tears running down her cheeks as she choked out the fumes.

'It's all right, Laura,' he managed. 'I'm a police officer. You're safe.'

She was already scrambling forward, coughing hard as she tried to claw her way up out of the pit. He reached down to help her, offering his hand as she pulled herself up on to the garage floor.

'Here, let me — '

But she swung at him, knocking his hand aside.

'Don't touch me!' she hissed, her eyes flaring wide. 'Get. off!'

Harland stepped back, startled. He watched as Laura forced herself up into a kneeling position, then lurched slowly to her feet, bending forward and coughing for a moment. Raising her head, she stared at him through her tangled hair.

'Help *him*,' she wheezed.

Harland frowned, not understanding, but she tilted her head back towards the pit, and he turned to look over the edge. There was another figure, crawling out from under the shadow of the cover, every movement an agony. He watched as it dragged itself forward; a grimy, bloody mess, struggling to pull itself upright.

Laura, her breathing laboured, moved to the edge of the pit, glaring at Harland in sudden fury.

'Help me to help him,' she hissed. Collapsing to her knees again, she extended a weary hand to the figure, just as it raised its head to look up.

'Oh God . . . ' Harland stared down, recognising the face despite the horrendous injuries to the mouth; the loose, horribly dislocated jaw. 'Nigel?'

Nigel looked up, blinking in surprise at Harland, then glancing across at Laura offering her hand.

'Come on,' she urged him. 'It's all right now.'

Crouching beside her, Harland swallowed hard.

'Laura.' He spoke softly, carefully. 'Do you know who this is?'

Nigel was staring up at Harland now, eyes pleading. A low whimpering sound escaped his damaged mouth as he tried to shake his head.

Laura frowned.

'Someone else that Frank and his sidekick grabbed,' she replied.

Tears streaming down his face, Nigel reached out to Laura, but Harland gently drew her hand away.

'No,' he told her. 'That's not who he is at all.'

Beneath them, his hand still outstretched, Nigel sank to the bottom of the pit and howled.

48

The door of the police van slammed shut and Frank's torrent of abuse was mercifully silenced. Imogen's shoulders sagged a little, but her muscles remained taut and her heart continued pounding. She turned away, cupping her hands together over her mouth and nose, bending forward for a moment to shut out her surroundings and take in everything that had happened.

They'd found their missing person — alive and relatively unscathed — *and* they'd caught a sadistic murderer before he could add to his tally of kills. She closed her eyes briefly, taking a long, deep breath, willing everything to slow down. The lane seemed almost peaceful without his angry shouts of protest, despite the crackle of police radios and the bustle of other officers moving around her. More importantly, there was a dawning sense of relief; months of fruitless searching, months of frustration and guilt, all bundled away with him into the back of that van.

She opened her eyes and stood up slowly, idly brushing down her clothes to remove some of the grime they'd picked up during her scuffle.

'Imogen?'

She looked round, then smiled in surprise as she recognised the overweight figure of Burgess approaching from the end of the lane. Squeezing past the van, his lined face broke into an uncharacteristic laugh and he ran the last few steps towards her, clasping her warmly by the shoulders.

'Well done,' he said simply, then surprised her by leaning forward and embracing her. She stood for a moment, unsure how to respond, then patted him awkwardly on the back as he whispered, 'You got the bastard.'

'*We* got him, sir.' She smiled at him as he drew back from her. 'You . . . DI Harland . . . all of us.'

'Of course.' Burgess nodded self-consciously, staring past her towards the garages. 'Where is Graham? I should really thank him before I head over to Filton Avenue . . .'

Imogen turned around, her eyes searching between the uniforms and the paramedics.

'Excuse me, sir,' she murmured. 'I'll be right back.'

* * *

She found him sitting on a slab of cracked concrete paving, leaning back against one of the locked garage doors, his knees drawn up in front of him like a barricade, but nobody was paying any attention to him. Smoke curled upwards from a cigarette held loosely in one hand; he seemed to be miles away.

'Sir?' She halted a few feet from him, waiting until he looked up at her and managed a slight smile. 'Burgess was asking for you.' She gestured over her shoulder. 'He's back there by the van.'

Harland inclined his head slightly, then lifted the hand with the cigarette, by way of an explanation.

'In a minute,' he replied.

Imogen looked at him, then nodded. Burgess could wait.

* * *

A dozen yards along from them, there was a scraping noise — old wood, grating across the concrete — as the two garage doors were pushed wider open. Moments later, a team of green-clad paramedics appeared, slowly wheeling a stretcher out into the lane. The prone figure was strapped down securely, the lower half of his face a bloody mess behind the oxygen mask, but their eyes met and Imogen recognised Nigel as he passed close by her.

She looked away, frowning to herself as she wondered about his role in things. Had he been Frank's accomplice at one point? Clearly, Nigel must have had a hand in Laura's abduction, but how had he ended up in the pit with her? Had Frank turned on him?

Her thoughts were interrupted by a shriek, and she turned around. Laura, standing nearby with a blanket round her shoulders, had seen who was being brought out. Jerking free of the medic who was attending to her, she struggled forward to block the stretcher's path.

'You piece of *shit!*' she cried, leaning forward and spitting on Nigel. Strapped in place, he still managed to flinch slightly, sudden tears streaming down over the oxygen mask as he stared up at her, distraught.

Harland had scrambled to his feet, and there

was a sorrowful expression on his face as he stepped forward to position himself between Laura and the stretcher.

'That's enough,' he told her softly, then turned to the paramedics. 'Get him out of here, please.'

Laura watched in silent rage as Nigel was wheeled away, before whirling round to glare at Harland, who held up his hands and moved back from her slightly.

'Let us deal with him now,' he said quietly.

'But he was the one who drugged me,' she hissed. 'He put me in that . . . that filthy *hole* . . . '

Imogen stepped forward, placing a hand on the girl's arm.

'And *this* is the man who got you out,' she said gently.

* * *

A crowd had gathered in Eastfield Road, and there were faces at the windows all along the street. Some people were standing on their raised front steps to see over the parked police cars, and a small gaggle of onlookers pressed in around the end of the lane itself, while two uniformed officers worked to keep them back. At the very front, Imogen spotted Mrs Hamilton, clutching Gordon in her arms. Beside her, Matt was waiting with his hands in his pockets, his face expectant.

'Quite a turnout,' Imogen noted, as Harland came to stand beside her.

'Well, it's a quiet neighbourhood.' He

shrugged, then winced and reached up to touch his shoulder. 'Usually.'

A second ambulance was waiting at the end of the lane, ready to back in once Nigel was driven away, but Laura insisted on walking out to it. They watched as she made her way out to the street with a paramedic following close behind, saw her slow a little as a muted ripple of applause rose from the crowd. Matt raised his hand and called out to her, but she didn't seem to notice him, walking straight on and stepping up into the ambulance without a word.

'It feels so good when they survive,' Imogen said, turning away.

'Certainly does,' Harland mused. 'And she had a lot of courage, that one. She *deserved* to make it out of there.'

He turned to face her, his grey eyes glittering.

'You did well,' he said quietly, and she could tell that he meant it.

'So did you, sir.'

Harland gave her a weary half-smile then turned away, massaging his injured shoulder as he walked back to the car.

'Are you all right, sir?' she called after him.

He stopped and looked around.

'Yeah,' he said, nodding. 'Nothing that won't heal.'

A FEW DAYS LATER

Epilogue

The pub was full, familiar faces packed into a cramped space that rang with loud voices and laughter. There had been a ragged cheer when the landlord brought out Linwood's birthday cake and placed it on the bar, but everyone had quickly lapsed back into their conversations and the cake remained uncut.

Squeezed in at a small wooden table, Imogen drained her glass and put it on the centre of the beer mat.

' . . . and he couldn't even speak when we found him. Dislocated jaw, missing teeth, a real mess.'

Sitting across from her, Andy Reed was his usual thoughtful self. His friend Josh was more animated — one of the Portishead lot — and seemed to know Harland quite well.

'Sounds nasty,' he said, with a little more enthusiasm than she liked.

'I almost felt sorry for him when I saw him,' she murmured. It wasn't the injuries — she'd seen worse over the years — more his expression that troubled her. Nigel Reynolds had looked so lost, so utterly defeated when the paramedics had carried him out . . .

'Sorry for him?' Andy was scowling at her, his arms folded.

'Well . . . ' She hadn't meant to say that. How could she explain? 'He wasn't really a monster. Not like Frank Guthrie.'

Andy raised an eyebrow, then sat back in his chair, shaking his head.

'You didn't see the guy he superglued.' His voice was cold with disapproval.

'You're right.' She lowered her gaze, awkwardly tracing one finger around the top of her glass. That was the danger of spending too long looking at monsters — you could lose your perspective on what evil really was.

Oblivious, Josh leaned forward, propping his chin up on the heel of his hand.

'One thing *I* was wondering,' he said slowly. 'How did you tie this Nigel Reynolds guy to the murder of the drug dealer bloke?'

'Oh, that was the GHB,' she explained. 'He had a whole stash of it . . . '

'Which he was using on the girl?' Josh interrupted.

'Yes.' She felt a prickle of annoyance at Josh's reference to *the girl*. 'He was using it to subdue Laura, and we think he also used it to drug her boyfriend — the downstairs neighbour.'

'It had Durand's prints on it?' Andy asked.

'Yeah, and traces of his blood . . . ' She trailed off, realising that this probably wasn't the place to discuss the details of the case. Andy was a good man, but she knew nothing about Josh and they'd all been drinking. 'Excuse me a moment, will you . . . ?'

She started to stand up, but Josh stopped her.

'Hang on a moment, looks like Mendel's up.' He nodded towards the middle of the room, where a solid-looking man was raising his hand for attention.

'Everyone shut up a moment,' he bellowed, smiling pleasantly as a hush descended and all faces turned towards him. 'Thank you. Now, I know it's Linwood's birthday, but I just wanted to take this opportunity to say congratulations to a couple of exceptional police officers, who've worked hard to score a really good result . . . '

Oh no . . .

Imogen shrank back into her chair, and glanced across the room to where Harland was watching the big man, a look of acute embarrassment on his face.

'Now, you all know these two,' Mendel continued. 'And I'd like you to raise your glasses . . . ' He held up an enormous hand, winked at Harland, then abruptly turned to face the other way. ' . . . to Sue Firth and myself, for wrapping up the Avonmouth truck robbery.'

There was a roar of cheering and applause. A blushing woman with straight brown hair — Firth, presumably — got to her feet and performed a brief, theatrical curtsy. She turned and smiled at Harland as Mendel raised his voice above the laughter.

'Certain coppers might get the headlines and the glory,' the big man intoned, gesturing towards Harland, who was wearing a strangled smile, 'but we all play our part, and it's *teamwork* that gets the job done.'

He paused, looking around at the assembled faces, and grinned. 'Now then . . . where's Linwood hiding?'

* * *

Several drinks later, Imogen emerged from the comparative quiet of the Ladies and pushed her way through the press of bodies. The birthday cake had turned out to be rather good, and she made a brief detour to pick up a second piece, holding a napkin beneath it to catch the crumbs.

'Back for more?'

She recognised the deep voice and turned around to find its owner smiling at her.

'You must be Mendel,' she said.

'James, if you don't mind.' He winked and offered her his enormous hand.

'Imogen.' She grinned, wiping her own hand on a napkin before shaking his.

He leaned up against the bar and regarded the remains of the cake.

'So you're the one who's taken over my old job . . . ' he mused.

'Your old job?'

'Looking after Graham.' He nodded across the room, to where Harland was sitting.

Imogen followed his gaze and frowned.

'I think it might be the other way around,' she sighed, turning away. 'If anyone needs looking after . . . '

Harland had trusted her, believed in her when it mattered most. He'd backed her up when she'd gone after Frank on her own . . . what had she been *thinking*? And then, after all that, he'd still fought her corner, and taken a lot of flak to bail her out with Pearce . . .

'What is it?' Mendel asked.

She shook her head.

'Let's just say I rushed into some stuff and

he . . . ' she looked up at him, ' . . . he had my back.'

'Yeah, well, Graham knows *plenty* about rushing in where angels fear to tread,' Mendel chuckled. 'Besides, you two got a result.'

Imogen gave him a rueful smile.

'That's nice of you,' she said, 'but . . . well, a lot of things didn't go the way I'd planned.'

'You're just getting started,' the big man told her. 'Give it time.'

His eyes glanced past her at someone standing behind her.

'Come on, let me introduce you to some of the gang.' He placed a friendly hand on her shoulder, turning her round. 'Imogen, meet Sue Firth . . . '

⋆ ⋆ ⋆

It was nearing the end of the evening. The crowd had thinned a little and the birthday cake lay on the floor in ruins, but nobody seemed to mind. Mellow with alcohol, Imogen squeezed behind Mendel, who was busy chatting to Pope, and found a space at the bar, raising her hand to get the barman's attention. To her left, Harland was perched on a stool, gazing across the room. She turned to see who he was looking at, then smiled to herself.

'Yes?' The barman nodded at her expectantly.

'Gin and tonic, please.'

Hearing her voice, Harland glanced round.

'Hey.' He smiled, sliding down off the stool. 'Let me get this one.'

He was a little tipsy. They all were.

'It's all right, sir.' She shook her head.

'I insist,' he grinned at her. 'And don't say 'sir' tonight. We're not at work now.'

It was good to see him happy — he deserved it after everything that had happened.

'Can I make a suggestion, then?' she asked.

'Anything,' he said, solemnly.

She looked at him, holding his gaze.

'Ask her out.'

Harland gave her a blank look.

'Eh?'

'You've been staring at each other all night,' she told him. 'And you don't work out of Portishead any more . . . I think you should ask her out.'

Harland turned to lean on the counter, bowing his head forward slightly as the barman returned with Imogen's gin and tonic.

'Who told you?' he said, after a moment.

Imogen smiled at him. Lifting her glass, she put her arm around his shoulder and gave him a friendly squeeze.

'Thanks for the drink, sir.'

* * *

The bell clanged for last orders, and Imogen pressed the phone closer to her ear, trying to drown out the noise.

'Are you sure?' she said. 'I can get a taxi . . . '

'It's all right.' Lucy didn't sound as though she minded. 'Where shall I pick you up?'

'We're still at the Ostrich,' Imogen explained.

'Meet me at the bottom of Guinea Street in ten minutes?'

'OK. Love you.'

Imogen smiled.

'You too,' she murmured, lowering her phone.

She turned and made her way over to Linwood, draping her arm around him and wishing him a happy birthday, before waving goodbye to the others. Then, feeling tired and happy, she pushed the door open and stepped out into the cool evening air.

It was dark now, and she stood for a moment, enjoying the quiet calm after the noise of the pub. As her eyes got used to the darkness, she spotted Harland and Firth, sitting together at one of the outside tables. They were leaning in close to one another, laughing at something, and that made her feel good.

Behind her, the door creaked and swung open. She turned around and found Mendel there, pulling on his jacket. He nodded to her as he stepped outside, then halted when he noticed the two figures at the table. Turning round, he studied her, a mischievous twinkle in his eyes.

'Was that your handiwork?' he rumbled, raising an eyebrow.

Imogen shrugged and glanced over at Harland.

'It's like you were saying before, about fools rushing in . . . ' She smiled to herself. 'Sometimes, the angels just need a little nudge.'

Author's note

Over the course of this series, which started with *Eye Contact* and continued in *Knife Edge*, I've done my best to find the right settings for the stories. I've tried to portray real locations in a realistic way and, from time to time, my characters have made unflattering observations about this place or that, but I want to make it clear that I wouldn't have chosen to write about these areas if I didn't love them and enjoy spending time in them.

Acknowledgements

I'm extremely grateful to Gary Stephens, and everyone at Avon & Somerset Constabulary who took the time to aid me with my research. The police rarely get the respect or thanks they deserve for their vital work; I only hope that any procedural inaccuracies in this book can be dealt with leniently.

I'm indebted to my first readers, Kate Ranger and John Popkess, who were kind enough to give me valuable feedback on early drafts of the story, and to Ian Paten for his copy editing.

As always, I'm grateful to the staff at Boston Tea Party and the Watershed Café, where so much of this book was written.

I want to thank my wonderful agent Eve White, and everyone at Hodder — Kerry Hood, Becca Mundy, Ellie Cheele, and especially my brilliant editor Francesca Best — for their hard work and support.

And finally, my thanks to Anna and Cameron, who have been unstinting in their patience and encouragement.

Other titles published by Ulverscroft:

EYE CONTACT

Fergus McNeill

From the outside, Robert Naysmith is a successful businessman, handsome and charming. But for years he's been playing a deadly game. He doesn't choose his victims. Each is selected at random — the first person to make eye contact after he begins 'the game' will not have long to live. Their fate is sealed. When the body of a young woman is found on Severn Beach, Detective Inspector Harland is assigned the case. It's only when he links it to an unsolved murder in Oxford that the police begin to guess at the awful scale of the crimes. But how do you find a killer who strikes without motive?

THE WRONG SIDE OF GOODBYE

Michael Connelly

Harry Bosch is working as a part-time detective in San Fernando when he gets an invitation to meet with aging aviation billionaire Whitney Vance. At eighteen, Vance had a relationship with a girl called Vibiana Duarte; but soon after becoming pregnant, she disappeared. Now, as he reaches the end of his life, Vance wants to know what happened to Vibiana, and whether there is an heir to his vast fortune. Bosch is the only person he trusts to undertake the assignment. Harry's aware that with the sums of money involved, this could be dangerous — not just for himself, but for the person he's hunting. But as he begins to uncover the secrets behind Vibiana's tragic story, and discovers uncanny links to his own past, he knows he cannot rest until he finds the truth.

MAGPIE MURDERS

Anthony Horowitz

Editor Susan Ryeland has worked with bestselling crime writer Alan Conway for years. Readers love his detective, Atticus PUnd, a celebrated solver of crimes in the sleepy English villages of the 1950s. But Conway's latest tale of murder at Pye Hall is not quite what it seems. Yes, there are dead bodies and a host of intriguing suspects; but hidden in the pages of the manuscript lies another story: a tale written between the very words on the page, telling of real-life jealousy, greed, ruthless ambition and murder . . .

BENEATH THE ASHES

Jane Isaac

The floor felt hard beneath her face. Nancy opened her eyes. Blinked several times. A pain seared through her head. She could feel fluid. No. She was lying in fluid. Nancy Faraday wakes up on the kitchen floor. The house has been broken into and her boyfriend is missing. Meanwhile, when a body is discovered in a burnt-out barn in the Warwickshire countryside, DI Will Jackman is called to investigate. As the case unravels, Jackman realises that nothing is quite as it appears — and everyone, it seems, has a secret. Can he discover the truth behind the body in the fire, and track down the killer, before Nancy becomes the next victim?

ARROWOOD

Laura McHugh

Arrowood is the most ornate and grand of the historical houses that line the Mississippi River in southern Iowa. But it has a mystery it has never revealed: it's where Arden's younger twin sisters vanished on her watch seventeen years ago — never to be seen again. Now that Arden has inherited the house, she returns to it determined to uncover what really happened to her sisters that traumatic summer. But Arrowood and the surrounding town hold their secrets close — and the truth, when Arden finds it, is more devastating than she could ever have imagined . . .

BURNED AND BROKEN

Mark Hardie

An enigmatic policeman, currently the subject of an internal investigation, is found burned to death in his car on the Southend sea front. Meanwhile, a vulnerable young woman, fresh out of the care system, is trying to discover the truth behind the sudden death of her best friend. DS Frank Pearson and DC Catherine Russell from the Essex Police Major Investigation Team are brought in to solve the mystery that surrounds their colleague's death — but when a dramatic turn of events casts a whole new light on both cases, the way forward is far from clear. Were the victims connected in some way? And just how much should Pearson and Russell reveal to their bosses as they begin to unearth some dark secrets that the force would rather keep buried?